WHAT LIES IN THE MIDDLE

BEKKI DIEFENDORF

DOGS AND COFFEE BOOKS

DEDICATION

This book is for my first fan, who read it at it's worst
and still told me it was wonderful.
I love you Dad!

CONTENTS

Prologue - Evan Harris

April 2045; South of Kansas City, Missouri, former USA

The sun is hot. The breeze is cool. The success . . . the success is intoxicating.

I maneuver our SUV around a fissure in the broken highway. What I wouldn't give to have driven this twenty-five years ago when it was a smooth stretch of asphalt that never crumbled beneath your tires. I'd have flown. Nothing but the power of my engine and an endless road.

Beside me Marcus stares towards the horizon, looking for danger or lost in his own head.

"They didn't think we'd get it all," he says.

"They didn't think we'd get half of it."

The cargo area is packed with everything from motors to chemicals to microinverters. The riches of a past age were just waiting for us. We knew they would be.

"Vindication," I say.

"Vindication," Marcus agrees, nodding. "But Evan, a word of advice. A little humility might help with Kessa's dad. Especially if you want her out gathering with us next time."

Kessa's absence is the only shadow on the day. She was pissed when her dad said she couldn't start gathering until her apprenticeship was over. But ultimately, she trusts him. We all do. So she'll finish, we'll marry, and then she'll travel with me. I tilt my face to the sun. Perfect.

"You're over there dreaming of making me the third wheel again, aren't you?"

"Whatever," I laugh.

Before I can say more, a cry splits the air.

Beside me, Marcus's eyes are wide

"That sounded human to you, right?" I ask. He nods in reply.

Ahead and to the right, barely visible behind a collapsing farmhouse, is the hood of a military vehicle. Without the shout we would have driven right past. We probably still should.

"We've got to, man," Marcus says. And I know he's right.

I veer off the road and around the building. Before us a crowd of men encircles a figure in the dirt. He groans as a boot connects with ribs. I shift into park, but keep the motor running.

"We've got visitors," says a small man leaning casually against the side of the truck.

"Looks like your friend could use some assistance," I say through my open window.

The small man spits a stream of dip and sizes us up. "Our friend is doin fine. All he needed was a lesson on keepin to his place. How about you boys move along?"

Well, that's not happening.

"He's not gonna be any use to you for a while," I say. "Why don't you send him with us?"

"I can't go about losin crew. Unless one of you wants to take his place."

His men tense and shift, but so far no one's made a move. I need to get this done.

"We've got people to get back to. Let us have him now, get him all patched up, and you can come for him later."

The small man smirks.

"Sure, why not?" he says. "Come take him."

It's too easy, but what choice do we have? I look at Marcus. Another nod.

"We make it quick," I say. On alert we exit the SUV and walk towards the body.

"Where you boys from, anyway?"

"El Dorado Springs. It's another fifty miles Southwest of here if you follow . . ." But I don't finish as the world goes dark.

Chapter 1 - Jace Morton

September 2045; Salida, Colorado, former USA

The Arkansas River beckons. One hundred more yards to freedom. I step out from the cover of the alley, place my skateboard on the sidewalk . . .

"Here he is now: the man of the hour. Jason, come join us, Son."

Caught.

Jason is my real name, but people who like me call me Jace. I tell myself the sweat trickling down my neck is because of the blaring sun, not Dad's summons. With a sigh, I pick up my skateboard and climb the stone steps to where he stands, surrounded by his puppets, before the ornate doors of town hall. I don't know if this is an official meeting, but the great Councilor Morton is obviously presiding.

"Look at this boy of mine. How could anyone ask for a better specimen? He's smart, handsome, and strong as his old man."

My "handsome" brown hair is in my eyes again. When was the last time I cut it? Dad's firm grip on my shoulder brings me back to the present. Around me the puppets smile and nod, eating up whatever my father is spouting. Ah, there's what I was looking for. Our town prosecutor scowls. He hasn't smiled at me since last year when Dad strong-armed him into dropping my arson charges. He's a good tether to reality in the midst of all the B.S.

Dad says something about a swap and "genes with value to them." Maybe I should be paying attention to this. But I'm too late. Dad makes a comment about how I must have more important things to do and dismisses me. Whatever.

I roll past moms with their kids on the playground to the concrete path that flows beside the bank. Scanning the river, I expect to find my bro, Cole, hitting the rapids for as long as he can while this heat holds out.

Instead, he's leaning against a boulder in the shade with his latest girl curled under one arm. She smiles at me like we're best friends, but I'm not friends with Cole's girls. Let her enjoy her moment in the sun. She's got another week, tops.

Cole, with dark skin and ridiculous confidence, is tall like me. Unlike me he makes movement look graceful. Once when I asked him what he planned to do after he dated every available girl in our town, he said he'd "join the family business." I think he meant it.

Cole's dad is a seed merchant. My father calls it a 'variation on the world's oldest profession,' despite the fact that new DNA is incredibly valuable now. But this means Cole only sees his dad every few years when he comes through town to offer his services. After a couple of months and some sage fatherly advice like "only women cry," Cole's dad is back on the road. At last count Cole thought he had twelve half siblings in Salida alone, but we don't know for sure.

The last time Cole's dad was in town, Cole asked if he could travel with him. His dad looked at him, said "Damn, I'm getting old," and walked away.

Today, Cole greets me with a fist bump and the kind of cool guy nod I can't pull off. His girl plays distractedly with the end of one braid.

"Sup, merchantman?" I say.

"You know it," he says with a cocky smile, pulling the girl closer to his side.

"You hear anything about a 'swap'?" I ask.

"A swap? A swap of what?"

"I don't know. Something Dad said."

I shrug it off as some of the other guys walk up. Dad's crazy can wait til later.

After hours of boarding I drag myself up the hill to our house. My grandfather built this "log cabin," as Dad calls it, as a monument to his success. Its enormous windows stare past me to Salida sprawled below. From this distance the red brick buildings look just like they did in 2020 before the world ended.

I go in the front door, under the antler chandelier that hangs from a beam in the ceiling far above me. Our massive fireplace takes up a whole wall but we won't light it until the nights turn cold again.

Dad and my brother Adam are in the kitchen filling their plates from dishes laid out on the island. A glance shows me flat iron steak, mashed potatoes, rolls. All my favorites. I load up then follow Adam to the long wooden table where my father is already seated at the head. Heaven forbid the three of us have dinner on the counter stools. I sit across from Adam on Dad's left.

"Adam and I have been talking about how far you've come since that trouble last year," Dad says. "We both think you're ready to handle some real responsibility for this family."

Suddenly, I'm reminded of the last meal given to criminals before an execution. A glance at Adam's expression tells me nothing. I take another bite to stall for time. Dad's looking at me, obviously expecting an answer. What do I say that won't piss him off or commit me to whatever's next?

"Thanks, Dad. That means a lot."

"Jason, I'm not a man who beats around the bush, so I'm going to come out and say it. I need your help. El Dorado Springs is sending a delegation to discuss ways we can be more connected for the good of both our towns. What they're proposing is something that could help secure Salida's future and move us toward our dreams of extensive city exploration. What do you think of that, son?"

City exploration has always been Dad's dream, not mine. But whatever.

"Sounds great," I say. "What do you need me to do?"

"I want you, and Adam, of course, to welcome them. Show them around and help us put out best foot forward."

There's something he isn't telling me. I force a smile.

"Whatever I can do to help."

It's eight thirty a.m. I'm showered, my teeth are brushed, hair sort of. No stains or tears on my pants. Adam woke me up this morning hours before my usual rise time to tell me that the delegation from El Dorado Springs arrived late last night. Apparently, Dad hadn't told either of us about welcome duty a moment before we needed to know. I make my way downstairs to greet the two delegates who will be staying with us while they're here.

Adam smiles warmly as I enter the kitchen. "Come meet our guests. Kessa McKnight, Henry Douglas, meet my little brother Jace."

"Little brother" is better than "Jason" any day, and I'm glad it's Adam doing the introductions.

I turn to the woman first. Kessa looks a few years older than me. Her dark hair is braided back and she has the build of a runner. She's very attractive in a put-together, so confident I would never in a million years have the cajones to ask her out kind of way. Adam's type, actually.

"Kessa works with her father inventing clean energy tech in El Dorado Springs," Adam continues. "You should see the SUV they came in. They drove the whole 650 miles on wind and sunshine."

"Lucky for us there are a lot of both on the prairie," Kessa says. She puts the glass she'd been holding on the counter, and reaches out to shake my hand. Her handshake is firm and her smile polite, not quite reaching her deep brown eyes.

Next, I take the outstretched hand of the middle-aged man beside her.

"Please, call me Henry," he says. "Unlike Kessa, I don't have a brilliant resume or a genius father. But I was able to get the time off, so they let me come." Henry's smile and shrug draw me in. I can't help grinning in return.

"Henry's being modest," Kessa says. "He's El Dorado Springs' resource manager."

"Oh yeah?" I ask. "What's a resource manager do?"

"It's changed over time, but mainly I help people find things they're looking for. Someone needs a crib, someone else has outgrown theirs, that kind of thing."

"He's simplifying," Kessa says. "Imagine doing that with every need in a five-thousand-person community, plus requests merchants bring from other towns and any components needed for my father's inventions."

I'd known that El Dorado Springs was bigger than Salida, but they have almost a thousand people on us. Dad's guess is that only about twenty thousand total survived the pandemic in the former USA. No wonder he wants to impress them.

"Do you rely solely on merchants or do you send people out to find specific things?" Adam asks. Henry's eyes dart to Kessa whose smile looks even faker than before. She turns her back to us as she refills her glass from the sink.

"We've sent people in the past," Henry says. "Two of our young men didn't make it back from a trip in April, so we've paused the excursions for now."

"I'm sorry to hear that," says Adam. He keeps talking before awkward silence can fill the space. "Jace, you and I have the privilege of showing Kessa and Henry around this morning. We'll meet up later with Dad and some others at the community center."

"Sounds great," I say. "Ready when you are."

The morning flies as we tour the town. Henry is my new favorite person. I'd be sad that the morning is over, except that I'm starving by the time we get to the community center. The lobby is crowded with people standing around talking. As usual, Councilor Morton is at the center of the largest group, the nucleus around which the town turns. Beside him are three strangers.

At our approach, the strangers break off. Henry smiles, clapping one of the men on the back. "Long time, no see," he says.

"Hours, at least," the man replies with a laugh. The woman beside him has pulled Kessa in for a quick hug and says something only she can hear. Kessa nods, smile firmly in place.

Henry introduces us, and while Adam talks to the merchant, the doctors ask me questions about river surfing. Apparently, they surfed the ocean on their honeymoon back when travel to the coasts was special, but not abnormal. As we talk my neck muscles loosen. I didn't realize they were tight, but my dad is in the room.

Eventually people start moving into the meeting space where tables are set up and a buffet lines one wall. It smells amazing. Can snag lunch before I go?

Adam hands me a plate. "Dad said we're supposed to stay."

Huh. Don't mind if I do. After getting my food I sit at a table near the back of the room. Kessa and Adam join me, and to my surprise so does Henry.

Henry's talking to someone, so I turn to Kessa on my left. "My dad said the delegation is here about a swap or trade or something. Do you know what that's about?"

Before she can answer, Dad calls for everyone's attention. He welcomes the delegates and begins his introductory speech.

Dad is at his best when he's playing "Councilor Morton." Today, he goes on talking about the great future of our two towns, "the mightiest surviving remnants of mankind," "havens of freedom," blah, blah, blah. When we study politicians and presidents of the old USA, I can't help but think my dad would have been a natural. He's the kind of guy who could have stabbed an ally in the gut, blamed it on a rival, and never taken his smile off the camera. And no, I'm not bitter.

The Mortons have ruled Salida for generations, but my grandfather, Robert Morton, had bigger goals for his son. Old railroad money, reinvested into tech companies at exactly the right time, gave him the ear of some of the most influential men in Washington and was well on its way to getting my dad a senate seat when the pandemic hit.

My grandfather was one of the first to know how bad things were going to get. He had Dad quarantine the town. No one in. No exceptions. It was already too late to save his own life, but my grandfather's warning is why Salida exists today.

One of the doctors from El Dorado Springs has started speaking. She thanks us for our hospitality and goes on about the need to "come together in both resource and intellect to see a prosperous future emerge." She says they also have an interest in sending teams to the cities, but want to establish codes of ethics to make sure the pandemic won't be re-released upon society. Humanity wouldn't survive a second round.

As she's saying this Kessa stands up, nearly toppling her chair, and rushes out the door. I look to Adam, wondering if we should do something. He rises and silently follows her. Would it look weird if I left too? There's polite applause as the doctor takes her seat. Shoot. I missed everything she said after Kessa left. I force myself to focus as Dad starts talking again.

"And, of course, a key part of this would be the swap that was proposed by our friends in El Dorado Springs."

The swap. My foot is bouncing and I force it to still.

"We are a democracy, as has always been the tradition of our great nation," my father, the great Councilor Morton, continues. "But as times and circumstances change, we must all adapt and evolve. Without an over-arching government to hold us together, we must find other ways to unite our communities, to further trade and mitigate any tensions that arise. On top of this, genetic material has, as we all know, become an important resource now with the population so diminished."

No. He wouldn't.

"Throughout history political alliances have been made through marriages. That is why I was so willing to consider the idea of a swap, not only of ideas and resources, but of young people who would bridge the gap between us. Our best and brightest will be empowered to choose from amongst the suitable young persons in their new home, not be forced into marriage with a stranger as with the political unions of the past. We can iron out the timing and age requirements together. And, of course, all participants must do so voluntarily, not by coercion."

Dad's eyes meet mine across the room, and everything switches to slow motion.

"In fact," he says, "my family and I are so committed to the idea of unity between our towns that my younger son, Jason, has volunteered to be our first ambassador to El Dorado Springs."

Every face turns towards me. They're clapping, but I don't hear the sound. Henry's big grin, so natural before, looks exaggerated and out of place as he reaches over to clasp my shoulder. Surely none of this is real.

Adam stands with Kessa in the doorway. It's clear from his expression that he didn't know this was coming any more than I did, but he covers it quickly. Time slips back into place as Adam mouths "Say something."

I stand and clear my throat. I don't know what to say. Maybe if I'd had time to prepare, but no. Dad wouldn't have risked me refusing. Now, I'm stuck. I can't tell the El Dorado Springs delegation that I didn't "volunteer" without risking trade and progress and everything else for both towns. As if I need more guilt.

"I'm honored that my town would consider me for such an important, um, honor. Nothing would please me more than to see our communities grow together to build a strong future for humanity."

What the hell am I saying? Is anyone buying this? Around me the smiling and clapping continues as though my whole life didn't just implode. I've gotta get out of here.

With a weird wave, I head for the exit, brushing past Kessa and Adam on my way out. Dad's speaking again, no doubt making some excuse for why I'm leaving, but I don't take the time to look back.

What just happened?

I knew my dad was doing something, but this? This is . . . what? It's brilliant, that's what. Councilor Morton managed to prove his dedication to the cause by parting with his own flesh and blood and get rid of his biggest source of embarrassment in one sweeping political move. I curse under my breath. Bravo, Dad.

He's trading me to El Dorado Springs like the bulls we stud out. I'm SEVENTEEN years old and they want me to get married? They'd better give me some time. I wonder if good old Morton has figured out what to do when they realize what a screw-up I am. Maybe El Dorado Springs will use this to get rid of their rejects too. It would serve Dad right.

I have to stop thinking.

My feet have taken me to the abandoned railroad tracks where someone's pre-pan cannabis garden grows wild. I haven't lit up since the night a year ago when Cole's shed burned to the ground. The fact that I could have been exiled on arson charges for something I can't remember was a wake-up call. But now I just want my mind to stop.

I pull off buds, popping them in my mouth. They taste like crap, but I don't care. Soon I won't be worried about anything.

CHAPTER 2 - KESSA MCKNIGHT

I COULDN'T STAY IN that meeting and listen to plans for city exploration. That was our dream, mine and Evan's. And Evan is dead.

My mind flashes to that last day, his hand on my jaw as he kissed me goodbye. Marcus hollering from the SUV. And now they're both gone . . .

I take a deep breath, which is a mistake since I've hidden myself away in a bathroom. Washing my hands and squaring my shoulders I look my mirror image in the eyes.

"You are not the girl who breaks down in meetings. You are fine."

I leave the bathroom to find Adam waiting in the lobby. He smiles and I tell my mouth to smile back.

"Hey Kessa," he says. "I wanted to make sure everything's alright."

"All good. Just the usual." I give a little shrug. Hopefully he'll assume I mean a restroom break, not that I'm always one wrong word away from losing my grip on "fine."

He doesn't look convinced, but he nods anyway. Thank God he's polite enough not to push. We walk in silence back to the meeting room. Adam opens the door for me, motioning me in ahead of him.

As we enter, Richard Morton announces that Jace has volunteered as an ambassador for the swap. That can't be right. Jace asked me what the swap was fifteen minutes ago. And sure enough, one look at his face shows me he had no idea this was coming. Is anyone else seeing this?

Jace stands up and stammers something about the honor of representing his town and then brushes past us out the door.

The official part of the meeting ends not long after that. I know I'm here as a delegate, but I can't manufacture a desire to stay and socialize today. When I claim a headache, Adam offers to walk me home to rest before tonight's dinner.

It was dark and I was half asleep when the SUV dropped us off last night. This morning, on the walk down, all I could think about was the stunning views that come with a house perched high above a valley. But now my back is to those views, I'm panting, and my stupid pride said "I'm good" when Adam suggested we stop for a break. I am a runner, but this altitude difference is real.

I finally make it up the hill and to my guest room, which had to be on the second floor. The blue and white quilt-covered bed calls to me. I stretch my tired self out, running my fingertips over the bumps and ridges of the stitching. Eyes closed, I sink into the pillow.

Before long Evan joins me, his body stretched out beside mine as we share a blanket on the beach. Strong fingers brush sand from my arm. Grey eyes take me captive.

A throat clearing behind him makes me look up to where my mom smiles at us from a low-slung chair. She's wearing sunglasses and a floppy black hat, but when she turns her gaze towards the lapping waves, her profile is paper thin. And when she turns back towards us, she vanishes completely, the hat and sunglasses falling onto the empty seat.

A scream builds in my throat, and I look to Evan, but he's gone too. The cross necklace he always wore gleams on the blanket.

I startle awake, clammy and breathing hard. My mom is dead. She's always been dead. And Evan is dead too. Why can't I be with them? Really on a beach somewhere . . . No, Kessa. Breathe. I rub my fingers over the cross at my neck, counting the strokes over its smooth surface. Aligning my breaths. Pulling myself back together.

It's Evan's cross. The search party found it on his body in the burnt-out shell of his SUV. Marcus, as always, was beside him in the passenger seat. In my mind they both died instantly, because I can't handle the thought of Evan burning and thinking of me. Or praying to a God who didn't answer.

Curling onto my side I tell myself to think of something else, and my traitor brain turns to my mom. Dream mom looked like she always does. Like my favorite photo from my parent's honeymoon. She died at my birth, and I know her like someone pre-pan would "know" a YouTube star, from videos and other people's stories.

It's probably awful to say this, but I missed having a mom more than I ever missed my mom. And really, until Evan died I pretty much had his mom. Before Evan's death, his mom her absence was a sorrow I'd feel every once in a while, but I didn't dwell on it. I'd never known any different, and Evan's mom was always there, with advice and cookies and hugs. who'd been my mom's best friend, took on the role in a lot of ways. But now every time she sees me her eyes fill with tears. And, as much as I want to share her grief, I just can't. I've got too much of my own to bury.

I must have fallen back asleep, because Adam wakes me with a knock on the door and lets me know we need to leave in half an hour. He's perfectly put together in khakis and a blue button-down the same shade as his eyes. Business casual tonight.

After a quick shower, I put on nice slacks and a silky scarlet blouse that makes my skin glow. I add earrings and a touch of lip gloss before heading down the stairs. When I join the men in the living room, Adam greets me with an appreciative "good evening."

Henry and Mr. Morton turn at his words.

"Well, then!" says Mr. Morton. "I was telling Henry that I'd forgotten how long it took to get somewhere with a woman in the house, but now I'm remember why it's worth the wait. You look lovely young lady! Simply lovely!"

"Thank you, Mr. Morton" I say with a smile. I hope it looks more authentic than his compliments.

"Please, call me Richard. Now that you're here, shall we go?" Richard makes a "ladies first" gesture towards the door.

"What about Jace?" I ask.

"He decided not to come tonight. Spending some time with his friends, I believe."

And with that Mr. Morton, Richard, offers me his arm and we walk out into the warm evening air.

After a blessedly short walk we reach a sprawling home with real candles in the windowsills. They have less reliance on electricity here, which probably means less ability to produce it. One more way that El Dorado Springs benefitted from my father's expertise.

Once inside, I'm introduced and reintroduced to people from this afternoon's meeting. Adam is the only other adult under thirty, and I wonder if they included him so I wouldn't feel awkward. He chats effortlessly with everyone, even getting high fives when the hosts parade out their kids. So maybe not.

The meal is delicious, but overly formal, like our towns are on a first date. I smile and chat and nod and answer the same questions again and again. It's still early when we walk home, and I hope I'll catch Jace before he goes to bed. I can't get past the idea that he was manipulated into participating in the swap, and that's not ok.

I consider waiting up for him, but I'm drained and there are more meetings tomorrow.

I drift off to sleep, wondering if I'll dream of Evan. Not sure if I want to or not.

Chapter 3 - Jace

Sunlight blares through the windows and my brain feels as crusty as my eyeballs. I'm glad I'm in my own bed, but not quite sure how I got here.

The clock reads 12:05. I guess I'm no longer needed at the meetings. I scrub my hand over my face without bothering to cover my yawn. After a few minutes of staring at my ceiling I get up and put on jeans and a shirt from the ground. They smell fine. Fine-ish.

The kitchen's empty today. No note. I grab a piece of bread and eat it on the way to the riverwalk. The temperature dropped overnight and only a few die-hards are on the water. The playground is still packed.

Cole and a couple of our friends are skateboarding at the amphitheater. I sit on the edge of the concrete stage. Why have I taken this for granted? My Bros. This river. These mountains. Do they even have mountains in El Dorado Springs?

"Where's your girl?" I ask Cole as he boards over. He shrugs.

"She's not gone. Well, maybe. We'll see."

Typical Cole. Not only does he not know if they're broken up, he doesn't care.

"Which line did you use this time? 'It isn't you, it's me'?" I ask.

"Nah, man. That's amateur. 'I've got some problems in my life I need to work out. I don't want to drag you down with me.'"

"Girls hate that one." This comes from Ben, who leans against the stage nearby.

"How would you know?" asks Cole.

"Because you used it to dump my sister a year ago, and I had to listen to her cry about how she wished you would open up and let her help you."

"Huh. Well, I'm an ass. I don't keep it a secret." Cole stretches his arms up over his head, not a care in the world. "It's not my fault every girl thinks she's the one who can change me."

"Yep, true that," Matt says. Matt is super smart. I can't tell if he just agreed with Cole that he's an ass or that the girls are dumb for thinking they can change him.

"Gotta go, bros," Ben says, standing up. "I'm meeting my girl and her sister for lunch. Anyone wanta join me? And by anyone, I mean anyone but Cole."

"Her sister is, what, fourteen now?" Cole says. But I know he's just messing with Ben. Cole's a player, but he follows a code.

"I just ate," I say.

"I'm in," says Matt.

I wait until they're out of listening range, then turn to Cole.

"Want to hear the latest on the great Councilor Morton?" I ask. That's usually how I intro it when Dad does something that sucks. Because that way it's about him, not me.

"Always," Cole says, taking a seat on a step.

"You know how I asked if you heard anything about a 'swap'?"

"Sure."

"Well, the swap isn't about trading stuff or information. They want to swap people. Like teenagers. For some sort of marriage trade alliance."

Cole laughs. "Bro, that's sus, even for Councilor Morton."

"Yeah. And guess who the first 'ambassador' from Salida is going to be?"

"By 'ambassador' do you mean what the word really means, or do you mean 'teenage marriage pawn'?"

"The second one."

"Who?"

"The younger son of the great Councilor Morton." I wait as this sinks in.

"Bro. No. Two days ago you didn't even know what the swap was. Now you're going?"

"I didn't have a choice. Dad volunteered me in a way that made it impossible to say no without calling him a liar in front of the whole town council and the delegates from El Dorado Springs."

"He didn't."

I don't say anything. I don't have to. Cole has been hearing Councilor Morton stories for years.

"That's wrong."

"Yep. But brilliant."

"Wait a minute," Cole says, pointing a twig he's been messing with in my direction. "Are you telling me you're going to get your pick of the ladies in the biggest known town in existence? How does that work, anyway? Do they line 'em up and parade 'em out or what?"

"They're still working on details, but they said everything had to be voluntary, so no parading. I've got to get someone to want to be with me."

"Bro, have you even kissed a girl since Torrie Wilson?"

Cole knows I haven't. And that was on a dare. In eighth grade. I don't bother to answer.

"Someone needs to tell your dad what voluntary means."

"Yep."

Cole doesn't mind silence the way I do, and right now I've got nothing left to say. We sit there, watching the river, until Cole says, "I could go with you."

"Yeah?"

"With me as your wingman, you could be the biggest stud El Dorado Springs has ever seen. All anyone there knows is that your dad's a bigshot."

"I'm not sure I want to deal with the fallout when you break the wrong girl's heart."

"Who knows." Cole shrugs. "Maybe true love's waiting for both of us. And if not, at least it's a fresh start. There aren't any do-overs nowadays. Who you are is who you were born to be."

Cole's back to staring at the river and the few surfers willing to brave the chill. They skim along the surface, not even thinking about what's going on beneath it. Like I have so often with my best friend.

"Bro, if nothing else, you have to come visit me," I say, standing up. When I think of this from Cole's perspective, maybe it isn't so horrible. And really, I don't have much to lose. "I should go see if the delegates are back at my house. If I'm going to be living with these people, I should start getting to know them."

"You go, stud," Cole says with a laugh. "But really, Jace, be yourself."

"Sure," I say.

But there's no chance I'm doing that. I don't even know who 'myself' is. But maybe if I can get far enough away from my father, I can figure it out. And until then I'm going to take a shower, get a haircut. Maybe go to whatever fancy dinner's happening tonight.

I'm not excited. More like resigned. But I know one thing. From now on Jace Morton can be whoever I want him to be.

CHAPTER 4 - KESSA

MEETINGS. SO MANY MEETINGS, with everyone posturing and nothing accomplished. I'm drained as Henry, Adam and I climb that dang hill towards home.

We enter the kitchen to find Jace lounging against the counter eating a sandwich. Something's different.

"Nice haircut," Henry says. Yep, that's it.

"Gotta look good for the ladies." Jace says with a shrug. Henry snorts and heads for the stairs.

I grab a glass from the cabinet and get myself water from the sink "We haven't seen you since lunch yesterday," I say. "That was quite an announcement."

"Well, we're quite a family. What are the plans for tonight?"

"Chili at the Prescott's. I'm told it's 'the best this side of the Rocky Mountains.'" I study Jace for a minute before continuing. "I'm glad you're coming, Jace." And I am. If nothing else, maybe I can find out what really happened when he "volunteered" for the swap.

The Prescott's house is a smart looking ranch style, less grand and more comfortable than where we ate last night.

Country music plays in the background. It's not in my top three genres, but tonight I'm hearing some new stuff that isn't half bad. The chili is as good as promised, but the best part of the evening is the stories. Everyone has one to tell, and the thrill of a new audience is tangible.

Henry looks at me with a grin and I groan inwardly. "I've got a story that involves our very own Kessa. Anyone want to hear it?"

There are several "yesses" and Adam raises his eyebrows as I slowly shake my head. "Looks like Kessa knows what's coming," he says.

"Oh, I'm sure she does. You see, Kessa here doesn't make mistakes often. But this one was a doozy." Henry looks to me to confirm this is ok, and I roll my eyes.

"Go on," I say. I can't very well stop him at this point.

"When Kessa was twelve, she decided she was ready to babysit. She made flyers and spent an entire Saturday handing them out at the general store. She even made a rhyme. 'Need a sitter? Leave it to me! I can take care of 1, 2, or 3!' And she drew the cutest picture of herself sitting in a chair surrounded by kids, giant smiles on every face."

I'm sure my current smile is more of a grimace.

"Unfortunately for Kessa, the spell-check feature on the school computer she was using had been modified by years of junior high schoolers, and it auto-corrected an additional letter 'h' into the word 'sitter.'"

I sigh deeply as realization dawns on the faces around me. Jace busts out laughing, and several others chuckle.

"Thank you, Henry," I say. "That is exactly what I wanted everyone in Salida to know about me. Oh, and Henry forgot to mention the best part. From then on, the entire junior high called me 'the sitter' but meant something else."

"That's brutal, Kessa," Adam says. "Hilarious, but brutal."

"It was a long time ago," I say with a shrug. "And I think I got some pity babysitting jobs, so it wasn't all bad."

Mrs. Prescott follows with a story of their daughter, Cacia, putting their long-haired tabby cat into an open tray of paint "just for a change," and then chasing it through the house to comb its fur.

"I'm glad we can laugh now," says Mrs. Prescott. "At the time I about killed my daughter. I scrubbed every floor in this house."

I picture the neat, comfy home covered in purple paint and can't help but grin.

"Where's Cacia now?" I ask. Unlike last night no children have been paraded through.

"She's helping Dr. Massman tonight."

I must look confused because Adam says, "Cacia's our age. She was one of my best friends growing up, and she's been Dr. Massman's apprentice for a couple years now."

I bite my tongue before a comment about how young Mrs. Prescott looks can get out. Instead, I say, "I look forward to meeting her," and the conversation moves on.

The evening ends late with no meetings scheduled for tomorrow, a Saturday. I walk home beside Jace. He's relaxed and I hesitate to bring up the swap, but this might be my only chance.

"Jace, can I ask you something?"

"Sure. What's up?"

"The other day at the meeting you didn't know what the swap was. But by the time I got back from the bathroom, you'd volunteered to do it. What did I miss?"

It takes Jace a minute to answer. "Yeah, that was weird, right?" He pauses again. "You don't know my dad, but he always finds a way to get what he wants. He wanted me to go to El Dorado Springs. So, he made it happen."

"So, you volunteering wasn't actually you volunteering?"

Jace shrugs.

"Maybe we can fix it," I say. "If I talked to Henry and the others, we could find a way for you to stay here without your dad knowing you told us. Fake a blood test and say your DNA's too similar or something."

"Maybe." We walk on in silence, and are approaching the hill to the house when Jace speaks again.

"My bro Cole said something, and I think he's right. Getting to start over isn't a bad thing. I'll miss my friends, but it might be nice to be away from Dad. Or even my perfect brother. Haven't you ever wanted to go somewhere that people didn't know you were nicknamed 'the sitter?'"

"Apparently that place isn't Salida, thanks to Henry," I say with a laugh. But I get what he means, and there's something to it.

I pant my way up the hill without another word.

Once we're inside, Adam is waiting in the kitchen in case I need anything. Jace mouths the words "perfect brother" with an eye roll and heads upstairs. I take a minute to study Adam. He is rather perfect in a Captain America way. Dark hair, blue eyes. I haven't noticed what a man looks like in years, not since Evan and I started dating.

Pain stabs through me, but this time I'm not letting it win. I accept Adam's offer of tea and sit down at the island while he pours our mugs. Licorice and chamomile waft from my cup. It's an unfamiliar pairing, but I suppose that's the theme of the night. New music, new stories. New starts.

As Adam settles onto the stool beside me, I can't help thinking that Jace might be on to something.

CHAPTER 5 - JAERISH

SEPTEMBER 2045; FORT RILEY, KANSAS, FORMER USA

MY FEET POUND THE ground, forward momentum creating the only breeze as I push on. The sweat and heat are as familiar as the trail before me and the litany rolling through my mind.

My name is Jaerish.

It's not my real name.

Cov-4N has stolen my memory.

Cov-4N has no cure.

I was alone when rescued.

I'm not alone anymore.

It's the last mile now. One more push is all that stands between me and a shower, a change of clothes, and a hot meal with the men from my barracks. I am not alone.

In the mess hall I load my tray and take a seat at a long metal table. Kelvin, a medic with nearly six years of memory, sits down across from me. He's trailed by a young Hispanic guy I don't recognize.

"Jaerish, meet Gideon. Gideon, Jaerish."

"Newb?" I ask, stretching a hand his way.

"How'd you guess?" Kelvin answers for him.

"Don't worry, Gideon," I say as we shake. "We all start with the same expression. It gets better." Gideon's blank look clears somewhat, until a rough voice calls from farther down the table.

"He's right kid. It gets better. Just don't forget the blue pill or you get to start all over again." Hayes is laughing. He loves to screw with the newbs. It's part of why I never sit near him. That and his tendency to skip the post-run shower.

"No one was talking to you, Hayes," I say.

"I've got nearly twenty years knocking around in this head of mine. You need to show some respect." He rises to his feet, makes a weird 'I'm watching you' motion and heads for the exit. Of course, he left his tray on the table for someone else to deal with. I'm scowling at his back when Kelvin's voice draws me back to our conversation.

"Sadly, Hayes is proof that having a long memory doesn't guarantee intelligence." Kelvin is confident and chill, which makes him the perfect choice for helping new soldiers acclimate. He did the same for me not long ago.

"How long do you have?" Gideon asks.

"Four months, twenty-six days."

The sound he makes is somewhere between laughing and choking. "I'm still counting in hours. One hundred thirty-two. But part of the time I was asleep."

"When you hit a week, we'll celebrate," I say.

"The thing to remember," says Kelvin, "is that we're all the same. Besides General Open Sky and the men on the rescue team, no one is immune. No matter what Hayes might say, he'd be as lost as you without the little blue pill."

"To the pill," I say, lifting mine from the tray and swallowing it.

"To the pill," they say, taking theirs as well.

"So why do General Open Sky and the rescue team still have memory?" Gideon asks.

"Cosmic payback," Kelvin says. "When the pandemic hit, people with a substantial amount of Native blood didn't catch it. The government tried to figure out why, but it was too late. *Cov-4N* is some sort of mutation of the original virus, so General Open Sky and those he sends on rescue missions are immune."

"How quickly do you forget if you don't take it? Has anyone done that?"

Kelvin glances at me with a nearly imperceptible shake of his head. He told me once about a soldier with a full twelve years who started questioning the need for the pills. Even made some sort of accusations publicly. The General hadn't had him whipped or imprisoned; he just took away the pills. Within a week the soldier was restrained in solitary, driven mad by *Cov-4N*. Not long after, he slit his wrists on his restraints.

"Don't waste time worrying about it," Kelvin tells Gideon. "If you miss a dose it won't kill you, although I hear it can be disorienting. Best not to risk it."

I haven't missed once, and I don't plan to. Five months is all I've got, and there's no way I'm losing it.

CHAPTER 6- JACE

OCTOBER 2045; EL DORADO SPRINGS, MISSOURI, FORMER USA

"IT'S NICE TO SEE you again, Mayor Cartwright," I say. I wipe my sweaty palm on my jeans before shaking the perfectly nail-polished hand of the woman before me. Sunlight floods through floor to ceiling windows and potted plants make this place look more like an office building than a high school lobby.

"Nice to see you, Jace," she says. "I don't think you've met my daughter, Mae. She's also a junior here so she'll be showing you around and helping you get acclimated."

Mae has long legs, styled hair and heavy make-up. She looks me up and down and says in a silky voice just like her mother's, "It's nice to meet you, Jace." All the hairs on my arms stand up, and I can't tell if it's in a good way.

"You too, Mae," I say. I attempt to harness my inner Cole as I give her a smile and a nod. I'm going for something like *I can roll with that* or *this is your lucky day*, but it probably looks like I have an itch on my neck and don't want to scratch it.

Mae smirks. "Are we done here, Mom?" she asks.

"Henry and I can finish up any unresolved paperwork. Why don't you two get to class?"

Henry's face looks perfectly agreeable, but I've gotten to know him pretty well in the last month. He's not loving the idea of paperwork. Or of more time with Mayor Cartwright. Maybe both. Still, he smiles.

"Have fun, Jace. Anne Marie will be here later picking up the kids from after care. You should keep her company on the way home."

It was nice of Henry not to mention that I'd probably get lost if I tried to get home alone. I've only been here a week, but I'm already part of the family. Anne Marie gave me a big hug the first time we met, and that was it. Plus, their kids are amazing. You'd think I was Spider Man for the hero worship I'm basking in.

"I've got your schedule," says Mae. She hands me a copy and I walk beside her down a long hallway lined with lockers. "This one's mine, but you're a late transfer so you're farther down with the sophomores."

When we get to my locker there's a cute Asian girl with an armload of books stretching to get one more from the top shelf.

"What are you doing here?" Mae asks.

The girl's eyes dart to Mae, and then to me. Her look is curious. I'm probably going to see that another four hundred times today. Returning her gaze to Mae she says, "This is my locker."

"No, it's not. It's Jace's."

"Number 304?" the girl asks.

I look down at the schedule I'm holding that clearly says "305." Before I can say anything, Mae says "Yes, number 304" in such a nasty way I'm shocked speechless.

The girl looks confused and maybe a little afraid, but she straightens up all of her five-foot-nothing self and says, "This is my locker."

Before Mae can reply, I say, "It's totally her locker. I'm 305."

Mae looks down at the paper she's holding. "Oh, right," she says. "Odd numbers are across the hall." Then she turns her back without another word. I try to give the girl an apologetic smile, but she's looking down and doesn't see it. By the time I follow Mae across the hall and look back, the girl's gone.

"You were kind of rude to her," I say.

"What?" asks Mae, distracted as she works on my lock. "Oh, that was just the Donor. It doesn't matter." Before I can ask what she means she says, "And tada!" as though instead of doing the combination to an empty tin box she's cracked the safe holding the crown jewels.

"Thanks," I say, when really, I'm wondering how soon I can ditch the mayor's daughter without offending somebody. Lucky for me, Mae is already in AP classes. The only period we have together is lunch.

Mae walks me to my first class, pushing open the door without knocking. "Mr. Perkins, I've brought you a new student," she says. "This is Jace Morton, from Salida."

Twenty-five sets of eyes are on me. I give my most convincing "Sup," and a three-fingered wave that I hope they'll assume is a normal thing back home rather than me not knowing what to do with my hands.

Mae looks around the room and points to a guy in baggy maroon sweats who's sprawled at a desk near the back.

"Stephen's in your next two classes," she says. "And he eats with my group at lunch. He can show you around."

I look at Stephen, wondering how he'll take this. He smirks and pulls out the chair beside him with his foot.

Stephen's laid back and sarcastic, but not mean. He doesn't object to me tagging along, and by the time we get to lunch, I think we could hang.

"Jace, over here!"

I've barely entered the cafeteria when Mae's voice shatters my good mood. The number of ways she makes me uncomfortable is roughly equivalent to the number of eyes now staring my way. I nod at the room in general, my hand making that same weird three-fingered salute I'd done in first period. They must think I'm the biggest dipwad on the planet.

Stephen chuckles. "You're so screwed."

I follow him into the cafeteria, yet another room flooded with sunlight from windows in the walls and ceiling. Instead of going to Mae, Stephen leads me to the food.

Fresh fruits and vegetables are kept cold on ice. Then there's a hot make-your-own burrito bar with meats and corn and grilled onions and cheese. Then dessert . . . oh the desserts . . . I can barely make everything fit on my tray.

"Where do we pay?" I ask. Stephen looks at me like I asked him where the ugly kangaroos skateboard. "You know, for lunch?"

"Dude, kids gotta eat," he says.

"You mean they give us this for free?"

Stephen shakes his head. "Salida must be one weird place," he says as he leads me to a table where Mae and some others are sitting. He puts his tray down beside a very attractive Indian girl who makes room for him on the bench and then leans in for a quick kiss.

"She's Stephen's girlfriend," Mae says unhelpfully. "And my bestie." Ah. Now I understand. Mae has saved a place for me, and I sit where I'm told like the good political pawn that I am.

The rest of lunch is uneventful. Mae hands me off to another guy for the afternoon, assuring me that should I need anything the office knows how to get ahold of her. When the new guy rolls his eyes behind her back, I'm hopeful the rest of the day will go as smoothly as the first half. Overall, not a bad beginning to life as the new me.

CHAPTER 7 - MICHAELA BARR

"SEE YOU SATURDAY, ENERY!" I say.

"Yeah, you will!" He hollers as he runs across the blacktop towards his bike.

Anne Marie Douglas was late for pick-up from after-school care. She apologizes as she stands from strapping Margi into her bike wagon. I wave it off. She was momming alone with two little kids while Henry was in Salida, and when he returned, he brought her a house guest.

As though my thoughts have conjured him, Jace Morton comes skateboarding around the building. *Fluid.* That's the word for him as he rolls towards us over smooth pavement. I realize I'm staring when I see Enery in my peripheral vision, on a collision course and pedaling hard. Jace manages not to get hit with some sort of magic sidestep.

"Nice ride, little man. I like the power." Jace puts out a fist to knock the rock.

Margi waves across the playground at them until Jace waves back, then she looks down smiling shyly.

"Have you met Jace yet, Michaela?" Anne Marie asks.

"Kindof," I say. Mae Cartwright did try to give him my locker this morning, after all.

"He might be around part of the time on Saturday. He's great with the kids, but we aren't asking him to babysit. It's not why he's here. Is that ok?"

"No problem," I say.

Jace notices me standing beside Anne Marie and gives me one of those cool guy head nods. I nod back, but I don't think it has the same effect. Anne Marie joins him and Enery, and I watch the four of them roll away, their laughter carrying back on the breeze.

I gather up playground balls and put them in their bin. What will I say to Jace if he's there Saturday night? He's barely acknowledged my existence the two times I've seen him so far, so I probably won't need to say anything. Now that I know him being here isn't going to cost me the Douglas' babysitting jobs, his impact on my life should be minimal.

Kessa's decision to stay in Salida though? Well, that hurt.

Two years ago, when Kessa was senior, she started mentoring me. I can't imagine how hard high school would have been without her. Kessa didn't care that my father is a seed merchant, and she always treated me like she valued what I had to say.

After Kessa's boyfriend, Evan, died things changed. Instead of her leading me through Bible studies, we'd bike or knit or sit and read. She didn't want to be alone, and I was glad I could be there for her, but I think I started missing her even before she left.

I lock up the balls and bike home. Mom isn't there when I arrive, which means a busy day at the doctor's office or that she's stopping by the store. A quick glance in the fridge and cupboards tells me creativity will be the main course tonight if she doesn't.

I'm sitting at our table working on a history essay when my mom walks in, cloth bags hanging from her arms. My stomach gurgles loudly and I jump up to help her carry.

"Sounds like I got here just in time," she says.

I grab some of the bags and put them on the kitchen island. Our house is a little bungalow with a front porch big enough for a swing, two bedrooms, a bathroom we share and a room that's kitchen, dining and living room all in one. It's all the two of us need, and anything else is "just more to clean" as mom likes to say.

The kitchen has the best possible pale-yellow cabinets and countertops that pretend to be granite but aren't. Mom and her husband gifted each other the farmhouse sink the last Christmas before the pandemic. They had plans to remodel every inch of this place, and no idea that within months most of the world would be dead.

As we sit down to eat, I notice the slump to Mom's shoulders. She's tired tonight. I volunteer to wash the dishes while she takes first shower. Her life would have been so different if her husband hadn't been away when the pandemic hit. When I was little, I'd look at their wedding pictures and daydream about the three of us as a family. I was ten years old when I realized that if he had lived, I wouldn't exist.

"Guess what?!?" Enery can barely contain himself, but its Margi who blurts out "Peeeza!!!"

I try to head off an argument with my enthusiasm for the news.

"Enery, pizza? Really?"

He shoots a sideways glare at Margi, but decides it's not worth it to be angry. Hopefully that's a good sign for the evening to come.

"Yeah, pizza! And dad says he brought back a super special movie and saved it just for tonight!"

Mental note: thank Henry Douglas. I've seen every kid's movie in this town at least ten times.

"It's called The Littlest Mermaid. There's a singing crab and an octopus monster and everything," Enery says.

"Well then, we should get to that pizza so we can watch! Go wash your hands." They run past Anne Marie on their way to the bathroom.

"Anne Marie! You look so good," I say. "Did Henry bring that dress back from Salida?"

"I sure did." Henry comes up behind her with a grin. "And it was worth every mile of the drive!" He nuzzles her neck, and she laughs, half-heartedly shrugging him off.

I love watching them like this. It seems like how a mom and dad should be.

"We'll be back by nine," Anne Marie says.

"Don't count on it," Henry says with a wink.

Enery and Margi come back, hands still wet, and give their parents kisses and hugs goodbye before sitting at the table. We've just started indulging in the hot cheesy goodness when Jace walks in.

"Enery!" Jace says. "Were you going to eat this whole pizza without me?"

"Yes!" Enery gives Jace a big sauce-covered grin.

"Margi, my main girl. You were going to let him?" Margi giggles and ducks her head.

"And you." Jace turns a mock serious face my way. "I suppose you were going to help them do it, weren't you?"

I've forgotten how to form words, but not how to blush. I'm doing that quite well, thank you. After an awkward silence, Jace nudges Enery with an elbow.

"Bro, who's your accomplice? Does she talk?"

Enery giggles and I manage to stammer "I'm Michaela. Barr. I'm watching the kids tonight."

"Michaela Barr. Why does that sound familiar?"

"Um, we have a class together, I think." We have two. He walks past me to get to his seat in the back row of Geometry every single day, but who's noticed, right?

"No, that's not it. I mean, yeah, we might, but that's not why I know your name. This is gonna bug me."

"Sorry about that. Want some pizza?"

"Now that, Michaela Barr, is a fantastic idea." Jace gets a plate and straddles a chair at the table, making Margi giggle again.

"Hats off at the table!" says Enery.

"Bro, are you trying to show Michaela my messy hair? You gotta give a brother a chance with the lady!" Jace sighs as he takes off his stocking cap, exposing a mass of dark hair. He shakes his head. "It's all over now. Thanks a lot, Enery."

"You don't have a chance with Michaela anyway," Enery says with a shrug. "She's way out of your league." I'm not sure if I'm more touched by Enery's sweetness or embarrassed by how backwards he has it.

"So, what's the plan for tonight, Michaela Barr? Is Enery taking you and Margi out on the town?"

"We're watching the tiniest mermaid!" chimes in Margi.

"Oooh, that's a good one. I used to watch that all the time."

"It's brand new for us, which is kind of fun," I say. "We haven't had a new kids' movie in forever."

"Three cheers for the swap," says Jace. It sounds forced.

"How do you like El Dorado Springs so far?" I ask. "Are you glad you're here?" As the questions leave my mouth, I realize how awkward it would be to answer honestly if he hates it. But it's too late to take it back.

"El Dorado Springs is cool. I miss my friends, but I like these guys." Margi and Enery grin. "And pizza. Your pizza is definitely better."

There's a pounding on the door. "That's my cue," says Jace. "If I'm not back before you leave, it was nice to meet you, Michaela Barr."

And with that, the ball of charm that is Jace Morton has left the building.

Enery and Margi choose seats on the couch while I put the pizza away and then we all watch "The Little Mermaid." Mental note: ask to borrow this for babysitting the Taylors next Monday.

Margi makes it nearly to the end, but not quite and I'm glad because it gets kind of scary. I carry her to her room and tuck her in while Enery picks a story. We're only a few pages into *Prince Caspian* before he falls asleep. I bring it downstairs with me so I can keep reading, but instead I stare blankly at the page and overthink what I said, and didn't say, when Jace was here.

Why can I hold a perfectly reasonable conversation with any adult or child, but not say five words to someone my own age without my brain shutting down? I'm still "reading" when the door opens at nine. I'm not disappointed to see Henry and Anne Marie instead of Jace. Really, I'm not.

I'm mounting my bike when a figure emerges from the darkness.

"Michaela Barr!" Jace says. "I was hoping you'd still be here."

"Oh yeah? Why's that?" Four words. Good start.

"Because I remembered why I know your name. And I have something for you. I'll be right back."

I stand, straddling my bike in the glow of the porchlight. What could Jace possibly have for me? He returns quickly, an envelope in hand.

"Kessa asked me to give you this. She said you were the most 'exceptional' girl in El Dorado Springs, which makes me wonder why I didn't look for you sooner."

"'Exceptional' isn't always a good thing," I say.

"True, but it was how she said it." Jace grins. "Have a great night, Michaela Barr."

There's an awkward pause, and then he's gone. Ten words. That's all I said. And six were to point out that I might be exceptional in a bad way. Fantastic.

As soon as I get home, I tear into Kessa's letter.

Michaela,

I'm sure me staying in Salida was a shock, and I hope you can forgive me. I needed to get away. Evan is still dead. That won't change. But when people here look at me, they don't know I'm broken. And if no one else knows, I can almost convince myself it isn't true.

I value your friendship more than anything else I left behind, with the exception of my Dad (and possibly my LOTR books, which I've been promised will be arriving with the next messenger). You've grown into an amazing young woman and I hope that we can write each other and stay in contact.

Forever your friend,

Kessa

PS- In a way you could say I'm here because of Jace. He's the one who pointed out that a fresh start can be a good thing. Having him deliver this letter to you is my way of repaying the favor.

Nothing about Kessa's reasoning is a surprise, but I'm still glad she wrote. As for introducing Jace to me as a favor to him, well, Kessa loves me. I'll take her words for the compliment they imply and leave it at that.

CHAPTER 8 - KESSA

I ENTER THE EVENT center with Adam. At least a hundred people I don't know talk and laugh in the crowded space, and I am so aware that my official "ambassador" duties have begun.

I didn't mention staying in Salida until three days before the delegation from El Dorado Springs left, despite several not-so-subtle hints from Richard Morton that it would be nice to have tangible assurance before sending his son so far away.

In the two weeks since, I've moved into my own place (a guest house belonging to the family that hosted our first dinner), and started my new job working on a plan to integrate Dad's alternative energy solutions into Salida's existing systems.

You'd think something that important would be top priority, but no. I've somehow been sucked back in time to the era of Pride and Prejudice, and now finding an "eligible match" for me is all anyone's able to think about. Hence the singles mingling. Oh, Miss Austen, if you could see me now.

Adam has been my running partner since my third day in town, and he offered to pick me up tonight so I wouldn't have to face this room alone. Now, as introductions begin, I'm more grateful than ever for his hero complex. Or gentlemanly nature. Whichever.

There's a brunette with a big smile greeting people near the door, and her eyes light up when she sees Adam. Throwing her arms around him, she hugs him tight as he laughs.

"You know you saw me two days ago, right?" he asks.

"I can count, Adam," she says with a grin. "But that was for business, not pleasure."

Turning to me Adam makes introductions. "Kessa McKnight, this is Cacia Prescott. Cacia, Kessa McKnight."

Her smile widens, if possible, and she puts out her hand, which I shake automatically. Her name sounds familiar and when it comes to me I blurt "Oh, the cat girl."

Adam is laughing at the confused look on Cacia's face, and I stammer out "I'm so sorry. Your parents told the story about when you put your cat in the paint . . . "

"Oh, that," Cacia says with a dismissing gesture and a laugh. "That's exactly how I want the only new person to this town ever to know me." She huffs a dramatic sigh. "Oh well. After that kind of intro, we're sure to be great friends." Her smile is genuine, and it gives me hope for the rest of the evening.

We move into the room and Adam sticks with me through introduction after introduction. Maybe I should request nametags next time. About half an hour in, Mr. Prescott appears and requests a moment with Adam, depositing Cacia in his place.

She continues to make the rounds with me, but I'm surprised when Adam doesn't return. It must be obvious that I'm looking for him because Cacia says "You probably won't see much of Adam again until it's time to leave."

"Really?" I ask her. "Why?"

"There are people who feel like he had an unfair advantage in getting to know you before anyone else was aware you'd be a swap ambassador. They want to make sure there's an even playing field moving forward."

"It's not like I come with a prize, you know," I say, slightly queasy to be discussing the strange political game that is my love life with such a new acquaintance.

"No, but there is prestige and connection, as well as new DNA, which could bode well for future marriage prospects."

"You're kidding?" I ask.

"Sadly, no. This kind of thing matters." Cacia shrugs. "Take it from someone with fifteen cousins in this town. Hopefully y'all send a guy next time." She says it without malice, steering me towards a table of refreshments.

"Does that mean that all of the singles in Salida are here tonight?" I ask scanning the room.

"For the most part. Ages eighteen to thirty-five. And no merchant kids."

"Merchant kids?"

"You know, people with a seed merchant father. They're considered 'ineligible' according to the rules of the swap."

This is news to me. We only have a couple of people in El Dorado Springs who have a seed merchant parent, at least that I know of, and my close friend Michaela is one of them.

"It seems like a bad precedent to treat people differently because of an accident of birth," I say. "Historically that kind of thing hasn't gone well."

"I agree," says Cacia. "I'll help you if you want to take it up with the Council. There's been some underlying prejudice for a while, but it's never been official before. We should address it now before you find yourself in a tragic love story."

If only she knew. Evan hasn't crossed my mind since I arrived tonight, and the guilt returns with a vengeance. Cacia's looking at me, waiting on an answer.

"Let's talk to the Council," I say. "My dad wouldn't want that type of prejudice involved. And besides," I force a smile, "I might miss out on the love of my life."

Adam arrives for our run at exactly seven a.m. He obviously jogged here, and while I appreciate his punctuality on principal, it takes second place to how good his faded blue t-shirt looks, slightly damp and stretched over broad shoulders. And, cue the guilt.

It pisses me off, because it's not like I'm in love with him and, quite frankly, Evan is dead. I can't spend my entire life never thinking a guy is hot, especially if I'm supposed to find one to marry. My anger propels me down the street away from my house and I welcome it. It's better than feeling nothing at all.

After half an hour we stop for a break. I lean against the painted brick "ghost sign" advertising coca cola and snowdrift, whatever that is. Adam takes a long drink from his water bottle then offers it to me. I shake my head. I'm not there yet.

"So, Kessa, why did you decide to stay?"

He asks causally, but it's such a loaded question. My deep breathing isn't about the altitude now. *Kessa, you are fine.*

"What do you mean?"

"Well, at first I worried that my dad pressured you into it. He isn't exactly subtle. But now that I know you better, I don't think you could be coerced, even by Richard Morton. You chose this. So why did you want to stay in Salida?"

There's something in Adam's eyes that I can't read. Is he hoping I stayed because of him? I don't want to hurt Adam, but I don't want to encourage him either. Do I? I decide to tell him the truth.

"My boyfriend, Evan, died almost six months ago. He and his best friend were on a gathering trip when their SUV went over a ravine and caught fire." I pause for a long time before I say it. "I was supposed to be with them."

Adam doesn't answer, just lets me gather my thoughts. "I did the swap because I needed a new start, somewhere that people weren't constantly watching to see if I was ok."

I've been staring at the brick and the ghost signs, and now I'm afraid to look at Adam, because I don't know what I'll do if I see "that look" on his face.

"Has it helped?" he asks. "Getting a new start."

Has it?

"I don't cry all the time now. But most of the time I don't feel anything." Except maybe guilt when I think about your broad shoulders. But I don't say that part.

"How long were you together?"

"Forever," I say with a shrug. "Our dads were best friends growing up, and when my mom died their family stepped in. Evan's mom took care of both of us during the day and then after school. We spent all our holidays together. Evan was like a brother, until one day he wasn't. I think the happiest day of his mom's life was when he took me to homecoming as an actual date, not just a friend."

I breathe deep, trying to keep it together as I remember Evan asking, all nervous like I might say no. By that point, I was so gone for him that he could have asked me to go cow tipping and I'd have agreed.

Adam doesn't break the silence, but he must know something's shifted because he reaches out, takes my hand, and pulls me into a hug. Before I know what's happening, I'm sobbing into his shirt. *I am not the girl who cries.*

His arms feel solid around me. Safe. I smell his sweat and I don't hate it. I wait for the guilt to come, but apparently I'm too exhausted to be mean to myself right now.

One of Adam's hands slowly strokes my shoulder. His lips are so close to the top of my head that I can feel his breath. I think he might kiss my hair, but he doesn't. And he doesn't make those shushing noises that are supposed to be comforting but actually mean "I can't handle your pain."

Eventually I pull back, aware again that I'm standing on a street in the middle of downtown Salida. Adam has angled himself between me and anyone passing by. My hero.

"I got your shirt messy," I say with an attempt at a smile.

"I had to wash it anyway." He shrugs, a small answering smile on his lips. "Are you ready to head back or do you need a minute?"

For the first time in months, I'm absolutely starving.

"Home," I say.

We jog back in silence, but when I've got one hand on the door he stops me.

"I'm glad you didn't go with them," Adam says. "On that gathering trip."

Despite how guilty it makes me feel, I realize I'm glad too.

Chapter 9 - Michaela

"Michaela, wait up!"

I'm leaving school Friday when Jace catches me on the steps. We've talked most days since he gave me Kessa's letter, and he's even started walking with me after geometry. This doesn't mean I'm comfortable with his attention, or the looks other people give me when I'm with him. I'm not. But I can speak in complete sentences around him now, and I'm counting that as a win.

Jace is asking me about a homework assignment when a trilling laugh interrupts him. Mae Cartwright walks up beside Jace and casually slips an arm through his elbow. I don't hate anyone, but it's a conscious decision with Mae Cartwright.

"Jace! I've been looking all over for you! Some of us are going to the pit tonight and I really want you to come with me. You will, won't you?" She looks up at him with big blue eyes under ridiculously long lashes. Auburn (yes, auburn!) waves fall over her shoulders and down to her perfect chest, covering a dark yawning chasm where her heart should be. No human male could resist such temptation.

I've been intentionally left out of the invitation, and Mae has actually stepped between us now, masterfully turning Jace so he would have to deliberately look past her to see me. Did she take a class in this?

I start to back away when I realize that Jace is trying to catch my gaze. *Don't leave!* his eyes shout, and I feel a smile forming at the corner of my mouth.

"I'm sorry, Mae, but Kayla and I have plans tonight. Maybe next time."

Mae turns to me, eyes narrowing as her fake smile widens. "Oh, Michaela, I'm sorry. I didn't see you there. Do you have a study session scheduled? We'd be happy if you came too if your plans aren't specific."

The same way a spider would be happy if the fly stopped by.

"Our plans are specific," Jace says before I can make my tongue work. "Thanks though." Mae turns back to Jace, already intentionally unaware of my presence.

"Well, have fun," she says, as though she thinks it's unlikely. "You know where I am if you change your mind." I watch her walk away, wondering how in the world she makes her hips do what they're doing.

I look to see if Jace is watching too, but instead he's grinning at me.

"Thanks, Kayla. Sometimes Mae makes me feel like I'm being hunted."

"I know what you mean. Well, not exactly. I feel more like an animal too small to be worth stalking. Not that she wouldn't eat me if I got in her way. Which I suppose I just did." Apparently, I have no words or all the words.

"Sorry about that. So, what are we doing tonight?"

I must look surprised because Jace says "You know, our 'specific plans.'"

"Oh. I thought you just needed an excuse not to go to the pit," I say. I can literally feel my cheeks heating.

"No problem. It's all good."

Jace is rubbing his hand on the back of his neck. He puts his arm back down quickly, like he's worried he might smell. This isn't the confident Jace

I'm used to seeing, and I think about Kessa's letter and him needing a fresh start. Be brave, Michaela.

"I'd love to hang out with you, but I'm babysitting the Fletcher twins tonight. I could use back-up if you wanted to come?"

Jace grins, kind of off-center. His eyes look like they're asking "really?" but not in a mean way. "That sounds perfect," he says. "Way better than a night as prey."

I find myself mirroring his smile. "You might change your mind after an hour with the twins. We babysit at six."

And just like that my Friday's gone from a night with ten-year-olds who have run off every other sitter in town, to a night with Jace, which is a million times scarier.

Jace is at my house at 5:30. Mom gives me a significant look but only makes an allusion to reinforcements before sending us on our way. The twins are in the front yard when we arrive, and I leave Jace to their dubious mercy while I go inside to tell Mrs. Fletcher we're here.

I find her in the foyer, purse in hand.

"Michaela, thank God you're here. If I'd been left with them another five minutes you might have been hiding bodies instead of babysitting tonight. Marshall had a last-minute patient, so I'm meeting him at the restaurant. There's food in the cupboard. The boys found my fudge stash and ate it all, so they're more likely to be sick than hungry. Just do your best."

We walk out together, and I can tell the moment Mrs. Fletcher spots Jace. She glances my way, trying unsuccessfully to hide a smile.

"So, Michaela, are you friends with Jace Morton now?"

"I am. Just friends. Kessa asked him to deliver a letter to me."

"Well, he's welcome to help, but I'm only paying one of you," she says smirking. "Boys, be good for Michaela and her friend Jace," she calls as she walks across the yard to her bike. "I've given them permission to bury you in the backyard if you give them any trouble."

The twins laugh and ignore her.

"Thanks Mrs. Fletcher. Where's the shovel? Just in case." Jace asks. Beside him the boys have a rope and the glances they send Jace's way do not bode well.

"Better help your *friend*, dear," says Mrs. Fletcher as she pedals away.

Besides a boiled over pot of macaroni and a scraped elbow the evening is blissfully uneventful. Jace even got the boys to bed without a fight by promising to tell them about how he broke his arm skateboarding down a mountain.

Once they're down, Jace and I watch *Toy Story* until Mr. and Mrs. Fletcher get home. They insist on paying Jace, despite his attempts at refusal, and then we head back towards my house. I bike and Jace rolls alongside me on what I now know is a longboard. The night air is cool but not cold, and a bright white moon peers at us through a hole in clouds that are somehow orange, blue and pink all at once.

This isn't a date. I know that. But I'm still nervous as we pull up to my house.

Mom left the porch light on, and we're standing just beyond its glow when Jace says "There's one more thing I want to do."

He's staring down into my eyes. Is he going to try to kiss me? I mean, of course he isn't. Right?

"Turn around," Jace says.

"What?"

"Just turn around."

I do and the next thing I know Jace shoves me.

"What was that for?" I glare at him, kissing now the farthest thing from my mind.

"You're goofy. I should have figured that," Jace says with a shrug.

"What? You're goofy! You're the one who pushed me!"

"On a skateboard, 'goofy' means you ride right foot forward. You can tell by which foot you step with when someone pushes you."

"Jace, I don't ride a skateboard."

Jace's eyebrow is cocked in a way I'm starting to know means trouble.

"No way, Jace Morton. Not gonna happen."

"Then I shoved you for nothing and I'm a complete jerk. You don't want to make me a jerk, do you Kayla?"

"I didn't make you a jerk. You did that yourself!" He looks at me with mock hurt. "Fine, you're not a jerk. But it's dark, Jace! And when did you start calling me Kayla? No one calls me that."

Jace shrugs again. "I like it. And it's not that dark. Try it once. Or maybe twice. If you hate it, we'll stop."

His face is so hopeful I can't say no. Jace breaks into a huge grin, knowing he's won.

"For the record," I say. "It is never ok to push a woman."

"I entirely agree."

Jace and I walk back to the road so we're standing under one of the solar powered streetlights, then he proceeds to tell me some basics. When I try it, I'm a little wobbly, but not bad. Jace jogs beside me as I pick up speed.

"Not bad!" he says. "Now drag your foot to stop."

"Drag my foot? How?"

He must hear the note of panic in my voice, because he quickly says, "Never mind." And before I know it Jace has jogged backwards a couple of steps and then lifted me off the board. Now he's beside me, kind of facing me, with an arm around my waist. He lowers me to the ground and my hand runs down his chest to his stomach as I attempt to catch my balance. I stand there for a second too long, looking up at him, before I step back and drop my hand.

"Have you done that before?" I ask, slightly breathless, into the nervous silence. "It was kind of impressive."

I can smell a whiff of Jace mixed in with the dried leaves and smoke from someone's fire. Part of me is wishing I hadn't taken that step backwards, but the other part is afraid I'm still way too close. Jace's arm drops to his side, and he turns to grab his board which has rolled a few feet away.

"Nope. But I watched my bro Cole do it about a million times. It was part of his repertoire for picking up the ladies."

"Literally," I say.

"What? Oh, yeah. Literally. Hah!"

"I guess I should feel honored. I'm the first lady to be picked up by Jace Morton."

"Yes, ma'am, you are."

We've walked back to my porch and my hand rests on the doorknob.

"Can I come over tomorrow to give you another lesson?" Jace asks.

"Only if you promise to teach me to stop."

"You'd have stopped in a few feet without my help. I just always wanted to try out that move. I'll be here at ten."

"I've got something at ten."

"Eight it is." He hops on the longboard and strikes a buzz lightyear pose. "To infinity, and beyond" he calls as he boards off down the street. I can't stop grinning as I walk through the door.

Chapter 10 - Kessa

My legs burn. My throat burns. But I feel good as I push through the crisp morning up the final stretch of hill to Adam's house. And then I see it. Turns out there's enough air left in my lungs to scream.

"What?" Adam asks, his gaze following mine.

"There, in that tree. Oh, God, it was a child." As much as I want to cover my face with my hands, I can't pull my eyes away.

Adam, beside me, makes a noise. Is he laughing?

I turn on him. "How is this funny?"

Adam doesn't answer. Instead, he walks to the tree, gently lifting down the skeleton.

"I don't think we should be touching that." I say, backing away as he approaches.

"Kessa, look. It's plastic."

"Plastic?" I hesitate, then step forward, and sure enough small plastic bones are held together with clear thread. "Why would someone hang that in their tree?"

"For Halloween?" he says. Like that should make sense.

"What do skeletons have to do with Halloween?" I ask.

Adam looks at me like I'm crazy, but I'm not the one holding a baby skeleton.

"Kessa, I can't picture Halloween without skeletons," Adam says. "That's the whole point. Skeletons, vampires, zombies. All the spooky stuff."

"That is not Halloween. Halloween is corn mazes and hayrides and fireworks. There's nothing scary about it. It's actually very hobbit-like."

"Hobbit-like? As in *Lord of the Rings* hobbits?"

"Yes. Halloween is the most hobbit of holidays. But we wear shoes."

Adam is laughing again. "You are totally geeking out on me, you know."

"Tolkein was brilliant," I say with a shrug. "Your Halloween sounds creepy."

"Yeah," Adam says. "It is." And then his face falls.

My lungs start constricting before my mind catches up.

"Wait. Are you telling me that until Halloween this town is going to be one big reminder of death?" I ask. My body's still coursing with adrenaline, and it comes out harsher than I intended. "I'm sorry. I'm not mad at you, it's just . . . oh God."

I close my eyes. Breathe in. Breathe out. And then Adam's arms are around me. But this time instead of feeling comforted, I feel trapped.

I push away from him, bending over with my hands on my knees. Breathe in. Breathe out. Count to five with each. Feel the curve of my kneecaps beneath my fingertips. Breathe in. Breathe out.

After what feels like a very long time, but probably wasn't, I'm ok again. Except for the embarrassment.

Adam is still standing here, his legs in my line of sight a few feet away. When I finally look up there's concern in his eyes.

"You ok?" he asks.

"I'm ok," I say, straightening. "It just looks like my plan to escape death has been thwarted." I try to say it lightly, but we both know it's not.

"Sorry about the hug," Adam says, looking past me at the tree line.

"It's fine. Hugs are nice. Just not during panic attacks. Which aren't something I have often, by the way."

Adam nods, his gaze back on my face, and then he opens his arms in invitation. I only hesitate a moment before I step into them. His warmth closes around me. Without snot and sobs as a distraction, I'm aware of his chest beneath my cheek, the muscles of his back under my palms. It still feels safe, but it's more, too. Like reading the back of a book with an intriguing cover and realizing the story might be even better than you hoped.

Eventually Adam steps away, stoops to pick up the skeleton, and returns it to the tree.

"That's going to take some getting used to," I say, staring at the little bones swinging in a breeze.

"In a couple of years, you won't even notice."

The fact that I will still be in Salida two years from now is finally starting to feel real. It's a new idea, but not a bad one.

I wait in Adam's kitchen while he changes clothes and we walk back into town together. We're passing the combo grocery and deli when we're joined by a tall, dark-skinned Adonis on a skateboard.

"Adam, my man. How's it going?" he asks.

"Going well," Adam says.

The young man checks me out with a grin then looks pointedly at Adam. Adam sighs. "Cole, this is Kessa McKnight, the swap ambassador from El Dorado Springs. Kessa, this is Jace's best friend, Cole Carson."

"It's nice to meet you, Cole," I say, extending a hand.

"Kessa," he says, drawing my name out with a silky voice. "The pleasure's all mine." He's taken my hand, but instead of shaking it he holds it gently until Adam clears his throat beside us. I pull my hand back, slightly shaken after all.

"Adam," Cole says, "I love your brother and all, but I think this swap might be slightly unbalanced." I'm suddenly aware of how rough I must look like in my running clothes and for a painful second I wonder which side he thinks the imbalance is on. Then he shoots me another killer grin and it's obvious he likes what he sees. Adam moves closer.

"You hear anything from Jace?" Cole asks Adam. He hasn't and the conversation ends soon after with Cole shooting us a "see you around" and taking off on his board. We continue our walk towards my house.

"So, what's the story on Cole?" I ask. "He hasn't been around for any of the events."

"He's too young," Adam says. "And he's a merchant kid."

"The age makes sense with him being Jace's friend. What are your thoughts on the merchant rule anyway?"

"I guess that depends," Adam says.

"On what?"

"On whether you're asking in general or because of Cole."

I laugh. "Why Adam? You jealous?"

He laughs with me. "Maybe a little. You should hear the stories Jace has told about that kid. He's quite the player."

"I believe it. But you're right," I say with a smile. "Way too young."

We're passing the playground, and I leave the sidewalk and sit down at an empty picnic table under leaves that are just turning gold. Adam takes the seat across from me. Around us parents chat as they watch their kids swing and climb.

"I have mixed feelings on the merchant rule," Adam says. "I understand not wanting to limit the potential influence of new genetic material, but I hate the idea of discrimination based on parentage. This town has a history of segregation. They'd fixed it by the time the pandemic hit, but now there's a stigma with the merchant kids. I get the impression my dad wouldn't want me dating one, although he's never come out and said it."

I'm stuck on the fact that I'm the "new genetic material" and barely register the rest of what he said.

"Cacia offered to go with me to the Council about it," I say. "You should come with us."

His "maybe" sounds a lot like a "no." I shift on the hard bench.

"How do you think they're handling it in El Dorado Springs?" Adam asks.

"I doubt it's an issue; there aren't many people with seed merchant fathers. I'm sure they'll take it case by case if it comes up."

"Do your laws work that way? Case by case?"

"Of course. Do yours not?"

Adam shakes his head. "Nope." This is almost as strange as skeletons at Halloween.

"You have to look at each case individually," I say. "If someone steals because they're lazy or greedy, they need character development, and have to own it. But if they steal because they lost their job and there wasn't another way for them to get food, that's societal opportunity and should be addressed by the community. If you aren't looking at the individual causes of crime, how do you bring about societal change?"

While Adam is thinking about his answer I'm distracted by the roughness of the wood beneath my fingertips. I clamp my hands together in front of me and lean in, elbows on the table.

"I guess our society mostly changes when people outside of the situation see what's going on and decide to do something about it. Sometimes that's through the Council, and sometimes it's just on their own. I'm sure we miss things that way, but there are a lot of good people around, so maybe not as much as you'd think."

We're both quiet now, watching the kids play until Adam says "What do you do about the first guy? The one who stole because he was lazy?"

"He has to work off his debt with interest. There's usually some sort of career path assessment or training involved in the hopes that he'll like the new job and stick with it. No more stealing needed."

"But what about punishment? Is there prison time or something?"

I'm surprised by the question. Adam loves history like I love "Lord of the Rings." He, of all people, should understand how poorly that system worked. My voice has some heat to it when I ask "Why?"

"What's to stop other people from stealing if there aren't consequences?"

"Trust me. In El Dorado Springs everyone knows everyone's business. There are consequences."

I look back to the playground. Happy kids. Happy parents, or maybe nannies. The occasional tantrum, but nothing out of the ordinary. Nothing to indicate a justice system based on fear and retribution.

"Do you have a prison here?" I ask. "I haven't seen it on the power grid diagrams."

"Well, no. Dad sees prison as a waste of resources."

"So what do you do for those 'consequences?'" I ask.

"For lesser stuff, community service." Adam shrugs. "For anything major, or repeat offenders, exile."

Did I hear him right? "Exile?"

"Yeah."

"Isn't that kind of like a death sentence?"

"Not really. But it is a strong deterrent."

Between Deathoween and the threat of exile I'm realizing how naïve I was to assume Salida would be just like El Dorado Springs. Our pasts were different before the pandemic and now they've diverged even farther. And if I'm honest, I don't like some of the directions my new home has gone.

Chapter 11 - Jace

"Good morning," I say, as I walk into the kitchen.

Henry nearly drops the pancake he's flipping. "Good morning to you. You do know it's Saturday, right?"

"Crazy, huh? I didn't know they made mornings this early on Saturdays, but here it is. Think I could have a pancake for the road?" I ask, taking one off the top of the stack.

"Only if you tell me who got you out of bed at this hour. I might need to hire them for school days."

"I'm going to teach Michaela how to skateboard. This is the only time she had."

"Michaela, huh?" Henry asks. "Michaela Barr?"

"I wanta go see Michaela!" Enery says from where he's coloring with Margi at the kitchen table.

"Me too! Me too!" chirps Margi.

"You'll see her at the church at ten." Henry says.

"That's four hours away!"

"Two hours, bro," I say.

Enery harumphs and then walks over and hugs me.

"That's sweet, buddy," I say. I'm touched.

"That's for Michaela," he says. "You'll have to give it to her for me since I have to wait four hours to see her."

I glance at Henry who's smirking. Thank you Enery. Don't mind if I do.

Kayla is waiting on her porch swing. Mornings are getting cold now, and for the first time I realize how much I like the look of a girl in a hoodie. We walk to the park, her carrying my skateboard and me with the longboard. Because I'm a gentleman. After an hour, she can stop on her own and no longer looks adorably terrified when she gets some decent speed.

We've taken a water break, and I realize if I'm going to give her Enery's hug, I'd better do it soon.

"I almost forgot. Enery asked me to give you something."

"Oh yeah?"

She looks at me expectantly, glancing at my hands which I hold up palms out. Then I step forward and wrap my arms around her.

Her whole body stiffens. I've somehow pinned her arms down so she couldn't return the hug even if she wanted to. This is not what I was going for. I give a little squeeze and step backwards.

"Enery wanted you to give me a hug?" she asks.

"Yes. Yes, he did."

"Ok, then. Tell Enery 'thanks' for me?" She definitely said that like a question. I stumble around for something to say.

"Yeah, I will. No, actually, Henry said you'd be at the church at ten, so you can thank him yourself. What are you doing there? Isn't church usually on Sunday?"

"It is. But we host a movie night once a month, and I'm on set-up. It's going to be packed this month because we're watching something Henry brought back from Salida, so no one but you will have seen it. But you should come anyway."

"Michaela Barr, are you asking me on a date?" I ask.

Kayla blushes. I like it when Kayla blushes. But she hasn't replied.

"I will take your silence as a 'yes.' And I'll raise you a 'yes' of my own."

Kayla's looking at me and her eyes are . . . stressed out? That's not what I was going for.

"If you don't want to, that's cool." I say. I feel like I've said this before. Stupid awkward hug.

"It's not that I don't want to. It's just, I don't know if you're allowed to go out with me."

"Allowed?"

"Yeah. With the swap. My dad was a seed merchant, so I'm practically the only person with a seed merchant dad in El Dorado Springs. And it's not like you're asking me to marry you or anything, but I don't know if there are rules about that. Gene pool stuff, you know?"

"Ah. I have no idea." And I don't. Because I skipped those meetings. All I know is that in the next five years I have to marry a girl from El Dorado Springs and stay here.

"Well," I say. "Why don't I go with the Douglases tonight, and you can sit with us. Enery and Margi will love that. And so will I. And if there are rules, we won't be breaking them." The old Jace liked breaking rules, but Kayla doesn't need to know that. She isn't the rule-breaking type.

"That sounds good," she says, grinning. I should have saved Enery's hug for now.

"I'd better get to the church. Set up to do and all."

"I'll come with," I say, and we're off.

Michaela's church is not what I was expecting. No pews. No stained glass. Instead, people are arranging couches and chairs in a big open space with basketball hoops on each end and a stage front and center. A band is practicing, and I'm nodding along to the bassline before I realize the lyrics are about Jesus.

I played bass in Salida, but our church was more the old lady with a piano type. Dad only made us go twice a year, which was fine with me. The Douglases go every Sunday, but I've never been up early enough, and they haven't mentioned it. Which is good, I guess.

There's a big screen and projector set up above the band. It's weird to think there used to be huge buildings only for watching movies, and if I ever explore cities, I totally want to see one. The irony is, I know such places existed because I saw them in movies.

These are my deep thoughts when Henry finds me. I'm also staring at Kayla who's setting up the refreshment table. Henry clears his throat, and I jump and look away.

"So, how was the skateboarding lesson?" Henry asks.

"It was good. She's a natural."

"Oh yeah. And did you deliver Enery's message?"

My face burns. "Yep, I did."

"And did Michaela send Enery a message back?"

"No. She asked me to thank him, but I told her she could do it here."

"Indeed, she can." Henry watches Michaela for a moment then speaks. "Michaela is a wonderful young woman. One of the best I know."

"Yeah, she is," I say. "Henry, am I allowed to date her?"

Henry chuckles. "Well, I think that would be up to her. And her mother."

"No, I mean, is it ok with the swap. You were in the meetings. She said she wasn't sure it would be because her dad was a seed merchant."

"Oh. I see." His brows knit. "You know, it was implied that it wouldn't be ideal in Salida, since the use of seed merchants is so prevalent that it could ultimately limit the effectiveness of adding new dna to the gene pool. It shouldn't matter here, though. Michaela's the only child her father had in El Dorado Springs."

I start to smile, but Henry's still talking. "She's felt the sting of it her whole life. Michaela's mom, Barbara, was a new bride before the pandemic. Her husband was on a work trip in Chicago when everything went down. They facetimed until the circuits crashed."

"Most towns that were able to quarantine had a 'shoot on sight' policy initially, so when word got out that El Dorado Springs was willing to take in survivors, people flocked here. Barbara set up the quarantine camps, and she didn't do it from a distance, either. Some people thought she was hoping to catch it when she took out food and supplies, but she never did. She also never married again.

"One day she shocked everyone by saying she'd taken a seed merchant into her home and was going to have a baby. Sure enough, seven months later, hello Michaela."

"The seed merchant left shortly after the birth and never came back through. We eventually got word that he'd been killed in the Dakotas on charges of defective seed. It's too bad. He was a decent guy, and probably would have won Barbara over in time."

Michaela looks up from organizing napkins and catches me staring. She quirks her head with a little smile and walks towards us. I watch her, looking for the sadness that should be there with that kind of backstory, but I just don't see it. She and Enery reach us at the same time.

"Kayla! Kayla!" he yells. She looks at him and then at me. Back at him.

"Hello Enery. When did you start calling me Kayla?"

"I don't know. Sometime," he says, shrugging. "Did Jace give you my hug for me?"

"Yes, he did," she says, with a hint of a blush.

"Good! Did you give him one to give me back?"

"No. I saved it for you." She smiles and leans down to hug the boy.

"It's not fair that he got to see you for two hours and I didn't," Enery says.

"It's nice of you to miss me, Enery. I'll tell you what. Why don't I promise to sit with your family at the movie tonight?"

Enery looks at Kayla and then at me. What is this little dude thinking? "Yep. That works," he says and runs off after a friend.

"That was odd," Henry says.

"Yep," I say. It sure was.

Set-up goes quickly, and I'm about as thrilled as Enery to have to go home and wait rather than watching the movie with Michaela now. I take a cue from Margi and sleep away most of the afternoon. I did get up early, after all.

Back at the church, Enery and Margi pick a bright green sofa in the front row. Henry sets up a couple foldable lawn chairs to one side. Suddenly Enery bolts for the door. He returns, pulling Michaela by the hand. Her mother follows behind.

The adults greet each other with hugs while Michaela hugs the children. I stand there awkwardly, wondering where I fit into this hug phenomenon. People I knew in Salida didn't do much hugging. Maybe it's because we're in a church. Barbara turns my way and, sure enough, I get a big hug from her as well. "Glad you could join us, Jace. I hear you helped with setup."

"Yes, ma'am," I say.

Henry chokes on a laugh. "Ma'am? Barbara what have you done to the boy?"

Barbara smiles. "I'm sure I have no idea." Michaela is blushing.

"Margi, Enery, do you want to go with me to get some popcorn?" Michaela asks.

"Yes!" says Margi.

"Nah," from Enery. "I'm going to stay here and keep Jace company."

"Bro, I'm all about popcorn," I say.

"Alright!" and like that he's halfway to the snack table.

This isn't how I pictured a first date, but I guess that's the point. At least Enery is on my side. He decided that since he and Margi can't both sit by both of us, the only fair thing would be to put us together between them. So now I have Margi curled on my left and Michaela on my right, with Enery beside her. The parents are in their fold-out chairs behind us.

The lights go down and the movie starts. It's one of my favorites, but I can't focus on the big-eyed dragon with its broken wing. There's half a foot of couch between me and Michaela, but I'm still distracted. Partly by her nearness, and partly wondering if I can scoot closer without it seeming weird. We must look like mannequins with our backs straight and hands on our own thighs.

Ten minutes into the movie Enery gives a loud huff. "Kayla, I need more room!" he whisper-shouts. This kid is a better wingman than Cole ever was. Is this intentional?

Kayla's moved closer now, her jeans-covered leg barely touching mine. I reach out and hook our pinkies together. She doesn't look my way, but I know she's blushing.

When the lights go on, Henry scoops up Margie, who fell asleep halfway through. Anne Marie folds their chairs. Enery is still awake, but barely. I'm not ready for the evening to end, so when I hear Michaela and her mom talking about helping with tear down, I jump on it, and volunteer to take Mrs. Barr's place then walk Michaela home afterwards.

"What a polite young man you are," says Mrs. Barr. She's smirking. "That would be fine.

And like that I've got more evening.

"That was some movie, huh?" I ask. Michaela and I walk along the well-lit street to her house. The night air is just cold enough to keep our hands in our pockets.

"Yeah. I'm guessing Enery is going to be playing 'dragon trainer' for weeks."

"Just wait until he sees the second one," I say.

"Did you know that if the pandemic had struck ten years earlier we would have more movies to choose from now?"

"Oh yeah?" I ask. Kayla's eyes shine when she talks about history. "It's true. In the 1980's movies were on tapes. Then came DVDs and blue rays, which we still have. But in the early 2010's people started watching movies through the internet, so fewer and fewer dvds were made. When the pandemic hit, the internet was one of the first things to go. No satellites, no cell signal, no internet. Electricity went quick, too, but Professor McKnight was able to fix that. Not even he can fix the satellites!"

"So, if the pandemic had struck ten years sooner, we'd have more movies now?"

"Yes! But we wouldn't have had Professor McKnight. Or we might have had a younger version of him who didn't know anything about alternative energy, so the chances of us having most of the town running off of solar power is slim to none." Michaela scrunches her brow. "Actually, how do you do it in Salida?"

"We have gas-powered generators for things like refrigerators and water heaters, but we also do a lot more candles, fireplaces for heat, that kind of thing."

"That sounds cozy,"

"The idea is cozy. The reality is a little cold and dark. I think that's one of the reasons Dad wants to build this relationship with El Dorado Springs. He's heard about your technology but hasn't witnessed it firsthand. He's going to be impressed."

"Do you think he'll come out to see for himself?"

That hadn't even occurred to me. "Yeah, probably."

"You don't look thrilled with the idea. Didn't he tell you if he'd come visit?"

"Nope. And if visiting me were the point, he wouldn't bother."

We walk a few steps in silence. I'm about to fill it with something, anything, but Michaela speaks first. "I never got to meet my dad. Mr. Douglas is the closest I've got. I've learned everything I know from watching him, and the dads in the other families I babysit."

"Henry's an awesome dad. Trust me, they're not all like that."

"What's your dad like?"

"My dad? I don't know. He's charming. And controlling. And nothing I do is good enough. He was glad to ship me off to El Dorado Springs, that's for sure." I didn't mean to say any of that. Here I am whining about my dad when she never even knew hers. We've reached her front porch, and Michaela turns towards me.

"If I meet your dad, I'm going to thank him. I'm glad you came to El Dorado Springs."

In the porch light I can tell saying that cost her another blush. She reaches out and squeezes my hand. "Good night, Jace." She turns to unlock the door.

"Wait," I say. "What are you doing tomorrow? Morning skateboard lesson?"

"I've got church, and after that Mom likes to keep Sundays as mother-daughter bonding time. Tomorrow we're making popcorn balls for the trick or treaters."

"Yum. How old do kids trick or treat here?"

"I don't know. Twelve maybe? But everyone dresses up for the barn party."

"Oh yeah? What are you going as?"

"You'll have to wait and see."

I raise an eyebrow. "A woman of mystery. I like it. I'm going to be a vampire. Perhaps I will suck your blood, bwahahah."

Michaela scrunches up her nose like something smells bad.

"What, you don't like vampires?"

Her shrug is adorable. "It's not a normal costume in El Dorado Springs. No one does the undead."

"Huh. I've been a vampire for the last three years. I'll tell you what. You tell me what you're going as, and I promise not to come as a vampire."

"But then I won't be a woman of mystery."

"No, but you will be a woman with a handsome non-vampire on your arm."

Michaela is blushing again. "Fine," she says, throwing up her hands. "I'm going as Flounder, from the Little Mermaid. Margi begged me and I couldn't say no."

I can't keep from laughing. "The woman of mystery is going as a fish?"

"Yes, yes I am." Michaela is laughing too.

"Michaela Barr, you may be the nicest person I know."

Her eyes are wide and warm. One hand is on the doorknob, but she hasn't turned it yet. I step closer and smell something flowery and sweet. Looking down at her lips, I bend towards her.

And the door opens from the inside. Taking a giant step back almost sends me falling off the porch.

"I thought I heard something out here," says Michaela's mom from the doorway.

"Hello Mrs. Barr," I say. Michaela is staring at her shoes. "Michaela and I were just talking about Halloween. I hear you're making popcorn balls tomorrow."

"Yes, we are," says her mom. "Thank you for walking Michaela home. It's always nice to see my daughter making new friends. Say goodnight, Michaela."

"Good night, Jace," Michaela says.

"Good night, Kayla. I'll see you Monday. Good night Mrs. Barr."

"Good night, Jace. Have a safe walk home." And with that Mrs. Barr closes the door.

Chapter 12 - Jaerish

Something isn't right. My muscles are tense as I listen for sounds in the dark barracks. All I hear is the men around me breathing, but then there it is, a shuffling to my right.

Suddenly a cloth is being shoved into my mouth. Hands grip my arms and I'm hauled from the bed.

I allow my attackers to pull me upright. They're going to regret it.

Plant my feet wide I jerk forward and slam my forehead into the face of the man in front of me. He cries out. A body hits the ground as I spit the rag from my mouth. The barracks is waking up around me, but I ignore everything but the men still holding my arms.

I roar into the dark. The man on my right loosens his grip and I easily yank free. My right fist connects with the forearm of the man holding my left arm and he screams as he lets go.

Light fills the room. As my vision adjusts, I can make out Hayes near my feet, groaning, with blood oozing between the fingers he holds over his nose. One of his buddies is on the ground near him, cradling his arm. To my right a man is backed against the wall, his hands held out in the universal sign for "don't hit me." Smartest thing he's done all night.

Adrenaline is still crashing through me and it's all I can do not to kick Hayes where he's fallen. I stand there counting breaths. Long in. Long out. Around me the barracks is a riot of flying questions and wrong answers. Kelvin takes charge from his position near the light switch. He sends someone for Captain Betner, someone else for an extra medic.

Kelvin walks to the bleeders and does a preliminary assessment. Then he turns to me.

"What happened?"

I scowl. "Something woke me up and then they were on me. So, I put em down."

"Yeah, you did," he says. "I didn't know you could do that."

"Neither did I."

Captain Betner arrives, appearing unphased despite the hour. Apparently, this isn't the first time he's been woken up in the middle of the night to handle a brawl. He scans the scene, intense eyes landing on me.

"It was two on one and you escaped unharmed?" Betner asks. "Impressive."

"It was actually three on one, sir," says Kelvin. "And Jearish here was asleep when it started."

Captain Betner looks me over. "Is this true, private?"

"For the most part," I say. "I think I took them by surprise."

Betner laughs. "I'd say you did. Everyone back to bed. No trouble." The last is said with a glance in Hayes's direction. "We'll handle this in the morning."

I've been told to remain on the commons after inspection. I expect to see Hayes and his crew, but instead four strangers join me. Their armbands designate them as Sergeant Major Open Sky's personal guard. They nod to each other, ignoring me completely, then position themselves at attention six feet apart. No one says a word.

Time stretches as we stand. I don't like waiting. I'm about to ask if they know why we're here when both Captain Betner and Sergeant Major Open Sky himself arrive.

The Sergeant Major, uniformed, with his long hair slicked into a low queue, looks at each of us appraisingly and then begins to speak.

"As you may or may not know, I have recently acquired a vacancy to my personal retinue. I asked Captain Betner to consider possible replacements, paying special attention to intelligence, physical prowess and the ability to act quickly in dangerous situations."

There's a cry and the man to my right is on his knees grappling with a blade protruding from his throat. I look up in time to see the giant beside him throw a second blade at my head. On instinct I pluck it from the air. Unphased, he pulls a third blade from somewhere. This one is smaller than the one I'm now holding, but still a good ten inches long.

"Orders, Sergeant Major Open Sky," I call, not taking my eyes off the giant.

"Carry on," he says.

What?

I stare at the two men before me. Two, plus a body. There should be three. . . The air behind me shifts and I pivot. My knife is now at the neck of the third man, making him a shield between me and the others.

"Stand down," says the Sergeant Major.

Like hell I will. Long breath in. Long breath out. I lower my knife slowly, eyes trained on the man who initiated this bloody contest. He grins, stretching the scar that puckers his dark skin from cheekbone to jaw.

"Malloy, Patner, deal with Fatim," says Sergeant Major Open Sky. The man before me looks over his shoulder and smirks like my blade wasn't just at his throat, then goes towards the body. "Captain Radley," the Sergeant

Major says to the giant, "it will be your privilege to show Private First Class Jaerish his new quarters and duties. Be in my office at zero nine hundred."

"Yes, sir," Captain Radley replies. "C'mon, Private. And give me my knife back."

Captain Radley and I stop by the barracks so I can grab my few camp-issued belongings then we continue on to the guard quarters. He talks casually as we go, and it's hard to reconcile this seemingly sane man with the monster in the field.

After a short walk, we arrive at a two-story house built of native stone. Unlike where I lived before, which was all about bunk space and footlockers, this is a home. Captain Radley introduces me to a couple of guys chilling in a common room watching a movie. He shows me through the kitchen, up a set of stairs and into a hallway lined with doors.

"This is you," says Radley, pointing to an open door on my left. "Patner, the one you used as a meat shield, is your roommate."

The room holds two twin beds, a nightstand with an oil lamp, a dresser and a closet. Several surprisingly well-done sketches hang above one bed.

"Was the dead man on the field today the vacancy in Open Sky's retinue?"

"You catch on fast, Jaerish. He was indeed."

"And this was his bedroom?"

Captain Radley nods confirmation.

"Is Patner going to have a problem with this?"

"Nah. Fatim was an ass. We were all waiting on the chance to put a knife through his neck."

"Lucky you." I put my belongings on my bed, feeling less than comforted by this new information. "Do many men leave the Sergeant Major's retinue this way?"

Captain Radley studies me before he speaks. "Jaerish, I can see that you have a healthy desire for self-preservation. In a battle, one rebellious soldier can mean the difference between victory and a bloodbath. Open Sky makes sure that those who have charge over the defense of his person are utterly trustworthy. Fatim was not."

Captain Radley seems to think this is all I need to know, and pressing for more information would go against that previously mentioned desire for self-preservation.

At zero nine hundred Captain Radley and I stand in Sergeant Major Open Sky's office.

"Private first class Jaerish, welcome."

"Thank you, Sergeant Major Open Sky," I say.

"Jaerish, you can now call me Open Sky when in private or surrounded by others of the guard. I allow some informality with those in whose hands I am placing my well-being. Do you like your new accommodations?"

"I do, sir. Open Sky. The house is very nice."

"It was a historic building even before the pandemic," Open Sky says. "A true testimony to the quality construction of our ancestors. And have you had the opportunity to meet some of your new comrades?"

"I have."

"Good. Next Captain Radley will see that you are armed. My personal guard alone is allowed to carry weapons within camp, so please choose whatever you deem necessary."

"Thank you for the honor, sir" I say.

"Welcome to the post. We'll have plenty of time to get to know each other in the months to come. For now, you are dismissed."

Captain Radley and I exit the office past two more men with the armband of Open Sky's personal guard. They stand slightly straighter and nod at Captain Radley as we go by. He doesn't stop to introduce me, and I can feel them sizing me up. After being attacked last night and fighting for my life this morning, I'd expect nothing less.

Captain Radley takes me to the armory, a well-lit warehouse with shelf after shelf of knives, guns, bows and swords as well as a sparring ring and shooting range.

"So, Jaerish, what's your pleasure," asks Captain Radley, gesturing towards the weapons.

I scan the room. "Would it sound stupid if I said I have no idea?" And I really don't.

Captain Radley smirks. "You've been with us, what, five months? You're barely out of the medic tent, but you disabled three soldiers from a dead sleep. You got the jump on Patner on the field. It's clear you had training before *Cov-4N*. We just need to figure out what that body of yours still knows."

Turns out my body knows a lot, and we spend three hours proving it. I can hit a target the size of my thumb at a hundred yards with a gun or a bow. Throwing knives, poles, swords, nunchaku. You bet. I'm sweaty and thrilled. I can't remember the hours I must have spent training. All I know is that weapons I don't recognize with my mind are lethal in my hands.

"Looks like you can pick whatever you'd like, bad-ass," says Captain Radley with a laugh when we've tried out every type of weapon in the arsenal. "What d'you want?"

"Strategy question," I say. "If anything happened in camp, we'd be fighting our own guys, right?"

"Most likely."

"Alright, then. I'll take a pole and a pistol. And a knife just in case."

Captain Radley agrees and I pick what I want from the racks.

"You'll need these as well," he says, handing me two armbands. "These communicate that you are a member of Open Sky's personal guard with all the privileges and responsibilities that implies. They also contain three pills. Two each of the blue, and a single red, which is a fast-acting poison."

"Things just got serious," I say.

"Things were already serious. Don't allow the lack of conflict since your arrival to cause assumptions that such precautions are unnecessary. There have been negotiations occurring that affect the future of each member of this camp, and we must be prepared should those negotiations go badly."

"What kind of negotiations?" I ask.

"No idea. Political curiosity is a liability in our profession. And liabilities are dealt with swiftly."

Chapter 13 - Michaela

Dreamy classical music floods my senses as I open my eyes to sunlight muted by gauzy white curtains. I'm swimming in good feelings. And then I remember why.

I spent yesterday with Jace.

Sundays have always been my favorite day. On Sundays I go to church and then spend time with my mom apart from the busyness of the week. I brush my teeth and put on clothes, lecturing myself on not being one of "those girls," the kind that need a boy to enjoy their life.

My resolve lasts all of an hour. Then, who should walk into church with the Douglases? Jace, of course. I'm not sure how I feel about this. Obviously, I'm glad he's here. But did he come to see me or because he wanted to try church? Either is good, for different reasons. When Mom sees him, she gives me a very significant eyebrow raise. I shrug in reply. But I blush too.

Jace is a couple rows away, but it's still hard to focus on singing. When the teenagers are released for class, Jace falls into step beside me.

"The music was different from church in Salida," he says. "I liked it. What's next?"

"How about 'Good morning, Michaela. Funny seeing you here?'"

"I'm surprised you didn't expect me," Jace says with a grin. "You did tell me this is where you'd be." Oh, the blushing. So much blushing.

"Next, we go to youth group. We're studying the book of Mark, but no one will expect you to say much since it's your first time."

"Hey. As far as you know all I did back in Salida was study the book of Mark."

Within minutes, I'm convinced Jace has never even heard of the book of Mark, but it doesn't matter. He can fit in anywhere. For the first time, I realize this funny, charming persona probably isn't the real him. Not on a deep level anyway. I wonder if anyone else has noticed this or if I've been thinking about Jace way too much.

When Jace and I get back to the main room after class, my mom is talking with Anne Marie Douglas. Anne Marie asks if we'd like to have lunch with them, and I'm surprised when Mom says yes. Then she makes it clear that she and I will be walking home to grab some cookies for dessert alone with a pointed glance Jace's way. Which means we're about to have a conversation.

We're less than a minute into the walk when she starts. "So, what's going on with Jace?"

The heat is rising in my face. "I don't know," I say with a half shrug. "I mean, I like him. He's funny, and nice, but there's nothing official."

"He's also cute," my mom says.

"Yes, he's cute," I agree. "Sometimes when we're with a lot of people, I feel like he's putting on a show. But I love who he is when it's just us."

"It must have been hard to leave home and come to a new place," Mom says. "That's very brave."

"Yeah. But I'm not sure he had much choice."

Mom studies me, but doesn't press for more information.

"El Dorado Springs is probably a good opportunity for him then. And I think he's good for El Dorado Springs too. At least my little corner of it." Mom is smiling.

"So, you like him?" I ask.

"I do, Michaela. And so do Henry and Anne Marie." I'm amazed by how much comfort I get from their approval.

We arrive at the Douglases' where Jace and Enery are throwing a football in the front yard. Enery trails my mom and the plate of cookies inside and Jace joins me on the front step.

"So, Michaela Barr, I have a question for you."

"Ok, Jace Morton. Ask away."

"This God your church talks about. You really think that you can sing to him, and he hears you?"

"Yes. Yes I do."

"And you can talk to him anywhere? Because he's there?"

"Yep."

"And does he talk back?"

"He does. But not always in ways we're used to listening."

"So right now I could ask him a question and he'd answer. The question is if I could understand him, right?"

"Something like that."

"OK, then," Jace says, looking up at the sky. "Oh, all-knowing God, does a guy like me stand a chance with the lovely Michaela Barr?"

I laugh. "You sound like you're talking to a magic eight ball," I say.

"A what?"

"It was a kid's toy pre-pandemic. It looked like the black eight ball in pool. But you'd ask it questions and a little cube floating inside would give an answer like 'it is decidedly so,' or 'my sources say no.'"

"Well, then. What does the eight ball say?" asks Jace with a grin.

"Let me see," I say. I lift up my hands and shake my imaginary eight ball, staring intently at the nothing I'm holding.

"Michaela, Jace! Lunch!" Mom calls from inside the house.

"Nooooo!" says Jace. "What's the eight ball say!"

I stare back into the non-existent eight ball. "Reply hazy. Ask again later."

"What does that mean?"

"Sorry, Jace." I shrug. "The eight ball says you're just going to have to wait and see." Grinning, I get up and walk into the house.

Chapter 14 - Kessa

A messenger arrived in Salida with my things just in time for Halloween. He brought a letter from my father with him.

Dearest Kessa,

I'm not surprised by your decision to stay, though selfishly I would always keep you close if I could. But I believe this is what God wanted.

You know I see all things as part of an intricate pattern, a weaving if you will. I was spared from the pandemic by my grandmother's passing because I was needed in El Dorado Springs, and in this new version of the world. Remember that He is always intentional, even when we can't see His purposes.

I don't blame you for being angry with God for Evan's death. Evan was a remarkable young man and always your clearest path forward. I would encourage you to take your questions to God and let Him be a comfort to you rather than blocking Him out. He's in Salida, just as in El Dorado Springs, if you're willing to look for Him.

Love always,

Dad

I put down the letter, frustrated. Dad's belief in God's overarching purposes used to be my own. Before Evan died, I knew God's plan for my life. And I assumed God could be trusted to do what it took to bring those plans about, including protecting Evan. Obviously that wasn't the case. I fold up the letter and tuck it in my drawer.

On a brighter note, Dad sent my Galadriel costume.

I feel elegant as I adjust the circlet of gold on my head. My long, white dress flows down to skim the tops of delicate sandals. I attempt my most queenly face in the mirror as I put on my pointy elf ears and end up snorting at the silliness of it. Then I walk out into the chilly night.

Holding up my hem, I crunch through leaves across the thirty yards from my guest house to the main residence. I enter through the back door to a cacophony of music and voices. This is not the sophisticated dinner party I attended at the Prior's my first night in Salida. Instead the lights are low, the couches have been pushed back against the walls, and the cleared space vibrates with people dancing, cups in hand. It looks like a frat party from pre-pan movies.

Next, I realize that I'm way over-dressed. Not like I'm the only one in a costume. But like I'm the only one whose costume is bigger than an acorn. Exposed skin is everywhere. Madison Prior, the hostess, glides over to me wearing high heels, an apron, and black lingerie. She has a feather duster in her hand and is apparently some sort of naughty housemaid. The part of me that isn't stunned notes how good she still looks after three children.

"Kessa! So glad you could make it," she hollers over the music. "Don't you look lovely. Are you a princess?"

"I'm Galadriel," I yell back.

"You're what?"

"Galadriel," I try again.

She looks confused and then dismisses it entirely. "Well, you look just darling. You should head over to the bar. Adam's there with Cacia and several other young people I'm sure you've met." With that she's on to other guests.

I skirt the dance floor and work my way in the general direction she pointed. And there's Adam, standing beside a young woman with very large hair and a very small bikini. He's laughing as he hands her a drink from the bartender. My throat catches and I'm not sure if it's because of how good he looks in his pinstripe suit and fedora or because of the adoration in the woman's eyes as she manages to squeeze even closer to him.

Beside them a guy in a toga and another in exercise shorts with boxing gloves around his neck are laughing with two women. One looks familiar, and I do a double take when I realize Cacia, the person who's quickly becoming my best female friend in Salida, is wearing her lab coat, a stethoscope and a minidress that covers less than my swimsuit. Really, Cacia? The woman beside her, whose name I don't remember, is in grey lingerie with a headband of cat's ears and a tail.

Cacia sees me and her smile is as warm as ever. "Kessa! I'm glad you found us! You look beautiful."

I try to smile in return, but I can't remember the last time I felt this out of place.

Adam has turned at the sound of my name, and I can see the smirk in the corner of his mouth. "Kessa, you do indeed look lovely. Galadriel?"

"Lovely" sounds childish and I feel anger overtaking my embarrassment as the bikini-clad woman beside Adam asks "Galadri-who?" and giggles like she's just made a joke. I tell myself this is why I feel such a strong sense of dislike for her, and that it's not because she's constantly finding excuses to lean past Adam and brush him with her barely covered breasts. Adam introduces her.

"Kessa, meet Amy Carson. This is her first time at the grown-up Halloween party as well, isn't it Amy?"

Amy lifts her glass, which I'm guessing from her slur contains one of the newly discovered grown-up drinks. "Cheers to Halloween!" she says, and several people around us drain their glasses.

"And what are you dressed as?" I ask.

"I'm beach barbie. See the heels?" She lifts one foot up, leaning into Adam to avoid tipping over.

"Yes, that explains them," I say.

"Amy is Cole's half-sister," Adam says. "I promised to watch out for her tonight."

"Well, I guess you have your hands full then." I force a smile. "I'm going outside for a minute. It's a bit warm in here."

Before Adam can reply, Amy grabs his arm. "Take me to dance, Adam!" she slurs.

When he hesitates the man in the toga pipes up. "If you're not interested, I'd be happy to dance with Miss Carson."

Amy giggles. Adam glances from me to Amy to toga-man. "Nope, we're good," he says and leads her to the dance floor.

I'm outside without a backwards glance and thrilled to feel the cool night against my skin. The air in the party was stifling, kept warm by all the bodies or for the sake of the half-naked women. Salida has never felt so far from home. And it's not just because I didn't know what to expect. It's because I have no desire to wear lingerie to a party. Who does that?

Back inside my guest house I frown into the mirror at my elven ears and long flowing dress. It's still lovely, but I can't imagine when I'll have a chance to wear it again.

Part of me hoped Adam would follow, maybe even expected that he would. But he doesn't. And why should he? He's never done anything that a good friend wouldn't do. I've probably just read into it something that wasn't there. And Amy Carson is cute. Hot even. Hot, half-naked, and drunk. Somehow, I'd thought better of him.

I change out of my dress, take off the ears and crown. I'm back in pajamas, back in the real world. But man he looked good in that suit.

Chapter 15 - Jace

I bump along in a wagon on the way to the Ridley farm. It's being pulled by the same solar-powered SUV that brought me from Salida, but now instead of riding in style I'm sitting on hay bales. Margi is on my lap and Kayla sits beside me. Not bad for a month.

I ditched my vampire costume for the rolled-up jeans and white shirt of Prince Eric. Margi's squeal when she saw me convinced me I made the right choice. Kayla is adorable in a yellow sweatshirt with blue stripes and fins on the sleeves. She even attached a Mohawk to the hood.

"Whatcha thinkin?" Kayla asks.

"I'm thinking that you make a cute fish." If she didn't want to blush, she shouldn't have asked.

We reach the farm, and pile off the wagon. I hand Margi down to Henry. Kayla is on the ground before I can offer her a lift. We follow the music to the barn doors where an older couple sits beside bundles of corn stalks.

"Hello Mrs. Ridley. Hello Mr. Ridley." I stop beside Kayla who gives each of them a hug.

"Hello, darlin," Mr. Ridley says. He turns to me. "And you must be Jace Morton."

"Yes sir," I say, reaching out to shake his hand. "How did you know?"

Mrs. Ridley laughs. "Well, son, don't attribute it to his vast wisdom. I have to live with the man!" She nudges her husband with an elbow.

"She means she gets to live with the man." His eyes shine. "Nope, Jace, I'm not that smart. You're just the only teenager here that I haven't watched grow since you were a babe wrapped in blankets."

That makes sense.

"Go on in and enjoy the party," Mrs. Ridley says. "You'll be the first one to see it with new eyes in quite some time." She waves us in and turns to greet someone behind us.

"I wanta be like them when we grow up," I say to Kayla. She blushes.

What did I say? Oh. When did I start assuming her into my future? I picture her with grey hair and wrinkles and can't keep from smiling.

Inside, haybales line the barn walls as seats, and several tables are set up with kids' games. One long table is covered in food, and I'm about to ask Michaela if she wants to see what's on it when someone calls my name.

"Jace!" It's Stephen, one of my new bros, and he's standing with some of the guys.

"I've gotta find Margi," Kayla says. She takes off into the crowd.

I walk to where the guys are standing near the apple bobbing. Kayla and I talk a lot at school, but she disappears when there's a group. She hasn't hung out with me and my boys the way Cole's girls always did, and when I ask her to have lunch with us, she's always got some project to do.

"Check out that one," Bruce says. He's laughing at a kid whose whole top half is underwater as he tries to pin an apple against the side. Bruce is not my favorite person.

"Do you always hang out by the apple trough?" I ask, fist-bumping my way around the circle.

"Just until the food table's full," says Kevin. He's thin as a pencil and always asking "you gonna eat that" in the cafeteria. He once finished my applesauce, which is a step too far for me, but whatever. Dude's hungry.

"Bro, did I see you come in with the donor?" It's Bruce asking, and my fists clench. He better not mean what I think he does.

"The donor? What are you talking about?"

"Shut up, Bruce," Stephen says.

"You shut up. He might not even know."

"Know what?" I ask.

"That Michaela Barr's dad was a seed merchant," says Bruce, as though that should matter to me.

"Yeah. So?"

"So?" asks Bruce. "Did you hear me? Her mom paid some dude to do the deed and get her pregnant."

Bruce starts making a pumping motion with his hips and I want to punch the ugly expression right off his face. Stephen looks at me and takes a step back. I close my eyes and start counting. Not because I don't want to see this guy bleed, but because I don't want to mess up tonight with Kayla.

When I'm confident I can talk without hitting him, I open my eyes and stare directly at Bruce.

"Back in Salida," I say, "there are a lot of seed merchant kids. Including my best friend who would totally kick your ass for that comment."

Bruce has stopped his motion, and now he's just standing there looking stupid as an awkward silence falls.

"So do they have caramel apples in Salida?" Kevin asks. He's staring at the food table. I don't know if he's so obsessed with food he missed what just happened, or if he's trying to change the subject. I'll take it either way.

We say everything that could possibly be said about fall foods. Then Stephen says, "Jax told me she and the girls have a special Halloween surprise for us if we cut out early." Jax, short for Jasmine, is Stephen's girlfriend and the "bestie" of Mae Cartwright.

"Oh yeah?" I ask. "What kind of surprise?"

"Jace, you know the definition of surprise, don't you?" says a silky voice behind me. A hand skims down my arm. It makes me shiver, but in the horror movie way.

I turn and Mae is there with Jax and a couple other girls I vaguely know. Mae's hair is down in waves. She's wearing a swimsuit top with fake seashells and a long shimmery turquoise skirt. She looks hot, and she knows it. Small glittery stars are painted near her eyes. I don't remember those in the Little Mermaid.

"Hello, Mae," I say, forcing a smile.

"I see you're here as Prince Eric," she says, sliding her hand into my elbow. "I knew we'd make a perfect pair."

"Actually," I say. "I've already picked my princess. Here she comes now." Margi runs up and tugs my arm right out of Mae's grip.

"Jace, you said you'd go with me for face paints. Wemember?"

"I do wemember, Margi. Sorry, all, but my princess awaits." Margi giggles and I'm happy to let her pull me across the barn to the face painting table.

Once we're out of earshot I tell her "You have perfect timing, Margi. You just saved me from Ursula the sea witch and her evil minions."

"I know."

"You do?"

"Oh yeah. Daddy sent me. He said you needed my help."

I look across the room to see Henry wink and wave. Now that is a good, good man.

Kayla sits at the face painting station with a line of children and a table full of colored paints. A boy gets up from the seat in front of her, transformed into a tiger.

"No bobbing for apples," she calls as he runs off roaring.

"Michaela Barr, is there anything you can't do?" I ask.

"Well, I'm a pretty lousy skateboarder, but I think I've suckered a guy into showing me the ropes. After that my plans for world domination should be complete."

"Does this sucker know he's aiding such a nefarious scheme?"

She looks at me, eyebrow raised.

"What? I can know big words," I say. She doesn't look convinced. "Fine, it's from a pre-pan video game."

Kayla laughs and keeps painting. Her next little customer, a girl in a pixie costume, now has a sparkly mask of flowers around her eyes. Soon it's Margi's turn.

"How about you, little mermaid?" Kayla asks Margi.

"I want little stars by my eyes like the girl Jace was with. She was a mermaid too."

"Oh yeah?" Michaela's face doesn't change, and she doesn't look up at me. She just starts painting small, shimmery stars around Margi's eyes. Apparently, she knew which girl Margi was talking about.

"She was a beautiful mermaid, Kayla. More beautifuller than me. But it's not fair because she has breasts and I don't."

Kayla starts and has to add a tail to a botched star.

"I think that you are more beautiful than her any day, Margi," Kayla says. She hands Margi a mirror. "What do you think?"

"I love it! Jace?" She turns to me, grin questioning.

"Perfect, Margi," I say. "Definitely the beautifullest mermaid here." Her smile covers her face.

"Your turn," says Margi.

Kayla looks up from cleaning her brushes. The raised eyebrow is daring me to do it. I sit on the seat in front of her.

"And what would you like, Prince Eric?" she asks.

Oh, how to answer that. . . Be clever. . . Be clever. . . Nope, I've got nothing.

"I don't know. You pick." Dang.

"That's a little bit dangerous," says Kayla, reaching for a brush. I squirm as she studies my face. At last, she looks right into my eyes. Then she gives a half smile and gets to work.

Michaela is so close, and I can't keep my eyes from her lips. They look soft and her breath smells like apples. After a time that stretches forever and still ends way too quickly, she sits back and smiles, handing me the mirror.

"Here you go, Jace. What do you think?"

She's painted my face like a Mardi Gras mask. A golden and blue crown is on my forehead. The lines of a theatric grin are at the corners of my mouth, but a tear is under one eye.

"I'm so easy to read, huh?" I ask.

"Not to everyone," she says as she wipes away the painted tear, but leaves the rest. "I just wanted you to know I see it."

Michaela's eyes are nearly green today. They change with her clothes or maybe her moods. I've been staring at them way too long, but I can't look away.

"Jace, it's my turn! C'mon!" Enery, dressed as a pirate, starts kicking the leg of my chair. Now that's a moment breaker.

"How long are you painting?" I ask Kayla.

"Someone's relieving me in half an hour," she says.

"I'll find you then."

But I don't find Kayla in half an hour.

Why? Because Stephen, Bruce, and Kevin, who said we'd only be in the corn maze for fifteen minutes, changed their minds when asked to stay alone in the dark with hot girls. And when I said I needed to get back, Mae swore she knew the way. So instead of bobbing for apples or whatever else I'd be doing with Kayla, I'm lost in a maze while Mae talks about how much she loves horses and squeals every time a stray leaf brushes her leg.

So, ok, Mae is hot. Her interest is flattering. And she's still in a bikini top even though it's freezing. If she didn't terrify me, maybe. But she does. And she's not Kayla.

At some point Mae realizes she's the only one talking and goes silent. I've given up on the paths and am crashing our way through corn walls towards the sounds of the party. If there are two barns full of people out here celebrating, we're screwed.

Right when I make it out of the maze, Mae trips in her flimsy sandals. I barely keep her standing as she leans into me. Warmth spreads to all the right places. Wrong places. Because I'm so not interested in Mae.

"Thanks Jace. You're my hero." I roll my eyes and walk towards the barn.

When I get to the face painting station, Michaela's gone. Her replacement says she just left, but I can't find her anywhere.

"I don't see why you're looking for her anyway," says Mae who's apparently following me. "You know she's just a donor, right?"

"What is it with you people and your weird thing about merchant kids," I ask. "It's not like kids choose their parents. God knows I wouldn't have picked my dad." I can tell I've said too much by the glint in Mae's eye.

"Why, Jace? What's wrong with your dad? I thought he practically runs Salida." Her voice is smooth like the purr of a cat. I'm the mouse being batted from paw to paw. She presses herself up against me and whispers in my ear. "I promise I won't tell a soul."

"Yeah, that's it. I'm out," I say and turn to walk away.

"Oh, Jace," Mae calls softly. I look back. "Your little friend saw us come out of the corn maze. Hopefully she didn't get the wrong idea."

Chapter 16 - Michaela

I rode back to town with the Fletchers. I somehow even managed to mumble something intelligible when the twins asked where Jace was, when all I wanted to do was yell "how should I know?" or "why would I care?"

I shower, trying to get the smell of campfire and hayrides and crushed hopes out of my hair. Then I get under my covers with a book. If I fill my head with something else, maybe I can crowd out the picture of Mae pressed up against Jace, her perfect features lit up by the barn lights and the obvious pleasure of being in his arms.

I close my eyes and take a deep breath in. Deep breath out. Distraction isn't working. It's time to face this head on and employ some logic. I push back my blankets and pace the bedroom.

First, I don't have an exclusive claim on Jace. He isn't my boyfriend. Yeah, he's held my hand, but what's that, really? I mean, it was a first for me, but it probably meant nothing to him.

Second, I've only known him a couple of weeks. Maybe he's a flirt. Or a player. I could be one of many. Obviously. But Mae Cartwright?

I make a sound somewhere between a groan and a growl and then jump at the knock on my door.

"Come in," I say on a sigh as I walk towards the door, ready to throw my arms around my mom and succumb to all the tears I've been fighting.

But it's not my mom in the doorway. It's Jace. The crown I painted is smeared on his forehead. Probably from his time in the corn maze. Whatever he sees on my face makes him wince.

"Your mom said I could come back, but we have to leave the door open," Jace says.

I should have told mom what happened, and she would never have let him in. I take the three steps to my bed so I can turn my back to him and try to screw my face into some semblance of normal. It's not working, so I sit down and put my forehead in my hands. Jace still hovers in the doorway.

"What do you need, Jace?" I finally ask. It sounds better than I was expecting. Not exactly neutral, but not like I'm on the edge of tears either.

"I couldn't find you after face painting. I thought we were going to do the barn stuff together."

Jace comes into the room, stands awkwardly, then sits in my desk chair.

"Yeah, well, when I finished you had other company. So, I left." I wanted to say it like it was no big deal, but I don't think it came out that way.

"Kayla?" he says. My name on his lips sounds as broken as I feel. But I still don't look up. We're silent for hours, which is probably only minutes. Then Jace says "I don't know what I'm doing in any of this. And I think you saw me with Mae by the cornfield, but it wasn't what it looked like. I went out there with the guys and they wanted to stay longer when the girls showed up. But all I wanted was to get back to you. Mae promised she'd take me to the barn. That's the only reason I was even with her."

"You weren't just 'with' her, Jace. She was draped all over you."

And now I am mad. Because if he's coming to my room and trying to explain this away, we're obviously more than just friends and he knows it. Which should make me happy. And maybe it does, but I can't figure out what I'm feeling right now, which is almost as frustrating as anything else that's happened tonight. Almost.

Jace's chair scrapes and he's right in front of me now. He reaches out and takes my hands. I should pull them away, tell him to get out of my room. But instead, I look up into deep brown eyes.

"I'm sorry," he says. "She tripped into me. I think she did it on purpose. I don't want anything to do with Mae. And I don't want to hurt you. Not ever."

And somehow, even through the fog, I believe him. Jace's eyes are searching, and he must have seen the shift because there's hope in them for the first time since he entered my room.

"Kayla," he says, "forgive me?"

I nod, and the look of relief on his face matches what's in my heart.

Jace's thumb reaches up and brushes my lower lip, which has curved into a smile to match his. Because, I realize, I'm staring at his mouth. His smile. His lips. When I lift my eyes back up to his they hold an entirely different question.

Slowly, Jace moves forward and then his lips are where his thumb was only moments before. I close my eyes, feeling their softness and the warmth of his breath. My first kiss, and it's with Jace. I grin as he pulls back. He tucks a strand of my still-damp hair behind my ear, running one finger along it. He's smiling too and we stare at each other, this silence so different from what came before.

But it's still silence, and he's still Jace.

"Wow. Yeah, ok," he says. "That's what I wanted to happen tonight. Without the stuff that came before it. We're good now, right?"

I laugh. I can't help it. And his look when I do is so cute that I reach out and take his face in both my hands and kiss him again. Second kiss, this one more about happiness than the first, which was kind of solemn. I laugh again and he grins.

"We might want to go out to the living room," I say. "I don't want my mother to hate you."

"No, we definitely don't want that," says Jace.

He stands up and pulls me to my feet, not letting go of my hand as we walk down the hall. We find Mom in the kitchen pouring popcorn into a big bowl.

"Jace, would you like to stay and watch a movie with us?" she asks.

"Yes, ma'am," he says.

"Do you want to know what movie? It might be a sappy chic-flick. We watch those around here pretty frequently."

"I'm in," he says, and Mom just laughs.

"I figured," she says, darting a glance at our hands. "*The Notebook* it is."

By the end of the movie, Jace's arm is over my shoulder. I'm snuggled up against his chest thinking how small today's trouble seem in the scope of things. The movie ends, and Mom stands up, turning on the lights.

"That's it for me. I'm headed to bed," she says. "Michaela, time for Jace to go home."

He pretends to snore on the couch.

"Very funny," I say, kicking his foot. I walk him to the door. Mom has made her way back to her bedroom, but I have no doubt she'll be out again if Jace isn't gone before long.

"Do I get to see you tomorrow?" he asks.

"Hmmm. I'll think about it."

He leans down and kisses me. Our third kiss.

"Yeah, all right," I say. Who knew I was such a push-over?

He grins, squeezes my hand, and walks into the night.

Chapter 17 - Jaerish

Parties rage across the base tonight.

I pass drunken soldiers stumbling from one garage or bunker to the next on my way to the mess hall. Inside it's chill, just a few guys playing poker. Minimal alcohol. I've been looking forward to this chance to hang with Kelvin and Gideon. While I fit my new role and new squad, being with these guys lets me relax and just exist.

I've barely arrived when a medic, the same one who showed up the night Hayes and his buddies jumped me, opens the door and scans the room.

"Kelvin, I could use your help. Yours too, Jaerish." With a nod towards Gideon, he's gone. So much for relaxing.

Outside there's a new buzz in the air. And the smell of smoke. We jog towards a blazing utility garage where men with buckets fight the fire. It's almost out by the time we arrive, but the sidewalk across from the building is littered with wounded. I expect burns, but instead see blood and bruises. And then I see Captain Forsworth.

The small man leans against a wall nearby. He's obviously made no attempt to help extinguish the fire. Several of his crew lounge on the ground around him.

Kelvin goes to him, surveying the scene. "I didn't know you were back in camp." The medic has begun checking Forsworth's men for injuries.

"Got back yesterday. Wouldn't want to miss Halloween." Forsworth says.

"So I see," says Kelvin. "Were you able to rescue any more *Cov-4N* survivors this trip?"

"Sadly, no," Forsworth says. "We might go out again before winter fully hits. If I feel like it."

And that's why I hate him. His team is the only one equipped to seek victims of *Cov-4N*, but he acts as though lives weren't at stake.

"What happened tonight?" Kelvin asks.

"I don't know," Forsworth says, rubbing his patchy blonde excuse for a beard. "My boys and I were in the garage here playing a friendly game of cards. Next thing I know people are shoutin and flippin tables. A lantern must have gotten knocked over in the confusion."

Captain Radley joins us, a military policeman beside him. Radley nods to me then greets Forsworth. "Captain," he says.

"Captain," Forsworth replies with a mocking smile. "What has you out on this fine evening?"

"Sargent Major Open Sky sent me to ensure this situation is handled without incident."

"You are just the perfect soldier, Captain Radley," Forsworth says. "Always obeyin orders." The words are neutral. The delivery is not.

Radley ignores the comment and nods to the policeman. "You may proceed with your questions."

The police officer looks at his clipboard rather than at Captain Forsworth. It's obvious he's weighing each word. "Captain, several of the men have mentioned a disagreement regarding the legality of a certain playing style within the card game as the trigger for tonight's event. Unfortunately, any evidence seems to have been burned in the fire. Do you have anything to add to that account?"

"I don't believe so," says Forsworth with a smirk.

The officer continues, "I've also noted that several of those who are more severely wounded have been cut with a blade. This type of weapon is not permitted on one's person within the camp."

Forsworth looks to his crew. Two of them hand him knives much like the ones Radley and I carry. "I'm sorry about that officer. When we're in the wild, the boys need these for protection." I swear Forsworth's eyes just flicked to Captain Radley's scar. Forsworth hands the knives to the officer. "They must have forgotten to turn them in."

"And is there anything you have forgotten, Captain Forsworth?" Radley asks.

"Me? No, Captain. I never forget anything." One day I will knock that smirk off his face.

"It seems we're done here," Radley says to the police officer. "Please take the knives to the weapons keep. Let me know if you need anything further."

"Yes sir," says the officer, glad to be dismissed.

"You need me for anything else tonight?" Forsworth asks Radley with an exaggerated stretch and yawn.

"I do not. I'm sure you'll enjoy resting in a comfortable bed for a change."

"That I will, old friend," says Forsworth, clapping a hand on Radley's shoulder. Then he walks off with his crew trailing behind him.

At this point I'm too mad for poker. I need to tell Kelvin I'm leaving. When I find him, he's instructing Gideon in caring for the wounded. Kelvin sees me and stands.

"Gideon would make a good medic," he says. "I'm going to ask Captain Betner to approve his specialization."

A glance Gideon's way shows him crouched by a man covered in blood and vomit. Even from here the smell makes me want to retch, but Gideon doesn't seem bothered.

"I could see it," I say. "I've got a question."

"Ok," says Kelvin.

"Why does Forsworth get away with this? He cheated at cards, started a fight and burned down a building. His guys were carrying illegal weapons. And nothing's going to be done about it."

Kelvin shrugs. "We all owe our lives to Forsworth and his crew of misfits. Apparently, if you rescue hundreds of people, you're allowed to live outside the law."

It pisses me off to owe anything to Forsworth. I remember waking up, disoriented from *Cov-4N*. "*That was a bitch, boy. But I've brought ya back.*" Dip pooled in the corner of his lip. My eternal first memory.

"Seems like they could pick someone better for the job," I say.

"You can't pick immunity. I try not to worry about things I can't change. You might want to consider it yourself." Kelvin says it with a smile, but there's a warning underneath.

The next morning Radley, Patner and I are called to Open Sky's office. Major Merritt, Open Sky's second, is there when we arrive. Unfortunately, so is Forsworth.

"Hello, guardsmen," says Open Sky. "You all know Major Merritt. And you've met Captain Forsworth, of course." We each acknowledge the men. "You are all aware of Captain Forsworth's role in the rescue of those afflicted with *Cov-4N*. He is also my primary means of communication with contacts in the rest of the country.

"The camp is running smoothly, despite last night's incident, and the timing seems right for me to confer with a colleague I haven't seen in many years. On the way we will do some scouting and enjoy a well-deserved break from the tedium of everyday life.

"I am leaving Major Merritt in charge of the camp in my absence. As I don't foresee danger beyond that which is always inherent in travel, the majority of my guard will remain here to ensure continuity and order. I have chosen the three of you to accompany me, as well as Captain Forsworth and his team, on this trip. We will leave in three days. Any questions?"

"Where are we going?" I ask.

Forsworth sneers. "Why would that matter to you?"

"No disrespect, Captain, but we all come from somewhere. I've been away from that somewhere for a relatively short period of time. If we're going near Kansas City, someone might know who I was before *Cov-4N* took my memory."

"Sadly," says Open Sky, "we are heading in the opposite direction, to Salida. Perhaps a traveling seed merchant or trader could give you information. You may certainly ask questions, so long as it's done circumspectly, but I recommend you not hold out much hope."

For the first time I wonder why victims aren't taken to nearby settlements when they're found. Surely someone there would know who they are and want them back. Surely someone, somewhere, is wishing I'd return.

I've trained my features to remain blank, but Forsworth sneers at me like he knows what I'm thinking.

"Thank you for the opportunity, Sergeant Major. I look forward to it," I say.

Open Sky nods. "Dismissed."

CHAPTER 18 - KESSA

MY HEAD THROBS AND my body's on fire.

I claw myself to consciousness, out of the flames and crumpled metal. But no, Evan is still in there. I can't leave him.

I push onto my elbows, barely registering my room in the early morning grey, before darkness drags me back to my pillow.

I keep burning.

Pounding rouses me. Sunlight scorches my eyes.

I force myself to my feet and stumble to the door. I lean against the frame, fumble for the knob, and then Adam is there.

"Hey, Kessa. I thought you'd forgotten our run. Whoa. You need to sit down."

He catches me as I slide to the floor.

There are voices. Adam and someone else. So soothing. At first I think it's my dad, but that's not right. I open blurry eyes and see Dr. Massman. He helps me sit up, listens to my heart and lungs. Takes my temperature. I shiver beneath my blankets.

"Aha!" he says and turns my arm to show me the inside of my elbow. There are several small, raised bumps. "You've never had chicken pox, have you, Kessa?"

I search my muddled brain, but everything is registering so slowly. Chicken Pox. Common childhood illness pre-pan. Nonexistent in El Dorado Springs. Worse in adults. Crap.

"No," I say. "We don't have it."

"Unfortunately, darling, it's still present in Salida. Most people catch it as kids and have an uncomfortable few days. You may take a bit longer to recover. You weren't having any symptoms yesterday, were you? No headaches or nausea?"

Was it just last night? It was awful. Humiliating to feel so out of place. But the ache in my stomach when I watched Adam take Beach Barbie Amy to the dance floor had nothing to do with illness.

"No. I wasn't sick yesterday."

"Honestly, when Adam fetched me, I thought you were going to be like most of my patients this morning. Not much to do for a hangover. But this is definitely chicken pox. I'll send Adam for supplies and be back to check on you this afternoon."

Before he's done speaking, I'm asleep.

Someone is shaking me gently.

"Take these." Adam's voice. "The sooner they're in your system, the more helpful they are."

I look up into concerned blue eyes. His brow is furrowed and shines with sweat.

"Oh no. Have you caught my fever?"

"Nope, just been running." Adam's smile is small. "Now take them." His arm is behind my back, helping me sit up. I swallow the pills and some apple juice before I'm out again.

Can't stop shaking. Clammy sheets cling to my legs when I try to roll over. So cold. Someone pulls back my blankets. Strong arms lift me and I curl into him. Into Adam. He carries me to my bathroom, and then I'm in the tub, clothes and all. I try to protest, but finding words is hard.

"I'm sorry, Kessa. But we have to get your fever down."

He lifts my head so gently and positions a folded towel behind my neck. I just want to stay in his arms, but he lays me back and begins pouring cool water over my burning body as the fever rages on.

Something is different. Nothing hurts.

I stretch everything, toes to fingers, and find myself weak but not in pain. I open my eyes and lift my arms in front of me. My skin is covered in bumps. Some of them have been smeared with cream, and others are bloody like my fingernails. Gross. I must have been scratching them in my sleep.

I push myself to sitting and there's Adam, sprawled in one of my armchairs, neck at an awkward angle. The stubble on his face contrasts with the innocence of sleep. I'm staring, wondering what that stubble would feel like under my fingertips, when his eyes open.

"Kessa?" He says my name like a question.

"Still me. What day is it?"

"Sunday. The third. You look better. How do you feel?"

"Itchy. And weak. And if this is better, I hate to think what I looked like before. I'm in old pajamas and covered in spots." That's when I realize that I'm not in the soaking wet pajamas of the bath.

It must have shown on my face, because Adam says, "Amy came over and helped change your sheets and clothes."

"Beach Barbie Amy?" I ask.

"Yeah. She's in her first year of training to be a nurse, so she was happy to help."

"I bet she was," I murmur under my breath. I'm not a murmurer, and I know it's ungrateful since this girl changed my sweat-soaked pajamas when I couldn't even move my own body. But I can't help thinking that she did it to look good for Adam, not to help me.

"What did you say?" Adam asks. I will not be repeating it.

"Nothing. How do I make these bumps stop itching?"

Adam approaches, handing me a jar of cream. "If you think you'll be ok for a little while, I'll go get us some breakfast," he says.

"That sounds great." I stand up from the bed without swaying even a little bit. "I'm going to take a shower. Hot this time."

My shower is the best shower in the history of showers. I feel the germs flowing away. I'm careful to clean the nasty dried blood from under my fingernails. Toweling off is a dangerous temptation, and it's all I can do not to give myself a good itch.

I dress, brush my teeth, and have just finished applying the cream to all the pocks I can reach, when there's a knock on the door.

Adam is back with breakfast. His stubble is gone and he's changed clothes.

"Adam, knocking seems silly at this point. You did force-bathe me."

"Yeah, well, I didn't want to assume. Now that you're coherent and all."

I laugh. "Really, Adam, thank you. I don't know what I would have done if you hadn't come by for our run. And thank Amy for me too."

"You're welcome," Adam smiles. "I'm glad I could help. And I'll let Amy know."

In true Adam fashion, he's swept three days of non-stop care aside as if it were nothing. Maybe for him it was. He says Amy's name so casually, like of course he'll be seeing her. I want to ask him if they're a couple now, but I don't. Because I'm not sure I want to know the answer.

How did I become this person? I used to be confident. Straightforward. Evan's death shook everything. I don't know when I started liking Adam as more than a friend, but I do. And even this new, wussy version of me is pissed at myself for being jealous of a drunk girl in a bikini and heels.

This is ridiculous. I'm going to find out. Now.

"Breakfast smells amazing, but I need to ask a favor first," I say, "Because you haven't done enough for me lately."

"Of course." He grins at me from the table where he's setting out a stack of pancakes that has my mouth watering. Maybe this can wait after all. But no, I won't be able to eat across from him without knowing.

I sit on my bed and hold out the jar of itch cream. "I've gotten all the ones I can reach, but there are some I can't get to. They're driving me crazy."

Adam walks toward me slowly and takes the cream from my hand. Is his face just a little redder than normal? I can't tell. I turn my back to him and pull my braids over one shoulder. The bed shifts as Adam sits behind me. The feel of his finger as he makes a tiny circle on each itchy little spot is so good that I can't help groaning.

Adam draws back. "I think that's all of them," he says. He's gotten my shoulders, but hasn't touched a spot beneath the cami. This is my last chance to bail and keep things normal. Friendly. No . . . Courage, Kessa.

"I'm sorry, Adam, but the worst ones are underneath." My father would be so disappointed.

I don't turn around to look at Adam, but I hear his inhale before he reaches for the bottom of my shirt. Warmth spreads from the point of contact as his fingers graze my skin. But as soon as it's there, it's gone.

"Listen, maybe this should wait until Dr. Massman gets here. Or I could ask Amy to come over and help you."

And there it is.

"Sure," I say, forcing a smile. "I didn't mean to make you uncomfortable. I'm just so itchy!" I turn towards him and he's closer than I realized. My leg bumps his and I don't pull it away. His eyes darken, and I think, just maybe . . . but instead he stands up and turns his back to me.

"Why don't we eat?" he asks. His voice is off.

I shouldn't have done it. Shouldn't have crossed that line, especially after he was so good to me while I was sick. I need Adam's friendship, even if he doesn't want more.

"Sure! It looks great," I say, trying to make my voice bright. I follow him to the table. "Thank you so much for getting breakfast."

"No problem."

We load the pancakes onto our plates in silence. We douse them in syrup. In silence. We spread the golden, creamy butter . . . yep . . . in silence. I take my first bite, that I know should be bliss, and it's flavorless. I might as well be eating my pillowcase. I've gotta fix it.

"Adam, I'm sorry. You've been wonderful to me, and I wouldn't have asked you to do my back if I'd known you're with Amy now. Please, I don't want to mess up our friendship over this."

Adam looks up from his plate. "I'm not with Amy. I was just looking out for her for Cole. Not every guy in Salida can be trusted with a drunk girl in a bikini. It's just . . . Do you even know I'm a man? You can't ask me to rub lotions on you and not be affected by it."

Adam, who is always so perfectly put together, is a little bit wild-eyed. Which I think must be a good thing. And I know this is the moment I choose whether or not to be the old me again. The brave, unbroken me. I take a deep breath and say it.

"Adam, I wanted you to be affected by it. At least, I hoped you would."

He frowns then tilts his head to one side, brows drawn. But he doesn't look away.

"I don't usually play games. And I'm sorry. I should have just asked if you were with Amy." My cheeks are burning.

"So, you're saying you asked me to put the cream on your back to find out if I was with Amy?"

"Well, yeah. Kind of." It sounds so stupid out loud.

His eyebrows go up, inviting me to continue, but I'm embarrassed enough without elaborating.

"And now you know I'm not with Amy," he says. His gaze flickers to my lips then returns to my eyes. "Do you still want help with your back?"

I nod, chew on my lip. What am I doing? I know I had a boyfriend for a long time, but I have literally no game. I stand, putting my napkin on the table, and walk to the couch. I turn my back to Adam, pulling up the bottom of my cami to just below my ribs. He sits down behind me, taking forever to uncap the cream.

"Just so you know," Adam says, "Amy, who is most definitely not my girlfriend, is the one who did this while you were asleep. This is a first for me."

I barely feel the cool air on my skin as Adam's finger works its way across my lower back. He pauses, and I almost wish I had more spots for him to cover. His fingers glide gently now in smooth strokes, the pretense of itch cream forgotten.

"Your back is beautiful, Kessa," Adam says, his voice close behind my ear.

I turn towards him, searching his deep blue, drown-in-me eyes. My mind flashes to Evan's eyes, steel grey like the sky during a storm. Adam's eyes are the blue after the storm has passed. I lean toward him, into his kiss. His lips are gentle on mine. I draw his bottom lip into my mouth, just the smallest bit, tasting maple and Adam.

He slowly pulls back, giving us space.

"Are you sure you're ready for this?" he asks, searching my eyes.

"For what?" I murmur.

"For us to be something other than friends. I don't want to rush you." I know he's asking about Evan, and I'm grateful.

"Yeah, I'm ready," I say, leaning back towards him for another kiss. I've somehow forgotten about the itching, but then my stomach growls. Loudly. I put my hand over it, embarrassed, but Adam laughs.

"You haven't eaten real food in days. I'm glad your stomach held off that long. C'mon." He takes my hand like it's the most natural thing in the world and pulls me to my feet, leading me the five steps back to the table where our pancakes are waiting.

They taste so much better this time, and I wonder if maple will forever remind me of our first kiss. Halfway through my plate I can't help but get up and kiss him again.

Five minutes later I'm sitting on Adam's lap, pancakes forgotten.

We both jump at the sound of a firm knock on the door. Adam's expression mirrors my surprise, and we laugh. I'd forgotten what this feels like, this easy happiness in small things.

I answer the door and find Doctor Massman on my porch. He smiles and enters, looking from me to Adam to the pancakes on the table.

"Kessa. I'm glad to see you up and around. How's the itching?"

"It's fine, except for a few I can't reach on my back."

Adam chokes on his juice.

"I can get those if you'd like," Dr. Massman says, oblivious as he holds my wrist and counts my pulse.

"I'll be alright," I say. "I'm finding ways to distract myself."

"Well, I'm glad to hear it. You should be back to normal any day now. Just take it slow."

Dr. Massman doesn't stay long, and as I turn from closing the door, Adam is standing before me. I slip my arms around his waist.

"I'm a distraction then, am I?" he asks.

"A fabulous one," I say, eyes trained on those perfect lips.

"Kessa," he leans back, catching my gaze. "I don't want to be a distraction from something else. I want to be what you want."

I think of making a joke, something to keep this light, but he's being honest, and he deserves more than that. And I'm willing to give it.

"Adam, you are exactly what I want."

He crushes me to himself and murmurs into my hair. "Finally, I don't have to make myself let go."

I'm covered in pocks, over-stuffed with carbs, and can't remember ever being this happy.

Chapter 19 - Jaerish

"That's nothin compared to your good buddy, Kelvin," Forsworth says with a nod in my direction. "Now Kelvin is a story I almost can't bear to re-tell. Except that it's so damn funny."

I make my face stone, but Forsworth needs no encouragement. For the third night in a row, he's dominating the campfire with rescue stories that humiliate the soldiers. Not even his men seem to enjoy them. Open Sky, as usual, has retired early.

Without Forsworth, the time we've spent on the road, scouting for resources and camping out, would have been the best time of my life. Or at least of the seven months I remember. Instead, I wish Open Sky had chosen to skip it all and make the trip in a day.

"Now Kelvin, see, we found him down in Oklahoma. It was middle of the summer, and we'd been followin a trail that looked like it had been thrashed through some brush, the way that Cov-4N victims sometimes do. It took us to a pond with a little beach and an island in the middle. And right there on the sand was a little blue miniskirt and tank top.

"Now, I've gotta say, as often as I might have seen some nice lookin women in the towns when I visit, I'd never come across a female Cov-4N victim. I don't know if women don't catch it, or what. But this was new.

"We're lookin out at the water and someone comes into view from behind the island. I holler 'Miss, I just want you to know we're here and don't mean you no harm,' thinkin a lady's not gonna wanta be caught skinny dippin, but to my surprise the lady starts swimmin our way. I'm standin there thinkin this might be my lucky day, when who should climb out of that lake but good old Kelvin. And all he's wearin is a pair of lady's panties."

Forsworth's doubled over, laughing at his own story. His men chuckle, but it sounds forced. I wonder if any of them would defend him if I broke his nose. I've decided it's worth it, even if they all jump in, when Radley puts his hand on my shoulder and uses it to push himself to his feet.

"Time for bed," he says. "Jaerish, Patner, let's go." I stand, thinking how much better Forsworth's smirk would look bloody. "Now, Jaerish." I follow him to the tent.

Inside Radley speaks quietly so he won't wake Open Sky. "I don't know why Forsworth is singling you out, but don't take the bait."

"What do you mean?"

"He means," says Patner, "that Forsworth is an ass, but he's not going anywhere. If it comes down to you or him, the only way you can win is if he's dead."

"What?"

"If you fight him and don't kill him," Patner says, "Forsworth will kill you in your sleep and get away with it. Or frame you for something so you'll receive camp justice. Either way, it's you who's screwed."

"So, you're telling me it's not worth it?"

"I'm telling you," Radley says, "that if you decide it is worth it, you'd better make it look like an accident. And I don't want to know about it beforehand."

I wake the next morning to find the campsite a mess of trash and dishes, and Forsworth's team gone. The guide they left behind spouts some BS about making sure the next town is safe, then spends several minutes grumbling into his coffee about a bar and someone named "Sweet Lucy." I'm shoving trash into a pack when Open Sky approaches.

"Good morning," he says, gathering dishes.

"I'll take care of it, Open Sky," I say. I'm pissed to be cleaning up after Forsworth, but there's no way I'm letting our leader do it.

"I have functioning hands and legs, Jaerish," Open Sky says. "And only a fool is too proud to share in honest labor." He walks with me to the nearby creek where we start washing off the metal plates.

"You've seemed pensive of late, Jaerish. What's on your mind?" What isn't? When I hesitate, he says, "Please, speak freely. If my guard cannot, who will?"

"I hate Forsworth's 'rescue' stories."

"It is difficult," Open Sky says. "Captain Forsworth speaks without discretion, yet we are all in his debt."

There's no way to ask what I really want to know without it sounding like an accusation. But Open Sky told me to speak freely.

"Why don't we take Cov-4N victims to the local towns when they're discovered?"

Open Sky is quiet long enough that I think he might not answer. Finally, he says, "Which is worse, Jaerish? To be given a fresh start or to remain amongst those who know you as someone you will never be again?"

"I think my family would want me back anyway."

"That depends on what kind of family you left behind," he says with a grimace. "But the question is moot. In the beginning we attempted to re-unite men with their past lives. We discovered in the worst possible way that the blue pill not only maintains memory, but also suppresses contagion."

Open Sky stares blankly into the creek as he continues.

"One of our earliest survivors was reunited with his village, a small place, maybe forty people. He had a supply of pills to last several months, but when we circled back just six weeks later, the entire population was dead.

"I can't be sure Cov-4N was the cause, but the town was carnage, as though everyone had gone insane. Bodies were found shot in bathtubs and cellars. The bar looked like the scene of a massacre. One man was tied into the branches of a tree, and I hope the birds waited until he died to pick his bones clean.

"I decided then that we couldn't take the risk again. Better to give a few men a new life at the expense of the old rather than to risk the many in a time when humanity is so diminished."

"Then why are you taking us to Salida?" I ask. "What if we spread Cov-4N there?"

"As long as you are taking your blue pill there's nothing to fear."

It's clear Open Sky would forget the horrors he saw if he could. Maybe there are worse things than having only seven months of memory.

<hr>

CHAPTER 20 - JACE

<hr>

"WE'RE HERE!"

Michaela veers off the main road and past a weathered sign. *Dogwood Canyon*. It's all I can do not to crash Henry's bike as I fly down the steep, pitted drive. Below us car skeletons rust away in a field full of brush and dead grass. A small booth to one side sags in front of a large timber building.

I stop beside Michaela, grateful I made it down without wiping out. Biking is still new for me, but Michaela insisted today would be worth it. And turns out I'm a sucker for anything that will make my Kayla happy.

She smirks at me as I barely manage to get off the bike without falling over. Then she turns to scan a paper tacked to what I can now tell is, or was, a ticket booth. She looks my way, grins almost wickedly, then reaches up and tugs the rope of an enormous bell. Its clanging sends a thousand birds into flight. And then everything goes silent.

"Hands where I can see them."

I've never had a gun pointed at me before, but movies have trained me well. My hands are high in the air before I can think about it. By the time I see the speaker, he's lowering his rifle. A smile splits his old, bearded face.

"Michaela, how are you doin, darlin? How's your mama? And who's this?"

"Hi Gregor. This is Jace. I wanted him to see the canyon."

Gregor has reached us, and I slowly lower my arms to shake his outstretched hand.

"Nice meeting you, Jace. I heard we had some new seed in town."

Well, that's awkward. "Is this place yours?" I ask.

"I watch over it and keep it safe for those who want to come learn about the past."

"My mom sent jam and fresh bread," says Michaela. She takes a cloth-wrapped bundle from her bike basket and gives it to Gregor. "We appreciate you." They both smile. Gregor takes a seat on a bench, already unwrapping the cloth.

I follow Michaela into the large building, which turns out to be a museum. The entryway is full of artifacts in dusty glass cases. I about piss myself when I see a lynx crouched above us, and laugh nervously when Michaela points out the hunters on an opposite ledge. They hold no weapons, which is when I realize that the only broken cases once held weapons too. I'm definitely a "town" kind of guy, and I'm suddenly glad of Gregor's gun-toting presence outside.

"I'm surprised your mom lets you come here alone," I say to Michaela.

"She doesn't. If you weren't here, she would be. And that only works because of Gregor."

I nod, understanding. "The paper?"

"He marks it every four hours or so. If it wasn't marked, we'd have left."

We wander into a gift shop. It's fully stocked with engraved shot glasses and keychains, but there isn't a bottled water in sight.

"This place was a big destination for tourists before the pandemic," Michaela says, "But now it's my own little paradise."

"Only you would have a paradise this educational." I reach out and take her hand, smiling.

"Just wait," she says.

We pass a giant mill wheel then leave the building and go back to our bikes. I'm honestly a little disappointed. The museum's cool, but I expected more from Kayla's favorite place. And that's when she turns her bike onto a covered bridge and we emerge into a whole other world.

A crumbling asphalt path rolls out before us, crisscrossed by a dry streambed. On both sides of us young trees in orange, yellow and red cover what Michaela says was once a flawless green lawn. In the midst of them a pioneer wagon tilts to one side, its wheel rotten away.

"We're seeing the remnants of a world that was recreating its past," Michaela says. "The people pre-pandemic had no more idea what the future held than the ones moving west in those wagons."

The trail ends at a pool where golden fish swim lazily through the reflections of autumn leaves and bright blue sky. Michaela packed a picnic, and we eat, taking turns tossing crusts into the water.

This setting is too romantic to waste. My inner Cole says "step up your game." I pull the cell my dad gave me as an it's-been-nice-knowing-you gift out of my backpack.

"Picture?" I ask. From Michaela's smile, I know she's thinking about how many people have taken selfies in this exact place over the years. Or maybe how much more cells could do before the pandemic.

"Do you have music on there?" she asks.

"Do I have music?" I pull up the playlist labeled *Get the Girl* and press play. "Dance with me?"

Michaela puts her hands on my shoulders as a sweet, sappy melody plays around us. She smiles and looks up at me as we sway. Slowly, I bend down and kiss her. I don't think I've ever been this happy.

On our ride back Michaela points out a chapel nearly hidden in the trees.

"My mom was married there. Want to see it?"

We park the bikes. Michaela moves aside a board so we can get in through a broken window. It smells musty, but it's still easy to see why people would want to start their lives together here. At one end of the room, a cliff looms behind double glass doors.

"There used to be a waterfall," Michaela says. "It's in all of my mom's wedding pictures. But it was man-made and the pump broke before I could see it. I was really disappointed the first time Mom brought me here."

I sit beside her in the front row.

"Mom was a newlywed when the pandemic hit. Just eighteen, and only married a few months. But she tells me she'd loved him for as long as she could remember. He was two years older and crazy smart. He'd already finished college and was traveling with an engineering firm when everything happened."

"Do you wonder what your life would have been like if he didn't die? If he'd been your dad?"

"I think about it for Mom, but I wouldn't be here. Different dna and all."

We sit in silence. It seems rude to say I'm glad her mom's husband died, but I am.

"I sometimes wonder what would be different if my mom had lived," I say. "People tell me she brought out Dad's best. I think he's convinced that if he'd pushed his obsession to get back into the cities sooner, he could have saved her."

"That's a lot to carry."

"Tell me about it. He's so driven now, like if he can restore medicine to what it used to be her death would have some grand purpose."

I sit on the hard pew, Michaela's hand in mine, thinking of our moms. Hers was married right here with no idea that in months her groom would die, along with the world she'd always known. My mom survived the end of the world, but woke up one morning with a cold and some bruises and was dead by that night.

I clutch Michaela's hand tighter, like that might keep her safe from some scary, unknown future. And for the first time I understand my dad just a little, because I already can't imagine what losing her would do to me.

CHAPTER 21 - KESSA

I SHOW UP LATE and slip into the back row, hoping to go unnoticed.

Around me people sing familiar lyrics accompanied by a single piano. It affects me differently than when a full band plays it back home. Or maybe this is the first time I've been ready to worship since Evan's death. There's something about declaring God's faithfulness when you've experienced real loss that I didn't understand before.

When the song ends, someone announces drinks in the back and a few minutes to greet a neighbor. Goodbye anonymity. I make my way to the tea table, which seems like a better alternative than sitting alone, trying to avoid eye contact with curious church-goers.

"Kessa. It's nice to see you here," says Dr. Massman as he pours cream into a mug. "How are you feeling?"

"Much better, thank you."

"Let me introduce my wife." Smiling he turns to the slightly plump woman with salt and pepper hair who stands beside him. "Amber, meet Kessa McKnight."

Before I have time to speak, Amber Massman has folded me into a squishy hug. She steps back, beaming.

"Hello, Kessa! How are you enjoying Salida? I hear you were sick last week. All better now? Where are you sitting? Oh, no matter. You can sit with us." She says it all without the slightest pause, and before I know what's happened, I'm sitting beside the Massmans in the second row.

The pastor's message is a good one about perspective and hope. It's not one of those "he's talking to me" experiences that sometimes happen, but it's familiar and comfortable, like slipping into my own coat again after weeks in Mrs. Prior's spare.

After the service I find myself at the Massmans' for lunch. Several people from church are there, and Amber mothers us all, keeping conversation going and plates filled.

It's almost one o'clock when I get home and find Adam sitting on my porch.

"Hey, you. Where've you been?" he asks with a smile as he takes in my fancier than normal outfit. He stands and plants a kiss on my cheek like we've been together for years.

I haven't mentioned church to him yet, assuming I'd be home by 11:30. Sunday is the one day that Adam sleeps in.

"I went to church and then over to the Massmans' for lunch. When did you get here?"

"Just a couple minutes ago." He follows me inside and sees the outfits and their hangers still lying across my bed. "Hard time deciding what to wear?"

"I was looking for something that wouldn't draw attention. It didn't matter once Amber Massman got ahold of me. She introduced me to literally everyone."

"You don't have much chance of going unnoticed anyway." Adam grins as he goes to the sink to fill a cup with water. I start hanging up clothes. "So, how was it?"

"Nice. Not the same as in El Dorado Springs, but good."

"Were you into church back home?"

"I was. Before Evan died. Since then, God and I have been on a break. But I think I'm going to go back. What about you? You've never mentioned church."

"You haven't been here for Christmas or Easter yet." He shrugs, taking a drink. "Mom took us when I was little, but Dad only did the big two. Did you know Amber Massman was her best friend?"

"Really? I would have liked to know your mom," I say.

"Yeah, me too. From everything I've heard, Lilian Morton was an amazing woman."

Adam's taken a seat in one of my armchairs now. I sit down on his lap and kiss him on top of the head. He turns his face to mine and I kiss him better.

"Mmmm. I like that," he says. I grin and kiss him again.

Minutes later I'm skimming my fingers down the column of his neck and across his shoulders, wondering what he'd look like with his shirt off. And I realize that we haven't talked at all about this kind of thing. The kissing and how far we want it to go.

"Adam," I say, scooting back so I'm practically perched on his knees.

"Yeah," he asks, a little breathless and blurry-eyed.

"I don't want to have sex until I'm married."

"Um, yeah. Ok."

"I mean, not that we were going to. But I figured that since I feel that way, we should talk about it. Before we get close." I sound like an idiot.

"Yeah. Good thing to talk about. Not exactly what I was thinking about right now, but important. Is this a new thing or an always thing?"

"What do you mean?"

"Well, did you and Evan . . .?"

"No. We were waiting."

"Ok," he says. "Do you wish you had?" His eyes are warm, genuinely curious. I take the time to think about my answer.

"I used to, when he was first gone. But not anymore. It would have messed things up between us. Besides, obviously Evan isn't going to be the man I marry, and I want to save that for him."

Adam is looking at me and I blush, wondering if his mind went where mine did. There's a softness in his look now as he lifts my hand up to his mouth and kisses my palm.

"I'm impressed that you guys waited. You were together a long time." He looks down, hesitates before going on. "I've had sex. I hope that's not a deal breaker."

"No, of course not," I say. I scoot closer to him. "Do I know her? You don't have to tell me if you don't want to."

"It's fine. Her name's Ally and she was a senior when I was a freshman. I thought it was forever, but she broke up with me to get back together with her ex-boyfriend. They're married now and have a toddler."

"I'm sorry, Adam."

He shrugs. I hate the thought of such a young Adam having his heart broken. I lean in and kiss him again.

"Anything else you want to talk about?" Adam asks. "Because talking about life-altering things was totally on my mind for today. Not how much I'd love to sit in a chair and kiss you, but international politics, the plight of pre-pan immigrants, the catastrophic toll of forest fires. . ."

"Shut up," I say and swat at his chest. He tries to go on, but I smother it with another kiss. Laughing, he kisses me back.

Chapter 22 - Jaerish

We reach Salida at dusk, driving up a rise to a mansion overlooking the town. A dark-haired man in a cowboy hat throws his arm over Open Sky's shoulder and loudly ushers us through the entryway into a spacious room complete with chandeliers and roaring fireplace.

"Richard," says Open Sky. "It's been a long time. Seven years, perhaps?"

"Indeed, old friend," Richard says. "And while I've enjoyed receiving your letters, this is better. Everything is coming together as it should, as if it were fated. But more of that later. For now, I'm sure you're exhausted. Would you and your men like to freshen up before dinner?"

"Perhaps we should," Open Sky agrees with his typical enigmatic smile. It's the first time I wonder what we must look like to this man, Richard, in his pressed shirt and polished boots. And what we must smell like.

Radley, Patner and I will be staying here with Open Sky while Forsworth and his men are set up elsewhere. I'll be glad of some distance, but I hope they don't do anything to get us all run out of town.

I'm last to shower. Despite the cooling water the marble-tiled room is pure luxury. I dress in an outfit reserved for arrival and comb my hair into a ponytail at the base of my neck. Do men here wear their hair long, or is that just a camp thing? I guess I'll find out.

Radley and Patner are gone when I return to our room. I hear voices downstairs and follow them, hoping dinner hasn't started without me. At the base of the steps, I realize the speakers weren't my friends, but Open Sky and our host, Richard Morton.

"Your report gladdens me," says Morton. "Twenty-five years and our goals are nearly accomplished."

"I'm hoping that after all of these years our goals still align. I'm not sure I understand the necessity of going to the lengths you're describing."

"Oh, it will all become clear," Morton says. "How trustworthy do you consider the men you've brought with you?"

"My guard is completely loyal. Dealing with Forsworth is like trying to tame a poisonous snake. He's insubordinate, and lately he's been testing his fangs."

"It's not hard to cut the head off a serpent that's outlived its usefulness. The size of our army is sufficient."

I'm about to cough to announce my presence when Morton continues.

"And how much does your guard know?"

"In regards to what?"

"In regard to all of it. *Cov-4N* and your immunity? Our purposes and methods."

"They know what the rest of the camp knows. It's not a secret I feel safe sharing, as my right to lead could be questioned. Forsworth and his team, who were chosen for their immunity, are the only ones who didn't join our army in the standard way. And only you and I know the army's purposes. Though it appears you know more than I do."

There's an edge to Open Sky's voice now. Why?

Patner's laughter interrupts my thoughts, and I realize I've listened for too long. Taking a few steps back from the doorway, I see both Radley and Patner descending. I laugh along with them. Radley narrows his eyes, but as Morton and Open Sky join us in the hallway Patner slaps me on the back.

"You seriously believed him," Patner says, still laughing. "You can be a real dumb-a . . . Hey Open Sky. Hello, Mr. Morton."

"Gentlemen," says Morton with a smile. "Call me Richard. I hope you're hungry, because my housekeeper has outdone herself."

I smile, saying something about enjoying the shower, while inside my mind is racing. My head fills with a new mantra, one of purposes and methods, secrets and headless snakes.

At dinner we're joined by Morton's son, Adam. He's a quieter version of his dad. Still engaging, still confident, but not as in your face about it. Less fake. But maybe that distinction comes from overhearing the older Morton's earlier conversation.

All through the meal I replay it. *"Our purposes and methods."* What is Morton's connection to the army, anyway? And what secret could possibly impact Open Sky's right to lead?

I want to ask Open Sky, but he's obviously been lying about something important. I have no interest in ending up like Fatim with a knife through my throat. I force myself to refocus on the conversation around me.

"So, Open Sky, how do you and my Dad know each other?"

"I met your father days after the pandemic began, though we've seen each other only a handful of times since," says Open Sky. "You might actually say that your father was my savior."

"Really?" Adam says with a laugh and a glance his dad's way. "That seems like a story I would have heard."

"Open Sky may be exaggerating," Morton says, launching in. "Adam's grandfather was active in politics at the highest levels, although he always chose a background role. He had big plans for me, and was preparing the way with his connections. 'Some men were born to rule,' he'd say.

"He was in Washington D.C. when the pandemic struck. I was a graduate student, but had come home to Salida to convince Adam's mother that a long-distance relationship was worth pursuing. So, in a way, she was my savior." Here he pauses slightly, and I notice his wife's absence for the first time. I'm so used to a men-only camp that it hadn't crossed my mind.

"In any case," he continues, "my father was one of the first in the world to know that the pandemic was upon us. He video-conferenced with the Council, telling us how to quarantine the town and guarantee its survival. 'No one in; shoot on sight,' he said. That's one thing I always appreciated about my father. He was willing to make the hard decisions.

"He knew he wouldn't be returning, that he probably had the disease already. He requested I stay on the video call after it ended, and no one questioned him.

"But he hadn't kept me for fatherly last words. Instead, he told me of a classified facility in the mountains west of here that was doing advanced testing on the brain and drugs to treat post-traumatic stress disorder. He said shutting it down was worth my life if the measures he gave me to guard against contagion failed.

"The Council trusted my father enough that when I said I had to go they supported me. They set up a quarantine area in the hopes that I would return, and I left the next morning. The pandemic had reached the facility before me. You can't imagine the things I saw, and I won't tell you." Morton shudders visibly.

"I wanted to turn around, but I'd given my word. I worked my way into the core of the building, and had just wiped the main bank of hard drives when I heard banging. I found Open Sky hitting a pipe in a quarantine room, the only person left alive."

Now Open Sky breaks his silence.

"I was a test subject, already quarantined when the outbreak began. I tell myself that the doctors who left me sealed in that room didn't intend to put me to a slow death with only my nightmares as company. That is, nevertheless, what would have happened had Richard not found me."

We're all staring at Open Sky now. He looks me squarely in the eyes as he says "So you can see, I am not exaggerating when I call Richard Morton my savior. I owe him not only my life, but my sanity as well."

"And now I understand why I haven't heard this story before," says Adam. "That must have been horrible."

"Everything about that time was horrible," says Open Sky. "The world was coming to an end." There's a pause, everyone quiet. What must it have been like to see everything you've ever known, gone?

"But it didn't end," says Richard Morton finally. "And now we have the opportunity to rebuild it as we see fit."

CHAPTER 23 - KESSA

His name out of my mouth like a breath. Like a sigh. Like life.

I've walked through the cold, dark morning to Adam's for our run, but when I enter the kitchen, he's there. Evan. Leaning against the counter, calm as anything. Coffee mug in hand. Not coffee. Evan doesn't like coffee.

Oh God. How is this possible?

"Good morning, Miss. Can I help you with something?"

It's Evan's voice. His hair is long, pulled back in a ponytail. His face is sharper. His eyes are the same steely gray.

But there's no recognition in them.

This must be another cruel dream. I haven't dreamt of Evan since Halloween, right before Adam and I got together.

Dream Evan is looking at me, brows furrowed, like he always used to do when he was trying to figure something out. I'm staring, but it doesn't matter. I can stare at him all I want to in a dream.

"Miss? Are you alright?"

And all I can think to say is "You don't like coffee."

He looks even more confused. And suddenly I'm feeling very awake. I can't breathe. Not a dream. A nightmare.

Adam comes into the kitchen. He kisses me on the head then looks from me to Evan who I'm still obviously staring at.

"Everything ok, Kess? Have you met Jaerish?"

I shake my head hard, trying to wake myself up. Too much.

Evan (Jaerish?) moves towards me, hand outstretched as though to shake mine. His expression is, is what? Wary? Polite? I don't know. But I can't stay here. I turn and dart for the door. Down the stairs. Wake up. Wake up. Wake up. Onto the road towards home.

Someone is running behind me. Evan following? No. Adam. Adam is calling my name. But I keep running. He catches up easily, runs along with me, like he would on any normal morning.

"Kessa, what's going on?"

There are no words. Just running. And Adam beside me. And Evan in his kitchen. Oh, God. My breaths are ragged now, forcing me to stop. But I stay upright, hands behind my head. I won't bend this time. Won't panic. Won't vomit. Won't be that girl again.

Adam isn't even breathing hard from chasing after me, and it pisses me off that he's still a better runner after the months I've spent here. Then I look at his eyes and my anger whooshes away. He's so obviously worried about me, and I'm mad that he's a good runner? What is my problem?

Oh, wait. My dead boyfriend is in Adam's kitchen. That's a problem.

"Kessa, what just happened?" Adam asks again. "Did Jaerish say something to you?"

"No," I almost sob the word. "He looks like Evan. Not just a little bit. Like a lot. Like, if Evan weren't dead, that would be Evan."

"Oh, Kess. I'm so sorry."

I propel myself into Adam's arms and cling to him. He holds my head against his chest and I breathe in clean, cold air mingled with Adam's skin.

I'm not thinking, just absorbing the comfort of being held. Until finally I pull back.

Adam wipes the wetness from my cheek with his thumb. "So, what do you want to do?"

What do I want to do? Curl up in fetal position and never leave my house again? Or maybe stand here and let Adam hold me forever? Neither is very practical.

"I need to go home."

Adam nods. "I'll walk you."

"That's ok," I say. Is it rude to tell him I need some time alone? Probably not, especially compared to literally running out the door when his houseguest offered to shake my hand. Whatever. "Maybe you can make up an excuse to the guy in your kitchen. He probably thinks I'm crazy."

"You are." I manage a half-hearted smile at Adam's attempt to joke. "Don't worry. I'm sure he thinks we're both crazy now with how I ran after you."

For the first time I look around us, aware that someone else might have witnessed my flight. But it's still early. The dirt road is empty in the new blue of morning, and the maple trees hold no judgment in their shadowed depths.

"So, who is he?" I ask. "Did you call him Darin?"

"Jaerish. He came to town with an old friend of my dad's. He's a bodyguard or something."

"Who needs a bodyguard?"

"I don't know. I'd never even heard of Open Sky before last night. Apparently, my dad rescued him from a bunker full of dead people right when the pandemic hit."

I shudder. "His name's 'Open Sky?'" I ask. "That makes 'Jaerish' sound normal."

"He's Native American."

"Oh." I'm crazy and a jerk.

"Kess, are you sure you don't want to go back with me? You were taken by surprise before, but I bet if you actually talk to Jaerish you'll see all kinds of differences."

I'm sure Adam's right, but I just can't do it. Not now, anyway. Adam must see it in my face because he leans over and kisses me gently.

"It's going to be ok. You'll take a hot shower and eat something salty and the next time you see him he'll look like a complete stranger. I'm sure of it." I nod, not nearly as convinced.

"I'll see you tonight, right?" he asks. "At the party?"

"Of course," I say, forcing a smile. "I wouldn't miss it."

Chapter 24 - Jaerish

Did that girl seriously just run away when I offered to shake her hand? Not a good sign. I'm still staring at the back door like a dumbass when Radley and Patner enter the kitchen.

"You look like you got hit by a truck," Patner says.

"Thanks," I say. "The bed was too good. I couldn't sleep."

Radley eyes me sideways. He didn't ask what happened in the hallway last night when they caught me eavesdropping, but I know he's watching me now. Once again my mind flashes to Fatim with a knife through his throat, and I look down at my mug, swirling the tea. *You don't like coffee*, she'd said.

"How rude would it be if I started making breakfast?" Patner asks, glancing around at the gorgeous kitchen.

"Depends on if you plan to set the place on fire," Radley says.

"It happened once," Patner says, scowling.

Adam walks back into the house alone.

"Sorry about that," Adam says to me. "Kessa remembered she'd left her oven on, so she went home to turn it off. She's kind of freaked out about fires."

Radley raises an eyebrow at Patner.

"Screw you, man," Patner says.

"No worries," I say.

"Who's Kessa? Is Jaerish scaring off the ladies with his ugly mug?" Patner asks. "Because I literally have no memory of a real live woman, and I'm looking forward to meeting one. Like, really looking forward to it."

"Well then, I'm glad Kessa, my girlfriend, is no longer here," Adam says with a laugh. "What do you mean you don't have any memories of women? Aren't there women on your base?"

Patner's eyes dart to Radley who says "This fool exaggerates. If you'd been isolated with these grubs for as long as we have, women would seem like a far-off dream to you too. We don't have women in camp, though. Early on Open Sky realized it would complicate things."

"I could see that," Adam says, "although it might hurt enlistment." I wonder if Radley's lie is as obvious to Adam as Adam's was to me.

Adam tells us about the schedule while Patner makes pancakes. Open Sky has meetings with Richard Morton and a few other council members this morning, so Adam will show us around town. He promises we will, indeed, get to meet women today.

I'm surprised we won't be with Open Sky in the meetings, but apparently he considers it safe. Or maybe he doesn't want us knowing what's discussed.

"By the way," says Adam as we finish up breakfast, "I don't think Dad wanted it spread around that you're part of an army. It might make people nervous. He's been telling everyone you're delegates from Junction City."

I wonder how much Adam knows. He's aware of the army and Open Sky's backstory, but probably not about *Cov-4N* since he didn't know about our memories. How would he feel about us bringing something so dangerous into his town? I put him in the "potential allies" column, but it's too soon to tell.

Something in me wakes up as we walk along Salida's main strip. It's not that anything particular is familiar, but what it represents feels like home. There are shops, diners, a doctor's office. Men and women walk together down the street. Two kids run by, obviously racing. This feels like life. Not army life or camp life. Real life.

A woman with stylish brown hair and a fitted red jacket exits a shop in front of us. She gives me a once over and I involuntarily straighten my shoulders. It's stupid, but I'm glad I don't send every woman running. Beside me Patner grins like a clown.

"Cacia," Adam says, "allow me to introduce some new friends. Radley, Jaerish, Patner, meet Cacia. She and I go way back, so watch yourselves."

His easy joking manner is tested when Cacia reaches out her hand to shake and Patner kisses it.

"I don't know where you found such gentlemen, Adam, but I'd like to move there," Cacia says with a laugh.

"Junction City would be happy to have you," Radley interjects smoothly.

Cacia walks with us, talking easily as we move down the street. We enter the bakery, the general store, the feed store. She even joins us for lunch at a restaurant and Adam charges it all to his father's account.

After we eat, Cacia announces that she has to get back to work. We return home with Adam for a couple hours of rest before tonight's dinner with some of the town's "most notable citizens."

"So, will Cacia be there?" Patner asks Adam as we prepare to leave. His mind has been on little else since we'd met her.

"I don't know. She is sometimes," Adam says smirking.

I want to ask if Kessa will be there, but you don't just ask a guy if his girlfriend will be at the party. Especially when the only other time she saw you she ran away in terror.

But now I'm thinking maybe it wasn't terror. Maybe Kessa recognized me. And if she did, I need to know. The problem is how. *By the way, I've got amnesia and was wondering if you can tell me who I am.* Worst pick-up line ever.

There are at least twenty people at tonight's dinner, but Kessa isn't one of them. Patner manages to score a seat beside Cacia when we all sit down at the huge formal table. The food is delicious. But Forsworth's presence ruins my appetite. What does he know that I don't?

After dinner we're introduced to council members and their spouses, business owners and school administration. When anyone gets too curious about Junction City, I compliment Salida and ask questions. It always works. From what I can tell no one knows about our army.

I slept badly last night, my mind chasing theories, each one darker than the one before. I wonder how long we'll stay tonight. Where's Adam gone? I find Richard Morton talking with a smiling older couple.

"Jaerish," he says, drawing me into their circle. "May I introduce Doctor and Mrs. Massman?"

"You can call me Doc," says the man. "And my wife goes by Amber."

He holds out his hand and I shake it then turn to his wife. She takes my hand and won't let it go, holding it while she gushes.

"We are just delighted to have you young people in town with us. First the delegation from El Dorado Springs brought us our sweet Kessa, and now here you are. It's a bit like it used to be, with young people coming and going."

Which means Kessa is from somewhere else. Mrs. Massman looks like she might cry through her smile but she doesn't. Instead, she finally drops my hand only to reach out and hug me. Which is awkward, but not un-pleasant. Better than crying.

"Well then," says Richard Morton. "Was there something I can do for you besides introductions?"

"Have you seen Adam? I was wondering how long we're staying, but I can't seem to find him."

Before he can answer Amber Massman pipes up. "Of course we know where he is. Kessa lives in the guest house right behind the Priors. He snuck off to see her as soon as dinner was over."

"Maybe he won't want us to wait for him then," I say. Knowing where to find Kessa seems like important information, although I don't know what I can actually do with it. I'd never just show up on her doorstep. My thoughts are interrupted by Mrs. Massman. Amber.

"Young man, I've said your name three times now. You are gone on your feet. I'm going to take you back to that guest house and we will gather up Adam so he can get you home."

I protest, but there's no arguing with Amber Massman. She leads me out a back door and down a stone path to a little house complete with a welcome mat on the porch. The curtains are drawn over lit windows, and muffled voices come from inside. I would turn back if I could, but that's not an option as Amber Massman reaches out and knocks.

Chapter 25 - Kessa

I barely remember today, except that I spent it at the lab engrossed in energy current diagrams.

Now I'm at home in the guest house instead of at the fancy dinner the Priors are hosting for the delegation from Junction City. I don't trust myself to see Jaerish in a room full of people, not after fleeing the kitchen this morning.

I bet if I really looked at him, I'd see a thousand differences. But I don't want to do that with an audience. I don't want to do it at all.

It's still early when I hear Adam's knock. He always does it the same way. Tap. Tap. Tap-tap-tap.

"Come in!" I call without leaving my chair. I'm re-reading one of my favorite books and have just gotten to a good part.

Adam enters and closes the door behind him. He starts to talk but I hold up a finger, eyes already back on the page.

I'm vaguely aware of Adam walking to my kitchen counter. When I glance up again, he's putting an enormous forkful of chocolate cake in his mouth. He makes an exaggerated moan, just to be sure I'm aware of how good it tastes. I close my book.

"Did the elf kill the dragon?" he asks.

"For your information it was a gilarabrywn, and the maiden slew it."

Adam shakes his head. "You're lucky you're so pretty."

"With comments like that, you're lucky you brought cake."

I stand up and give him a quick kiss. He pulls me closer, kisses me deeper. Then he realizes it's a dud. No fire at all.

"Hard to kiss me when you've been thinking about your dead boyfriend all day?" he asks.

"Intentionally not thinking about my dead boyfriend, but yeah. Seems to be affecting the kissing."

"I get it, Kessa." Adam cups my face in his hands and looks down at me. "It's ok that you still miss him." He kisses my lips very gently then pulls back. "Want some cake?"

"You always know exactly what to say." His smile melts me. "How about cake and then I read to you?" I ask. Because I'm not ready to be done with this book for the night.

"Sure. But you're going to have to tell me what a gilarathingy is."

"Gilarabrywn. And you don't even know what you're asking for."

The cake is gone to the tiniest crumbs. I've been reading aloud to Adam for about twenty minutes when there's a knock on the door. Adam gets up to answer it.

I hear Amber Massman's distinctive voice. "Adam, I knew we'd find you here. This young man is dead on his feet, and I told him I was sure you wouldn't mind getting him home."

Amber has walked right in, of course, but the man she mentioned is still on the porch. Adam looks my way, and when I nod he steps aside so Jaerish can enter.

Amber continues prattling on, something about the differences in the decorating since she'd last been in the guest house. I'm trying to study Jaerish's features without being too obvious, but I don't think I'm succeeding. He still looks exactly like Evan, besides the long hair and thinner face. The smooth surface of Evan's cross glides beneath my fingertips.

Amber stops talking abruptly.

"Why, Kessa! Silly me. It didn't even occur to me that you probably haven't met Jaerish yet. Kessa McKnight, this is Jaerish . . . what did you say your last name was?"

Jaerish seems taken off guard by the question.

"We don't bother with them much in Junction City, Ma'am. Not enough people to need two names."

"Oh, yes, ok then. Kessa, meet Jaerish."

He hesitates then stretches his hand forward, no doubt wondering if I'm about to bolt for the door. I put my hand in his.

He has callouses in the same places Evan did from hours using weapons in his dad's martial arts studio. Jaerish's eyes hold a question. They really are the exact steely grey . . . I've been looking at him too long. Or time has stopped. I drop his hand.

"It's nice to meet you, Kessa," he says.

"Yeah, you too," I manage to mumble.

"You do look tired, Jaerish. Why don't I get you home?" Adam clasps a hand on Jaerish's shoulder. Always looking out for me. Or maybe also thinking I'd held this stranger's hand a little too long.

"Thanks, Adam," Jaerish says. "I can probably find my own way back if you want to stay."

"Nonsense," interrupts Amber. "What kind of hosts would we be if we left our guests to wander alone in the dark? Adam's mother would have been mortified."

"Besides, a gilarabrywn might get him," Adam says with a wink my way.

Amber Massman looks confused, but Jaerish laughs.

"I didn't know you had those around here," he says.

Adam's eyes widen, but he doesn't acknowledge the comment. "Are we still running tomorrow afternoon?"

"Yeah, sounds good."

Adam nods, then positions himself before me, back to Jaerish. His eyes ask if I'm ok. I force a smile then reach up and give him a quick kiss. Amber swats him out of the way, and engulfs me in a hug.

"Sorry to steal your boyfriend, dear. But I'm sure he'll be back soon enough."

From the doorway I watch both Adam and Evan, no Jaerish, as they're swallowed up by the night and tell myself that tons of people know about gilarabrywn. It didn't mean anything.

Chapter 26 - Jaerish

Radley offered to stay with Patner, who won't be leaving Cacia until he has to. I'm walking through the dark December night alone with Adam. Seeing his girlfriend again was almost as weird as the first time. She didn't run, but she stared. Then when she shook my hand, she dropped it like it was on fire.

If she recognized me, why wouldn't she just say something? It's hard to imagine Adam with a girl this socially awkward.

The silence surrounding us is uncomfortable, and I'm relieved when Adam breaks it.

"You know we don't actually have gilarabrywn around here, right?"

He asks straight-faced, but he has to be joking. "I know you don't have mythological flying lizards?"

His smile looks forced. "Just making sure."

"O-kay. So, my turn to ask a question."

"Sure."

"I didn't want to say anything with the guys around, but what actually happened with your girlfriend this morning? She looked like she'd seen a ghost." I'm pushing, but I need answers.

Adam glances at me then away. "You look like her dead boyfriend."

"What?"

"Before Kessa came to Salida she was dating a guy who looked like you, but he died. It wasn't all that long ago, so seeing you was hard on her."

"How did he die?"

"He was out gathering supplies with his best friend and their car went over a ravine. Their bodies were burnt past recognition, but he was wearing the necklace he always wore. The one Kessa's wearing now."

"That cross?"

"Yeah."

I feel Adam's eyes on me. This has to be weird for him too.

"Amber Massman said Kessa came from somewhere else," I say.

"El Dorado Springs. Former Missouri. Kessa came with a delegation this fall. They proposed the idea of creating marriage alliances to ensure peaceful trade and build up the gene pools. So my brother, Jace, went to El Dorado Springs, and Kessa stayed here. She thought getting over her boyfriend's death might be easier somewhere new."

"Good thing you're here to help her with that," I say. There's an edge to my voice. I school my features to cover the anger, but Adam doesn't look my way.

Could I be Kessa's dead boyfriend? If so, Adam's helping my girlfriend get over me. Which, yeah, sucks but is minor compared to a planted body and someone faking my death. *Our purposes and methods*
. . .

"You all right?" Adam asks.

"Sure, man. Just tired," I say. We walk the rest of the way in silence.

For the second night in a row, I'm not sleeping. Is Kessa awake too, thinking about me? Sometime long into the night I realize Kessa doesn't know that I have no memory.

Those first few days nearly killed me. Riding with Forsworth and his crew through the plains of former Kansas with no idea what was going on except that I'd been saved from a disease. Knowing that my memory, and with it my life, was gone forever. That my only hope was in the blue pill they'd given me.

What did Morton and Open Sky mean about joining the army in the 'standard way'? Just that we all have *Cov-4N*? And then my skin goes cold. I force myself to follow the thought.

Morton rescued Open Sky from a medical facility doing advanced PTSD testing. If what they were working on targeted suppressing traumatic memories . . . there might not be a disease. Just a little blue pill . . .

But no. Kelvin told me about the soldier who went mad when he went off the pills. *A man who somehow managed to kill himself while tied up in solitary.*

I can barely breathe now, thinking of Forsworth and his smirk. His disregard for the victims. Would he be willing to drug and enslave an entire camp full of men? I cringe away from the resounding "yes" that echoes through me.

And Open Sky. . . I've respected him. Protected him. I felt honored to be chosen as his guard. He wouldn't do something like this. He saved us. He tried to return that man to his home, and saw a whole village dead.

Or so he said.

If any of this is true, Open Sky's behind it all. No. Morton, his 'savior,' would be behind it all. The pieces fit too well. *Our purposes and methods.* This can't be true. But if it is . . . Why? Why would Richard Morton go to this extreme to create an army?

I must have eventually fallen asleep because I wake up to Patner's voice and a pillow thrown at my face.

"You're getting soft, Jaerish. Sleeping in like a queen. We've got things to do!"

"You are not a morning person," I say, groaning.

"He is when there's a lady involved." This comes from Radley who sits on a bed tying his boots.

"You're so jealous," Patner says. Radley doesn't bother to reply, and Patner continues. "We're fly fishing with Cacia. Apparently the Arkansas river has big trout this time of year."

"It's way too cold for that," I say.

"No colder than home. And what's the weather when you've got love?"

"Yeah, I don't have love. I'll stay here." I settle back onto my pillow.

Thirty minutes later I'm alone in the kitchen. I hesitate, but take my pill.

Adam joined Radley and Patner on the fishing trip, which makes this the perfect time to talk to Kessa. If I'm not really her dead boyfriend, and there was no body set up to look like me, then all of this could be nothing but too little sleep two nights in a row. And the fool's hope that my life might not be gone forever.

But if it is true, recognizing me might put her in danger.

I walk to Kessa's and knock on the door. Two solid raps. I wait and knock again. I'm second guessing this whole thing when she answers.

Kessa's hair is perfectly braided. Her lightweight shirt sticks to her skin like she's just out of the shower. She's wearing slacks, but barefoot, and something in my gut tightens at the intimacy.

Kessa stares, searching my eyes. My face. Her gaze darts down my body.

"Can I come in?"

CHAPTER 27 - KESSA

I'VE SHOWERED AWAY A restless night of fitful dreams and sorrow-filled waking and am buttoning my shirt when there's a knock at the door. There he is on the porch. Evan. No, Jaerish. Jevan?

I search his eyes, and something is different today. Maybe it's that he's searching back.

"Can I come in?" he asks.

I hesitate. Do I really want to let a strange man into my house? But another look at his face has me stepping out of the way. I close the door behind him. Jaerish looks around the room then turns and faces me.

"Can we sit?" he asks, gesturing towards my dining set.

"Yes. Of course. I'm sorry." I'm also rambling. "Would you like something to drink? I have apple juice and coffee."

I stammer a little at coffee, hoping it won't send his mind back to my strange comment yesterday morning.

"No, thank you," Jaerish says. "I actually don't like coffee. I was drinking tea when you first saw me."

He's searching my face again. Watching for my reaction. Breathe.

"So, what can I do for you?" I try to sound cheerful, polite; like how a person normally sounds with a stranger. Meanwhile my foolish body can't understand why Evan isn't already holding me.

"On the way home last night I asked Adam why you seem unsettled around me," he says. "He told me I remind you of someone you used to know."

My face heats. I don't know if I'm cool with Adam telling him that.

"You do." I manage. I'm surprised when my voice comes out calm.

"And this person died not long ago? In a car accident?"

"Yes."

"How long ago?"

Seven months, 12 days, 5 hours since I heard the knock in the middle of the night. Since I stumbled down the hall and saw my dad's face, contorted in the porchlight. Since I knew Evan was never coming home.

But that's not Jaerish's business.

"We don't know exactly," I say. "The search party found his body about seven months ago. But they could have been dead for a while before that. We don't know."

The man before me shudders. He closes his eyes before looking at me again.

"Kessa, will you sit with me?" he asks.

It's only now that I realize I'm still standing, and I seat myself in the chair across from him. I hold my hands together in my lap.

"Kessa, I need to tell you something. It might put you in danger, but at this point not knowing might as well. We aren't from Junction City. We're from an army base. There are over five hundred of us, and none of us can remember anything about our lives before we got there."

He's staring at me intently, waiting as this sinks in.

"You have no memory?" I ask. He shakes his head.

"How long have you been there?"

"Seven and a half months," he says.

A sound scrapes out of my throat and I crumple forward. I would have fallen from the chair, but Evan catches me and lowers me into himself on the ground. I'm shaking, strong arms surrounding me. The dead body doesn't matter. It could be anyone.

This is Evan. My Evan. And I knew it since I first saw him, impossible or not.

Tears are running down my face as I pull back to stare at him. His eyes, his jaw. His hands cup my shoulders, and he's searching my face intently. One hand moves towards my cheek, maybe to wipe a tear, but he holds back an inch away.

"I'm sorry, Kessa," he says. "I wish I could remember everything. I wish I remembered you. I'm going to try."

I lean my cheek into his hand. He smells like himself, the way I remember. And Adam's soap. Adam. Adam has no place in this moment. I push the thought of him away. Evan is here. Alive. Holding me.

But he doesn't remember me.

Slowly the idea of an army invades my mind. An army of men like Evan, with no memory of their old lives. And the warning that I might be in danger. I take a deep breath and release his hand, allowing it to leave my face and drop back by his side. We're both on the ground, nearly beneath my kitchen table, where he caught me and lowered me when I broke.

"Evan, why is your memory gone? Why are all of your memories gone?"

Now it's him taking a deep breath. "So, my name's Evan. I don't feel like an Evan."

"You thought it was a nerdy name back then too, but I like it," I say. His left hand still holds mine, his thumb absently rubbing over my knuckles, as though it, at least, remembers me. Oh, God. Evan's alive.

"I don't know why our memories are gone. We're told it's a disease, but I don't believe that anymore."

Evan tells me of a mutated strain of the original pandemic that causes memory loss, and a pill they all take to keep symptoms at bay. But maybe the pill itself is erasing memories. Because someone set up a fake body, so he wasn't just found wandering in the wilderness. And those same people might do something to me if they find out I recognized him from before.

"Evan, if I wasn't so very certain that you are you, I'd think you're crazy."

"Yeah, well, I was starting to think that, until you told me seven months."

Seven months. Seven months of thinking Evan was dead, when he was alive. Seven months of trying to convince myself and everyone I loved that I was fine, really. I left my dad and friends and town. All for a lie.

"Who'd do any of this?"

This new Evan obviously can't read me like the old Evan could, because he can't tell I'm boiling on the inside.

"If I'm right, a man named Forsworth and his crew do the actual drugging and abducting. But my commander, Open Sky, would have to know. And I'm guessing Richard Morton."

"Richard Morton's involved?"

"He's the real leader. And the one with plans for the army."

"What kind of plans?"

"Who knows? The kind of plans a man willing to drug hundreds of people makes."

Why would Morton need an army? Hardly anyone travels, and there are plenty of resources if someone's willing to go get them. Adam told me his dad was interested in going back to the cities. Maybe he'd want to send in the army to retrieve things?

Adam. I'm sitting on the floor with Evan holding my hand. Evan alive. And Adam knows I recognized him.

"Adam knows about you," I say.

"Adam knows you think I look like Evan," Evan says. "But do you think he knows about the rest of it?"

"The rest of it? No. He didn't even know Open Sky existed until a couple days ago. And he wouldn't have anything to do with something like that."

I'm offended that Evan would ask, and I pull my hand away without thinking about it, but once I do it feels so empty. I want to reach back out and take Evan's hand again, but instead I fold it in my lap with the other.

"Adam is one of the kindest, most moral people I've ever met. He wouldn't have anything to do with this."

Evan flinches as I defend Adam, and I'm suddenly flooded with guilt. This whole time I've been so focused on my pain that I haven't even thought about what it must be like for Evan. First to have no memory and then to find out even what you thought you knew was a lie. And here I am, sobbing and questioning and soaking up the comfort he offers and giving none in return. I reach back out and take Evan's hand. He stares at our hands, together, for a long time.

"Even if Adam wouldn't hurt anyone intentionally," Evan says, looking up, "he could mention something to his dad without knowing the damage it could do. And that could go very badly for both of us."

I'm gazing at his face, so lost in the impossibility that I'm truly seeing him again, that I almost miss what he's saying.

"We've got a choice. You can either convince Adam that you've decided I'm not Evan, that after seeing me again, I'm nothing like him. Or we can tell Adam everything and ask for his help."

I try to imagine what this would sound like to Adam. Suddenly my girlfriend's dead boyfriend is alive. My father is abducting and drugging men to build a secret army. I wouldn't believe any of it if I were him. I wouldn't want to, and as far as I can tell there isn't any real proof beyond my certainty that this is Evan. But if Adam did believe, or even if he was willing to check into it without telling his dad, he could help us figure out what's going on.

"Have you talked to anyone else about this?" I ask.

"No. I needed to find out how long ago your boyfriend went missing."

He pauses, looking at our hands again.

"The only way I can think to test this is to stop taking the pill. I can't describe how awful the first few weeks with no memory were. If I stop taking the pill and I'm wrong . . . Well, I had to make sure it was worth it."

I swallow and look from our joined hands into Evan's grey-sky eyes. Eyes I never thought I'd see again except in dreams that left me weeping. He has no memory. I'm a stranger, the weird girl who ran from the kitchen the first day we met. How could I be more?

"And have you decided?" I ask.

He's staring at me, his knees almost touching mine. His free hand reaches up and fingers one of my braids. And then he leans forward. As though in slow motion he brushes my lips, so softly, with his own.

He sits back, blinking like he might cry too.

"It's worth it."

Evan didn't stay long after the kiss. I saw the familiar resolve in his eyes as he stood to go. I was only able to tell him the most basic of things about his family and our life in El Dorado Springs, but he drank it in desperately.

He can't go off of the pill while he's still in Salida. If we're wrong and there is a disease, it could infect the entire town. We can't take that risk. Which means he won't remember me until he's gone. We didn't talk about what happens then. All I know is that for now we have to keep up the appearance of being strangers. Both of our lives are at stake, and probably a whole lot more.

Evan held my hand the whole time we talked, but he didn't kiss me again.

When Evan's gone, I put on enough make-up to cover my restless night's sleep and head to my meeting. Richard Morton is there, and it's all I can do to focus on the solar cell modifications when my brain keeps screaming *"Why does he want an army?"*

After the meeting Morton approaches.

"This solar cell is magnificent! Your father is truly a genius, Kessa. But, speaking for myself and, I'm sure, my family, you are still by far the most valuable part of this swap between our great cities."

Morton's charm is thick today, and I do my best not to cringe as he places a hand on my shoulder. My smile is forced, but luckily for me Richard Morton never requires much encouragement.

"Kessa, I owe you an enormous apology. I have erred in a way that impacts you greatly."

Is he about to confess in the middle of the meeting hall? That would make things a lot easier.

"What is it, Mr. Morton? I can't imagine what you could be talking about."

"Kessa, please. Surely you can call me Richard by now. We're practically family."

He pauses and I wonder if he's waiting on an affirmation of wedding bells. I just smile tightly, willing him to go on.

"I sent gifts and correspondence to my son Jason in El Dorado Springs without even thinking to ask you if you'd like to send anything with my messenger as well. Now I'm afraid that there's no chance of you doing so before the holidays. Can you find it in your heart to forgive me?"

Well, that's certainly not the worst thing I've heard him accused of today.

"Oh," I say with a small laugh. "That's no problem. It sounded like you were about to confess to murder." Or worse.

"I am many things, my dear, but I can't say I have that on my conscience," Richard Morton replies. "I'll tell you what. I'd be more than happy to send my man back to El Dorado Springs when he returns. He's paid by the trip, so I'm sure he won't mind."

"Thank you, Richard," I say forcing another smile. "That sounds wonderful. I hate to admit it, but with my new life here I hadn't given much thought to sending gifts home. This will give me a little time."

"I'm glad to hear we've been able to make your time with us so pleasant."

When I show up at Adam's for our afternoon run, he's waiting on me outside. He gives me a quick kiss and I feel like a fraud, my lips tingling with the whisper of Evan's kiss this morning. The kiss of a ghost.

I don't make up an excuse to go inside and see if Evan's around. While I want that reassurance with every fiber of my being, I can't let Adam suspect anything, at least until I've decided whether or not to tell him the truth. Everything needs to appear completely normal, and the Kessa who ran from Evan yesterday wouldn't want to see him now.

We're jogging slowly, warming up, when I say "Your dad sent a messenger to El Dorado Springs with gifts for Jace. I wish you'd told me. I would have loved to send something to my dad and Michaela."

Adam laughs shallowly. "It's cute how you assume I knew." The attitude somehow reminds me of Jace, which in this case is encouraging. Maybe Adam sees his dad more clearly than I gave him credit for.

"He didn't tell you?" I ask. "That's weird."

"I guess." Adam shrugs. "It's just my dad."

"But wouldn't he think that you'd want to send something to your brother? It's not like you've got many chances."

He doesn't reply, so I go on.

"Sometimes I wonder about your dad." I say it lightly, but when I glance at Adam, his jaw is clenched.

"What do you mean?" he asks.

"I don't know. He's so charming, but sometimes . . ." Now I'm the one shrugging.

"Sometimes what?" There's an edge to his voice, and I hesitate. "What, Kessa?"

"I don't know. Sometimes I don't think he's very nice."

Adam stops jogging, and turns to look at me. He's frowning as he measures his words carefully before saying them. *Just like his dad would.* I ignore that thought.

"Kessa, has my dad ever done or said something unkind to you?" It's not an accusation; it's a question. But it feels loaded.

Not unless you count kidnapping and drugging my boyfriend so I think he's dead for months. But, of course, I don't say that.

"No."

"Then I'm not sure you should be talking about him this way." Adam starts to jog again, like this conversation is over.

"Adam, wait. That didn't come out right."

He stops again, gives me his attention. Why didn't I just keep my mouth shut?

"It just seems like some of the things your dad does are for the sake of politics rather than anything else. Like volunteering his messenger since I'm an ambassador, but not asking if you want to send something to your brother."

I can't tell from his face if I'm just making it worse. Finally Adam lets out a deep breath.

"I guess I'm just used to it. Dad's always been that way. And I'm sorry I got defensive. It's been easy to ignore my Dad's flaws without Jace around to point them out." He says it with a short laugh, but again it's not the funny kind.

"Your dad and Jace didn't get along very well, did they?"

"Dad volunteered him to go live in another town. What do you think?"

This is the first time Adam has mentioned what happened with Jace and the swap. Does he resent his dad for it or see it as a problem solved? And why was Richard Morton in such a hurry to send Jace gifts when they got along so poorly?

An idea is niggling at the back of my mind, but it flees with Adam's next words.

"Dad asked me why you weren't at the party last night."

"Oh yeah?" I say, managing to keep my voice even. "What did you say?"

"I told him you were just tired," Adam says. He reaches out and takes my hand. "Kessa, how are you after seeing Jaerish again? Is there anything you want to tell me?"

Adam's beautiful eyes search mine. He knows me so well already, and I don't want to lie to him. But I don't think I can tell him the truth. Not after how he reacted to my suggestion that his dad wasn't "nice." What would he do if he knew what I'm really thinking?

"I'm better. Really. It can't be him, right?"

Adam looks away. "He knew what a gilarabrywn was."

"Lots of people know that," I say lightly. "You just haven't read the right books."

I step into Adam and his arms go around me. I could tell him the truth. Just blurt it all out. Maybe he'd believe me and help us figure out what's really going on.

But I don't. Because if he doesn't believe, he might tell his dad. And maybe because I don't want to risk losing him. Which is stupid because I can't keep them both. But I'm not ready to choose. Not when I've just gotten Evan back.

I hold Adam closer, wanting to make up for the distance I know my lie is putting between us. I rest my head on his chest.

"There's nothing to tell."

CHAPTER 28 - MICHAELA

I love Christmas.

I love the songs and the food and how everyone is just a little nicer to each other. I love the extra babysitting jobs that come with Christmas parties. I *really* love the music. If it's July and I'm feeling down, I listen to Christmas carols.

And this year, I have a boyfriend. Which can only make Christmas better.

"Sooooo, you want to know what I got you for Christmas?" I ask Jace.

We're walking home from school through the first slushy snow of the year. Snowmen already stand guard in several yards, surrounded by patchy brown and green streaks of dirt and dead grass that have been stripped of their white glossy blanket. Snowmen go great with Christmas.

"Christmas is three weeks away," Jace says.

"Yes, it is. I'm lousy at surprises. Do you want to know?"

"No, I want to wait. At least until Christmas Eve. Then you can give it to me."

"If you're going to make me wait that long, you're going to have to wait until Christmas."

"OK."

"Jace! That was supposed to make you want to know now!"

"Sorry. Kayla, will you please, please, please, tell me what it is now? But don't, though. Because I want it to be a surprise."

"You missed your chance anyway."

Jace grins as he kicks a chunk of ice down the road in front of us.

"What did you get me?" I ask.

"Nope. You're going to have to wait until Christmas," he says.

"No pressure or anything, but this is my first Christmas with a boyfriend."

"You have a boyfriend? Man, just when I thought I had a chance." I shove him and he laughs, grabbing my gloved hand in his. "I'm not worried about the pressure. You're going to love my present."

"What is it?" All I get is a look. I roll my eyes. "It was worth a try."

We're at my house, but Mom isn't home yet. Jace can't come inside when she's not there, so he sits down on the porch swing while I run in and make us hot chocolate. I hand him his mug and take the seat beside him.

"To Christmas," I say, holding up my drink.

"To Christmas," he says, tapping them together. "This is my first Christmas away from home. Obviously, I guess. It seems like it should be weirder, but it's not. I feel kind of bad for not missing my family more."

I don't know what to say, so I scooch closer to him and lean my head on his shoulder. He's not quite so tall when he's sitting down.

"What's your brother like?" I finally ask.

"Adam? He's a great guy. Solid, you know. You can always count on him to do what's right, unlike the old man."

"Are you going to send them something when a merchant comes through?"

"I probably should. Do they make any El Dorado Springs souvenirs?"

"We could paint '*I heart El Dorado Springs*' on a t-shirt."

"Maybe."

Jace shifts, putting his arm around me and tucking me against him.

"They used to do that with cities all the time pre-pan, you know," I say.

"I didn't know. You know a lot of weird facts about the pre-pan."

"That's because it's fascinating. There were so many people going about their lives, and they thought it would always be that way, so no one even appreciated what they had. Then, in weeks, it was all gone and something completely different took its place."

"Sounds like my life," Jace says.

"Kind of does."

He squeezes my shoulder and smiles. "I like my new life better."

I'm blushing again. Not that it's all about me, but some of it is. Jace sets the swing into motion with his foot.

"Let me know if you're going to send Adam something. I'll send something for Kessa too."

"Sure. And I want to send Cole some music," Jace says.

"We should send Cole Mae Cartwright."

"He'd send her back broken."

"Yeah. And?"

"Michaela Barr! I don't think I've ever heard you say something so close to being mean. I kind of like it."

"I don't like it. But she's become a lot less pleasant since she stopped ignoring me. I hope you're worth it." I nudge his side with my elbow.

"Hey. If Mae wanted a chance at this," Jace says, motioning to his chest with his cocoa mug, "she should have been less scary."

"Scary is her brand. She can't help it. Does that mean you picked me because I'm non-threatening?"

"And because your mom makes excellent popcorn balls."

I laugh. "Remind me to thank her."

Jace puts his empty mug on a side table and turns so he's mostly facing me. "So, why'd you pick me?" he asks.

"I thought it was my best shot at meeting Cole." I shrug. "That guy is legendary."

"If we were in Salida, I'd believe you. It wouldn't be the first time I thought a girl was into me only to find out Cole was her real target."

"Seriously?" I ask. Jace nods. "Girls in Salida must be stupid. Or blind." That makes Jace smile. Man, I love his smile.

"Have I mentioned how much I love your smile?" I ask.

"I don't think so. Not today, anyway."

"Well, I do. Every time you smile, I want to kiss the corner of your mouth. Right here."

I kiss my finger and put it right where his lip tips up on the side. It makes him smile wider. If I weren't sitting on my front porch . . . My mom's smart to make him stay outside when she's gone.

I don't know where this wanting to kiss Jace all the time is coming from, but it's a little bit scary. Not Mae Cartwright scary. 'I could get swept up in this and not come back down' scary. Because someone else having this kind of power over me . . . I shudder.

"You ok?" Jace asks.

"Just cold," I say.

His brows furrow. There's no way I'm going to tell him what I'm thinking. Because liking him this much, this quick is crazy, and he doesn't need to know how crazy I am. But I don't want to lie to him either.

"Just thinking about how much I like you," I finally say.

"You looked a little too concerned to be thinking happy thoughts," Jace says. "Are you worried about liking me?"

Maybe about liking you too much. But I don't say it. "Maybe a little," I say instead.

He looks like he's thinking now. Not happy thoughts. Crud.

"What are you thinking," I ask.

"That if you're worried about liking me, you must know me even better than I realized."

"Jace, that's not it."

The 'I know I'm a screw-up' look is back in his eyes, even though he's smiling. That's the worst look of them all and getting rid of it is probably the only thing that would make me choose to be this vulnerable.

"Jace. I'm worried that I like you too much," I say. "I like you enough that I could get really hurt if you decide you're done liking me."

"Why would I ever be done liking you?" Jace asks, like it's the most ridiculous idea in the world.

"I don't know. But it happens with people all the time. I've never let someone get close enough that it would matter much. Except my mom, and she doesn't count. Moms aren't allowed to stop liking you. And maybe Kessa. But she left."

Huh. Well, there's a pain I haven't processed yet.

Jace takes the mug from my hand and sets it beside his on the table. Then he holds both of my hands in his. He looks at me with his deep brown eyes and says "Michaela Barr, I am never going to be done liking you."

And there I go, melting, just like the slushy snowmen, back into the ground.

CHAPTER 29 - JACE

We've just finished dinner when the doorbell rings. I volunteer to answer it, and find a scrawny blonde man on the porch with a box in his arms. Enery looks on curiously as Margi hides behind my legs. There aren't many strangers in El Dorado Springs, even to a kid her age.

The man smiles, maybe trying to be friendly, but it just looks predatory.

"I'm lookin for Jace Morton. And I'm assumin that's you."

"Yeah, that's me," I say.

"The name's Forsworth, and your daddy sent me from Salida with some Christmas cheer."

My laugh causes Enery to pull his eyes away from the box and look at me. For him a father sending a Christmas gift is a no-brainer. Forsworth is studying me, and I can't tell if his eyes are slitted or if he can't be bothered to open them all the way.

I'm grateful when Henry joins us at the door. Until he starts talking.

"Jace, don't make a guest stand out in the cold. Please, Mr. Forsworth, come in. You're welcome to join us for dessert."

I, more than anyone, appreciate the Douglas's hospitality. But I don't want this man in our house. Maybe it's the fact that he claims to know my dad, but I've never seen him before. Or maybe it's how he smirks like he knows a secret the rest of the world can't handle. Whatever it is, I'm glad when he turns down the offer.

As soon as dessert's done I take the box to my room, all the while telling that voice inside, the one that keeps hoping my dad won't suck, that it needs to cool off. Dad sent something. That's better than forgetting me entirely. I open the box.

Inside are three packages. One is plain cardboard, tied with string. My name is scrawled across the flap in black marker. I remind myself that it's what's inside that counts. Or maybe the thought is what counts? Something like that.

The next one is beautifully wrapped and labeled for the Douglasses. Looks like they're getting our housekeeper's famous baklava and fudge Christmas assortment. That's dad's standard gift to people he wants to impress.

The last box is a cube, a little larger than my fist, wrapped in gold foil. The gift tag reads "Professor Gary McKnight."

There's nothing from Adam or Cole. Tucked to one side is an envelope marked "open immediately." I consider putting it off, just to prove that Dad can't control me, but curiosity trumps defiance.

Jason,

I hope all is going well in El Dorado Springs and that you're keeping your eyes on the goal. Shouldn't be difficult, since the goal is to find a young woman and fall in love. That's the desire of every teen boy, isn't it? Make sure she's well-connected.

I plan to visit you in El Dorado Springs with a delegation once travel is easier, most likely mid-March or thereabouts. My main purpose will be addressing the opportunities surrounding seeking medical advancement in the cities. We've waited long enough to see this dream become a reality, and the technology El Dorado Springs possesses is key. If you have any reason to believe that El Dorado Springs will be opposed, let me know asap.

Along those lines, I need you to find out information on a young man named Evan Harris who was killed in a car accident while exploring last summer. It's important that I know if his death will influence El Dorado Springs's position. Also, on a more personal note, Evan was Kessa McKnight's boyfriend. Her relationship with your brother has been progressing nicely, and I want to make sure nothing hinders it.

Send your reply with the messenger. He'll be returning to Salida in three days and knows to expect something from you. Feel free to send any gifts as well. His fee has been handled.

Your Father,

Richard Morton

PS- Open your package alone. There's a second gift in it that you can open publicly.

This letter would make a great "Councilor Morton" story if Cole were around to hear it. First he calls me Jason. Then he tells me to make sure the girl I fall in love with has good connections. And to top it off, he wants me to spy on my new town. I'm actually glad he didn't say "Merry Christmas." No need to try to pretend this letter was something it wasn't, like a father who missed his son.

How am I supposed to know how El Dorado Springs feels about exploring cities? Sure, Henry's the resource manager, but it's not like the

Douglases sit around the dinner table and talk about it. He probably sent the gift for Professor McKnight so I'd have an excuse to visit him. It might even start the conversation for me. I think of unwrapping the present to see what it is, but I suck at wrapping and it would be obvious it was opened.

I should write Dad back now. "I don't know how they feel about any of it or how a dead boyfriend could mess up Adam's chances with Kessa. PS - My girlfriend has zero connections."

For the first time since I've moved to El Dorado Springs I want to light up. Just forget for a while. But that's the old Jace. I just need to think this through.

Dad is coming in the spring. There's nothing I can do to change who Michaela is connected with. And I'm not changing Michaela, regardless of what Richard Morton has to say about it. But I can go over to Professor McKnight's and see what he thinks about exploring. And I can ask him or the Douglases about Kessa's boyfriend. Two out of three will just have to be good enough.

And then I think about Dad's weird P.S. I might as well open my "secret" gift now. I struggle for a minute with the string but eventually get the box open. It's easy to tell which gift is the "public" one. Setting aside the paper-wrapped package with a tag lettered in our housekeeper's neat hand, I reach for the plain, cloth drawstring bag

The bag's heavy for its size, and when I look inside I nearly drop it. What the? Why would Dad send me a gun? I reach in and then reconsider. Maybe Dad's framing me for murder from half-way across the country. But that makes no sense. Still, I'm not touching it. I just stare into the bag. My dad never took me hunting, or even target shooting, so why in the world is he giving me this?

There's a box of ammo too, but nothing else. Definitely no explanation. I take the ammo out and stash it in my underwear drawer. Then I wrap the bag around the gun and put it as far back as I can under some clothes on the top shelf of my closet. I reread the original letter, hoping for a clue, but there's nothing.

My stomach hurts, and I wonder if I should tell Henry. It doesn't seem right having a gun he doesn't know about in his house. I can hear him down the hall, still putting the kids to bed. Maybe this isn't the right time. Instead, I go to the kitchen with the baklava and leave it on the counter for the Douglases to discover. At least our housekeeper is sane.

I walk to Professor McKnight's after school. His house is smaller than I expected, probably because everything my dad does is for show. It does have a wrap-around porch with some sort of automatic heating system that comes on when I walk up the steps. That's very cool. Or, well, warm.

The front door is opened by a man with warm brown skin and a salt and pepper goatee. I search his face for traces of Kessa, and find it in the same intent gaze, although he looks through wire framed glasses.

"Professor," I say. "My name's Jace Morton. How are you today?"

I sound like a salesman. It would have been nice if some of the famous Morton charm had come my way. Lucky for me the Professor doesn't seem to mind.

"Jace, Henry has told me good things about you. Please, come in."

The Professor motions me into the entryway and closes the door behind us. On my right is an office with a desk covered in blueprints and piles of books. Professor McKnight chuckles.

"Perhaps we should use the living room instead," he says, and leads the way into the room on our left. It's bright and comfortable, as neat as the office was messy. This room seems like it's just for sitting. There's a fire in the fireplace and a mug on a side table. The professor gestures me to an armchair.

"Can I get you something to drink, Jace? I wasn't expecting visitors, but Barbara stopped by with cookies, and I'm willing to share."

It takes me a minute to realize "Barbara" is Michaela's mom. I guess I shouldn't be surprised that he's friends with the adults in my life, but it's kind of weird.

"No thanks," I say. "I'll be there tomorrow, so I'll eat their cookies."

"Very thoughtful of you," says the Professor, sitting in the chair by the mug. "What brings you by today, Jace?"

"I brought you a gift from my father," I say. I hand him the box.

"That was very kind of him. I'll save this for Christmas." He puts the box aside. "How do you like El Dorado Springs so far?"

"I like it very well, sir. I can see how your technology has built a thriving community." That sounded like something dad might say.

"Yes," he says, a small frown on his face. "My daughter wrote to me about you, Jace. She's rather fond of you. Seems to think you have a lot to offer, and that getting away from Salida would be of benefit. Do you know what would have given her that impression?"

Maybe the fact that my dad's an over-bearing bastard who wants to run my life, even from hundreds of miles away, and your daughter was smart enough to see it? But I can't say that. "Maybe she just knew that sometimes people need a fresh start," I say. It's true, and she might have even told him something like that.

"Perhaps," he says. "It was very nice of you to drop off this gift, Jace. Is there anything else I can do for you?"

Crap. I've learned nothing. Maybe I'd better just go for it.

"Well, yeah. I did have one question."

Professor McKnight waits, looking at me like he can read my thoughts. Which would make this easier. And then it wouldn't be my fault if I screwed it up. I push on.

"Ever since my mom died of meningitis, Dad's been planning to get back to the cities. He thinks if medical knowledge can be restored, other people won't die from things that could once be cured like she did." The Professor's eyes soften, which I take as a good sign. "He thinks your technology would be helpful with that goal. Do you think it would be?"

Professor McKnight sits back in his chair, mulling the question over. He doesn't seem like the type who'd give a thoughtless answer about anything.

"The technology we've developed here would be useful in any context," he finally says. "The question isn't in its usefulness, but in the accord of our thoughts regarding the exploration of the cities.

"The preventable death of someone so loved would be a great motivator. I'm very sorry about the loss of your mother." When he says this, I believe him. I have to push back down things I haven't let myself feel in a long time.

"That notwithstanding," he continues, "the re-emergence of the pandemic would devastate our species beyond recovery. I won't say that El Dorado Springs wouldn't be willing to discuss this further, but at this point I wouldn't feel comfortable allowing our technology to be used in a way that might endanger the future."

"But you've had people go out and explore the cities, haven't you?" I ask cautiously.

"We have. Minimally and for very specific essential resources. The last expedition ended in tragedy. You may or may not know, but Kessa's boyfriend and his best friend died in that excursion. I don't think Kessa has yet forgiven me for not allowing her to go as well, though in hindsight I cannot regret the decision. Both Evan's and Marcus's bodies were burnt beyond recognition and the families did not even have the opportunity to see their faces one last time. As you can imagine, this has not increased my eagerness to continue exploration."

I swallow. "It sounds like you and Evan were close," I say.

"His parents are my best friends, his mother a surrogate to Kessa after my wife passed. On top of that, Evan and Kessa dated for nearly four years. They would have married already had I not counseled they wait until their apprenticeships were complete."

It's obvious what Professor McKnight is sharing is painful. I feel like a jerk for even considering telling my dad any of this. I need to go. I stand up.

"I'm very sorry for your loss, sir. From what my father writes, Kessa and my brother, Adam, are dating. He's not Evan, but he is a great guy."

"I'm sure he is Jace." The professor stands to his feet. "There tend to be larger purposes at work than what I can understand. Maybe there's something here as well. I have to believe that. Thank you again for the gift. And please send your father my thanks and greeting."

His words are polite. Kind even. But somehow I'm sure he knows. I don't think I've lied once since I came to El Dorado Springs, but one letter from my dad was all it took to bring back the old Jace. Great. I'm about to leave when I realize I should let him send things with the messenger.

"I'm sending gifts with Dad's messenger in three days. He can carry anything you want to Kessa too."

"Thank you, Jace. It seems your courtesy extends beyond that of your father."

That's something anyway. It was strange for dad not to let Kessa send gifts. Knowing Councilor Morton, there's a reason.

I don't know what I'm going to tell my dad. The Professor really isn't into exploration right now, and I don't blame him. But my dad's going to hate it. For now I'm going to do what I do best. Procrastinate. I've got a couple days before I have to write the letter, and I have gifts to make.

Chapter 30 - Michaela

THE WORLD IS WHITE, pristine snow as yet unmarred by any feet but mine. A full moon reflects off tree limbs and rooftops alike. I close my eyes and breathe the icy air into my lungs as I savor the silence. On mornings like this, it's easy to imagine that only the stillness exists.

"Kayla, wait up!" Jace shouts. Jace and stillness don't do well together.

I stop and watch him come towards me, brown hair peeking out from under a beanie and face flushed with the cold. I would pick Jace over silence any day.

Normally Jace is like a puppy in the snow. You'd think that he'd have gotten enough of it, being from Colorado and all, but he can't just walk through it. He has to interact with it, to scoop it up and throw it at a tree or kick a drift or knock it off a branch.

But not this morning. This morning he's just walking, hands shoved into pockets.

"What are you doing up so early?" I ask as he joins me.

"I slept lousy last night, so I finally gave up. I was eating breakfast when I saw you walk by. Where are you going?"

"Bible study before school," I say.

"Cool. I'll come too."

"Girl's Bible study. Well, one girl. I started mentoring a seventh grader, like Kessa did for me."

"Oh yeah? That's cool," Jace says. "Speaking of Kessa, my dad sent a messenger, and he's supposed to take stuff back to Salida for me. So if you want to send anything, I got you."

"That's awesome, Jace! Did your dad send your Christmas gifts?"

Jace hesitates. "He sent a couple, and a letter too." Something in his voice is off.

"Oh yeah?" I ask as casually as I can. "What did it say?"

Jace shakes his head, and the defeated look is back in his eyes. If his dad can do this from hundreds of miles away, I can't imagine what it was like for Jace to live with him.

"Well, among other things, he said that he's planning to come visit in the spring."

"It's going to be interesting to meet him," I say, trying to sound cheerful. Jace sighs.

"My dad's a jerk, Kayla. So if he's rude, just know it's because he's him, and it has nothing to do with you."

"Alright," I say with an awkward laugh. It's kind of unsettling that Jace is already expecting his father to dislike me. "You know, Jace, not to brag or anything, but grown-ups usually think I'm pretty great."

"That's because you are pretty. And great. But my dad is neither, and generally disapproves of everything I do. You might have stood a chance of him liking you if I didn't already like you so much."

Jace saying he likes me "so much" is just about all my heart can handle.

I stop in the snow, in the middle of the street. When he turns, I put one gloved finger to his lips before he can say anything else.

"Let's not think any more about your dad today," I say.

And I kiss him. No dads. Just me and Jace and the stillness.

On Saturday morning, the first day of Christmas break, Jace comes over, and we paint "I heart El Dorado Springs" on a t-shirt for Adam. We make Cole a playlist of music that will be mostly new to him. Jace has finally decided to give his dad a record of the all-time best jazz that's been at the general store for as long as I can remember. Apparently, jazz is his dad's least favorite type of music.

The gift I've been working on for Kessa is what used to be called "fan fiction," where people would write stories with characters from other people's books. Some authors from the past liked it, some didn't, but nobody cares about intellectual property rights since the world fell apart, so I'm not worried. I know Kessa will love it.

"I didn't know that you write," Jace says. "Like stories and stuff. How did I not know that?"

"I don't usually show it to people. Besides Kessa, who is, of course, not here."

"You could show it to me," Jace says.

Hmmm. Now that is a nerve-wracking idea. It's not like I can tell him it's too personal after all of the kissing we've been doing lately. But the thought of letting someone else read my writing . . . Eek.

"I'll make you a deal," I finally say. "If you read all three of the original books, plus the prequel, I'll let you read mine."

"You're going to make me work for this, huh?"

"Yep. But I'll loan you the books if you want." Jace grimaces, and I think I'm safe for a while.

My mom returns to the kitchen with a jar of her prized apricot jam for Jace's father and Adam. I see Jace hesitate but finally take it. I don't think he's written his dad since arriving, so they might not even know about me.

I guess jam is one way to introduce ourselves. I make a label for the jar, drawing an apricot tree in the sunshine and a big ripe fruit.

"Did your dad's letter say how Kessa is doing in Salida?" my mom asks.

"It said that she's dating my brother, Adam, now."

"Oh yeah?" Something like worry flits across her face but she covers it quickly. Jace must have seen it because he rushes to speak.

"Don't worry, Mrs. Barr. My brother's nothing like me. He's the real catch in the family."

My mom laughs. "It's not that, Jace. If your brother is half the young man you are I'm sure Kessa would do very well with him. It's just that she was with Evan for so long. It makes it hard to think of her with anyone else."

"What was Evan like?" Jace asks. "I mean, I only met Kessa for a little while, but it was obvious that she was sad about something. He must have been a great guy."

"He was a great guy," I say. "And he was, well, I don't know. He was Evan. He worked with his dad at the martial arts school, and he always wanted a new challenge, something to conquer. He wrote poetry, but most people didn't know that. He was probably the most determined of anyone to get back to the cities."

"And he died trying to do it," Jace says.

"Yes, he did," says my mom, her mouth set in a grim line. "He died trying to do something he believed in, but I think most people wish he'd stayed put."

We're all quiet for an awkward moment, and then I ask Jace "Are you going to make something for Kessa too?"

"I guess I should, if she might end up my sister-in-law. What would she like?"

"You could write her a story like I am," I tease.

"Sure. Why not?" Jace says. He stands up straighter, and with a mock serious face grabs the open sides of his flannel shirt like a politician of old might have held his lapels. "Once upon a time there was a beautiful princess who lived with her mother. One day, as she was watching the children of the local huntsman, she was met by a friendly wood troll who asked her to help him make his Christmas gifts. Then they all lived happily ever after. The end."

My mom snorts. "Yeah, maybe you'd better leave the writing to Michaela," she says with a smile. "That's it for me. I'm crashing early tonight, so make sure you clean up whatever you mess up."

"Good night, Mom." I give her a kiss on the cheek.

"Good night Mrs. Barr," Jace says and pats her awkwardly on the arm. She rolls her eyes and heads down the hall.

"So, really, what should I give Kessa?" Jace asks, turning my way. "I don't want to send her something lame like a rock or something."

I can't help the smirk on my face.

"What?" Jace asks. "I mean, of course I'm not going to send her a rock. But I couldn't think of something lame to say."

"Oh, you thought of something lame to say," I say with a laugh.

He grins and pulls me up against him, his arms around me.

"Anyway, how do you know I didn't get you a rock, huh?" I ask, staring up into his face. For a second Jace looks nervous, until I burst out laughing. "Don't worry. If I'd gotten you a rock, it would have been the coolest rock ever and you'd have been eating your words."

"I'd rather be eating your words," Jace says and bends down to kiss me. Right there in my kitchen with my mom down the hall.

"Mmmmm," he says, pulling back. "Your words taste way better than mine."

That kiss was pretty intense, and the humor that's normally in Jace's eyes has been replaced by something that makes me blush and look down.

I bite back a squeal of surprise as Jace lifts me up and sets me on the kitchen island.

"I've been wanting to do that all night," he says.

He's so tall that even with me on the island he still has to lean down a little to kiss me. And kiss me he does. I don't know how long it lasts. At some point I stop worrying that my mom's going to come back out and catch us. All I can think about is Jace's mouth. And his hands. One is on the counter, but the other is on my waist, one finger tracing the top of my jeans.

I can feel myself getting swept up in the kissing, and then I feel something else against my leg. Oh gosh. It's Jace. And a part of him that I don't want to think about is definitely thinking about me. It freaks me out enough that I pull backwards. He starts to follow me, and for a second I wonder if someone actually could do that on a kitchen island. Which freaks me out even more.

I put my hand against his chest and push gently.

"Jace, wait," I say.

He pulls back and stares right into me, and I wonder if my eyes are telling him to stop or to keep going.

"We need to stop." I'm not sure how I make my lips form the words but I do.

Jace nods and then he turns around, his back to me, and leans against the other counter. He's almost panting, and I realize I am too.

"Jace," I say.

"Yeah, just a sec." He's taking a deep breath. In a minute he turns back around. I'm still sitting on the counter.

"I'd offer to get you down, but I think I'd better not touch you right now."

"Yeah. That's a good idea," I say, still trying to figure out what in the world just happened.

"I should go," Jace says. "See you tomorrow?"

I nod.

"Okay then."

Jace gets his coat from the back of the couch and puts it on. I watch silently as he pulls his hat down over his head and takes his gloves from his pockets. He walks to me and tries to kiss me gently, but he can't. He's kissing me hard, and I'm barely breathing when he stops and without a word walks out the door.

Chapter 31- Kessa

I'VE NEVER CARED ABOUT gifts. I mean I like them and all, but they aren't a big deal to me. This year, though, is different.

Do I want to get Adam something special? Of course.

But the real priority here is finding a gift for my dad. Something that says "Evan is alive and part of an amnesiac army controlled by my new boyfriend's father." Mrs. Prior's stories have raised pre-pan online shopping to legendary status, but I'm betting this would have been a stretch even back then.

And, of course, I'm working with the assumption that anything I send will be scrutinized beforehand. Because why wouldn't it?

Involuntarily I picture Adam's clenched jaw when I said his dad might not be nice. Imagine his reaction if I accused Richard Morton of leading a kidnapping ring and wanting to take over the world. Or whatever else someone does with an army. I've got two amazing (and alive) boyfriends and still no one to strategize with.

Deep breath. Freaking out is wasted energy.

I let my mind follow rabbit trails for too long last night, and by one o'clock I was convinced Adam was only dating me as part of his dad's endgame. Because really, no one's that amazing. In daylight, I know it's not true. If it were, Adam would have told his dad as soon as I recognized Evan, and the whole thing would be over already.

And you wouldn't have to deal with any of this.

I shut that voice up. It's the same voice that kept me in bed for days at a time after Evan died. But Evan's alive and I refuse to listen again.

It's Sunday, so instead of my usual run with Adam, I'm going to church. Which is why I'm surprised to see him climbing my porch stairs as I step outside.

"Hey, Kess! I thought I'd come with you this morning, if that's ok."

"Of course," I say, giving him a quick kiss and slipping my hand through his elbow. "Any reason?"

"Nope. I just know it's important to you," he says, making my heart do a little flip.

We enter late and stand in the back for the music. During the tea break Amber Massman beelines our way. I'm surprised she manages not to call out until she's almost upon us.

"Adam! I'm so glad you're here. It's not even Christmas yet. I knew our sweet Kessa was going to be a good influence on you."

"Yes, ma'am, I believe she is," he says.

"Did you just 'ma'am' me, Adam Morton?" she asks and he grins. "That young Jaerish has been doing it all morning. I must be way older than I feel, but that's what they say . . ." Amber keeps talking, but I've stopped hearing, despite my mask of polite attention.

Adam squeezes my hand, then nods towards the front left of the church where Evan stands beside a dark-haired guy I don't recognize with an obviously military posture. How does everyone not see that? Evan's friend is so intent on whatever Cacia is saying that I'd be surprised if she isn't already dreaming of life in Junction City.

I shift my gaze to Evan and our eyes meet briefly before his flick behind me to Adam and quickly shutter. Evan nods our direction.

"Want to go over, Kess?" Adam asks.

"Nah," I say. "We can say 'hi' after church. Let's get a seat."

Amber has wandered off to talk with someone else, which is great because it means I can stay near the back today. We choose a seat. Once we're settled, Adam turns my hand palm side up on the back of his thigh. He smooths his hand over it once. Twice. Then begins tracing the lines along the insides of my knuckles.

"My mom used to do this to keep us quiet in church," he says with a small smile.

I can see it. Little Adam and Jace in this place, maybe even this pew, not so long ago. When Adam still had a mom. His touch skims over my skin and I want to purr like a cat. I barely hear the pastor's sermon. And then I think of Evan. Great, now I feel guilty towards both of them.

After the service Adam smiles and deflects comments about me "getting him to church" and when to expect a different type of ceremony. Meanwhile it's all I can do to keep my eyes from darting Evan's way. We're nearly out the door when Cacia waves us down and introduces me to Evan's friend, Patner. They want to know if we'll be going to the Massman's for cookie decorating. I shake my head, all peopled out.

The air as Adam walks me home is crisp, but not bitter. The silence is the same.

Chapter 32 - Jaerish

I ONLY WENT TO church to see Kessa, but being there felt right. And I need all the help I can get.

I should have asked her if I believed in God when I had the chance. I bet I did, because through all of this I've been talking to someone in my head. Or maybe that's just a side-effect of the blue pill.

Today felt real, though. I was even into the pastor's message until I noticed Patner holding Cacia's hand. After that all I could think about was Kessa sitting with Adam. Was she holding his hand too?

I agreed to decorate cookies at the Massmans in the hopes that Kessa would be here. She's not. Instead a blonde in a reindeer sweater has been talking at me non-stop for hours. Fine, half an hour. Patner's no help. He's too busy staring at Cacia to notice my pain. Eventually I excuse myself and head back to Morton's alone.

I'm at the base of the hill when I hear him.

"Jaerish, maybe you are useful for somethin." Forsworth shoves a heavy bag into my arms. "Carry this, will ya?"

It's not a request, and as he falls into step beside me I want to throw it on the ground.

"Why am I carrying this?" I ask.

"Because you're so big and strong," he says mockingly. "And because I'm worn-out deliverin gifts for the boss."

"You're Santa Claus now? Scary."

"Scarier than you'd ever guess, boy." Forsworth says it like a joke, but I shudder.

"Where'd you get this stuff? Doesn't seem like your type of assignment."

"The boss's son's in El Dorado Springs now, and he needed some holiday cheer."

"Open Sky has a son?"

Forsworth's look says I'm an idiot. Then his words do too. "How can you be stayin in Morton's house and still think that Open Sky is boss of anythin?"

And, yeah, I knew this, but it's different to hear it. Forsworth's side-eye isn't subtle, and I'm glad I've trained myself to keep my emotions hidden.

"It's not my business anyway," I say.

When we reach the house, Forsworth walks around to the back door and enters without knocking. I trail him to Morton's office where we find the man himself behind his desk, a map nearly as large as its surface spread out before him. He doesn't attempt to cover it as we enter. I scan for only a moment before lifting my eyes to find him watching me.

"Interesting, isn't it? Come around and see." He notices the bag I'm carrying and looks to Forsworth.

"It's all here. Gifts from Jace and Professor McKnight and some letters. You need me for anythin else? The bar scene in El Dorado Springs is lackin and I've got some catchin up to do."

"You are aware that our bars don't open until 6pm on Sundays, aren't you?" Morton says with mild disapproval.

"I've been around long enough to know where to find what I need."

Morton makes a motion like shooing away gnats and Forsworth leaves without a glance in my direction.

"Put those on the floor by the wall, Jaerish, and come look at this with me."

The map is of the USA before the pandemic. It's marked with two thick, black lines. One crosses the whole continent, separating California from Oregon, Colorado from Wyoming, slicing Nebraska in half on its way to skirt below the Great Lakes, through Pennsylvania and New York to the Atlantic Ocean. The second encompasses what used to be Texas and Oklahoma.

In the middle section, in red and blue ink, are handwritten names and numbers. The other sections have only a few names, all in black.

"These are the towns that remain," Morton says. "Blue numbers are population pre-pandemic, red my best current estimate."

"What about the black?"

"Those aren't my concern."

There are more red numbers than I would have expected. 350 here, 700 there. Only a handful are over 1000, with the biggest two by far being El Dorado Springs and Salida. I see 'Junction City' marked as 550, which seems about right.

"Are you in contact with each of these?" I ask.

"Yes. Some more than others."

"And are there others like Fort Riley?"

"In what way, son?"

Are there others that have been kidnapped? Drugged? Forced into an army?

"I suppose in regards to *Cov-4N*, sir. Or in regards to our training?"

I say it like a question, but inside I'm boiling. I want to ask how many people he's enslaved for his purposes, whatever those might be. I keep my face carefully neutral.

"Interesting question," he says appraising me.

Maybe I'm giving away more than I thought.

"Junction City" (he stresses the name) "is unique in both of those aspects." He looks like he'll say more, but we hear the outside door open followed by Patner's voice and female laughter.

"Thank you for carrying these in, Jaerish. I believe there may be other, more enjoyable ways for you to spend your Sunday than chatting with me."

With a final glance at the map, I nod and take my leave.

Chapter 33- Kessa

It's Monday afternoon, and Adam is on my doorstep in a Santa hat with a bag over his shoulder.

"You can kiss the messenger if you want. I've got gifts from El Dorado Springs."

I do kiss the messenger as I usher him inside, and then I reach for the bag which he holds just slightly beyond me.

"Now, Kessa, these are Christmas gifts. Are you sure I should give them to you ahead of time? It's only the 20th, after all."

I don't even hesitate, just go for his ribs, which I know from first-hand experience are highly ticklish. His shriek is less than manly as he pins me into a hug. We're both laughing and I feign relaxing into his chest before going for the ribs again.

"Fine, take it!" Adam says, flinging the bag onto the couch.

I retrieve the bag then empty the contents onto my desk and sort through it as Adam watches. There's a manilla envelope from Michaela, a small box from Evan's mom, two gifts from my dad and even something from Jace. Adam picks up Jace's gift, which flops forward. T-shirt, maybe?

"Your present from Jace feels like mine. We might want to open them at the same time so we don't ruin the surprise."

"Good call. Did you decide what you're sending him?"

"Yeah. I've got this baseball cap that he's wanted forever. It used to cause real fights because I'd see him wearing it out places and he'd just grin and take off on his board because he knew I couldn't catch him without looking like an idiot. I think I'll send him that."

"That's very sweet," I say, turning from the gifts to wrap my arms over Adam's shoulders.

Just last week I could lose myself in his kisses, but now they taste like guilt. Guilt because I'm lying to him. Guilt because Evan's alive. I'm obviously distracted and Adam pulls back, rubbing the back of his neck and sitting down on my bed. He pats the spot beside him and I sit.

"Are you going to open your gifts or save them?" he asks.

"I'll do one per day. Five days til Christmas, five presents."

"Good plan."

The silence between us grows awkward, but I know Adam well enough to know this means he's building up to something. Finally, he speaks.

"Kess, since Jaerish showed up I've started missing you, even when we're together. You know you can tell me anything, right?"

I don't know that. Not about this. But that's not what I say.

"I know, Adam. Seeing him around is just a constant reminder."

He studies me, searches my eyes for long enough that I'm sure he sees the lie. But as always, he's a gentleman. He won't force me to tell.

"OK, Kessa. I trust you."

I hug him so I don't have to look at him. I'm such a fraud. Here I am, leaning into his warmth and keeping this secret. I have to tell him.

"Adam I . . ."

"Kessa, I love you."

He pulls back and looks at me, chuckles a little.

"I sure hope that wasn't going to be 'Adam, I need to take a break.'"

"It wasn't," I say and swallow.

"Kessa," he says again, looking into my eyes, "I love you."

And I know it's true. Which makes it worse and better all at once.

"I love you too," I say. How have I gotten myself here, loving this boy but with something so important between us? And still loving Evan, too. Maybe. When Adam leans in and kisses me I throw myself into the moment, pushing the rest from my mind.

His kisses are deeper, and for a little while, I forget everything else. Then, out of nowhere, Adam stands up and walks across the room. He sits in my reading chair, eyes closed.

"Adam?"

"Give me a second," he says, taking long slow breaths.

What in the world? Why would he just leave me like that? But when he looks up, the intensity in his eyes makes my stomach flip over.

"You told me you want to wait until you're married, Kessa. I just had to back off and remind myself."

Wow, ok. I appreciate being respected and all, but . . . "We weren't anywhere near that."

"We were in my head." He's grinning. He might be kidding. But his eyes say otherwise. "Besides, it's like your Christmas gifts. I want to spread it out and enjoy everything you share with me. There's no rush, and I have infinite patience."

If I weren't the one who asked for these boundaries, I'd take that as a challenge. But now that I'm not in the middle of the kissing, I can acknowledge that Adam has a point. Especially with Evan back in the picture.

A distraction wouldn't hurt. I walk to the gifts on my desk. Which should I open first? Maybe Michaela's. Or Jace's. "Do you want to do Jace's today?" I ask.

"I don't have it with me. How about after our run tomorrow?"

"Sure."

I pick up the manilla envelope from Michaela. Inside is a folded piece of paper that I hope will be a long letter. Under that is a typed story. A quick scan makes me smile.

"She's been writing and re-writing this forever and never thought it was quite good enough. I'm so glad she finished it!"

"I can tell that my entertainment value just plummeted," Adam says. "I ought to get home anyway. I'll see you tomorrow?"

"Of course," I say with a quick kiss, my mind already on the papers in my hands. Adam shakes his head with a grin as he leaves. I sink into my reading chair, still warm from his body heat. Letter first.

Dear Kessa,

You know I'm shaking right now at the thought of you reading this story. It's like putting my baby on display and saying 'isn't she beautiful.' Please lie if needed.

Jace asked me if he could read it and I told him not until he read all four of the others. That could take a while. Jace has many amazing qualities, but he is not a reader. He is . . . my boyfriend now. (Squeal!) Did you have this in mind when you sent your letter with him? It sounds like something you'd do.

Will this be a problem for the swap? Henry thinks it's fine, but from what Jace said his dad might not like it because of my dad. If you wanted to be subtly nosey, I wouldn't mind.

Jace is wonderful. I wish you were here because I have about a thousand things I want to ask you about boyfriend stuff, but since you're not I might have to break down and ask my mom. Which could be embarrassing. So please make sure you write back with lots of advice. The more the better.

Jace said you're dating his brother, and I'm really happy for you. From everything Jace has said Adam sounds amazing. Speaking of, have you met Jace's buddy Cole? It seems like he was the lady's man back there. Obviously he's younger than you, but I kind of wonder after some of the things Jace has told me what your impression would be. I picture you patting Cole on the head and saying "nice try, kiddo." But I don't tell Jace that.

OK, this is going to be as long as my story if I don't quit writing. I'm sure you'll get letters from others too so I'm not going to keep you reading mine.

Your friend forever,

Michaela

PS- If you married Adam and I married Jace, we would be sisters!

PPS- Merry Christmas! (Almost forgot!)

It shouldn't surprise me that Michaela writes an entertaining letter, all of the things she's too nervous to share aloud spread out across the page. Something about my move has put us on equal footing. Or maybe it was the months she spent giving quiet support while I was a shell of myself.

If I married Adam. . . I flash to the kisses, the desire for more. Married we wouldn't have to stop. How can I be thinking this after only knowing him a few months? I was with Evan for years, and I never wanted him this much. The accompanying stab of guilt has so many aspects I can't begin to dissect them all.

I told Adam I love him and made out with him, and meanwhile I'm lying to him about Evan being alive. And I'm pretty sure he knows it, but he's not pushing me. Which is one more reason I love him.

I'm glad Evan isn't dead. Of course I am. But somehow Adam now owns my heart, and I have to tell him the truth, no matter what comes of it. Tomorrow. Tomorrow I'll tell him.

Chapter 34 - Jaerish

THERE ARE FOUR DAYS until Christmas; five until we leave Salida. The holiday festivities have been going non-stop, and I should be having the time of my short, forgotten life. Instead, the lights and cheer just highlight the anxiety that's been building since I overheard that conversation.

Our purposes and methods.

I'm no fun at a party, unlike Patner who's jolliness incarnate. Even Radley's a Christmas elf compared to me. I spend the evenings hiding my scowl and pretending every fiber of my being isn't aware of Adam and Kessa across the room. He touches her arm, casually, like it's nothing. When she leans towards him, I want to punch something.

Kessa and I agreed to this. It's safest for her to pretend. But when I see them together it's all I can do not to claim her as mine. And what if she's not acting? I need to talk to her alone, but that would risk everything. What I really need is proof.

Which is why I'm in Morton's office, in the middle of the night, long after everyone else is asleep.

A full moon glows brightly through the giant windows, and I feel utterly exposed as I walk behind his desk. I hesitate, then pull out my flashlight, not sure I need it. Around me are hundreds of places to hide things and I don't even know what I'm looking for.

I open a couple of desk drawers and then turn my attention to the bookshelf. Maybe he's tucked something in a book, hiding it in plain sight. I reach for a copy of Machiavelli's "The Prince," which seems like a very Morton thing to read. Pulling it out I glance behind it on the shelf, as though I'll find a hidden panel.

"Are you after my money, my bourbon or something else entirely?"

I turn quickly and see Morton standing in the doorway, his face unreadable in the moonlight.

"A book, sir," I say, holding up the copy in my hand. "I couldn't sleep." I hope my lie is convincing.

Morton walks into the room and lights the oil lamp on his desk. He glances at the book in my hand.

"Interesting choice. I knew there was something I liked about you."

I casually turn off my flashlight and slip it into my pocket.

"It's not wise, Jaerish, to search through another man's belongings in the dark. What if I had shot first before assessing the situation?" Morton sets a gun beside the oil lamp with a solid thud.

"Yes, sir. I see that now."

"Have a seat, Jaerish," he says, motioning to an armchair before his desk. It's not unfriendly, but also not a request. I obey.

"You were looking for a book and chose Machiavelli. Do you think that would have been your ultimate selection had I not interrupted?" His words are casual and his tone matches. We could be friends discussing philosophy on a sunny day for all the tension he shows.

"I don't know sir. To the best of my knowledge, I've never read it." It's the perfect opening for him to ask about my memory loss, but instead he studies me long and hard.

"I'm a man whose eyes are always open, Jaerish, and I think we have that in common." I don't know how to reply, so I don't say anything. Morton continues. "What do you think of Forsworth?"

"Forsworth, sir? In what way?"

"Oh, just your overall impressions. Who is he as a man?"

I scoff. At best Forsworth is a "guy," not a man. At worst, a monster. Morton's gaze is questioning.

"I apologize, sir. I don't have the highest opinion of Forsworth."

"And why is that?"

"He's not trustworthy."

"An ironic statement, given our current circumstances."

"Fair enough," I say without flinching.

"Come, now, Jaerish," he says, sitting forward at his desk. "Tell me why you hold such a low opinion of Forsworth."

"He causes chaos because the rules don't apply to him. He taunts and humiliates the men with things they can't remember." I shrug. "He's an ass. It makes it impossible to be grateful for the rescues."

Morton sighs. "Forsworth has certainly wasted the opportunity he was given. A bigger man would not have."

I don't fully understand Morton's meaning, but I'm distracted as he reaches into a side drawer and pulls out the map I'd seen before. He slowly spreads it across the desk, holding it down with objects on each corner. I stare, trying not to seem too eager.

"This, Jaerish, as I mentioned before, is the world now, or at least our little corner of it. The pandemic was in virtually every nation before anyone closed their borders. If there's a surviving superpower out there, I've seen no sign, and as you can tell, I am intentional about gathering information."

"Open Sky tells me that you were rescued only recently from the Kansas City area."

Morton points to a place on the map with *2.5 mil* written in blue. I can't even begin to comprehend that many people. There is no red number. No remaining population?

"There's no red," I say.

"No, there is not. Two point five million lives wasted, gone in a matter of weeks because leaders led with no plan for the salvation of their people. There were surely some of the indigenous tribal population who were immune living there, but they seem to have left the area. But I digress. We were talking about you."

His eyes pierce mine briefly then he leans back in his chair, friendly, casual tone in place.

"Your rescue near this unpopulated metropolis makes me think you were an adventurous soul before *Cov-4N*. Perhaps you and I share a common dream, one of re-entering the lost cities and discovering what once made this land great. Imagine what could be gained by such a venture. We could rebuild, and with the right leadership, make this nation a place to be proud of again."

He pauses, clearly expecting a response.

"I appreciate your vision, sir. Who doesn't love the grand utopia? But with only a few months of memory I'm still trying to rebuild myself. The adventurous man you envision could have been a lost seed merchant for all I know."

"*Cov-4N* is such an odd condition. It still astounds me in its devastating simplicity." He's looking at me like a test subject in a lab. "You truly have no memory of your former life?"

"No, sir." I swallow hard.

"That must be difficult. Please forgive me for pursuing such an unpleasant subject."

Well, if we're discussing unpleasant subjects . . . "Mr. Morton, I've asked Open Sky why they don't try to find the homes of the men when they're rescued. He told me a horror story of *Cov-4N* destroying an entire town. Do you know anything about that?"

"Sadly, I do."

Morton points to writing about midway between Kansas City and Fort Riley. *Meriden, Kansas. 780. ~~780~~.*

"A tragic loss of life," Morton says. "Particularly because it could have been prevented so easily."

"It surprises me that you allow something so dangerous within Salida."

"I suppose it would. But that is the confidence I have in Open Sky. I trust his judgement completely regarding those he has selected as his guard. That is, of course, the reason you do not currently have a bullet in your thigh."

Which brings me back to now, in Morton's office, where he caught me looking through his things in the dark.

"Thank you for that," I say.

Morton receives my words with a nod, then looks at his watch.

"Despite how much I've enjoyed our time, Jaerish, it is late. If you'd still like to read, you may do so in the sitting room. The fire is still smoldering, and you may rouse it to new life."

"Thank you, sir. I think I'll sleep for now. Can I borrow this for tomorrow?" I point to *The Prince* on his desk.

He picks it up and tucks it under his arm. "Not this copy, but I'll find you another."

He turns to the bookshelf, and for a moment I consider grabbing the gun from the table and forcing him to tell me everything. The idea is gone as quickly as it came. Sure, I could do it, but what then?

Morton turns back around and hands me a different copy of *The Prince*.

"Here you are, Jaerish. I hope you enjoy it as I have." A broad smile; the gracious host.

"Thank you, sir," I say as I leave the room. Morton doesn't follow, but sits back at his desk, rolling up the map and putting it away.

I'm no closer to the truth than I was before, but considering how Morton found me, that could have gone worse.

If I learned anything tonight it's that Morton can do with a conversation what I can do in combat. He had me fully disarmed and in his power within moments, and it had nothing to do with the gun.

Chapter 35 - Kessa

I walk through the cold, dark morning to Adam's house filled with resolve. Today I'm telling him who Evan is and our suspicions about his dad. He won't want to hear it, but he loves me. And more than that, Adam cares about truth.

But when I get there, Evan's in the kitchen. I haven't seen him alone since that first morning in my house, and I have to remind myself to breathe. Evan is alive. And I love him. Like a brother or a best friend. But not like Adam. Not like someone I can't live without.

Evan, on the other hand, is looking at me like a lifeline. And I suppose I am. The only link to a past he can't remember. This is the boy I thought I'd always be with. We were building our lives together before we even knew what that meant. The responsibility of it washes over me and it's all I can do to find a smile, fake as it may be.

"Good morning, Kessa," Evan says evenly. His voice is all that would be expected of a stranger, a house guest with no ties. It's his eyes that give him away.

"Good morning, Jaerish. Is Adam around?"

He winces, and there's the guilt.

"I haven't seen him this morning," he says. As if on cue Adam enters.

"I thought I heard your voice."

Adam cups my face and kisses me. Not long and lingering, but firmly. It echoes of "mine."

When he pulls back Jaerish is washing his mug in the sink, to all appearances oblivious to Adam's show. I don't blame him. Either of them. What a mess.

"Ready to run?" Adam asks.

I'm out the door without a backward glance.

My resolve to tell Adam has weakened, and as we run I think of armies. Why would Adam's dad need an army? Maybe I'll feel like I'm doing something if I start there.

"Last time we talked about your dad it didn't go so well. But if he's going to be in my life long-term, I want to know more about him."

"What do you want to know?"

"Anything. What's he like as a dad? He's always very professional with me."

"Yeah, me too."

"Really?" I glance Adam's way as he shrugs.

"He doesn't show much real emotion. I think it started when mom died. I remember them laughing and being goofy together, but I haven't seen that side of Dad since."

"How did she die?"

"Meningitis. One morning she woke up feeling like she had the flu, and by that night she was dead."

"I'm so sorry, Adam. I can't even imagine how hard that would have been."

"You kind of can," he says. "That's what happened with Evan. There, then gone."

I should tell him now. Just say it. *Evan's alive.* But instead we jog on in silence. Eventually I break it.

"So that's why your dad wants to go to the cities so badly? For the medical tech that would have saved your mom?"

"Partly. People died of meningitis pre-pan too, so having the tech wouldn't have been a guarantee. But this goes deeper. My grandfather raised Dad with big expectations for what he'd accomplish. I think when my mom died, Dad saw it as a pivotal moment in his grand narrative. Like a wake-up call that he wasn't the leader his people needed, or he would have saved her."

"Really?"

"'All the world's a stage and Richard Morton's in the spotlight.'" Adam laughs, a short, harsh sound. "Jace used to say that. I spent so much time defending Dad to Jace that I don't think I let myself see his flaws clearly. My little brother wasn't always wrong."

It means so much to me that Adam's willing to share this, especially after our last conversation about his dad.

"Do you think he'd ever take it too far, this need to get back to the cities? Would he hurt someone who stood in his way?"

I glance at Adam. He's clearly trying to hear me and not be defensiveness.

"Violence has never been my dad's style, if that's what you're asking. And he runs this town. How would anyone stand in his way?"

"I don't know. My dad's got a lot of technology that could help him, but he's pretty set against going back to the cities, especially since Evan and Marcus died. Would your dad be mad about that, now that we're doing the swap and building more between the towns?"

Adam's silence lasts longer than I would have hoped, but I appreciate that he's thinking about the question rather than just answering.

Finally, he says "I don't think my dad will let anything keep him from getting back to the cities. But he always does things politically, and the swap seems like a great first step in that. Besides, my dad couldn't force yours to do anything."

I think about a secret army and something must show in my face because Adam stops jogging and takes hold of my elbow.

"Kessa, wait a sec."

I look into those deep blue eyes that have always given me such reassurance. But he doesn't know anything about the army. I'm only confused for a moment before his next sentence takes things to a whole new level.

"My dad's not a monster. I'm sure he would never threaten you to control your father. It's not who he is. And if he tried, I wouldn't let him."

Crap. It's so obvious, I wonder how the possibility never crossed my mind before. I attempt a smile.

"Of course not," I say. But it does nothing to calm the freak-out inside.

I take a quick shower, my mind on the gifts and messages I need to send El Dorado Springs. Why didn't I read more spy novels? Then maybe I'd have a better idea where to start.

People in those books always had codewords that meant danger. The only thing I have is "buttercup," which Dad and I used to get out of boring conversations or commitments. Like Dad would say "I don't know, buttercup, what do you think?" And then I'd say "We can't. You promised to hang my bookshelves today." And then we wouldn't get stuck helping Mayor Cartwright re-paint her white walls for the tenth time. It's not much, but it will have to do.

I decide to open Dad's Christmas gift in the hopes that it might jog some ideas. The package is small but heavy. Inside I find several red wax sticks and a seal of a capital *K* in elaborate calligraphy along with a letter.

Dear Kessa,

It is my prayer that in this season of peace you are finding peace with the past.

Jace brought me a gift from his father and allowed me the opportunity to send this along to you, for which I am grateful. Mr. Morton seems to have more connections with messengers than I, as we've remained for the most part content to develop El Dorado Springs without extensive contact with others. Perhaps now the world is changing once again, and I must look beyond our borders and personal tragedy to bring our town into the future.

Jace tells me that you are dating his brother. I know that any young man who has so quickly gained your notice must be a truly remarkable person, and I hope that you will settle for nothing less. You have taken upon yourself a great responsibility in volunteering for the swap, and I am proud of you, but you will always be my little girl. If you decide you are happy with this young man, I will be happy for the two of you. But if not, do not sacrifice yourself to politics or a sense of obligation.

In a letter to Richard Morton I have expressed the same feelings, letting him know that I am optimistic that this relationship will continue to develop, but that any swap ambassador must be free from coercion. I also let him know I would like to be present for such a joyous and momentous occurrence as my daughter's wedding, were it to progress that far, and that nothing else would be acceptable to me.

My love is always with you. I hope you like my gift. I thought it would be practical in our new reality, as well as capture that sense of the romantic that you seem to enjoy in your novels. Please make sure you use it so I know that it was received and appreciated.

All my love,

Dad

I read and re-read the letter, trying to decide if Dad is writing anything between the lines. The most obvious thing is that it contains none of his normal crossing out and writing over which makes me think it was scripted out and rewritten, possibly because he suspected it might be read by someone other than me. I don't think he used a seal that was removed, or he would have mentioned it, so maybe he left this open on purpose. More than anything I feel safer, knowing that even far away my dad is looking out for me. Now I need to find a way to look out for him.

Chapter 36 - Michaela

It's nearly midnight on Christmas Eve. The lights are dimmed, and our voices are accompanied by a single guitar.

Tonight we celebrate the ancient mystery that God entered the world as a human, born into poverty, with a quest to rescue us all. And this year Jace sits beside me, filling a space I didn't know was empty.

The Douglas family went to an earlier church service with the kids who are now off dreaming of sugar plums. Jace isn't touching me, but he's close, and my mind flashes back to my kitchen the other night just as the hymn reaches the part about a virgin mother. My cheeks burn. Which they totally shouldn't. But I have no idea how they managed to wait after they were already married. I force my focus back to the song.

At the front of the room the pastor lights his small candle from the large one on the altar. He takes the flame to someone in the front row, lighting the candle they hold. The flame passes from one person to the next, a picture of Christ's love spreading among us.

I light my candle from my mom and turn to Jace. When he tips his candle into mine, it feels intimate in a way I've never noticed before. The flame catches.

Am I doing a good job of showing Jace God's love? Something's been off since his dad's gift arrived, but when I ask him about it, he switches into charming-Jace mode and won't let me behind the mask. It reminds me of the teardrop jester I painted Halloween night.

Jace catches me staring and smiles, but even in this low light I can tell his heart isn't in it. The music swirls around us, promising peace. More than anything else that's what I want this Christmas. Peace for Jace.

I hold my candle in one hand and take his hand with the other.

"Open your eyes," I tell Jace.

We're in the shed behind my house on Christmas morning. I cleaned it last night after putting the finishing touches on Jace's gift. It's a little chilly, but still a decent showcase for the present I've been working on the past month.

"No flipping way!"

I'm pretty impressed myself. I sanded or replaced nearly every piece of that old bike, and finished it off with a super-detailed paint job. It looks good.

"You know I've never owned a bike, right?" Jace asks.

"Of course I do," I say. "I told you my gift wouldn't be lame."

"To be fair, you told me if you gave me a rock it wouldn't be lame. You didn't say anything about a bike."

"If I'd given you a rock, it wouldn't have been lame either."

Jace is straddling the bike now, but the snow is thick outside and riding it will have to wait for another day. He hops off.

"My turn," he says with a grin.

Jace pulls a small black box from his pocket. It looks like a jewelry box from an old movie. Oh my gosh; is he proposing? Because we're still in high school, and there's no way my mom would go for that. He hands me the box and I open it to see a necklace with a purple gem surrounded by glittering diamonds.

"It's an amethyst," he says. "My grandmother's."

I gently run a finger over it.

"Jace, it's gorgeous. I've never seen anything so beautiful."

"Well, I've never seen anyone so beautiful," he says, staring at me.

"OK, cheese-boy," I reply, laughing. But, as usual, I'm blushing too.

"Can I put it on you?" he asks, lifting it by the delicate silver chain.

I nod. Jace steps behind me and I pull my hair out of his way. He only fumbles with the latch for a moment, and then he leans down and kisses my neck.

"I've wanted to do that for weeks," he says, his breath hot and voice rougher than normal.

I turn around and he's right there. And then Jace's arms are around me. He's pulled me close and there's the kissing and all I can think is that I wish he were closer. But there is no closer, except there is, and my mind is going there and my mouth is still kissing Jace and my hands are on his back, but maybe a bit low on his back, and then somehow we're sitting on the old car seat against the wall of the shed and I'm not sure where my hands are when the door opens.

We spring apart, and I turn to see my mom framed in the doorway, her face indiscernible.

"Pancakes are ready," she says. "Come get them while they're hot." She walks out, leaving the door open behind her. It's a clear indication to follow.

I don't know what to do with this. This getting caught. Jace reaches over and takes my hand. He brings it to his lips, his gaze steady on mine.

"Michaela, I love you," he says. And it leaves me as breathless as the kissing.

"I love you too."

Gently I brush my lips against his. Then he pulls me to my feet, and, never dropping my hand, we head towards the house and breakfast.

It's not until I'm falling asleep that night, fingers tracing along Jace's grandmother's necklace, that I realize Jace did give me a rock for Christmas. And it wasn't lame at all.

Chapter 37 - Jaerish

I FLEX MY FINGERS, trying to retain feeling, as I crouch behind a row of evergreen bushes outside Kessa's house. Her laughter cuts through the cold night air. She still hasn't sent Adam away. Instead they're saying long goodbyes on her front porch. Through my frosty breath and a bare patch in the hedge I see him lean in to kiss her. Again. Merry Christmas to me.

Gravel crunches and I sink further into the bushes as Adam finally leaves. Kessa has turned off her porchlight. It's smart; hopefully it means she knows I'll be coming. But it still makes me feel like her dirty little secret.

How have I become the "other guy," skulking in the dark at my girlfriend's house? One more side effect of being dead. I shake off my anger. I can't stay long and don't want to waste this time.

When I knock Kessa opens the door, glances behind me, and pulls me inside. As soon as I'm in, I wrap her in my arms. Something about her smell makes my muscles relax. Home. My body remembers her, even if my mind doesn't. I force myself to let go and take a step backwards.

"I'm leaving tomorrow."

"Adam told me. I'm glad you were able to come. Have you figured anything out?"

Right to business then.

"Not much," I say. "Morton has a map with population before the pandemic and after. It's divided into sections, and he only seems to care about the middle. I asked about the town Open Sky said was wiped out by *Cov-4N*, and he pointed it out."

"Morton was showing you the map?"

"Yeah. After he caught me in his office. I told him I was looking for a book."

Kessa's shoulders tighten, but she doesn't speak, so I continue.

"He asked what I think of Forsworth, and warned me not to look like I was sneaking around. Then he took the book and gave me a different copy. I don't know if that means anything or not."

"What book was it, in case I get a chance to check it out?"

At my hesitation, Kessa narrows her eyes. "What? You're allowed to take risks and I'm not?"

"Yes," I say. I know it's the wrong answer, but the thought of Morton doing something to her is more than I can handle. Bad enough to think what his son's been doing. With that I reach for her hand.

"We could leave," I say. "Let's go back to El Dorado Springs and warn them. I'll go off the pills and hopefully remember something helpful. If nothing else my parents will know I'm alive. And you'd be safe."

She won't meet my eyes, and I know her answer before she gives it.

"I can't, Evan. We don't have any proof yet. I don't think I even want you going off the pills. What if your memory doesn't come back and you lose the time you do have?"

It's my biggest fear, but I don't see any other way.

"Besides, I don't have a spare car around and would rather not start my life of crime quite yet. Just be careful, and I promise I will too."

She doesn't mention Adam.

"So what book is it?" Kessa asks.

"Machiavelli's *The Prince*, one with a red fabric cover. I lost a lot of arguments to you, didn't I?"

"Of course not," Kessa smiles. "You were just good at seeing the error of your ways."

I can imagine my life even if I can't remember it. Joking with her feels right, and I long for this. For her. Before I can do something stupid, I ask, "Did you think of a way to get word to El Dorado Springs?"

"I think so. Morton said I could send gifts, and I'm putting some messages in. It's hard because everything I want to say sounds crazy, but I think I've figured out how to let them know you're alive with no memory and that there's an army. Dad sent me a wax seal, so at least they'll know if someone else reads my letters. The gifts will leave when you do."

"That probably means Forsworth's delivering them. I have no idea why Morton trusts that man."

An awkward silence falls. My mind goes to Kessa and Adam on the porch. Adam, the unspoken elephant in the room. I should ask what she's planning to do once I'm gone, if she'll keep dating him, pretending I don't exist? But I can't. I don't want to know.

"I'd better go, before someone misses me," I say.

She nods and walks me to the door. I don't know how to tell her goodbye, so I draw her into my arms again, hold her close. Then I walk out. I'm about fifteen feet down the path when she calls my name.

"Evan! Wait."

She walks to me quickly, wearing slippers in the snow. Her hand comes to my cheek, and she searches my face, memorizing me. Then I lean in slowly, bringing my lips to her lips. She responds, lifting up on her toes, making the kiss into something more than I'd intended. It doesn't last nearly long enough, and when she pulls away her smile is sad.

"Be safe," she says, then walks to her house without looking back.

CHAPTER 38 - KESSA

Evan is gone.

Again.

Not that I'd been able to spend much time with him, but just knowing he was nearby and safe was something.

And then last night . . .

Last night's kiss wasn't the soft, whispered kiss he'd given me when we first knew who he was. It wasn't the safe, familiar kisses we shared so often in another life. And it was nothing like the passionate kisses that have been growing between Adam and me this week. No, this kiss tasted like history and possibility and goodbye. Because he was leaving and everything was changing.

Again.

I wouldn't have initiated the kiss, but I did kiss him back.

Except that's a lie.

I was the one who called Evan's name and followed him into the dark. I initiated that kiss, and I'm still no closer to knowing what it meant except that he's gone and the possibility that I'll never see him again feels nearly as real as it did the day of his funeral.

Now as I get ready to run with Adam I think about movies where the main character turns out to be a ghost. Or dead. No one else can see them and no one else has seen them. Like I'll mention Jaerish in conversation and everyone will say "who?"

Adam arrives and waits in the doorway while I finish tying my shoes. As we start to run he asks "How's the headache?"

It takes me a second to remember my excuse from the previous evening, when I was hoping Evan would find a way to see me and wasn't sure how else to ask Adam to leave.

"Much better. Thanks," I say. "What did you do the rest of the night? Did I miss anything exciting?"

"No, you didn't miss anything. Did I miss anything?"

"What would you have missed?" I ask.

"I don't know, Kessa. You tell me."

It takes me a few steps to realize Adam isn't beside me. He's stopped running, and when I turn his face is a mask, blank, jaw clenched. His eyes blaze with a mixture of hurt and anger. Oh God, he knows.

We're on a side road and no one is around, but this isn't a conversation I can have where anyone might pass by.

"I think we should go back to my house," I say.

"Yeah? Why's that Kessa? Are you thinking we can reenact it? You can give me a play by play? Because you don't need to. I saw it the first time."

I have no idea what to say.

I'm sorry. He's Evan. I can explain. But can I?

All of it is stupid and not enough. I've chosen not to trust Adam over and over again, and now all he knows is what he saw last night. I reach for Adam's hand, but he puts it in his jacket pocket.

"He's Evan," I say. Because I can't look at Adam as he stands, radiating pain, and give him anything but the truth.

His doesn't look shocked. He probably covered that last night. Probably heard me call Evan's name before he saw . . . Oh, God. I've messed this up. Adam's walking away from me now. I chase him down and grab his elbow. If he runs I'll never catch up. Pulling his arm free he reels to face me.

"Evan is dead, Kessa. He's dead and Jaerish is just some army guy who took advantage of knowing he looked like your dead boyfriend."

"No he's not. And what do you mean army?" How does Adam know about the army?

Adam must have finally realized this isn't a conversation to have on the street because he says "C'mon" and directs me down a side trail into the woods.

We walk in silence to an old service shed where he opens the door and makes an "after you" motion. It's colder inside than out, lit only by daylight coming through an empty square where a window used to be. The kind of place you'd stash a body, if you did that kind of thing. Breathe, Kessa. This is Adam.

But how did he know about the army? Has he been working with his dad the whole time? Has everything with us been fake?

But no. When I look at him in the low light all I can see is pain. Pain I caused.

"Kessa, tell me what's going on."

He chokes it out and I wish I could take him in my arms, comfort him like he did me all those times. But I don't know if my heart can handle him rejecting my touch again.

"Sit with me?" I ask.

Adam scans the shed, gives me a look that I translate as "really?" then lowers himself to the dirty concrete floor with his back to the wall. I sit beside him, shoulders not quite brushing. Where do I start?

"Did you know none of the guys from Fort Riley can remember anything before they arrived there?"

"What are you talking about?"

"Patner, Radley, none of them have a memory of their lives before they came to Fort Riley. They think they have a disease, and can only remember as far back as when they started taking these pills that are supposed to keep the disease in check."

"I've never heard of a disease like that."

"Me either."

Adam is quiet and then says "So Jaerish says he's Evan with this disease?" I nod. "Why didn't you tell me?"

I could put it all on Evan, but that would be one more lie, and I'm so sick of lying. But I still don't know how he'll react if I tell him I didn't trust him because I think his dad's involved.

"Jaerish is Evan," I say. "But they found Evan's body, wearing his cross." I finger the cross that's never once left my neck since the day his body came home to El Dorado Springs. *A body* came home to El Dorado Springs.

"That doesn't make any sense," Adam says. But I can see he's thinking, trying to put it all together.

"Adam, Evan is alive. With no memory and a drug he takes every day. And someone's body was set up to look like his. We think the drug is really suppressing their memories, but he can't stop taking it until he's gone because if we're wrong the disease would wipe out Salida."

"What?"

"The pills are also supposed to suppress contagion."

"No wonder they didn't tell anyone about their memories. If they really have a disease, they risked all of our lives just by being here."

"We think their leader knew there was no real danger. Because there is no disease."

"So Open Sky wasn't worried because he knew they couldn't actually hurt anyone?"

I take a deep breath. "We aren't sure what Open Sky knows. But Evan thinks your dad knows about everything."

Adam jumps to his feet.

"I don't even know what you're accusing my dad of at this point, but there's no way he would have let anything hurt Salida. Keeping this town safe is his life. And you still haven't told me why you were making out with Evan, even if that was him. I saw you, Kessa. Is that it then? Evan's back and I'm no longer needed?"

I have no idea what to say. My brain that used to be so reliable is trudging through options but nothing works.

"Adam, I don't know," I finally say. "He was leaving, and it's probably dangerous. He's going to stop taking the pills. In three days he might not remember the name 'Jaerish,' let alone anything about the last seven months. Or the last three weeks."

Adam's eyes soften. Barely. Or maybe it's just the light. There's as much distance between us as there can be in an eight-by-eight shed.

"It's a lot Kessa. I need time to think."

I swallow back more words and nod.

Adam reaches down and helps me to my feet but drops my hand as soon as I'm standing. When we get to the main road Adam turns towards his house, the opposite direction from mine.

"I'll come by tonight," he says.

"Adam," I say, halting him. The mix of pain and hope when he looks back nearly kills me, but all I say is "Don't tell anyone else until we get to talk, ok?"

His eyes dim but he gives a short nod before turning and jogging away.

'I love you,' I think. But I don't say it.

I stumble through work at the lab. I've never had this much trouble putting aside distractions, not even right after Evan died. Or didn't die.

I go home early, claiming a return of last night's headache. I clean out my fridge, scrub the bathroom, take a shower. But really, I'm waiting for Adam and the nebulous "tonight," when he'll be here. I try to pray but can't get the words out.

Will Adam forgive me? Will he help me? Or has he already told his dad? By the time Adam arrives my house is spotless but inside I'm a wreck.

He brought dinner.

"I thought you might have forgotten to eat," Adam says. And I had.

I get plates as Adam unpacks the bag. The smell of fried chicken and biscuits fills the space as we sit on opposite sides of my table. He's so calm on the surface, but his eyes are red and something about his face seems worn in a way I can't quite describe.

"Why don't you start from when Jaerish showed up and tell me what's been going on?"

I take a deep breath and tell him everything. Well, not everything. I tell him about the disease and how Evan's had no memory for the right length of time. About how he heard Adam's dad talking with Open Sky and how he's going off the pills once he leaves town. I don't mention the late-night conversation with Morton or the map in his office.

"So what happens once Jaerish goes off the pills?"

"I don't know," I say. "He thinks his memory will return and he wants to keep it secret so he can find out what the army is for."

"And how will he tell you what's happening?"

"We couldn't think of a way to do that. I was hoping you might be willing to help me here, to see if there's anything we can figure out."

"So you were planning to tell me eventually," Adam says. "I'm back to being useful when Jaerish isn't around."

"It's not like that."

"It seems like it from here. From what I can see Jaerish didn't say anything before he knew your boyfriend was dead. He didn't tell you how long his memory was gone until you said how long Evan was gone. And you only think my dad was involved because 'Evan' said so."

"What are you saying, Adam?"

"I'm saying it's pretty convenient that he couldn't go off his magic memory pill until he left town. I think 'Evan' is just some guy who saw a way to get with an attractive girl for the holidays."

"He didn't 'get with' me. The only thing we ever did is what you saw."

And that first kiss, him holding me, right here. But I ignore that, because I'm angry now. Angry that Adam doesn't believe me. And yeah, I know I'm a hypocrite for it since I've been lying to him for weeks. I didn't start this conversation as my best self, despite having most of the day to think about it. Or maybe because of that. So I say what I know I shouldn't.

"You just don't want to believe your dad could be involved in something like this."

"You're right. I don't. And you just don't want to believe that Evan is dead." Adam's words hang there, suspended with the no longer pleasant smell of our untouched chicken.

"Kessa, I" but I cut him off.

"No. I don't want Evan to be dead. But I'm also not delusional. I knew Evan my entire life, and I'm not stupid enough to be tricked by some army con man. You've only known me four months. Wouldn't you know if I was me, with or without a memory?"

"Kess, of course I would know you."

Adam rubs his hands over his face, and then he walks around the table to sit beside me. He tentatively reaches out and takes my hand. It's the second time he's voluntarily touched me since he saw the kiss, and I force myself not to pull away.

"You get that this is happening to me too, right?" he says, looking down at our hands. "I kept asking and you kept saying nothing was wrong until I convinced myself I was making it up. But I knew. And then last night I saw you kissing him." Adam looks up, blue eyes filled with pain. "Why didn't you trust me?"

And I have no good answer. Just my own fear.

"I'm sorry," I say. And I am. "I almost told you so many times."

He's still holding my hand, stroking his thumb along my finger.

"We'll figure this out," Adam says, and my heart starts beating again.

"Adam, I am so sorry." I'd say it a thousand times if he needed me to. He squeezes my hand.

"I know," he says with a small smile. "I just don't know where we go from here."

Chapter 39 - Jaerish

I carried that first pill around for hours. Whenever I reached for it, I'd think of Kessa's kiss. Remember her hand on my cheek. The brush of her lips.

Throwing away the second pill was easier.

Now it's day two, and I'm eating breakfast with Patner. He's a big ball of sunshine since leaving Cacia, and Radley's patience is just about gone. We knew this trip was short-term, a vacation, not a life. But that was because of the danger of spreading *Cov-4N*. If I'm right, there's no reason for Patner to be going through this. He could be planning a future with Cacia right now.

It's easy to skip this dose, hiding my pill until I can bury it along with my waste.

This morning our group is splitting up. Forsworth is going to El Dorado Springs on a side gig for Morton while his men head back to base. Kessa's gifts and messages should be in Forsworth's pack. I offer to come along and get a sarcastic reply about the size of my stones, which is laughable coming from such a small man.

Open Sky says he left something necessary in Salida and has to go back for it. Radley objected to his going alone, but ultimately obeyed orders. He, Patner and I will continue to Colby, Kansas, an uninhabited town along our route, and wait for Open Sky there.

Either going off the pills has me paranoid, or Radley's watching me. Either way I can't shake the image of Fatim with Radley's knife through his neck.

A few hours later I'm in the back seat of the truck, eyes closed, when I see it. Remember it.

I'm sparring in a ring with an older man who looks a lot like me. A door opens and in the moment of distraction my staff is on the ground. Kessa stands in the doorway smiling.

"Still can't best me," the man says.

"Your time is coming," I reply with a laugh.

"I'm sure it is."

"Dude, are you crying," Patner asks, looking at me over the front seat.

"What?" I say, wiping at my eyes. "No. Allergies."

"Whatever," he says.

But now I know for certain that what we've been told is a lie. I have a life waiting for me back in El Dorado Springs and the only thing keeping me from it is a little blue pill. And an army. And the fact that my girlfriend's already started over with the son of the man responsible for it all.

I can't intentionally call up memories, but the flashes are getting more frequent. My parents, Kessa, and her dad are in so many of them.

So is Marcus.

I'd hoped that I'd know him by another name, someone else brought into camp with no memory. That both bodies had been planted and he was still alive. . . But I don't. My best friend is dead.

I'm there with him in an SUV. He's giving me grief about something. Then we hear it. A man screaming. I turn the wheel towards the sound . . .

Several men from Forsworth's crew kicking another man on the ground. Forsworth watching from the side, looking up as Marcus and I approach.

We were fools. Sheltered . . . arrogant . . . fools.

It happens so fast. The conversation. The blinding pain in the back of my head. The empty blackness. And then Forsworth looking down at me, dip pooling in his lip.

"That was a bitch, boy. But I've brought you back."

Then I knew nothing, not even my own name. But now I'm sure of it. Marcus is dead. And I'd bet the man we were trying to rescue was the second body in the ravine.

If Forsworth were here I'd kill him. No question. But instead he's headed for El Dorado Springs, towards everyone I love. Everyone except Kessa who's in Salida with the monster's keeper.

CHAPTER 40 - MICHAELA

JACE AND I HAVE been sticking to the living room the past few days since we got caught kissing in the shed. Mom's been staying up late with us rather than turning in at her normal nine o'clock, but she hasn't said a word. When I walk into the kitchen, I know that's about to change.

Mom is sitting at the table before two mugs and a plate of cookies. I embrace the inevitable, grab milk from the fridge and sit across from her.

"Do you want to start, or do you want me to?" she asks.

"You go ahead," I say.

"OK." Mom nods. "I know that you and I have talked about sex, and how it's a gift meant for marriage, despite the specifics of your conception."

Oh God. Maybe I should have started.

"Mom, we're not having sex. What you saw was the farthest we've ever gone."

She stares at me like she's reading my soul. Finally, she speaks.

"I like Jace," she says. "And I really like you. The things you're feeling are normal, healthy even."

"Mom! Please stop."

"If we don't talk about this, who are you going to talk about it with?"

"I asked Kessa's advice in my letter."

"That's actually a great idea. But we're still talking about it."

I groan and drop my head down onto the table.

"Honey, this is new for you. It's new for me too. But it's important. You need a plan or you're asking for trouble, and I'm too young to be a grandma."

My cheeks burn, but I know what she's saying is true. I always assumed I'd wait until I was married, and the thought that if Mom hadn't walked in my first time could have been in our shed makes me nauseous.

"Fine. What's the plan?" I ask.

"The plan is you pray and find out what God wants you to do. You know what I think that is, but you are not going to care what I think when Jace's pants are off."

"Please kill me."

Mom laughs. "Sorry, hon. If you're old enough to consider having sex, you're old enough to talk about it."

"I wasn't considering having sex," I say. But Mom's stupid raised eyebrow disagrees.

"Once you decide what you want, you have to tell Jace."

"And what if Jace isn't ok with that?"

"If he respects you, he'll respect what you want. If he doesn't, he's not someone you should be with."

Which seems too logical to argue, so I don't.

"By the way, you have to respect his boundaries too. If he draws a line, you can't tempt him to cross it."

"Mom!"

"Girls do that. It makes them feel powerful. But it brings shame into the relationship, and sex and shame shouldn't go together."

I don't think I can handle any more of this conversation. I'm practically squirming in my seat when there's a knock at the door.

"Are you expecting anyone?" Mom asks.

Oh, God, please don't let it be Jace.

"Nope, not expecting anyone."

Mom goes to the door and there's a short, rough looking man standing on the porch.

"Can I help you?" Mom asks.

The man slowly looks her up and down with a leer that makes me want to punch his face. Mom is still as a statue, and I wonder if she's thinking about the pistol we keep in the coat closet. I know I am.

Then the man grins, which isn't any better. "I'm here with a delivery for Miss Michaela Barr. From Kessa McKnight."

"Ah, I see," says mom. She reaches out her hand and the man gives her a small package.

"Merry Christmas," he says without leaving the stoop.

"Merry Christmas," my mom says. "Have a good day." With a forced smile she closes the door and locks it behind her.

Mom turns to me, gift in hand. "I'm guessing you'll want to open this now?" she asks with a real smile. "Let's pick up our conversation later."

"Sure thing, Mom," I say, hoping we will never have to pick up that conversation again.

I open the padded envelope and pour out its contents. There's a small box wrapped in red paper and an envelope with a wax seal.

Gift first.

When I open the small box, I stop breathing. It's a gold and black pen. Evan's pen, or an exact duplicate. This has been passed through four generations of his family. Besides the cross around her neck, it's Kessa's most precious possession. She sobbed when Evan's dad gave it to her after the funeral, saying her children were as close as he'd get to grandchildren now, and that he wanted her to carry on the tradition.

Why in the world is she sending this to me?

I turn to the letter, hoping for answers. I'm about to break the wax seal when my mom slides me a knife.

"Along the top," she says.

Ah, yeah, that's better. I slice through the envelope. Inside is a card, and inside the card another piece of paper.

Dear Michaela,

First things first. I loved your story. And I'm totaly taking credit for all your talent since I'm the one who got you into writing.

I'm glad you're dating Jace. I could see the two of you being good for each other. I know Adam is good for me in ways I never knew I needed. As for boyfriend advice, be honest with him. And if you love him, make sure he knows. Talk about your boundaries before you cross them.

I did meet Cole. To quote Miss Austen, "He is tolerable; but not handsome enough to tempt me." Not with Adam around, anyway.

I think rather than asking here about any potential problems with the swap, you should go to my dad. I'm sure he can make your dad's status a non-issue. The two towns will need to have meetings soon anyway. In fact, I'd guess those meetings would take place in El Dorado Springs this spring, unless my dad prefers to travel here.

I'm sure you opened my gift first and hope that you value it the way I would. I wrote a poem with it to tell you my heart in this new season. I think my dad might like the poem as well, so please share it with him.

Your sister regardless,

Kessa

Value it the way she would? I still don't understand. This pen was everything to her. I open the paper that was within the card. In a beautiful script I read:

"A poem in the style of the Psalmist"

I left my home as one who mourns,
As an Israelite, starting over in a foreign land.
The Judah of my exile has now become my refuge
And love has sprung up in the barren place.
I dwell in peace.
What could disturb my soul?

The Writer lives,
The past forgotten.
Alive beyond doubt or hope.

My words are a lamp;
Listen well
And let them dispel all darkness.

"Trust in the Lord with all your heart, and do not lean on your own understanding. In all your ways acknowledge Him, and He will make your paths straight." 2 Chronicles 26:11

It's beautiful, but I know I'm missing something. Or I'm reading too much into it because of the pen. *"Always notice details."* That was Kessa's mantra when she tutored me in poetry interpretation my freshman year. I grab my notebook and recopy the poem so I can write on it.

The beginning seems straightforward, although the *"Judah of my exile"* part is weird. Then I underline the question. *"What could disturb my soul?"*

"The Writer lives, the past forgotten. Alive beyond doubt or hope."

Evan's pen is heavy in my hand. If the question isn't rhetorical . . . But there's no way. It's only when I set the pen down on the table that I notice my hand is shaking.

And then I see it. 2 Chronicles 26:11 is written below the Bible verse. That verse was one of the first ones Kessa and I memorized together, and it's in Proverbs. I grab my Bible from my bedroom and find the right place in the book of Chronicles.

"2 Chronicles 26:11 'Uzziah had an army of well-trained warriors ready to march into battle unit by unit. This army had been mustered and organized by Jelel, the secretary of the army, and his assistant, Maaseiah. They were under the direction of Hananiah, one of the king's officials.'"

Well, that didn't clear up anything, but it did keep the ominous vibe going. If it weren't for Evan's pen, I'd be sure this is all in my head. But she would never give that pen away, except to her kids someday.

I re-read the letter. I think she wants me to take this to her dad. Before I can ask to go to Professor McKnight's, Mom tells me it's dinner time. I'm quiet, pushing things around my plate as I run through it all in my head. When I look up, Mom is studying me.

"This isn't the response I'd expect from you getting a gift from Kessa. Want to tell me what's going on?"

Before I can there's a knock at the door.

"We're a popular place today," Mom says, getting up to open it. "Gary, what can we do for you?"

Professor McKnight stands in the doorway.

"I received gifts from Kessa today. She asked if I could check in and make sure Michaela got hers as well."

"That was a nice thought," Mom says, ushering him inside. "It did arrive, although I can't say I approve of the messenger." Professor McKnight's brow knits, and my mom says "Oh, nothing happened. He just gives me the creeps is all."

"And the once over," I add. My mom rolls her eyes and the professor scowls, but I continue. "Professor McKnight, Kessa asked me to show you the poem she sent. I'm going to grab it."

Mom has cleared our plates, and she starts making tea as I lay the pen and letters on the table. The professor picks up the pen, startled.

"Yeah," I say. "That was Evan's."

Professor McKnight pulls a letter from his pocket, then sits.

"Why don't we swap?" he asks. We both sit, and there's silence while we read.

Dear Dad,

Merry Christmas! It's so strange not to be with you, but it lets me practice the fine art of letter writing and I feel I must do Ms. Austen proud.

I'm so glad that Mr. Morton gave me the opportunity to send you this package. He's been very charming this whole time and I like his son, Adam, very much. Perhaps the swap was truly meant to be. I know you always tell me that things happen for a reason, and I see reasons I could never have imagined unfolding.

I hope you're finding ways to entertain yourself without me around to drag you out of your office. Give Evan's parents my love.

Your Buttercup,

Kessa

PS- I sent a gift to Michaela as well. Can you check in and make sure she received it?

I finish first and wait while he intently studies both letter and poem.

When he looks up, I say "I've never heard you call Kessa 'Buttercup.' Is that a thing?"

"That was a code for when we needed an excuse to get out of something."

"You're going to have to change your code word now or I might end up offended next time you decline a dinner invitation," my mom says. Professor McKnight looks vaguely uncomfortable. Mom places tea in front of us and sits down.

"I took it as Kessa's way of drawing attention to the fact that something wasn't as it should be," Professor McKnight says.

"Do you think she needs you to get her out of the swap?" I ask and the professor sighs.

"If so, she underplayed it, leaving only that one word and instructions to check in with you. Unless you see more that I'm missing. Your gift, on the other hand, is more telling."

I hand him my copied poem with its notes and underlinings.

"You're one hundred percent sure this pen was Evan's?" he asks and I nod. "Well, that does change things."

CHAPTER 41 - JACE

CHRISTMAS BREAK IS ALMOST over. I'm in my bedroom, flipping through a comic, when the doorbell rings.

Usually I'd ignore it, but Henry and the kids are gone, and Anne Marie's in bed with a headache. I rush to the door to keep whoever's there from ringing again. It's Dad's messenger. And I totally blew off Dad's question. Still, sending this guy back seems like overkill.

"What's up, little prince?" The messenger sneers.

"Little prince, huh?" What the hell is that about?

"I got a package for you from daddy," he says as he hands me a small box. "I'm leavin two days from now and your pops said I wasn't supposed to return without a reply from you. He said you needed to be more specific this time."

I don't even try to stop my eye roll.

"Anything else?" I ask.

"You got a pretty sweet set-up here, kid. But why not, right? Your daddy's always had big plans. Just remember whose side you're on when it all goes down."

"Dude, I have literally no idea what you're talking about, so I'm just going to go ahead and shut the door."

That scary little man has finally lost it. Opening the package, I find two envelopes and Adam's favorite baseball cap. I used to wear it just to piss him off, but now when I put it on I feel homesick for the first time since leaving Salida.

If I got something from Adam, I bet Michaela got a present from Kessa too. I grab my coat and shove the envelopes in the pocket. Soon I'm knocking on her door. Her mom answers and seems surprised to see me, which is kind of weird since I'm here all the time.

"Good evening Mrs. Barr. Is Michaela around?"

She looks behind her, like she has to check.

"Of course, Jace. C'mon in."

Michaela is sitting at the table with Professor McKnight. She looks at me and smiles, but its forced. Which is weird, because she usually likes the professor.

"Sorry to interrupt," I say. "Dad's creepy messenger came by my house and I thought maybe he'd brought you something from Kessa. I know you were looking forward to that."

Michaela looks at Professor McKnight who barely shakes his head.

"Um, yeah. She sent me a pen and a poem. And a letter."

The silence is awkward until the Professor fills it.

"It's always nice to see you, Jace. We were just discussing some family matters, but we've finished. Please, join us, and tell us what the messenger dropped off to you."

"Sure," I say, taking a seat. "This hat is from Adam. And there are a couple things I haven't opened yet." I take the envelopes out of my coat pocket and glance at the front of each. "This one's from Adam, and I'd guess the other's from my dad, but it doesn't say."

I drop the unmarked envelope onto the table, which is probably a bad idea since the last thing Dad sent me was a gun.

Adam's letter is short. He says dad's the same as ever, and that I'd better appreciate the ball cap. Kessa wrote too, and she tells me that setting me up with Michaela was her present and I'm welcome. She's also claiming big sister privileges early. If I hurt Michaela, she's going to come to El Dorado Springs and pound me. I laugh out loud because I know she'd try with all five foot five of her ferocious being.

Michaela's looking at me funny. "Kessa's going to come pound me if I break your heart."

"What?" she says. "Let me see."

I hand over the letter. She scours it, but doesn't seem to think it's as funny as I did. Something feels off.

Michaela passes my letter to Professor McKnight, who looks at me before reading it.

"May I?"

"Yeah, sure." It's got to be hard to be separated from a child you love. You'd probably want any hint of them.

Which makes me think of Dad's envelope. Not because he loves me, but there are still similarities. And that stupid hope I can't seem to crush. But now I'm wondering if I should open it here.

"What did your dad send?" Michaela asks.

I pick it up. Here goes nothing. Maybe if it's something insane they can help me figure out what's going on.

I pour it out on the table. There's a letter and a cool watch with a built in compass. I pick up the watch and look it over. I don't recognize it as anything from our house, so maybe Dad went to some effort for this gift. I pick up the letter and unfold it.

Son,

I know that you and I haven't always seen eye to eye, but I need you to know that in all things blood is thicker than water. Our world is always changing and we are about to enter a new era, one that will bring mankind into a place of prosperity to rival that existing before the pandemic. In fact, the quality of life for those who remain has the potential to surpass any that has come before with no concerns for resources or overpopulation.

I need to know that in this you are with me, even if things occur that you may not understand. I am your father and family is where your loyalty lies. Please send word back with Forsworth that you can be counted upon. Eloquence is not necessary. Just your promise.

The watch I sent is one that was issued to paratroopers who were going behind enemy lines so if they got turned around they could always find their way back. Hopefully you don't need that, but please wear it always, in remembrance.

Your Father,

R. Morton

PS- I hear you have a girlfriend and that she's wonderful in all ways except that she is the daughter of a seed merchant. In this situation I'm fine with that. Who am I to stand in the way of young love?

When I finish, Michaela's looking at me expectantly.

"Just when I think I've got old man Morton figured out," I say. "Weirdest letter ever. But he's ok with us dating, so that's all I care about."

I smile, but her returning smile is off.

"Was there a question that your father would have a problem with you dating Michaela?" Professor McKnight asks.

"Well, Michaela wasn't sure since her dad was a seed merchant."

"I suppose it's a good thing Kessa is interested in your brother then. I understand that the use of seed merchants is more prevalent in Salida."

"It is. But I think my dad had Kessa pegged for Adam from the beginning. He's like that."

"Like what?"

"I don't know. He's always talking about the 'bigger picture' and trying to make people fit into his version of how it should be."

Professor McKnight gives me a long look and I hurry on.

"Don't worry, though. Adam's amazing. I just meant that Dad probably had Kessa stay with us in the beginning so she'd get to know Adam first, you know. Give him a head start or something." I make myself stop rambling.

"Is this a quality you admire in your father, Jace?" the professor asks. The question is straightforward, but there's enough compassion in it to make me answer honestly.

"It's hard to admire someone who's tried to control you your whole life. One of the best things about moving here was getting away from him. Until he started writing, anyway."

"What do you mean?" Professor McKnight asks.

"Well, like in his last letter he told me to make sure my girlfriend has connections and then in this one he said it doesn't matter and that he'd never stand in the way of true love. What kind of mind game is he playing?"

"May I see the letter, Jace?" Professor McKnight asks.

I freeze. Part of me wants to show him and see what he thinks of my dad's crazy godfather bull. The other part wonders if dad would consider that 'betraying the family.'

"It's got some personal stuff in it," I say and tuck the letter into my pocket. "What do you think of the watch? He said they used to issue them to paratroopers so they could find their way back home."

"It's a beautiful piece," says Professor McKnight, picking it up and examining it. "Very well maintained, although the back of the face isn't original. It was probably repaired at some point and the original back lost."

I take the watch and latch it onto my wrist. It feels heavy, like the secrets Dad is making me carry. Why did he send me a gun before, and now this weird letter about my loyalties? I look around the table. If anything my loyalties are to these people, and to Henry. They've made me feel more welcome than I ever did at home. I'm going to do it. To tell them. Screw Dad. But before I can Professor McKnight pushes back his chair.

"I'd better go. I'll see you all tomorrow at the New Years' Eve celebration, won't I?"

"Wouldn't miss it," Mrs. Barr says.

Michaela's mom walks Professor McKnight to the door. I turn towards Michaela, lean in and press my forehead against hers.

"Michaela, you'll tell me if something's wrong, won't you?"

She nods, which is kind of awkward with our foreheads pressed together. It makes her laugh, which breaks the tension, at least a little.

"Of course, I will," she says. "It's nothing." She gives me a little kiss and her mom clears her throat behind us.

"Jace, it's going to be a long night tomorrow. Time to call it an evening."

"Sure, Mrs. Barr."

She hasn't dismissed me like that in a while. Maybe ever. I glance at Michaela who just shrugs. She walks me to the door, gives me one more quick kiss, and then I'm back out into the night.

The ride home feels longer than the one there. What went wrong? Hopefully I'm just being paranoid, but the sinking feeling in my gut is familiar. It means Councilor Morton is about to screw up my life.

Chapter 42 - Kessa

Adam's house is dark and silent as we slip in the back door and up the stairs. It's ten o'clock on New Year's Eve. Adam didn't correct his friend's assumptions when he told him to cover for us if anyone noticed we'd left the party, but that's not the sort of sneaking around we're doing tonight.

We've been cautious with each other since Adam found out the truth about Evan. Really, I'm not sure we agree on what that truth is, but tonight Adam surprised me by suggesting we take a look around his dad's office since we could guarantee he'd be gone.

Our first stop is Adam's room to mess up the bed in case we need an alibi. He lies on the comforter and I settle in beside him, his arm beneath me so my head can rest where his shoulder and chest meet. I relax into his warmth, wishing I could pretend nothing crazy is happening. He's holding me like this when a door closes downstairs, followed by voices.

I look at Adam, eyes wide. He stands quietly, a finger to his lips, and reaches a hand down to me. Together we walk to the hall and stop just before the landing.

"Can you truly ask why I question this?" The voice is familiar but I can't quite place it. "I've let you lead me blindly for too long as it is."

I can hear Morton's voice in reply, but can't make out the words. I tiptoe forward, but Adam stops me with a hand on my arm. I give him a look, hoping he can read *"but this is the best and maybe only chance we will ever get"* from my eyes. Apparently not because he shakes his head, unmoving.

We stand in silence, straining to hear, but there's nothing. Then we hear a thud like something large hitting the ground. My heart plummets and as I look at Adam I see my surprise mirrored on his face. Before we can decide what to do Morton's voice calls from below.

"Adam, bring Kessa down and help me move this man."

Adam's face goes pale.

"Kessa, it's not what it looks like."

What it looks like? I have no idea what it looks like, but it doesn't look good. How did Morton know we were here?

"C'mon, Kessa. Let's go down." He hasn't let go of my arm and now he leads me gently down the steps. What the hell is going on? Should I pull away? Try to run?

Open Sky is lying face down on the ground in Morton's office. I thought he left with his men days ago.

"Good evening, Kessa," Morton says, as though there weren't a body on the floor. "I'm sorry you need to be involved in this, although from what Adam's told me you already are."

Adam swallows, runs a hand through his hair before speaking.

"Kessa, I thought we should talk to my dad and ask him what's really going on."

"What's really going on? I told you what was 'really going on,' and you told your dad."

"Now, Kessa, you're over-reacting," Morton says. "There's nothing to get upset about?"

"Oh yeah? What about the body on the floor? Or your army?"

"Ah," says Morton, with a glance at Adam. "It seems my son hasn't told me everything." And I realize my mistake. Crap. What has Adam told him?

"Kessa has a lot of crazy theories, but I told her I was sure that's all they are. We can talk and clear it all up."

The look Adam sends my way is pleading and I clamp down on my anger at "crazy theories." I know I'm right now more than ever, but this isn't the time to fight him about it. I don't even know whose side he's on, but I need to start playing this smarter, and fast.

"I do have a lot I want to ask you about, Mr. Morton, but don't we need to get help for Open Sky first?"

"He'll be fine. He just needs to sleep it off. Adam, I'll need your assistance carrying him. Kessa, please go to the bookshelf and pull out *The Art of War*. It's the third shelf down. There's a button behind it, if you could press it please."

I do as he says, hoping it's not some sort of trap that's going to inject me with a paralyzing drug or something, but when I press the button a section of the bookcase swings out to reveal stairs going down. No wonder he was suspicious to find Evan here.

"Ladies first," Morton says, gesturing into the stairwell, and I have no option but to obey.

Lights turn on automatically and at the bottom there's a door. Behind me Morton and Adam are making their way down, carrying Open Sky between them. Maybe I can do something while their hands are full but I don't know what and then it's too late.

When they reach the bottom Adam supports a limp Open Sky while Richard Morton turns to a glowing keypad. He types in a code and then swings the door open.

I'm not sure what I was expecting. A sterile room filled with computers, or a medieval dungeon, maybe? Instead I see a cozy apartment, which is almost creepier in its own way. There's a kitchen off to the left, a dining table with chairs, a couple couches. Several colorful rugs cover the floor and an open doorway shows a bed and bathroom beyond.

"It's a safe-room," Adam supplies. "Somewhere we could go if the worst happened. My grandfather built it into the original house when everyone thought the world would end in nuclear war."

They lay Open Sky on one of the couches. He looks peaceful, like he's sleeping, except for the handcuff that Morton attaches from one wrist to a metal ring imbedded in the concrete floor.

Morton walks over and closes the door to the staircase. It shuts with an ominous beep, the word "secure" appearing on the lock screen.

"Now, let's have a seat, shall we?" Morton motions to the table. "Would you like a drink? Hot tea maybe?"

"No. Thank you," I say, rocked by how meek and dutiful my voice sounds.

I sit across from Morton with Adam on my left. I can't look at him. He puts a hand on my leg under the table, maybe to reassure me, but I pull away.

"So, Kessa," Morton begins. "Adam tells me you believed one of the men who was here with Open Sky to be your boyfriend who passed away last summer while exploring the cities. Is that correct?"

"Yes sir."

"But this man had no memory of you or anything to do with your town or his life before?"

"Yes."

"Adam thinks this man was taking advantage of you, a con man of sorts, with an endgame of enjoying a pretty girl's company while traveling. Is that what you believe, Kessa?"

"No."

Adam interrupts. "Of course she doesn't. It's natural for her to want to believe Evan's alive."

I still haven't looked at Adam, afraid that if I do I'll either scratch his eyes out or burst into tears. This means I have no way of gauging how much he told his dad. After my big mistake upstairs, my best bet is to keep my mouth shut.

"Well, Adam, I also don't believe that, so Kessa and I have something in common." Morton says. "Kessa, I believe that man had other motives that go way beyond a winter fling."

I can feel Adam cringe and remember the pain on his face when he confronted me about kissing Evan. But I can't soften now.

"As you apparently know, Open Sky and I have been working together to create a force capable of protecting that which remains of civilization in our portion of North America. We are not the only ones organizing on this continent, and I fear the cohort to our North will not be content with our current treaty lines forever. Suffice it to say, they are not nice people."

My mind wanders to the map Evan mentioned, the one with the black dividing lines.

"All of the men in our force, or 'army' as you called it, are there voluntarily. They live a communal and mutually beneficial life, supporting themselves through their labor just as those anywhere do. To the best of my knowledge there is no memory loss among them, nor disease of any kind. I certainly wouldn't allow men with such a horrible condition to enter Salida, particularly after having undergone the extremes needed to prevent the first pandemic from wiping it out."

My eyes dart to Adam. He had said as much when I told him about Evan.

"My suppositions about Jaerish, though, are different from my son's. Adam is primarily focused on this man's attentions to you. How could he not be? But Kessa, I'm looking at a much bigger picture. What could this man's motives have been in the grand scheme of things?

"Here we are, at the beginning of a new era. Trade is being restored. Open communication once again exists between the two greatest remnants of civilization. Soon we will be allied not by words only, but by the bonds of marriage and blood. Who would stand to gain by interrupting such progress?"

"I have no idea, sir."

"Of course not. You are young and haven't had to think beyond El Dorado Springs until recently. But I think of this entire continent and have for decades, nearly my whole life. The North, Kessa, sees us striding forward, and they are working to stop it."

"Why would you think that?" I ask.

"I caught Jaerish looking through my office in the dead of night, Kessa. I chose to show him a map I have with very vague numbers for the North, to allow him to believe our intelligence of their efforts is limited, per the original treaty. That is not the case. And I know they watch us for weaknesses as well. At this point, I don't know whose loyalty to trust."

I follow his gaze to Open Sky, passed out on the couch, wrist secured. None of this makes any sense. I want to ask questions, but don't know where to start.

"Kessa," Morton says, "Did Evan give you any indication that he truly was who he said? Any proof at all?"

"He couldn't. His memory was gone."

The look Morton gives me is so patronizing I want to smack it off his face.

"Something is happening Kessa, and we must be prepared. Sometimes the few must protect the many, and you are a part of that few."

I'm suddenly exhausted. Open Sky is unconscious on the couch behind me and I wish it was me instead so I wouldn't have to wade through any of this.

"You've been dealing with so much on your own, Kessa," Morton says, shaking his head, "especially with that man filling your mind with his stories. I wish you'd come to me sooner. But now I need to get back to the party for the commencement of the new year. Let's all talk again, once you've had time to process this new information."

I stand to my feet, head swimming. When Adam takes my arm to steady me, I don't pull away. We go back up the stairs, leaving Open Sky locked in the room below. It could just as easily be me.

But if any of what Morton said is true, there's a real threat building in the North, and however this army was assembled it was done for protection. But Evan, his memory . . . Nothing lines up anymore.

The walk home is silent until Morton leaves us with a last "We'll talk soon."

Adam escorts me to my porch, but when he tries to speak I hold up a hand. I can't. Not tonight. I shuffle inside, fall onto my bed and sleep, deep and dreamless.

Chapter 43 - Jaerish

We've driven through the dark for hours, outpacing an ice storm. The lopsided sign welcoming us to Colby, Kansas, "the Oasis of the Plains," is a beautiful sight, peeled paint and all.

Radley pulls our truck under the hotel overhang as the first pinging drops fall. We stopped here on our way to Salida, wedging plywood under the doorknob on our way out. It's still in place.

We enter the hotel, following our flashlight beams across worn hardwoods through the lobby and into a dining area stacked with dusty tables and chairs. Broken furniture is piled beside the decorative gas fireplace, now filled with ashes. Patner moves to it immediately. It will take a while to warm up this space with its high ceilings and wall of windows, but the guest rooms don't have fireplaces. And some have skeletons.

"Did Open Sky say how long we're supposed to wait for him before going on to Fort Riley?" I ask.

"We're here indefinitely," Radley says. "And this ice storm could slow him down further. We might as well settle in."

Radley and I push aside tables and lay out sleeping bags. I'm wired, despite the hour, and wander the space until I find a shelf filled with dvds and books for guest use.

"You ever see this?" I ask, walking towards Patner and the fire. "This cat was hilarious."

"Kind of young for the base collection, don't you think?" Patner asks.

"Like you don't like cartoons?"

"Jaerish, I'm going to need you to take a seat." Radley's voice is stone cold. When I turn he's eight feet away pointing a gun at my chest.

"What the hell, man?" Patner says.

I've raised my hands in the air, but there's no way I'm going down like Fatim.

"We need to have a conversation," Radley says. "This fool is too badass for his own good, and I need truth. Open Sky's orders."

Patner falls into line. And I'm not fighting both my friends until I'm out of other options. I sit in the chair Radley points out, and even let Patner tie my arms. Mainly because he's piss at knots.

"Sorry, man," he says as he stands and walks to Radley. I don't reply.

"Open Sky told me to keep an eye on you," Radley says. "He knew something was going on in Salida, and for all I know that's why he went back. So tell me why you were snooping in Morton's office and always watching his son's girl?"

"Now I can get tied up for watching a hot girl? Please. Patner did way more than watch Cacia."

"You know that's not what he's talking about," Patner says. "You might as well just tell us what's going on."

And that's when Radley pulls out a bottle of the little blue pills.

"I've kept my eyes open, Jaerish. And do you know what I've seen? I've seen someone who's willing to endanger others for his own mad ideas. That type of person doesn't make a very good soldier."

He opens the bottle and pours a single pill onto his massive palm.

"What if we'd arrived in Colby and found people here? Innocents just trying to live their lives. You'd have infected them. And why? Because you thought you knew better than what you'd been told."

The anger in his eyes takes me off guard, but it shouldn't. It's exactly what I should have expected from Radley, who always follows the rules.

"The pills are a lie," I say, injecting as much calm into my voice as I can. "It all is. They don't save us. They steal our memories and make us into slaves."

"I don't feel like a slave, Jaerish," Radley replies.

"They don't take your free will. But they steal who you were and make you dependent and trapped. We don't have to be. We could go home."

"Fort Riley is my home," Radley says. "And you're talking like a mad-man."

"Patner, you could know who you were," I say, turning to him. "And you could go back to Cacia. Or anywhere. You could go home and there'd be nothing to stop you."

Patner glances at Radley who raises a brow.

"I think we've heard enough, Jaerish," Radley says. "Time for your pill." He approaches, pill and canteen in hand.

"You can't do this," I say. "I remember everything. My parents. And Kessa. Adam's Kessa was my Kessa once. Before that damn pill."

Radley's face is stone, but Patner's lips are pressed, the way he does when he's thinking.

"Patner, help me. What if I'm telling the truth? It was Forsworth who kidnapped me. He probably got you too."

Patner draws in a breath. He knows Forsworth would do it.

"Radley, hold up." The gaze Radley turns on Patner is as cold as the ice battering the windows. "Did Open Sky tell you anything other than to watch him?"

"He told me to watch him and detain him here if needed. But my men are under my jurisdiction."

"Did he tell you to make him go back on the pill?" Patner asks.

"He did not."

"Then let's hold off and let Open Sky make the decision."

Patner and Radley have a wordless conversation that ends in Radley nodding and turning his back on me. Suddenly I can breathe again. They don't need to know my hands are free, and they were about fifteen seconds from unconsciousness.

"Thanks for that," I say to Patner.

He pulls a chair in front of me and sits down.

"You see this one?" he asks, holding up a dvd from the pile in his lap. I haven't. He shows me another, and it's a no. But the third is a yes.

"What's it about?" he asks, reading the back as I tell him. Radley joins us, another stack of dvds in his hands and we go through ten, four that I've seen, before Radley swears and walks away.

Patner follows. I can't hear them, but I can tell Patner's pressing and Radley relenting. Eventually Patner comes back and sits in the chair beside mine. Radley follows with more rope.

"What are you doing?" I ask.

"Patner's going off the pill," Radley says. "And this is the only way I'll let him do it."

CHAPTER 44 - KESSA

January 1.

The new year has just started, and I already wish it was over.

The fact that I'm not locked up with Open Sky highlights the impossibility of my situation. Morton isn't even afraid of me telling someone, because really, who would believe me? Last night his words hypnotized, but now the fog has cleared.

I know Jaerish is Evan. Morton is full of it.

I'm still in bed when Adam knocks on the door. I should just put my head under the pillow and stay there until he leaves. But as confused and frustrated as I am, I don't want him to go. I open the door then crawl back under my covers.

He doesn't have pancakes this time, no peace offering to give. Maybe he knows this is bigger than pancakes, or maybe he's sick of trying so hard to comfort me. He lays down on the bed beside me, above the covers. His eyes are red, like he didn't sleep much, or maybe like he was crying.

"Hey," he says.

"Hey," I say. I roll onto my back.

"Thanks for letting me in."

"Yeah, well, what else could I do?"

"Ignore me until I left?"

"Would you have left?"

"Maybe. Eventually."

"It's not like I can avoid you for long anyway."

I feel him wince but I don't take it back.

"Kessa, I'm sorry," Adam says.

"I know," I say. And I do.

I glance sideways. He's on his back now too, staring at my ceiling. We're still not looking at each other, not touching, the blankets making it impossible for me to reach out and take his hand, even if I wanted to.

"So what all did you tell him?" I ask.

"I told him you thought Jaerish was your dead boyfriend and asked him if he knew of any disease that might give someone amnesia. He didn't, but he suggested we all sit down together and talk it out. I figured if he got to the house before we started looking through his office, I wouldn't have to betray either of you."

"You figured this after you told your dad my secret?"

"I told my dad the night I saw you kissing Jaerish."

"Oh." And that's all I have to say.

We lay there silent for a long time. I'm on the verge of sleep when Adam rolls onto his side and looks down at me.

"What now?" he asks.

"I don't know. I'm too tired to know anything."

He leans forward, putting his arm over me and drawing us together, the blanket still between us, and somehow like that I fall back asleep.

Chapter 45 - Jace

For the first time ever I'm glad winter break is over. Being back at school gives me less free time to obsess about whatever's going on with Michaela.

Maybe she's embarrassed because of her mom catching us in the shed on Christmas. Or maybe it was me telling her I love her. Or maybe I screwed up in some other way I can't even guess at. I don't want to be the needy guy, so when she tells me nothing's wrong, I pretend I believe her.

"That pervy little guy over there is staring at me."

Sure enough, Forsworth is waiting outside the school. He's clearly staring at Mae Cartwright, and instead of his usual smirk, he's leering. Bruce, who's dating Mae now, starts towards Forsworth, his hands already fists. I stop him.

"Bro, that guy works for my dad, and he's not worth the effort. I'll go see what he needs."

I leave Bruce on the steps making out with Mae like he's got something to prove while everyone else tries to ignore them.

"Did you need something?" I ask. "It's creepy when old dudes size up teenagers."

"Boy, that girl's tasty. I don't care about her age."

There are so many things wrong with that I don't even know where to start.

"What do you want?" I ask instead.

"You owe me a message for Daddy. Then I can get out of this town and be on my merry way."

Right. I'll be glad to get rid of him, but I still have no idea what to say to my dad. I take off my backpack and grab paper. *"Sure, Dad. Whatever. You know me,"* I write and then sign my name.

I hand it to Forsworth and he reads. "This is seriously what you want me to take back to Morton after he made me wait around for your answer?"

I take the paper back. *"PS- Forsworth says this is a crap answer and not worth his time, so hopefully this will satisfy him and he will leave. You know I'm dedicated to you, our family and the future of mankind and that I will always work in its best interest. Your devoted son, Jace."*

"Better," Forsworth says. "See ya around kid." He starts walking away then glances at my wrist. "Nice watch," he says with a smirk. And he's gone.

"Was that your dad's messenger?" Michaela asks. I jump. When did she get here?

"Hey, you." I smile and pull her into a hug. "Forsworth wanted an answer to my dad's letter. Hopefully now that he has it, he's leaving town."

She shudders. "I'm glad he's going. What did you say to your dad?" The way she asks is casual, but Michaela can never hide anything.

"He wrote some weird stuff last time and wanted a reply. Actually, can I show it to you?"

Michaela glances at her watch. "Let me just tell aftercare that I can't stay today."

"We can do it later. It's no big deal."

Michaela thinks about this for longer than seems needed, then nods. "I'll come to your house at four thirty."

I pull Michaela close and plant a kiss on her head. I love holding her. My internal optimist tries to reassure me that the awkwardness I've been feeling is all in my mind. Unfortunately, that's when Bruce hollers "get a room." Michaela, blushing, jumps from my arms and flees to the school.

The afternoon drags and by four thirty I'm all anxiety. Things are already weird with Michaela, and now she's going to know my dad's insane. Not that I haven't told her that already, but this seems different.

I'm coloring with Enery and Margie when Michaela arrives. There are hellos and hugs and then whining when Anne Marie won't let the kids follow us to the living room. Then I'm alone with Michaela. And my dad's letter.

I hand it to her and clasp my hands together so they won't fidget. As Michaela reads, her face gets pale, and my hope that I was reading too much into it fades.

"Jace, let's go see Professor McKnight."

"Why?"

"Kessa sent us news in her letters too. And I think you need to know about it, but I'd rather he tell you."

"OK," I say. "But you know you're freaking me out, right?"

"Yeah, I do. I'm sorry. But why don't we go over now and then you won't have to worry long."

My stomach growls.

"Anne Marie's making enchiladas," I say. "She said you could stay."

Michaela looks undecided so I take her hand and pull her up off the couch. She's not bossy by nature, but I've never seen her this uncertain.

"Let's see how much time we have."

Anne Marie told us dinner was still an hour away, so I grabbed a granola bar and demolished it on the way to Professor McKnight's. After a couple knocks, the Professor opens his door.

"Hello, Jace. Michaela. Welcome. What brings you by?"

"Professor," Michaela says, "Jace let me read the letter from his dad today. When you put it with the others, it seems important."

"Oh?" he asks with a glance between us. "Let's go to my office. I've just straightened up."

Unlike the last time I was here, the office is completely in order. There isn't a stray paper in sight. It's also wonderfully warm after our cold bike ride. I give Michaela the seat nearest the heater and sit myself. Professor McKnight settles behind his desk and I find myself, once again, handing over Dad's letter.

This is probably the opposite of what Dad meant with the whole "blood is thicker than water" thing. As I watch the Professor scan the page, I realize I don't care. I trust him more than my dad any day.

"Jace, did you already reply to this letter?" Professor McKnight asks.

"Yeah, I gave an answer to Forsworth this afternoon. Seemed like a good way to get rid of him."

"Indeed. And what did you say?"

"I said that of course I was devoted to him and the good of mankind. But how weird is it that I'd ever have to tell my dad that, right?"

"Jace, Kessa sent us some disturbing news with her Christmas gifts. I'd be interested in your interpretation of what it could mean."

"Ok. Sure."

Michaela pulls a letter, a card and a pen out of her bag and puts it on the desk. Professor McKnight takes a letter from a drawer and hands it to me.

I read his letter, then Michaela's. I love that Kessa thinks Michaela and I are good for each other. The idea that Professor McKnight read her advice about setting boundaries makes me squirm.

I read the poem last. It's nice and all. When I'm done, I pick up the pen and look at it. Looks like a fancy pen to me. Michaela and Professor McKnight watch me expectantly, and I'm not sure what to say.

"So, my dad's note is still the weirdest, right?"

Professor McKnight gives a polite chuckle.

"Did you notice anything of interest in Kessa's letters, Jace?"

I feel my face heat, thinking of the "boundaries" we've already crossed.

"Nope?" I say. "What am I missing?"

Michaela's shoulders relax, and Professor McKnight lets out a long breath.

"Jace, is your father a religious man?" he asks.

I can't stop my laugh. "Only in the sense that he thinks he's God."

Professor McKnight nods. "Michaela, may I explain what we've put together or would you prefer to?"

"Go ahead," Michaela says. She reaches out and takes my hand.

"Jace, we believe that your father may have created an army."

"A what?" I ask. That's the last thing I expected to hear.

"As you know, Kessa's long-term boyfriend died last year on an exploration trip to Kansas City. His body, and the body of his best friend, were found burnt beyond recognition in their jeep at the bottom of a ravine."

"It's why Kessa decided to stay in Salida, right?" I ask.

"Yes, it was." Professor McKnight has picked up the pen, and seems to be contemplating it. "I saw no need for exploration. I'm not an ambitious man, and El Dorado Springs has the technology and population we need to carry on indefinitely. The risk didn't seem worth it, and I've never had much sense of adventure.

"There's a contingent here that feels differently, and both Evan and Kessa were part of it. They'd been pushing for this excursion, and while I have much influence, ultimately it wasn't my decision. When Evan and Marcus didn't return, I wept for my friends who mourned their sons, while thanking God that Kessa had ultimately chosen to honor my wishes and stay home.

"My letter from Kessa contains no hidden messages except the name 'Buttercup' which was used by our family as a code that we needed extraction from an awkward conversation or situation. That and the instruction towards the gift she'd given Michaela."

I glance at the pen that still just looks like a pen to me. Professor McKnight holds it up.

"This is just a pen," he says. "But it was also Evan's, and it was very important to him. Can you see why that might make a difference, Jace, in this context?"

I think back through what I'd read, knowing I'm missing something.

"The Writer lives," Michaela says under her breath.

"What?"

Professor McKnight repeats it. "*The Writer lives, the past forgotten, Alive beyond doubt or hope.*"

I pick up the poem, re-reading the lines. "How is that possible? I thought you found his body."

"We found two bodies," Professor McKnight says. "One was wearing Evan's cross, the other a bracelet that Marcus always wore. We had no reason to believe it would be anyone besides them in Evan's car. But Kessa seems to be saying not only that Evan is alive, but that he has no memory."

"You've got to be kidding me."

"I am not."

"So, Evan's alive, and maybe Marcus too for all we know. Someone set it up to look like they're dead. And Evan has some sort of amnesia. Am I following this?"

"Yes."

"So where does the army come in? Or my dad?" Not that I feel any need to defend him.

"I was relieved to hear that your father is not a religious man," Professor McKnight says, "because Kessa also put a message into the Bible verse. The one she quoted isn't in Chronicles. It's in Proverbs, and she knew Michaela knew that."

Professor McKnight passes a Bible to me, and I look at a page with a single verse underlined. It's something about warriors and their commander.

"That's kind of random, yeah?" I ask.

"It's not one I've ever noticed before," Professor McKnight says. "But King Uzziah was King of Judah, which Kessa calls the land of her exile, whereas Judah would have actually been the Israelite homeland. I can only guess that she wanted us to know that it was the 'king' of Salida who has amassed an army."

"You think my dad has an army under his control? Is it somehow connected to Evan being alive and having no memory? How would Kessa even know that?"

"We don't know," Professor McKnight says. "Honestly, there's only enough information to create questions, not enough to answer them. I was hoping you might have something to add."

"If Dad has an army, he didn't tell me about it, but I wouldn't put it past him. And his latest note sounds like he's finally lost it." I consider stopping there, but I'm in this now. "He sent me a gun the first time Forsworth came through."

"He sent you a gun?" Michaela squeaks. She sounds as freaked out as I feel.

"Yeah. Merry Christmas, right? I hid it in my closet, with the bullets in my drawer. Professor McKnight, that was right before I came to see you the first time. Dad wanted me to find out if Evan's death would get in the way of exploring the cities. And he said he's coming with a delegation in mid-March."

"And he sent a gun."

"Yeah."

"I'd like to see that letter at some point, if that's all right, Jace. But for now I need you to tell me if you think your father would ever be a threat to Kessa."

I take a minute to think about it. This is a big deal and my normal saying whatever comes into my head isn't what he needs. Michaela's leg bounces beside me, and despite the whole "my psycho father might have an army" thing, I'm glad I finally know what was wrong.

"I don't think he'd hurt Kessa, sir. I've never known my dad to use physical violence. If he can get what he wants with charm or social pressure, he always does that first. I'm sure her being with Adam is enough for him."

"And if they were no longer together?"

"I still don't think he'd do anything to her physically. Honestly, I don't think he'd see her as a threat. He's like that with women."

Professor McKnight relaxes into his chair.

From beside me Michaela says "Like what with women?"

I shrug. "He underestimates them. Treats them like pretty dolls. It's probably his biggest blind spot."

"We can use that," Michaela says. The professor is already nodding.

"Do you think Forsworth's left town?" Professor McKnight asks. "Michaela might need to send a letter back to Kessa. You know those chatty teenage girls."

"Forsworth won't want to camp an extra night if he can drink and sleep in a bed, but I bet he'll leave early. I can check the bar and make sure he waits for Michaela's letter. But if Henry hears I was there, you're backing me up."

Professor McKnight manages a small smile with his nod.

I glance at my watch. "We're actually supposed to be eating with the Douglases in about five minutes."

"It's probably time we brought them into this," Professor McKnight says. "Why don't you and Michaela head there now, with a quick bar stop on the way. I'll be over when their kids go down and we can talk more."

Michaela and I agree and go outside to our bikes.

"So, this is why things have been off the last week, right?"

She nods, and I give a sigh of relief.

"I'm sorry I couldn't tell you, Jace. And I didn't think you were in on anything with your dad, but Professor McKnight wasn't completely sure, so he said we needed to be safe."

"You thought I'd be in on something with my dad?" I ask, and I'm sure the hurt comes through in my voice because her eyes are panicky.

"No," she says, shaking her head. "I just said I didn't. I trust you, Jace. Always."

I force a smile, but she sees through it. Michaela grabs my jacket and pulls me down so I'm looking her right in the eyes.

"Jace Morton, I trust you with my life and with everything that's important to me. You're a million times better of a man than your father will ever be. And I love you."

It's great to hear her say that, but it doesn't change who I am. I know I'm a screw up. Why didn't I tell someone when Dad sent me that first letter? If Forsworth's left town it's going to complicate things even more.

"I love you, too, Kayla," I say, and I give her a soft kiss on the lips.

I don't know why a girl this amazing has chosen to be with me. I squeeze her hand and give her a big super-hero grin.

"We're off to save the world, one bar-stop at a time" I say.

But her smile back is as fake as mine.

Chapter 46 - Michaela

We made a quick stop by the only truly seedy bar in town and Forsworth agreed to take my letter to Kessa.

"Anything for such a cute little bite."

The memory makes my skin crawl. We were only slightly late to dinner at the Douglases, and I'm helping Anne Marie clean up when Professor McKnight and my mom arrive.

"Sorry we didn't knock. I didn't want to wake the kids," the professor says.

A peal of giggles sounds from the bedrooms where Jace is "helping" Henry with nighttime routines.

"Looks like we could have been polite after all," my mom says, giving me a hug.

"You both know you're always welcome. But you can't see the kids tonight or they'll never sleep." Anne Marie hangs her towel on the sink. "Can I get you some tea?"

We talk about nothing until Jace and Henry join us. Then Professor McKnight lays out our thoughts along with each item that led us to those conclusions. Henry and Anne Marie read the letters and poem, eyes straying to Evan's pen on the table.

"Henry, you've met Jace's father. What do you think of all of this?" the professor asks.

Henry thinks before replying. "Richard Morton was all charm. He seemed like a man on a mission regarding city exploration, but there was nothing to cause alarm or I would never have condoned Kessa staying. Now I suppose it's good she did."

"What do you mean?" Jace asks. "Isn't Kessa being there a problem at this point?"

"Kessa's smart. She knows how to handle herself," Henry says. "And if she didn't stay, we would have been completely blindsided when whatever this is played out."

"I agree," says Professor McKnight. "I assume that's what she meant when her letter referenced things happening for a reason. Kessa knows that a belief in God's providence has always governed my life. I hope she now sees it in her own as well."

Oh, God, let Jace hear this. He needs to know he's here for a reason too.

I'm praying without realizing it and have to reorient myself to the conversation. Henry is looking at Jace's watch, and as he removes the back cover he lets out a low whistle.

"Man, I was hoping I was wrong," Henry says. "Hold on." He goes to a cabinet, quickly returning with tweezers. Carefully he pulls a small vial of liquid from the inside of the watch.

"What is that?" Jace asks.

The professor has taken the watch now and is looking at the mechanisms inside. "It looks like the watch has a remote trigger," he says.

"What does that mean?" I ask.

"It means whoever holds the remote could cause this vial to be injected into the wearer with the push of a button," Professor McKnight says.

Jace's face crumples. "My dad was going to poison me?"

"I don't think it's poison," Henry says. "My guess is a tranquilizer."

Am I the only person watching Jace as this unfolds? His eyebrows are drawn, lips pinched. A muscle twitches in his clenched jaw.

"What made you think to look for that?" my mom asks Henry.

"It was the paratrooper reference. I saw a history channel special that showed these. They were a last resort for soldiers who could choose the injection over capture."

"So I could have been messing around with my watch and unintentionally knocked myself out?" Jace asks, voice cracking.

"I don't think so," says the Professor. "That feature's been modified for the remote trigger."

"God forbid I do it accidentally and F- up Dad's plans," Jace says. Between the bitterness and the language all eyes are on him now. "Sorry. I've gotta go."

Jace stands abruptly and heads down the hall to his room. I want to follow, but Anne Marie stops me with a hand on my arm.

"It's a lot, Michaela. Give him a minute."

Professor McKnight suggests we start on my letter to Kessa, but all I can think about is Jace. The look on his face when he first saw the vial. How much he's hurting right now. I've contributed nothing, and after a couple of minutes and some glances between Anne Marie and my mom I'm allowed to leave. With barely a nod I rush down the hall.

Deep breath. *Lord, help me.*

My knock gets a muffled response, and I let myself in. My beautiful boyfriend sits on the bed, staring down at the gun in his hands.

"Hey," I say.

Jace doesn't look up as I close the door behind me.

"Is that the gun your dad sent?" I ask, sitting beside him on the bed.

"Yeah," Jace says. "It isn't loaded."

"That's a relief. Guns freak me out."

"Me too." Jace says. We're silent. Eventually he continues. "How did I not know any of this was going on? And seriously, what kind of dad has a plan to take out his son if he gets in the way?"

"Maybe the kind who's building an amnesiac army?"

"Is that what we're thinking now? I mean, he's got an army. And we know Evan doesn't have a memory, but are they all like that?"

"I don't know. I feel like we hardly know anything. But it seems like the more we find out the worse it gets."

"Welcome to the world of Councilor Morton."

I reach out and take the gun from Jace, placing it carefully on the side table. His hands are curled into fists now, but I take the one closest to me, and lay it's back on my thigh. I uncurl it, smoothing my fingers over his palm and down.

"Your dad sucks. But I love you. And God loves you. And the Douglases and Professor McKnight and my mom all do, too. No one blames you for any of this."

"Yeah, well, that's great. But it doesn't change anything. How could he send me here and expect me to betray everyone on his command?"

"I don't know."

"I mean, who does that? And wasn't the swap your town's idea? Was he planning this army thing anyway and throwing his son into the mix was an afterthought? I mean, he's my dad. What if you guys had decided to hold me hostage when you found out? Did he even think of that?"

I don't know what to say to any of this, but I think of what Professor McKnight was saying about God's providence and go with it.

"Jace, your dad had plans, but so did God. You were supposed to be here. Without the swap, your dad could have shown up with an army and we would have had no warning at all."

"Seems like God could have made this plan a lot simpler if he'd stopped my dad from making an army in the first place."

"He could have stopped the pandemic too. And a million awful things that happened before it. I don't know why He didn't, except that He lets people make their own choices."

"God should take a lesson from my dad," Jace says with a humorless laugh.

"You wouldn't want that."

"Right now I would."

Jace's head is down now, fists in his hair. I lay my head against his shoulder and we're quiet for a minute before he breaks the silence.

"I've never been good enough for my dad. I want to believe in this God you and Henry talk about, but I can't be good enough for Him either."

My heart hurts. I turn and wrap my arms around this amazing boy that I love so much.

"You don't have to be good enough, Jace. That's the whole point."

I want to go get the Professor or Henry, but then I hear the whisper. *You've got this, my love.* All the anxiety washes from my body. It's time.

"God is Holy, Jace. Everything about Him is perfect and pure and beautiful. Compared to Him, none of us is good. We can't even exist in His presence."

Jace doesn't joke or put on his mask. Instead, eyes intent, he says, "There's got to be more. Because you all live like you know Him."

Oh, my heart.

"There is more. God knew there was nothing we could do to save ourselves, so He sent Jesus to do what we couldn't. He lived an innocent life and then took our punishment in death."

"That isn't fair."

"No, it's not. But Jesus chose it. He chose to give up His life in exchange for ours. And He offers us the same choice. We can give up our old lives and live a new life where we're connected to Him and the Father. We can live in His 'good enough.'"

Jace is silent. Jace doesn't do silence.

Finally he says "I want to know that kind of God."

I can't help the grin that spreads over my face. "Then we pray."

"What do I say?"

"Just talk to him." I shrug. "He's a person, not a math problem."

And so Jace prays. It's simple and a little goofy and self-conscious. But it's real. And this boy I love will never be the same.

CHAPTER 47 - JAERISH

"I have a little sister," Patner says. "She's nearly a woman by now."

My body is stiff from two days tied to this chair with minimal bathroom breaks. Having this much time to process has made one thing clear.

"How are we going to kill Forsworth?" I ask out loud.

"Slow down," Radley says from across the room. "I'm ready to believe you, but we need to think this through before we move on it."

"My name's Houston," Patner says. "My sister just said so. We lived on a cattle ranch." He grins. "I think I'm a Texan."

"You would be," I say with a laugh. As horrifying as this whole thing is, there's something about being in it with my crew again. I'm not alone anymore.

Radley scoffs from his position near the windows. "Evan and Houston, huh? Y'all got some pansy names. I'm sticking with the ones the camp gave you."

"We should probably do that anyway to make sure we don't slip up in front of anyone else," I say. "So when are you untying us?"

Radley's brows lower. Finally he says "I'll untie you both if you swear you won't take off. I'm hiding the keys and your weapons, and if I think you're looking for them, I end you. Understood?"

"Yep," I say.

"Got it," from Patner. Houston.

When Radley leaves I turn to Patner. "Houston's not a pansy name," I say.

"I wouldn't care if it were. I never thought I'd know my name again, let alone my family. Am I going to remember everything?"

"I can."

Patner's eyes are closed, head laid back, when he says "I don't think Cacia will like it if I've got a girl back home."

"Adam didn't like it much."

"Bro. That had to be hell."

"It was, but I couldn't remember anything specific then. It's worse now."

Radley comes back and starts untying Patner.

"Do we get to tie you up while you go off the pills?" Patner asks.

"Who says I'm going off?"

"Why wouldn't you?" Patner says. "Don't you want to know who you are?"

"I know who I am. I've been the same person for fifteen years now, and I've got enough to deal with. Besides, I can't imagine I've got a home to go back to at this point."

"Your call," I say. "How long do we wait for Open Sky before we start worrying?"

"Why would we worry?" Patner asks.

"Because, if Morton's behind all of this, and Open Sky starts asking questions, he might not be as safe in Salida as we thought," I say.

"I'm not sure I care as much about his safety as I thought either," Patner says. "He might have been in on this whole thing with Morton."

Radley's eyes narrow in the tense silence that follows. I'm glad we're already untied.

"We have to allow for both possibilities," I say. "We can't travel right now regardless."

We all look to the enormous windows where a dawning sun glints off ice stretching to the horizon.

The sun has set but still Radley paces by the windows like a caged panther. His patience melted away with the ice, and he's spent the day scanning the brown stretches of field for Open Sky. Patner and I play cards and ignore him. When Radley leaves to check the front doors yet again, Patner speaks in a rough whisper.

"We need to find our weapons. There's no way in hell I'm going back on that pill. Or back to the army."

"If Radley catches you looking, he'll end you."

"Maybe they can tell everyone we died and let us leave," Patner says, laying an ace on my king. "They wouldn't want us spreading the word about Forsworth and the pills at camp."

"Yeah, well, they wouldn't want us telling anyone else about an army either. The only reason we're alive right now is because Radley doesn't act without orders. Once Open Sky's here, all bets are off." His ten falls to my queen.

"Then we're back to needing weapons." Patner's quiet as he shuffles his deck. "We could take out Radley now, while he's alone."

"I can't do that when he hasn't moved on us."

"I could. With getting back to my family at stake. We could both be back where we belong in just a few days. Open Sky wouldn't even know what happened."

"Could you live with not telling the guys at camp? Besides, Cacia isn't going to move to Texas with you after knowing you a month, and you can't stay in Salida with Morton."

We play in silence until Radley returns.

"Open Sky should be here by now, even with the storm," he says. "We give him one more day then go back to Salida to find out what's happening."

I look at Patner then back at Radley.

"We take three days," I say. "And the only way we're doing this is if you go off the pill."

Radley looks between us.

"Two days. You want to tie me up?"

"No need," I say. "The only one you'll be a danger to is Forsworth."

And maybe Open Sky, I think. But I don't say it.

CHAPTER 48 - KESSA

WHEN I OPEN THE door, Richard Morton's on my porch. Adam stands behind him. If the dark shadows under his eyes are any indication, the two days since I last saw him have been as hard on him as they have on me.

"Kessa," Morton says, "I'm glad to see you up and around. I thought it time we continued our conversation from the other evening. Couldn't stand to see my boy moping any longer."

Morton steps past me, his presence shrinking my house like a wizard in a hobbit hole.

"I was actually just leaving," I say. "They're expecting me at the lab."

"Priorities, dear," Morton says, surveying the room then making himself at home in my armchair. Reluctantly I close the door and sit on the sofa. Adam takes the seat beside me, leaving a good ten inches between us. I look to Morton expectantly.

"I'm sure the events of New Year's Eve were unsettling," he begins. It's a ludicrous understatement, but I don't reply. "My only intention that night was to have a private conversation regarding Jaerish and his claims. Obviously Open Sky's presence complicated matters."

"Is Open Sky all right?" I ask.

Morton's eyes widen. "Of course he's all right," he says. "Why wouldn't he be?"

"Are you kidding? I saw you carry his unconscious body to a hidden room. You tell me?"

"Kessa, what do you think of me? Open Sky had too much to drink. He came into my office making wild accusations and then passed out on the ground. Adam and I carried him downstairs to sleep it off."

"Yeah, downstairs through a bookshelf and a locked, coded door."

"That room is nothing sinister. It's just a saferoom and not even a secret one. Adam, Jace and even Cacia used to play there all the time as children."

I look to Adam and he nods. "It was our fort until dad decided we were too old."

I have a momentary spark of jealousy about Adam's shared history with Cacia, but I shove it aside and refocus on now.

"I saw you handcuff Open Sky to the couch."

Morton brushes that away like it's nothing. "It was for his own safety. He was intoxicated and I couldn't stay to babysit him. We spoke the next morning, when he was sober, and everything's fine. Open Sky returned to Salida alone because he had suspicions regarding Jaerish that he wanted to discuss."

"I want to talk to Open Sky," I say.

"That's not possible. He left after our conversation. As I mentioned the other night, this goes beyond just you. Open Sky has an insurrectionist to deal with."

Dread settles on me as I think of Open Sky "dealing with" Evan. I run my fingertips along the creases in my pants as I focus on keeping my expression blank.

"What about the blue pill and their memories?" I ask.

"Open Sky knew nothing of either. I'm afraid those were fabrications. Lies."

"I'm sorry Kessa," Adam says from beside me. "This has to be hard to hear."

Adam believes his dad. Of course he does. Who would believe in an army of drugged, kidnapped amnesiacs when there was a more logical explanation? Could I have been fooled by someone who looked like Evan? No. NO. Evan is alive. But I can't process this now. Because now I need to convince Morton I believe him. I fold my fidgeting hands together and lean forward.

"I appreciate you telling me this, Richard. But I do have one question you haven't resolved. Why did you keep the army a secret rather than tell El Dorado Springs, especially once we started the swap? An army's a big deal."

"It is, Kessa. I agree. And I should have been upfront about it. I've been keeping this secret for a very long time, and beginnings are fragile things. I didn't want a perceived imbalance of power to complicate matters, and as I understand it, though your technology has advanced in remarkable ways, none of that research has gone in a military direction."

Unfortunately, Morton is right, although I don't know how he got that information. The sheer size of our town had negated the need for protection beyond a largely inactive militia and some physical barriers.

"Are there any other questions I can answer for you, Kessa?" Morton asks.

"No. I just need to process. I'm sorry I didn't come to you sooner."

"Entirely forgiven," Morton says with a benevolent nod. If he were closer, he'd be patting my hand. "Seeing Jaerish, with his resemblance to your deceased boyfriend, must have been a shock. I regret that he caused you such pain and uncertainty. But now things can get back on track. Please, in the future, seek me out when problems arise. I'm always here for you."

Morton stands but motions Adam and me to remain seated.

"I'll stop by the lab and tell them you'll be late, Kessa. The two of you have things to resolve. Please don't be too hard on Adam. He had your best in mind."

As soon as the door closes Adam rises and watches his dad through the window blinds. I have no idea what to say. I won't lie to him again, but anything I say now will sound like I'm pining for a con man.

After a few moments Adam turns around and takes a deep breath. "He's gone. The liar."

Wait, what?

"Adam?"

"I'm sorry I didn't believe you in the first place." Adam's expression is tight, his eyes sad. "I had to step back, try to see it from the outside. Of course you would know if it was Evan."

My whole world shifts back into place. I join Adam at the window and sag into him as he wraps his arms around me. For a while I just stand and breathe.

"So what now?" I ask.

"If Dad's telling the truth about Open Sky, we need to warn Evan. And then we have to make sure El Dorado Springs knows there's an army."

"I think I took care of the last part," I say, telling him about the messages coded in my Christmas gifts.

"You're brilliant, Kessa," Adam says. "It's a good thing Jace is the one in El Dorado Springs. He won't hesitate to tell them how awful our dad is. I'd have been defending him."

"And you wouldn't be here with me." Adam leans in for a distracted kiss.

"You'd probably have hooked up with Cole," he says.

I bark out a laugh, his lips still on mine. It's awkward and he chuckles along with me.

"You know, Cole's not a bad idea."

"What?" Adam asks, the laugh still in his voice.

"Cole was Jace's best friend, right? His opinion of your dad can't be that great. He might believe us if we told him what your dad's doing."

"What would that get us?"

"Maybe he could warn Evan. Or even go to El Dorado Springs."

"I don't think Cole's ever left Salida, but he's talked about it a lot." Adam's nodding now. "If he did go, no one would question it. Cole's a great idea." Adam pauses, absently running his thumb along my arm, then asks "Are we ok?"

I burrow into him.

"We're ok. I should have trusted you while Evan was still here. We could have worked together and come up with a better plan."

"That wouldn't have been awkward," Adam says. "We'd have figured it out though. When I saw him kissing you and thought he was some lying creep, I was so angry I almost punched him right there. I would have if I'd been sure you would choose me. Now that I know Jaerish is Evan, I'm terrified of losing you. But I'll help you, either way."

Adam is peering into me, his deep blue eyes hopeful and vulnerable.

"I love you, Adam. I'm choosing you. That isn't going to change."

I cup his face with my hands and draw him into a drawn-out kiss.

"OK," he says, his forehead resting on mine. "Now we tell Cole."

Chapter 49 - Jaerish

I drive the truck over pitted grey highway through stretches of barren fields, then foothills, and then mountains. Beside me Radley is silent. Staring. He's done little else the past two days as his memory returned. Patner snores in the backseat.

With each mile closer to Kessa the dread settles deeper. I put a fist to my chest, pressing at the anxiety gathered there. Radley glances my way but doesn't ask.

How could I have left her there? Now that I remember Kessa from before, the unafraid, open, teasing girl she was, I can see how my death broke her. And I left her alone with a madman. And his son.

We're crossing a scrub-filled valley when a bright red jeep appears between us and the ragged mountains. I pull to the roadside, angled for a quick exit. When the SUV doesn't divert its course, Radley motions for us to switch seats. Patner is awake now, and we all have weapons available, but nothing drawn.

The Jeep pulls up alongside us. The driver is young, maybe eighteen if that. Dark skinned. He jerks his head in a nod.

"S'up," he says, like this is his first trip out of town and he has no idea it's a big bad world out here. He looks past Radley to me. "You Evan?"

Radley shoots a glance my way.

"You know him?" he asks.

"Nope."

At that Radley pulls a gun and the kid's hands fly into the air.

"Whoa, whoa, whoa," he says. "What's that all about?"

"I'm just wondering why you're calling my buddy here Evan when that's not his name. And besides, he says he doesn't know you."

"Bro, my mistake. Obviously, I've got the wrong person. I'll just move on. No harm, no foul."

"I think not, son," Radley says.

By this point Patner is opening the jeep's passenger door and sliding in beside the boy.

"Wouldn't want you to think of taking off," Patner says. "Until we get to talk."

The kid floors it and the jeep speeds forward about fifty feet before skidding to a stop. Radley raises a brow my way then drives to where Patner's half out of the jeep and tugging the teenager's body into the passenger seat.

"He's alive, right?" I ask.

Patner scoffs. "He's fine. Let's get somewhere out of the way and camp like we planned. Then we can figure out how the kid knows your name."

I join Patner in the jeep in case the kid wakes up, and we drive West for a couple more hours. As the light fades we park under the cover of a pine forest. The cold, scented air fills my lungs and relieves some of the pressure.

The kid doesn't wake up as I drag him from the vehicle and lay his slumped body against my pack. Soon I have the fire going and Patner puts folded foil packets with our dinner into the flames. Radley pitches the tent, but still the kid sleeps on.

"How hard did you hit him?" I ask Patner.

"I didn't. Just a little knock-out juice. He should be back anytime."

"He's been awake for the last five minutes listening to you fools talk," Radley says. "Kid's not quite as naïve as I thought. Are you, kid?" he asks.

"Naïve's a new one," he says sitting up and stretching his bound arms in front of him.

"Why you listening to us, Kid?" Patner asks.

"We making S'mores?" he replies with a nod at Radley who's sharpening a stick for no apparent reason.

"Nah," Patner says. "I thought I'd go ahead and pierce my tongue like yours. You inspired me."

The kid sticks out his tongue and clicks the bar between his teeth. "The chicks dig it," he says with a cocky grin.

"Kid," Patner says, "you get that you're in the middle of the woods with three armed men who just drugged you and took you to a secondary location, right?"

"I do. Not my day." He sighs. "And it started so well."

I'm honestly impressed by the kid's stones at this point, but I can tell Radley's not. If he clenches his jaw any harder, he's going to break a molar.

"How about this," I say. "You tell us why you're looking for someone named Evan, and we'll see if we can help you find him. Assuming Radley there doesn't kill you. He's having a bad day too."

The kid looks at Radley who continues making stroke after smooth stroke with his knife. Looking back to me he says "Sure, man. Any chance you could untie my hands first? And maybe we could eat?"

Radley reaches out, quick as a viper, and slices his ropes. I roll my shoulders. The tension has returned, and from what I can tell this kid has a death wish.

"Food can wait," I say.

"Take me somewhere these two aren't listening and I'll tell you anything you want to hear."

"You're in no position to bargain. But I'll do it because Radley gets grumpy when he has to clean blood off his stuff."

I walk the kid away from the fire. When we're a decent distance he says "The name's Cole. And you, my new friend, are most definitely Evan. Kessa said if you didn't believe she sent me to tell you there's a mitten-shaped birthmark on your left thigh. That way even if your memory didn't return you can check my story."

"Who's Kessa?" I ask.

"Whatever man. We don't have time for this. Stuff's going down."

It's obvious Kessa sent this kid. I drop the act.

"Is she safe?"

"She was when I left, but Morton knows she's on to him. She's pretending to believe the bull he's spouting, but that won't last."

A glance towards the campfire tells me my time alone with Cole is short.

"What about Open Sky? Is he still working with Morton?"

"Kessa said they argued on New Year's Eve, and Morton locked him in a basement. But later he told her Open Sky was just drunk and they worked it out. Said he left town to go deal with you because you work for some bad dudes up North."

I knead the back of my neck.

"How long ago did Open Sky leave?"

"Maybe four days? But Kessa doesn't believe it. She and Adam think he's still in the basement, and they're going to get back down there as soon as they can."

"Adam? What do you mean Adam?"

"You know, Adam. Her boyfriend."

"She told him?"

"Adam's a good guy. If you care about this girl you should be glad she's got someone there. Especially since you left."

I want to punch the little punk, but he's right.

"So, Kessa sent you to find me. Then what?"

"I was going to Kessa's dad. Finding you was a happy accident, except for the kidnapping part. Kessa figured once I got to El Dorado Springs, they'd figure out how to warn you. Plus then I can catch up with my bro, Jace, and check out the ladies."

"Did you really just say that?" I ask.

"Say what?"

"You're on your way to tell the leader of the biggest town left on this continent that a madman with an army of brainwashed soldiers is holding his daughter captive. How are you thinking about 'checking out ladies?'"

"Cause I'll be the hero," Cole shrugs. "And heroes always get the girl. Not that that was ever a problem."

I can't believe I'm having this conversation.

"Think dinner's ready?" Cole asks. "It's cold out here."

"I've still got questions."

"If you trust those guys, I'll spill whatever you want. If you feed me."

Cole and I rejoin Patner and Radley around the fire. True to his word, Cole answers every question we ask around bites of venison and swigs from his canteen.

"So, who's going with the kid?" I ask.

"I've got this," Cole insists, but the grown-ups ignore him.

"You know it should be you," Patner says. "It's not even a question."

"I'm not abandoning Kessa again."

"You didn't abandon her the first time. Besides, you think she's going to be happy you came back instead of warning El Dorado Springs?"

I set my jaw and lock eyes with Patner across the fire. I know I'm the obvious choice, but I won't do it. Patner looks away.

"If you two don't resolve this," Radley says, voice low and measured, "I will end whoever would be least helpful in retrieving Open Sky. El Dorado Springs can burn for all I care."

It's Cole who breaks the silence.

"Kessa seemed happy with Adam. And she knows you're alive."

I tell Cole what he can do with his observation. If Kessa's happy with Adam, there's no way in hell I'm leaving them there alone.

Finally, Patner stands. "Kid, you're with me. We drive early, so sleep now."

I stare into the flames long after everyone else is down for the night. It's no problem to take first watch; I wouldn't be sleeping anyway.

Will my parents understand why I didn't go to them? Everything makes sense if I do. The pain they must be in is almost enough to change my mind. Almost.

Even the next morning, as we pack up and head in opposite directions, I wonder if I'm making a mistake. I guess I'm more like Radley than I thought though, because if it comes down to Kessa or El Dorado Springs, the town can burn.

CHAPTER 50 - KESSA

"AH, KESSA. WHAT A lovely surprise."

I'm sitting on the Morton's front porch, working at the twisted tongue of my shoe while I wait on Adam for our run. My back stiffens before I can stop it, and I attempt to cover with a stretch and shoulder roll. Standing, I greet Richard Morton with a big smile.

"Good morning, Richard. Great day for January, isn't it?"

"Indeed," Morton says. "We have these gems periodically to remind us that all hope for a glorious spring has not abandoned the world. I just heard the shower turn on upstairs. Are you early? Why don't you come inside?"

I check my watch. I'm not early, but maybe I confused the time. While I don't want to go inside, our current gameplan is pretending everything was a big misunderstanding. Which means pacifying Richard Morton. So I follow him to the kitchen and take a seat at the counter while he puts on water for tea. We talk about what it would take to mass produce my dad's solar battery and I silently will Adam to hurry up.

Morton offers me milk and honey, and he must load it up because it's so sweet I feel like I'm drinking candy. But its warmth is soothing, and I can feel my anxiety slipping away. I cover my yawn with one hand and am thinking maybe I'll take a quick nap while I wait for Adam when I look up at Morton. He's nodding slowly, a pained expression on his face.

My head is foggy as I swim back to consciousness. I snuggle into the soft pillow, thinking I'll rest just a little longer, when I smell something. Bacon. I can wake up for bacon. But when I open my eyes nothing is familiar.

Getting out of the bed, I see my shoes on a chair beside a closed door. The handle turns silently and I peek my head out. I'm in Morton's saferoom. Adam is frying bacon in the kitchenette. Open Sky sits on the couch, bent nearly double, head in his hands.

What's going on? I rub my fingertips across my eyes and take in a shaky breath.

"Hey," I say, surprised by how normal my voice sounds.

Adam takes the pan off of the heat and comes to me.

"Hey," he says, cupping my face to look into my eyes then drawing me into a hug. Which is nice and all, but I stiffen and pull back to look at him.

"Adam, what's going on?"

His mouth is pinched as he pushes a hand through his hair. He sighs.

"My dad put us here. He tricked me and drugged you and now we're trapped."

"What?" My heart sinks. "Did they catch Cole?"

"They didn't catch him, but they know about him."

Before Adam can say more the door to the saferoom opens and Morton walks in followed by a short, greasy man with a gun. At first I think Morton himself is in trouble, but then he turns to the man and says "Do you think that's necessary?"

The man assesses us then slides the gun into his belt. Apparently, we're not a threat.

"Kessa, so glad you're awake," Morton says in that friendly chat voice I despise. "I apologize for taking such drastic measures to get you here, but Forsworth overheard Jace's worthless friend conspiring with Jaerish, who's now headed this way. I wouldn't want you running into him on the street. For your own good of course."

"You're insane," I say, incredulous. "You just drugged me. Are you seriously going to try to keep up the façade of benevolent ruler? You are literally a madman."

Morton sighs. "People of small ideas cannot be expected to see the big picture. And you're a woman." He shrugs. "I won't hold your lack of vision against you, my dear." Before I can sputter a reply he continues. "I'm going to need to ask the three of you to move into the bedroom. I'm expecting more guests."

"Like hell I'm moving into the bedroom," I say. "Why would I do that? Why would I ever do anything you want?"

"The simple answer, dear, is that Forsworth has the gun. But if you need something else, you will see that my desire to keep you safe is key in negotiating with your father. A fail-safe in case the army isn't incentive enough."

"It's Open Sky's army," I say, but a glance in his direction melts my defiance. Morton also looks at the pale, crumpled man on his couch then back to me.

"Kessa darling, you're smarter than that. It's always been my army. Now, into the bedroom. And I'm thinking I can't trust you to keep your mouths shut, so we'll take care of that as well. Forsworth."

Adam, who's remained silent to this point, turns to his dad.

"Dad, we've got the swap and new trade relationships with El Dorado Springs. Why are you bringing the army into play now?"

"Son, do you truly think El Dorado Springs is going to allow things to continue as they were once they find out how my army's been established?

I don't know what Open Sky was thinking bringing those men along, especially one who'd been with the camp for such a short time, but it has ruined everything."

"Well, Dad, seeing as he didn't remember why he shouldn't you can't blame him, now can you? I guess that's what happens when you keep your pawns in the dark." I dart a look at Adam, wondering what he's talking about, but his attention is solely on his father.

Morton motions to Forsworth who takes Open Sky's arm and leads him into the bedroom. As soon as they're out of sight I bolt for the exit. I pull the door hard, but it doesn't budge. Morton hasn't moved, and neither has Adam.

"From the inside it uses voice recognition," Adam says. "And dad's reprogrammed it only to respond to him."

Forsworth, Morton's toady, comes back out smirking. "Who's next?"

As Adam and I walk back together, a strange peace settles over me. My dad has never let me down. Cole is on his way, so El Dorado Springs will be warned. There's nothing left to do.

The peace vanishes when I see Open Sky tied to the desk chair, his mouth gagged.

Forsworth is shaking the headboard, and he must decide it's solid enough. "Looks like I'm doin you a favor, Adam," he says, leering. He motions to the bed with his gun. "Up you go."

Morton followed us in and Forsworth hands him the weapon while he ties first Adam's and then my hands together, securing us to opposite sides of the headboard.

"Huh. I guess not quite a favor. But you could still play footsie, I suppose," the creepy little man says. I try to kick him but he jumps back with a laugh. "I knew you'd be a wildcat in the sack," he says, winking at me and earning scowls from Adam and Morton alike.

I tell him what I think of him ever getting a real woman into bed and he just tsks and ties a gag around my mouth. Right before he leaves, he tosses a pink envelope onto the dresser.

"That's from Jace's little girlfriend. It'll help you pass the time once you're freed."

There's nothing we can do but watch as they leave the room, closing the door behind them.

Chapter 51 - Jaerish

Radley and I parked outside of town and hiked in, hoping to avoid Morton's notice for as long as possible. We're on a side street, nearly to Kessa's house, when a familiar female voice cuts the air.

"Radley! Jaerish!"

Cacia, unaware of our need for caution, is calling to us from twenty feet away. I turn and smile, putting a finger to my lips and motioning her our way. She tilts her head and wrinkles her brow, but complies.

When she's close, she stage-whispers "So why are we being quiet?"

I force a little laugh. "Because we aren't supposed to be back in town." I act like it's a joke, but I don't think she's buying it.

"Where's Patner?" she asks, looking around like he'll suddenly materialize. I feel Radley tense beside me and try to move this along.

"He's not here. But he sends his love."

Cacia blushes. Shoot. They might not be there yet. Whatever. I've got more to worry about than Patner's love life.

"So, where are you headed?" Cacia says, walking along with us. I wish Radley would give her one of his trademark scowls and send her running.

But he likes Cacia. We both do. And a fleeing female would probably draw attention we don't need.

"We're on our way to Kessa's," I say. "There's something we need to ask her about."

"You're going the wrong direction then. I saw her headed to Adam's house less than an hour ago. They jog, among other things." I refuse to acknowledge what her smile implies.

"Thanks," I say. "We might wait for them at Kessa's anyway. It's probably best that Richard Morton not know we're here."

Cacia's gaze holds questions now, and Radley shoots me a look.

"You'll keep this on the downlow for us, won't you C?" Radley asks. I don't know when he started calling her C, but she smirks.

"Yeah, yeah. I've got your back," she says and something I don't catch passes between them.

"Thanks, Cuz," he says with a little nod.

She kind of half laughs and rolls her eyes then says "I've gotta go to work anyway."

"Anything you want me to pass along to Patner?" I ask.

Cacia reaches up on tiptoes and plants a kiss on my cheek. Which I swear is now on fire. Stupid.

"That'll do," she says with a smile.

Radley smirks. "Probably won't be the same coming from Jaerish."

"Probably not," Cacia agrees. "Actually, can you stop by my place before you leave town? I've got something else to give him, and no idea when I'll get another chance."

While I'm wondering how this will affect our stealth mission, Radley agrees. He's strangely compliant where Cacia is concerned. We wave as she heads down a side street.

When we arrive at Kessa's, we find Forsworth, slouched as always, against the corner of her house.

"Hello to you, too," Forsworth says. "Is that how you greet your friends now?"

Sure enough, one of Radley's knives is in his hand.

"You have never been my friend," Radley growls.

"True," Forsworth says, unphased. "But you still don't want to do anything with that knife, pretty boy. You won't find who you're looking for without me."

My body goes cold. Does he mean Kessa or Open Sky? The fact that he's waiting for us here doesn't bode well.

Radley slips the knife back into his belt. That wouldn't slow him down if he chose to use it, but it satisfies Forsworth.

"Good," he says. "Follow me."

With that the fool turns his back on us and starts walking. I look at Radley with a raised eyebrow. Can we kill him now? Radley shakes his head and we fall into step behind Forsworth.

"We could find them some other way. It's a small town," I say.

"You could try." Forsworth doesn't even glance back.

"I know what you did to Marcus," I say.

"Marcus? Never did know his name. I guess you're smart enough to know it doesn't pay to be a hero, then, aren't you?"

That would have been the end of him, were it not for Radley's side-eye. That fast, no more Forsworth. I've played out his death a hundred ways in my mind. The old me wouldn't have approved, but the old me had a much less complicated life.

We're at Morton's house and Forsworth walks around back through the kitchen door, just like when he brought Morton the gifts from El Dorado Springs. Did he already deliver Kessa's messages and come back or was that a lie too? I don't ask.

"This would have been our next stop," I say. "Looks like we don't need you quite so much after all."

"Oh, I think you do," Forsworth says. We follow him to Morton's office where he steps behind the desk and pulls a gun from a drawer. Radley's knife is in his hand.

"It's just insurance," Forsworth says. "No need for that." He doesn't even bother telling Radley to put the knife away this time. I never knew how intensely I could hate someone's back until Forsworth turns his toward us again.

With the hand not holding the gun, Forsworth pulls a book from the shelf. It's red with gold lettering, but when he tosses it on the desk the cover says *The Art of War.* So not *The Prince*, after all, but a similar binding. No wonder Morton was suspicious.

Forsworth reaches into the space left by the book and a portion of the shelf swings out to reveal a well-lit, narrow stairwell. He leads the way down. Radley right behind him.

Suddenly Forsworth cries out and drops onto the stairs. He contorts his body in an attempt to see, or maybe reach, the dark red stain spreading beneath his right shoulder blade. The gun has fallen from his limp right hand and clattered to the ground several steps below him. Curses, crude and unoriginal, pour from his mouth.

Radley is unphased. He leans over Forsworth, bloody knife in hand, and pins his left arm to his body. Then he carves a long, clean line down Forsworth's cheek.

"Just returning the favor, pretty boy," he says. Radley straightens and without another glance continues down the stairs, picking up the gun as he passes.

Forsworth writhes on the step, moaning and attempting to reach for his shoulder with the arm that's still working. I can't leave him here and risk him taking off, but I need to know what's downstairs.

"Radley, what did you find?" I call. There's no reply.

Before I can decide what to do, Forsworth's face goes pale and he passes out. It's probably the most helpful thing he's ever done. I toss him over my shoulder, trying not to get blood on my clothes as I go down the steps.

At the bottom Radley is scowling at a complicated keypad with tech I've never seen.

"You try the knob?" I ask.

It turns easily in Radley's hand. Beyond is a cozy, well-lit apartment. Do I smell bacon?

I follow Radley in and dump Forsworth on the floor of the kitchen area. Sure enough, there's a pan of bacon congealing on the range. A loud beep sounds behind me, and I turn. The door we entered through is closed.

Morton's voice fills the space from a speaker on the wall. "I thought you were Open Sky's elite guard. You've done a rather poor job thus far."

"Where is he?" Radley growls.

"He's in the bedroom, with your other friends. I put all the vipers in one pit."

Radley is already moving towards a lone door on the far wall.

"Your man Forsworth is wounded," I say. "He needs help or he'll bleed out." I couldn't care less if he does, but it's the only card I have.

"There's a med kit in the cabinet above the microwave, if you think he's worth it," Morton says through the speaker. "He was getting hard to manage anyway."

"You're just leaving us here?"

"It shouldn't take long for me to wrap things up in El Dorado Springs, not with the army and Kessa in the bargain. I'll let you out when I get back."

"What do you mean Kessa in the bargain? What did you do to her?"

"Oh, Jaerish, she's fine. I would never hurt Kessa. She's way too valuable to me."

"She's in here," Radley calls from the bedroom.

"Yes, she is," Morton says. "I considered bringing her along, to prove she's unharmed, but too late now. This place was set up to house a family of four for twenty years. I'm sure the month I'll be gone will fly by."

"Morton," I say, trying desperately to think of something that will make him open the door. There's no reply. "Morton!" I shout. But he's gone.

I leave Forsworth bleeding on the tile and join Radley in the bedroom. He's crouched, holding a sobbing Open Sky to his chest. Adam is on the bed hovering over Kessa. Her eyes shoot to me and I read guilt. Or embarrassment? What in the . . . ?

"Evan," Kessa says quietly.

Adam turns, gives me a quick nod, then goes back to what he was doing, which I can now see is untying her hands from the headboard. Something else is passing between them, but I can't see her face with how Adam's repositioned himself. I'm not watching this.

"I'm going to make sure Forsworth doesn't bleed out."

"We'll be right there," Adam says.

Radley nods once as Open Sky continues to shake in silence.

Back in the kitchen it's all I can do not to kick Forsworth where he lies. I find the med kit, well stocked and exactly where Morton said it would be. Looks like Forsworth will live. Unless Radley finishes what he started.

I grab disinfectant, bandaging and a military grade wound sealant. Hopefully I can get this done before he regains consciousness. I'm washing Forsworth's blood off my hands when Kessa and Adam finally come out of the bedroom.

"That's the guy who overheard your plans with Cole and set this whole thing up," Adam says with a nod to Forsworth.

"He's also the one who kidnapped and drugged us all," I say, "so ratting us out is low on the list of things he'll have to pay for. I'm sure Radley will be happy to take care of his tab."

"Radley do that to him?" Adam asks with a nod towards the stab wound.

"On the way down."

"Good."

"Where should we put him?" Kessa asks.

I glance around the space.

"Not many options," Adam says. "This room, bedroom and bathroom."

"Let's use the metal ring Morton handcuffed Open Sky to. And if he talks, we can gag him." That was from Kessa. It's dark for her, but I approve.

"There are drugs in the med kit that can keep him knocked out for a long time," I say. "His chances of staying alive are better if he doesn't open his mouth."

Adam and I push the couch aside so we can attach Forsworth to the ring without wasting good seating.

"This is cozy," Adam says once Forsworth's secured. "There's bacon if you want some."

Kessa is seated at the table, reading something on pink stationary. We both go to her.

"Kess?" Adam puts a hand on her arm, and I crack my knuckles to distract myself from the desire to knock it away.

"They figured out there's a problem from my Christmas gifts," Kessa says. She looks up at us with the smile I remember from every time she solved a tough equation first or beat me at Othello. "If I'm reading this right, they're reinstating the militia and strategizing next steps."

I walk to the other side of the table. Otherwise I'm going to do something stupid like kiss that smile just to stake my claim.

"Patner went with Cole," I say. "He's off the pills, so he can tell them what Morton and Forsworth have been doing firsthand."

"He remembers?" Kessa asks.

"Yeah," I say. And she knows that I remember too.

Then she's around the table and in my arms, hugging me, half crying and half laughing. I hold her tight and it feels like it used to. Too soon she pulls away and starts pacing the small space.

"That's all good news. If we can just figure out how to get out of here, maybe we can take Open Sky to the army before they follow Morton to El Dorado Springs. If nothing else, my dad needs to know I'm safe so he won't give in to any of Morton's demands."

"I'm not sure how much use Open Sky's going to be," Radley says from the bedroom doorway. "Did you say the kit's got something that can knock someone out? I don't think Open Sky's slept since Morton locked him down here and took away the pills."

"Open Sky was on the blue pill?" I ask. "What about immunity?"

"That was the secret you heard him talking to Morton about," Kessa says. "That he wasn't immune. He thought if anyone knew they'd question his right to lead."

"But really," Adam says, "there's no disease to be immune from. Twenty-five years ago, when the pandemic was killing the whole world, Dad found Open Sky quarantined in that medical facility. His future army needed a general, so Dad offered Open Sky a choice. He could be that man with or without knowledge of the 'recruitment' process."

"And Open Sky chose ignorance?" I ask.

"Open Sky was trapped in a room while everyone around him died," Adam says. "That's traumatic enough without whatever caused him to volunteer as a test subject in the first place. All he wanted was that pill and to forget. I'm not gonna be the one who judges him."

I might. But I hold my tongue.

"Once he was a blank slate, my Dad told him the same things you were told about *Cov-4N*. If Open Sky stepped out of line, Dad controlled him with the threat of exposing his lack of immunity. Open Sky was his slave like everyone else, but with the added shame of his secret."

The silence that follows is broken by a moan from Forsworth.

"That piece of filth, on the other hand, was always a willing participant," Adam says, and the rage on his face mirrors my own. In different circumstances, the two of us could have been friends. But not now.

"You sure know a lot about your dad's plans," I say.

"Yeah, well, once Forsworth overheard you guys talking with Cole in the woods my dad brought me down here and locked me in. I had plenty of time to listen to him monologue through the intercom while waiting helplessly for him to trap my girlfriend. So thanks for that."

"You're blaming me for this?" I ask.

"Us being locked in here? Yeah, that's on you," Adam says.

My fists are clenched when Kessa steps between us and gives Adam the "quit it" look I know so well. Adam frowns and lets out a breath.

"I'm sorry. This is my dad's fault. All of it. I just meant things would have played out differently if Forsworth hadn't come across you. Or if you'd noticed him and gutted him there."

"Plenty of time for gutting him now," Radley says.

Kessa's eyes go wide and I shoot Radley a look. "No talk of gutting in front of Kessa," I say. Radley's mouth turns down, but he nods.

"Keep going," Kessa says to Adam. "What else did your dad tell you."

"There's not much left. Open Sky came back and confronted my dad after Evan started asking questions. Dad seemed to think that taking away the pills and leaving him here, trapped like when he first met him, was a fair exchange for what he deemed disloyalty. Open Sky's been like you saw him since I was locked in early this morning."

"Why was your dad telling you any of this?" I ask.

"Because words are his weapons. He wanted me to agree that what he's doing is right."

"And did you," I ask.

Adam narrows his eyes. "I'm here, aren't I?" he asks. "And I'm not a psychopath."

I make a noncommittal sound. "Fine. So what now?"

"Now we wait."

Chapter 52 - Jace

"Sup, Bro?"

No way. I turn and there's Cole, grinning.

"What the . . . ?" and I'm pulled into a bro hug. "What are you doing here?"

"Well, I didn't just come to see you," Cole says with a laugh. He glances around the room. "Introduce me to McKnight."

"Do you have word from Kessa?"

"I do," Cole says. "And this is Patner. Patner, my bro Jace."

I notice the man in army casual for the first time. Patner nods as Cole lowers his voice.

"Patner is friends with Evan."

Cole's looking at me like he wonders if I understand the significance. My eyes dart to Patner.

"It's real then?"

"Way too real," he says.

"C'mon."

I take Cole and Patner to where Professor McKnight is having a conversation with someone I don't know. The room has started clearing out from tonight's meeting about increased security measures and a second delegation to Salida. The people who are still here have noticed us, and I see Evan's mom eying Patner, lips turned down.

"Professor McKnight," I say, "I have a couple of people I need to introduce you to."

The Professor looks my way then ends his conversation with a smile and an excuse.

"This is my friend Cole, all the way from Salida. And this is Patner. You have a friend in common."

"It's nice to meet you gentlemen." The Professor is studying them and seems to reach a conclusion quickly. "Have you eaten? Perhaps, you'd like to come to my house for dinner and conversation after your long journey?"

"That would be appreciated, sir." Patner says.

"Jace, would you mind escorting them? There are a couple more people I need to speak with here, but I'll do it quickly."

"Sure thing," I say. "Could I bring Michaela too? She and her mom already left, but we could stop there on the way."

"Yes, that's fine. Bring them both, if they're able. I'll let the Douglases and Harrises know as well."

"Sir, I wasn't anticipating a large gathering," Patner says. "We do need some time to speak with you alone."

"Don't worry, son. I'm just saving you from repetition. We've been working in the dark, so to speak, but everyone in attendance is aware of all we do know."

In less than an hour, we're all sitting around Professor McKnight's dining room table. The story Cole and Patner tell makes the wristwatch of death seem almost sane in comparison. Marcus was murdered. Evan was kidnapped and drugged. There's an entire army with a fake disease and no memory. And, of course, my dad is behind it all.

Mrs. Harris, Evan's mom, has been crying from the start, and Michaela isn't far behind. I reach out and take Michaela's hand under the table. As Patner talks, I sink further into my seat. I can feel the weight of Dad's sins on my shoulders. Michaela squeezes my hand.

Cole has noticed Michaela's hand in mine. He gives me an approving nod, and I'm sure in other circumstances he'd be fist-bumping me right now. Which, yeah, seems a little disrespectful, but I did do pretty well. Michaela is the good I'm clinging to in all of this. Michaela and this newly-found God. And the Douglases. And Professor McKnight. Even now, with everything my dad's done, I know they won't abandon me.

It's late when the questions and strategizing finally end. The professor offers Cole his guest room, but Cole says he'll crash on my floor instead. The Harrises insists Patner stay with them. On the way home Cole talks with Henry and Mrs. Barr, proving himself almost as good of a wingman as Enery.

Michaela and I walk slowly, her hand in mine. As we get close to her house, I tug her behind a big evergreen bush. I just need to hold her for a minute to feel myself relax.

After a few breaths Michaela draws my face down. Instead of kissing me like I think she will, she turns my head and whispers in my ear.

"So, that's Cole, huh?"

I startle back and look into her grinning face.

"Don't worry. You're still my favorite," she says with a laugh. Then she gives me the kiss I was anticipating and pulls me from behind the bush. I drop her at her house and catch up with Cole and Henry.

"Not bad at all," Cole says.

"What isn't bad?" asks Henry with a smirk.

Cole shrugs. "I was just thinking that my bro here seems to be doing well in his new hometown. I'm looking forward to getting to know El Dorado Springs during my stay." He absently clicks his tongue bar.

"Unfortunately, some of that 'getting to know' will involve defending the town from an army," Henry says. "But when that's not happening, El Dorado Springs is great."

"Typical Councilor Morton." Cole rolls his eyes, like of course my dad would ruin his vacation.

Back at the house I get Cole set up with some blankets on my floor. I offer him the bed, but he shrugs me off, saying this is better than where he stayed last night.

"Seems like you're really happy with your girl. She's cute. Has she got a friend you want to hook me up with?"

"You do know we're on the brink of invasion, right?" I ask.

"I mean, we don't know that for sure." I can hear his shrug in the dark. "Morton's had the army for a long time. Besides, that won't mean less access to the ladies."

"Really?"

"Nah, man. I'm joking. How one-dimensional do you think I am?"

Before I can reply I remember our conversation before my move. The one about how no one gets a do-over.

"You know, Cole, you could have a fresh start here too. Michaela knows you were a player back in Salida, but no one else does."

"My bro, you act like being a player is something to deny. I've always worn it proud."

"Yeah, but here you wouldn't have to."

Cole doesn't reply. Did he fall asleep mid-conversation? He used to do that when he'd stay over in Salida, too. I roll onto my back and stare into the dark.

"It's some craziness that's going on. Even for your dad."

I guess he wasn't asleep. Just thinking.

"Yeah. It is."

"How are you doing with that?"

"He sent me a godfather letter about family loyalty and a watch that can knock me out remotely. Oh, and a gun. Take a guess how I'm doing"

I'm sure Cole's asleep this time, but I'm wrong.

"I used to wish my dad was around more, but your Councilor Morton stories cured me of that. For years I've figured all dads suck, and I was better off without one. But Henry seemed cool, and so did McKnight and Harris. Maybe we both just got the exit end of the stallion."

Maybe I should tell Cole about how I've started talking to God, and how Michaela claims He's the perfect Father. But I don't. It's too new. Eventually Cole's breathing evens out.

I'm left awake and alone with my thoughts. We're doing everything we can with the militia and checkpoints, but if Evan doesn't convince the army not to follow my father, I don't think it will be enough.

CHAPTER 53 - KESSA

WE'VE BEEN LOCKED IN this room for two and a half days and Morton's never returned. Somehow, I know he's gone. Off to get the army and then to my home.

We spent the first few hours mimicking Morton's voice, but the locking mechanism wasn't fooled. In a different context it would have been funny, but in this one it reeks of desperation. Ironically, from the outside all it takes is the turn of a handle.

Open Sky is barely lucid. Sometimes he recognizes Radley, but no one else. He begs for the pill that we can't give him, and since we can't let him forget, we keep him sedated. It's the only mercy we have to offer.

We've been drugging Forsworth too. It only seems fair. Besides, if he saw how Radley looks at him he'd wet himself, and then we'd have to deal with the smell or let him wash up, and no one wants to supervise that.

I'm aware that the Kessa of a month ago would be appalled, but she's not here.

We eat what Adam cooks. We play cards and watch dvds. We even found an exercise video and work out to the encouragement of the ultra-positive blonde on the screen. She and I are the only girls, so it's nice to have her around.

Adam and Evan have managed an unspoken truce. Neither of them touches me, and I miss Adam's arms. I know he's doing it to be respectful, but I'm locked in a tiny space with five other people and I still feel alone.

We're at the table playing cards when the stairway door opens.

"There you are," Cacia says.

The normalcy of it is disorienting, and for a minute everyone is perfectly still until Adam bolts up and runs for the door. He grabs a chair, propping it open, then pulls Cacia into a hug.

"Nice to see you too," she says.

"How are you here?" Adam asks as the rest of us start moving. Radley is headed towards the bedroom to get Open Sky. Evan glances towards Forsworth but instead turns back to Cacia and interrupts her answer.

"Where's Morton?" Evan asks.

"Gone," she says. "He's on his way to El Dorado Springs. He told the Council he'd gotten a letter from Jace that needed his attention, and that he'd sent Adam and Kessa ahead."

"How long ago?" I ask.

"He left yesterday morning."

"And how are you here?" Adam repeats. "I appreciate the rescue, but what made you think to look for us?"

"Radley and Jaerish promised to stop by before they left town. Couple them vanishing with your uber-responsible girlfriend not canceling her doctor's appointment before her trip, and I knew something was off."

Adam laughs and grins at me.

"It's rude not to cancel if you're not going to show up," I say, but I laugh too. The relief of getting out of this room is intoxicating.

"So what now?" asks Evan, and with that reality crashes back in.

Just then Radley brings Open Sky from the bedroom. He's pale and thin, barely even aware of his surroundings.

"I'm getting him out of this room," Radley says.

"Can we leave Forsworth here?" Evan pokes him with his boot.

"Tell me that man isn't dead," Cacia says.

"We're not that lucky." I shoot Evan a glance and he winces. He probably didn't mean to say that out loud.

Cacia leans over Forsworth, checks his pulse and glances quickly at the shoulder where his shirt is cut away. "Let's leave him here until we decide what to do next."

"Ata girl," says Evan. We all head upstairs.

Adam is walking up behind me, and his hand finds my waist. I pause, long enough to let him step up close, then lean into him, grateful for his warm, solid presence at my back.

"I've missed this," he whispers, nuzzling the space behind my ear. I take a deep breath, savoring the feel of him before continuing up the steps. I need Adam to know I'm with him, but I can't throw it in Evan's face. After everything he's been through, I have to tell him gently. Somehow.

We walk through Morton's office and into the living room where Radley has laid Open Sky on the couch and covered him with a throw blanket. The afternoon light from the windows shows how much he's aged, and he looks tormented even in sleep.

"Someone should tell me what's going on," Cacia says.

Adam gives her the super-short version, promising to tell her everything once we figure out who else needs to be involved. We decide to approach the town prosecutor responsible for Jace's arson charges rather than the sheriff who was always Morton's lapdog. We need Dr. Massman too. Cacia volunteers to go get them while we stay here, out of sight.

Once she leaves, Adam asks Evan to help him with something upstairs. There's an awkward moment, then Evan follows.

Radley sits in an armchair, staring into space, near Open Sky who's asleep on the couch. I'm making tea in the kitchen when Dr. Massman arrives. He examines Open Sky, then I take him down to the secret room to check on Forsworth. When we get back to the kitchen, Cacia and Lucas Vega, the town prosecutor, are there with Adam, Evan and Radley.

We tell them the whole story, answering questions as we go. If Open Sky were in his right mind, this would be as simple as racing Morton to El Dorado Springs and telling the army the truth before any fighting starts. But as it is, we can't count on Open Sky for anything. And who knows what kinds of traps Morton may have set in case we got out of that room? He's been three steps ahead of us this entire time.

Lucas Vega agrees to take custody of Forsworth when we leave. Dr. Massman is hesitant to allow Open Sky to travel, so Cacia offers to come with us as medical aid. I'm sure seeing Patner sweetens the deal.

Instead of splitting up, we'll go to the army base first. If we're lucky they haven't deployed yet, and if not we have a better chance of convincing someone about the pills without Adam's dad around to spin things his way.

Once we've decided on our plan, we have just a few hours to rest and prepare. I thought the safe room was close quarters, but at six tonight I'll be crammed into a truck with Adam and Evan, plus Radley, Cacia and Open Sky, non-stop for 650 miles. Uncomfortable doesn't begin to describe it.

I'm about to go upstairs when Adam stops me.

"Kessa, we wanted to talk to you."

We? Evan stands behind Adam. They both look serious. Maybe even nervous. I walk with them to the ornate dining room table and take a seat. I wish I could think of something funny to say to dispel the tension, but I can't. So instead I trace the decorative carvings of the chair arm with my fingertips. It's Adam who speaks.

"Kessa, we both love you," he says. "But there's too much at stake. If you're ready to choose one of us, we've agreed to respect your choice. But if not, we'll be able to focus better on what needs to be done with both relationships on hold."

"And this is what you talked about upstairs?" I ask. They both nod. I want to be mad that they discussed my future without me, but what's the point?

Besides, I've already chosen Adam. I've never been more certain of anything. And I can tell from how he's sitting, like a man resigned to do what's right, even if it kills him, that he doesn't know. It hurts to see him this way, but I can't blame him. Not with how I lied to him. And not with knowing about that stupid high school girl who told him forever then left him for her ex. He must be afraid it's happening all over again.

But then there's Evan, with the jagged, angry edge that's come since he realized what's been stolen from him. Marcus's death is still brand new, and we have no idea what's going on with his parents, or even his new friends in the army. How can I take away his hope?

"Give me half an hour to rest and sort things out. Then I'll talk with each of you alone."

They agree. What else can they do? I go upstairs to the room that was mine when I first came to Salida. It's still the same, which seems wrong in the face of all that's changed. Laying down on the quilt I stare at the ceiling and I cry. Not loud tears that anyone outside could hear, but slow, quiet tears for the man I love and the man I loved.

The half hour passes. I debate taking a shower, but putting this off won't help. Instead, I go to the kitchen where Adam is cooking. Evan eats at the counter. I wonder if they both stayed here, just waiting. Adam puts scrambled eggs and a piece of toast with jelly on a plate and hands it to me. Evan frowns but quickly wipes it away.

I thank Adam and sit. He follows with his own plate and the three of us eat in silence for a minute that seems to stretch forever.

"Who would you like to talk with first?" Adam asks.

"I'll talk with Evan first," I say.

"OK," Adam says with a nod. "I'll take this upstairs and get a quick shower. Someone let me know when you're finished."

And with that he's gone. I take a deep breath and look at Evan. Once I see his eyes, I know I can't tell him the truth. Not all of it, anyway. But is it worse to string him along and give him hope where there isn't any? Surely that's worse.

Evan reaches for my hand, and I let him take it.

"Kessa, I remember us. I remember a thousand moments of you and me together. Do you remember when we made that boat and sank it in the pond outside the Ridley farm?"

I laugh. "I remember telling you it would sink and you convincing me to get in anyway."

"We could both swim," he says, a smile in the corner of his mouth.

"That's been your excuse since the fifth grade."

"I know. And now I remember. It's me, Kessa. I've always been yours. You've always been mine. You can't let Adam's dad take that away too." Shadows have filled his eyes.

"I can't imagine what it was like to have your memory gone and then to remember so much. Evan, what happened to Marcus? Are you sure it was him in that ravine?"

Evan sighs. "As sure as I can be. I've scoured my mind since my memory returned, and I never saw him at the base. We were headed to El Dorado Springs with a huge haul when we found Forsworth and his gang beating the crap out of one of their own. Marcus and I tried to intervene, and the next thing I know, I'm in the back of Forsworth's truck with no memory. We were such newbs. And Marcus is dead because of it."

"I'm sorry, Evan."

He squeezes my hand. "I don't think there's a way it could have ended differently. Not unless we'd just driven away, and neither of us could have lived with that. Knowing that helps."

"If you'd driven away and none of this had happened, who knows what Morton and his army would have done. El Dorado Springs would have been completely unprepared."

"If you hadn't moved to Salida, I'd have been in that army."

We're quiet, both thinking about the "what if's" that got us here. He takes my other hand.

"Kessa, I can see how good has come of it, but I won't count any of this as good if I lose you too. My best friend was murdered; I was kidnapped and drugged and lied to. You brought me back. If you can't choose me now, give us time. We'll be friends again through this thing, and when it's done, I'll remind you of why it was always us in the first place."

I hadn't known what I would do, but I can't look at him now and tell him no. So I nod.

"We'll be friends until this is over," I say.

"Thank you."

He leans his forehead onto our clasped hands. I close my eyes, bracing myself for my conversation with Adam.

It feels wrong, asking Adam to wait, to give some other guy a chance to win my heart when he's all I want. But I couldn't steal Evan's last bit of hope.

I knock on Adam's door and push it open without waiting for an answer, but he isn't inside. I glance around at the books on his night table, the clothes hung neatly in his open closet with shoes lined up beneath. Everything in order. I'm about to go look for him when he enters the room, toweling his wet hair. When he sees me, he smiles, steps inside and closes the door.

My heart lurches in my chest. Adam is beautiful. I'm suddenly hyper-focused on a trickle of water making its way from behind his ear down to the collar of his t-shirt. Before I can stop myself, I've reached out a finger and am tracing its path.

Adam gently reaches up, takes my hand and brings it to his lips, kissing the fingertip that was so recently on his skin. I look into his eyes and electricity courses through me. I breathe in the smell of him, soap and mountain air, missing the hint of sharpness that's there when I'm in his arms after a run.

"Do you want me to step out for a minute so you can finish drying off?" I ask.

Adam grins, but it's not the nice boy grin I'm used to.

"You probably shouldn't know what I want right now Kessa," he says. "I've been doing everything I can these last few days to be respectful of Evan and this whole situation. But if you stay in this room for another moment,

I'm not going to let you leave it for a very long time. And there will be no doubt that we were doing more than talking."

I close my eyes, but the image of him in front of me stays imprinted on my eyelids. I try to make my feet walk to the door, but as I take a deep breath to steel my determination the scent of him is too much and instead I reach out and place my palm on his chest. Before I can think his mouth is on mine and all the anxiety and confusion that's been building dissolves as I lose myself in his kiss. After I don't know how long, Adam pulls away.

He's staring down at me, hands cradling my face, eyes burning into mine with a question I can't quite make out. Whatever it is, my answer is yes. He must be able to read that because his mouth is on mine again. I've missed this. I've missed him. Nothing has ever felt as right as this moment.

Which is interrupted by a knock on the door.

"Kessa, are you in there? I wanted to see if you need anything from your house before I go."

It's Cacia. I physically push back from Adam, both hands on his chest. He reaches up, taking hold of my wrists and drawing my eyes to his.

"Yeah, just a second," I call. But I can't break our gaze. Time must have passed because Cacia hesitantly speaks again.

"Kessa?"

"Coming."

To Adam I say "I'm going to give her a list of things to pick up, and then I'll be back."

His eyes are blazing, but he lets go of my wrists. I take a deep breath before stepping out to talk with Cacia.

When I return Adam is sitting on his bed. He's picked up the towel from the floor where he dropped it and folded it neatly. I pull over his desk chair and sit in front of him.

Adam takes my hands, and I lean my head down onto them before straightening and looking into his face.

"I hope this means you've chosen me," he says. He's joking, but not only joking, and his vulnerability pierces me.

"Yes, I've chosen you," I say. "I love you."

He grins, but a shadow quickly follows as he searches my eyes.

"I love you too Kessa," he says. "But I hear a 'but' coming."

"There's no but. I choose you. 100% just you. But," he raises his eyebrows and I rush to get it out. "Evan asked that if I couldn't choose him now I'd give it time and not make my decision. So he could have a chance when all of this is done."

Adam's jaw clenches.

"And what did you tell him?" he asks.

"I told him ok."

Adam swears. Just one word, but it's the first time I've heard him say it. His voice, when he continues, is sharp with pain.

"Are you asking me to be your secret boyfriend, Kessa? You want me to pretend we're just friends and let Evan keep hoping he's got a chance, even though you love me and want to be with me?"

It sounds so bad when he says it that way.

"Yes? No? I don't know. They stole everything from him, Adam. His identity. His best friend. His future."

"Do you want it back?" he asks. "Your future with Evan?"

"No," I say, shaking my head. "I want you."

His blue eyes are intent, almost pleading.

"If you want me, I'm yours. All yours. Heart. Body. Future. Past. Everything. And I'll be respectful of Evan's feelings. But I won't hide it from anyone. I will never give you a reason to think I'm ashamed to be with you."

I will never give you a reason to think I'm ashamed to be with you. There's something there, something wounded, but I don't press. He's right regardless. It's unfair of me to ask him to hide it if we're together.

"OK," I say.

"OK, what?" Adam asks.

"I won't ask you to hide us. I'll let Evan know I've chosen you."

He closes his eyes and brings our hands to his lips, kissing my fingers.

"Thank you, Kessa," Adam says. It's so sincere and I'm ashamed that I made this amazing man practically beg for something I should have given him freely.

"Why do you have to do that?" I ask.

"Do what?"

"Make me be better than I want to be."

"Maybe because I know who you really are." He leans in, putting his forehead against mine. "You're brave and kind and full of integrity. And I won't see that change for anyone."

CHAPTER 54 - JAERISH

Kessa's been gone too long. When she comes down the stairs, I know everything's changed. She's chosen him.

I can see it in her flushed cheeks, her slightly swollen lips. Memories of other times I've seen her like this flood in to torment me. For a second, just one, I think of the blue pill. I don't have to remember.

That same coward voice wonders if I can leave before she opens her mouth and steals away the hope I've been clutching like a lifeline. She can't meet my eyes. Before she speaks or I bolt, Radley walks in.

"Jaerish, if you're done with breakfast can you go sit with Open Sky while I take care of a few things?"

"Sure. Unless Kessa needs me for something."

Kessa smiles weakly. "I'm good," she says. I escape upstairs.

Open Sky looks better than he did in the saferoom. Our prison. His color is back, and his face is thinner, but in sleep it's not so tormented. But then he thrashes and calls out.

Radley didn't tell me what to do if this happened. Should I wake him? I stand here, hovering and useless, waiting to see if it gets worse before reacting. Slowly he calms and settles.

I sit across from Open Sky on the bed that was mine. The last time I was in this room I was a drugged pawn, but didn't know it. I was just finding out that this beautiful girl knew me, that somehow I'd been important to her. And now I'm on the verge of losing her all over again.

There's a knock at the open door, and Kessa walks in.

"How is he?" she asks.

"Not great, but better."

Kessa looks at Open Sky, her brow creased.

"I can't imagine what this must be like for him. To find out a decision you made twenty-five years ago has damaged everyone you know and care about . . . I wouldn't want to face it either. I'd say let him have the pill, but we need him to stop the army."

Kessa sits on the bed beside me. She closes her eyes, and when she opens them they're begging me to understand. But I'm not going to make this easy. She has to say it. And she does.

"Evan, I'm sorry. But I love Adam. I'm choosing him."

I was expecting it, but the pain is still deep and instantaneous.

"How did he change your mind?" I ask. "You just told me you'd give us a chance."

"He didn't change my mind. You did. In the kitchen. Because when I was there with you I couldn't stand the idea of hurting you after everything else that's happened. But it's not fair for me to drag it out and give you hope that isn't real."

"What in this has been fair, Kessa? The kidnapping? Marcus's murder? Definitely not the killer's kid getting my girl."

She winces, and I know I'm not playing this right. I need to be smart if I want to have any chance, but I can't stop the words that are pouring out of my mouth.

"And now you've betrayed me too. You lied and said you'd give us a chance, but now you won't even do that. After everything we were you won't wait a couple of months to let me try to win you back? You're as bad as your future father-in-law."

She looks at me shocked, like I'd reached out and hit her. At first I think she's going to burst into tears, but instead she stands up, eyes narrowing. Her hands go to her hips.

"This wasn't only hard for you. I don't know who you are now, but you're not Evan after all. He'd never let himself get so lost in self-pity that he'd intentionally hurt the people he claimed to love."

With a final glare she's gone. A roar explodes from me, and before I realize it, I've punched the wall. There's a gaping hole where my fist went through, and I shake out my hand. I don't feel the pain. Open Sky thrashes again, and I want to punch him too. He's one of the people who did this to me and everyone's acting like he's a victim here.

I've gotta get out of this room. Adam is in the doorway, probably coming to see what the noise was. I push past him hard, heading down the stairs and outside before anyone can stop me.

I don't know where I'm going; I just go. I run, like if I run hard enough I can outrun my life. I finally stop beside an old tree, bending double and desperately dragging knives of frigid air into my lungs. It's all still with me. My damn, broken life. Kessa was the last piece intact, the lynchpin holding me together, and she's gone.

I hit the tree. I sob and I roar. I pant and I spit. I break off a branch and slam it against the trunk. It doesn't help. Nothing does. Nothing will.

Exhausted, I collapse at the base of the poor tree I've just ravaged. My knuckles bleed. The cuts on my palm throb. I lean my head back against rough bark, peering through black, leafless lines at a too blue sky.

I hope it's ok in the spring, that the branches grow back and the wounds heal. I hope the same for myself, but how could my branches grow back when Kessa's been my every breath for as long as I can remember?

Somehow my anger morphed into sorrow, but now even that's worn thin. It's late afternoon, I'm numb with cold and I have to get home. Not to Morton's or the army base. To El Dorado Springs. Even without Kessa or Marcus it's still home, where my parents live and all my regained memories take place. There's no way in hell I'm letting Morton destroy that too.

When I get back, everyone's in the dining room. Not just Radley, Kessa and Adam, but also Dr. Massman, Cacia and Lucas Vega. I wanted to slip in unnoticed and clean up, but instead all eyes are on me.

"I'll be right back," I say, rushing past.

The man in the mirror has wild hair and hollow eyes. My shirt and hands are bloody. I wash quickly, embracing the sting of hot water on numb fingers and fresh wounds. I pull my hair back and change shirts. Then I brace myself to go back downstairs. I can do this. I'll just act like nothing's happened.

But as soon as I enter the room, Vega says, "Forsworth's dead."

I keep my face blank as I take in this information.

"Dead? How?"

"His throat was cut from ear to ear. No sign of struggle, so he was probably unconscious when it happened."

Which is a gruesome way to die. Not that he didn't deserve it.

"Who did it?" I ask, realizing they all saw me covered in blood and looking like a madman.

But I don't need to worry long.

"It was Open Sky." This comes from Kessa, and I flinch away from the sympathy in her voice. "He disappeared when you took off. We found him sitting by the body with the knife still in his hand. At first, we thought he was dead too, but he wasn't."

Radley's eyes tell me where I stand. If Open Sky had been harmed, I'd be Fatim right now, no questions asked.

"While we need to incorporate this into our plans," says Vega, "it actually simplifies things. We won't need to involve the sheriff to avoid kidnapping charges. I'll take Cacia's place as we approach the army, and Open Sky will be considered in my custody until this situation is resolved."

I like Vega. He doesn't give a damn that Forsworth is dead. Cacia looks disappointed, but she has her whole life to be with Patner once this is over.

"There's one more thing," Radley says, handing me a small brown bottle. "We found these on Forsworth."

I swear when I read "***Dose 1***" scrawled in black marker.

"Before the pandemic there were all kinds of 'breakthroughs' in the suppression of trauma, and just as many ethical debates on their use," Dr. Massman says. "While everyone who knew exactly how these pills worked is long dead, I'd guess this was an initiating suppressant and the blue pills a maintenance agent."

At this point I don't care how the pills work. But this is one more piece of proof for the army. Radley slips it back into his pocket. We have a town to save.

CHAPTER 55 - KESSA

I'M CRAMMED BETWEEN ADAM and Evan in the front seat, which isn't awkward at all.

Radley and Lucas flank Open Sky in the back, neither one willing to risk him jumping. Somehow, I can't see the nearly comatose man doing anything that dramatic, but I suppose Forsworth's ghost might say otherwise. Luckily not even a ghost could shove himself into this over-crowded truck.

Only five months ago I was staring vacantly at this same valley, mind numb with grief over Evan's death as I travelled west to Salida. Now Evan sits beside me, his thigh involuntarily bumping mine, and somehow, he's farther away than when I thought he was dead. Adam's on my other side. I hadn't even met him then, and now all I want is to hide in his arms and hear him tell me everything's going to be ok.

Eventually I drift off. I wake up leaning against Adam's shoulder, my body instinctively curling into him. As my mind clears, I realize that we've stopped. A glance around the cab shows everyone asleep except for Open Sky who stares forward, unseeing, with haunted eyes. And Evan. It must have been the cold air coming through the open driver's door that woke me. I slide across the seat and out. Stretching, I shade my eyes and blink at the rising sun glinting off endless snow-covered hills.

"Beautiful, isn't it?" Evan asks as he secures a gas can into the truck bed. I nod in silence.

"The first time I saw snow, back when I was on the pill and it was brand new again, I swore I'd never take it for granted. Never take a sunrise for granted. Never take a moment of this life for granted. Being able to experience everything for the first time with adult eyes brought a whole new perspective."

"When you think of it that way it's almost a gift," I say.

The look on his face is the same one he wore in seventh grade when I spit on him, thinking it would be funny. I'm not sure why I thought it then, or why I said it now. But unlike then Evan doesn't wipe it away and move on.

"Kessa, let's get something straight. When I thought I had an incurable disease I was trying to find anything that was positive about my new life. And I did. I made good friends, all of us in this together and creating a community that worked. But that life is about to disappear as thoroughly as my first one.

"How do you think these guys are going to handle the news that they were kidnapped and drugged, some of them for decades? At least I have something to go back to. Had something to go back to. It's what kept me going through the anger and confusion of those first days as my memory returned. They might not have that. And some of them will hate me for taking the illusion away from them. Because I'll be stealing the only life they've ever known as thoroughly as Forsworth did.

"I've lost two lives now, and I don't feel much like building a third, so quit trying to pretend there's a silver lining."

I can't move. Or find anything to say. I can't even look at him as I screw up my face and refuse to cry.

"Evan, I'm sorry." I don't even know what I'm apologizing for. And there's nowhere to go from here. Evan stares at me, nearly as blankly as when he first saw me in Adam's kitchen.

"Let's keep driving while everyone's still asleep. Once they wake up Adam's going to take my place."

And there it is. I know he means driving, but that's the heart of it all.

I climb into the truck, shoving myself across the driver's seat and back into the middle. Adam, eyes still closed and breaths even, turns his hand up and grasps mine. I cling to the connection as my heart breaks for Evan, for his pain and the man he's becoming.

CHAPTER 56 - JACE

"JACE. COLE. WAKE UP. There's an army at the Southern checkpoint."

Henry's voice drags me from sleep. It's still black outside my window, so stupid early.

"My dad?" I ask.

"Unless you know of another army. Get dressed, and we'll see what we can find out."

Cole lets out a massive yawn. "We should have known Councilor Morton would schedule his invasion on a Saturday morning."

People are gathering in the icy air of town square. They stand or sit in groups of twos and threes on the cold metal benches near the gazebo. Just last month this square was full of music and twinkling Christmas lights. Welcome to town, Dad. You know how to bring the party.

Cole and I go with Henry to the community building where Professor McKnight, Mr. Harris and Mayor Cartwright and a couple of people I kind of recognize are talking with Patner.

"How could you have known about this and not told the Council?" Mae's mom asks.

"The Council was aware of everything that we knew, Mayor Cartwright," Professor McKnight says calmly.

The Mayor's shoe tap, tap, taps against the floor. Who wears heels to an invasion? It's six a.m. and she has makeup on. My tired brain can't process this.

"You told us only that you suspected an army had been assembled. You said nothing of it targeting El Dorado Springs," she says.

"We had no reason to believe that it would," Professor McKnight replies.

"You also said nothing about his father being involved." The emphasis on *his* and the glare she sends my way make me want to vanish into the cold morning air.

Cole narrows his eyes, and I already regret whatever he's going to say. Fortunately, Professor McKnight speaks first.

"Now, Arabelle, surely you of all people know better than to judge someone based on their parents."

She glares but doesn't argue.

"Fine. What do you propose we do now that the wolf's at the door?"

"We've already sent a detachment of the militia to the Southern checkpoint. Now we find out why they're here. And hopefully learn something of my daughter."

Two soldiers come forward from the army with a flag of parley. They stop 100 yards from the checkpoint and stand at attention. Behind them are two more men. One is my father. Which means any chance that this was some nightmarish misunderstanding is gone.

Henry and Mr. Harris go out to meet them. We can't hear what they're saying, but Henry's usual grin is missing. I wait near Professor McKnight and Mayor Cartwright for their return.

Michaela joins me, slipping her hand into mine. Cole stands on my other side. Despite his talk of seeking out "the ladies" he hasn't left me. I can do this.

Henry and Mr. Harris return from the parley with my dad's demands.

"That was Richard Morton, and a man named Major Merritt. They're requiring the safe return of Jace and of their army general, Open Sky," Henry says.

"Why do they think we have their general?" Mayor Cartwright asks. "We don't have him, do we?" She says this with resignation, like at this point anything is possible. I don't blame her.

"Last I knew, Open Sky was on his way to Salida," Patner says.

"Which means that either Morton has lied to them, or he and the Major are allied." Professor McKnight says. "It wouldn't be the first time a Major has been promoted to General in a similar fashion."

All eyes turn to Patner, who's shaking his head.

"I don't think so. Major Merritt is a 'by the books' kind of guy. He wouldn't knowingly be part of that."

"Maybe they'll just take the boy then," Mayor Cartwright says.

Michaela's hand tightens in mine, like she could physically keep that from happening.

"Nobody's taking Jace," Professor McKnight says, "although a meeting with him to establish his safety is a reasonable request. I would certainly wish to see Kessa were that a possibility."

"Morton said Kessa remains in Salida, unaware of this situation," Henry says. "His exact words were 'There was no need to distress her delicate sensibilities.'"

"Because she's a woman?" Mayor Cartwright asks.

"He didn't elaborate," says Henry.

Mayor Cartwright's face is a thundercloud as Henry continues.

"Obviously we can't give them what we don't have, but if Open Sky's welfare is what's keeping them from attacking, I'm not sure we can reveal that he isn't with us."

I've given up hoping that my welfare might figure into this, at least on Dad's side of things. The watch on my wrist feels even heavier than normal.

"We can show them I'm ok," I say. Michaela takes a quick breath, but she doesn't object, although my fingers are starting to go numb from her grip.

Mayor Cartwright turns my way with Mae's catlike smile and practically purrs her thanks. I can tell Henry doesn't like the idea, but he keeps his mouth shut, waiting on Professor McKnight. After a long moment, the professor nods.

"It's a good idea, Jace. We'll send you well guarded as a spokesman. You can tell Major Merritt of your treatment here. Henry will go with you."

"And if my dad tries to activate the wristwatch?" I ask.

"Maybe don't wear it today. Best to keep that particular piece out of play for the moment."

At noon I walk with Henry and a guard of six militia men to a tent set up where the parley was held this morning. My father's eyes narrow as I tell both him and Merritt that I've had no ill treatment during my time in El Dorado Springs.

"And where's the watch I sent you, Jace?" my father asks. He does it casually, like he's just checking in.

"It's at home on my dresser. I didn't want it to get scuffed up."

"I'd love to see it on you," Dad says. "Make sure you wear it next time."

Bastard.

I know I'm just a kid to Merritt and that my dad's going to tell him I'm rebellious and whatever else the moment they leave, but the thought of the watch pisses me off so bad that I can't help what I say next.

"Major Merritt, my dad can't be trusted. He manipulates and lies to everyone, and he's good at it. He's doing it to you right now."

And just like that I know it's all over for me with Councilor Morton. Good thing I was the disposable son all along. I don't stay to hear Dad's response. Instead, I turn and walk back toward El Dorado Springs, my real home and my future.

Chapter 57 - Kessa

It's nearly noon when we drive through the town of Ogden, just outside Fort Riley. Adam pulls behind a house that looks like it was already abandoned pre-pandemic. There's no way to cover our tire tracks through the miles of pristine snow. If someone wants to find us, they will.

Radley insists Open Sky be kept away from camp until we know what kind of trap Morton might have set for us, and when it comes to Open Sky's safety, Radley doesn't budge. Evan and Lucas start the hike in to gather information and hopefully bring back someone willing to listen before pronouncing judgement.

Once they're gone, Adam and I decide to explore the nearby buildings to see if there's anything useful, but really to distract ourselves while we wait. Radley doesn't argue, just hands Adam a gun and asks if he knows how to use it. Adam's "yes" is followed by a pause before he tucks it into the back of his pants.

Adam and I walk behind several houses, look inside a metal-work shop and enter a gas station long cleared of anything valuable. One register drawer gapes open, still filled with piles of worthless paper money. To think people used to steal that.

We walk to the library, and I pause in the entrance. As my eyes adjust to the to dim light, I'm met with row upon row of metal shelves half-filled with books and discs. It's hard to comprehend the wealth of information and entertainment available in just this one small building in one small town.

A pang shoots through me as Adam takes my hand. Exploring the cities was my dream with Evan, and now I'm sharing this with someone else. I pull my hand away, as though needing it to reach for a book. I don't think Adam's fooled, but he doesn't ask.

Wandering towards a rack of music Adam says, "I heard your conversation with Evan when we stopped."

"You were awake?"

"I woke up when you got out." He's looking at the shelf, not me.

"I don't think Evan would have wanted you to hear that," I say, swallowing.

"I know. I shouldn't have listened. At first, I was still half asleep, and then I wasn't sure how to tell you I was awake." He takes a deep breath. "How are you? He was pretty harsh."

"He's not who he used to be," I say. "The Evan I knew was confident and driven, but always kind." The silence stretches until Adam takes my hand again, drawing me to look at him.

"Kessa, I know how big the stakes are. But all I could think about on the drive here was Evan's leg bumping against yours. I couldn't even blame him if he left it there longer than he needed to." Adam closes his eyes. Opens them. Takes a deep breath.

"As selfish as it makes me, I wouldn't give you up to him for even a moment. Not to heal him or this whole world. Hell, I wasn't even willing to stand aside so you could sort this out because I was so afraid if I did, you'd choose him. What kind of person does that make me?"

He's looked away now, hiding in the midst of his vulnerability and shame. Reaching up, I turn his face towards mine.

"Adam. You're a good man. I'd already made my choice. All you did was ask me to do right by him. It would have been unfair to give him false hope, and you know that. What's this really about?"

Adam's struggling to force the words out. Finally, something breaks.

"My dad can justify anything. He convinced himself it was right to kidnap men and create this army and then to force your dad into giving him his technology. He's made himself the sole arbiter of right and wrong, based entirely on his own desires. I'm terrified I could become that.

"Maybe I should have let you give Evan time and decide later, but instead I turned it into a moral issue. I said it was for him, but it was for me because I was afraid. Because you are what I want. That sounds just like my dad."

"Adam, you are what I want." I say it slowly, each word distinct. "You aren't forcing me into anything. You're not controlling me or manipulating me. And you're certainly not drugging me." I try to make it light, like a joke, and he tries to force a smile. Neither works.

"I love you. I choose you. Evan isn't even the person I used to know anymore, and I'm not going to be the one who fixes him. What I need now is you."

I reach up onto my toes and kiss him. His arms are around me, and our kiss is soft and lingering, like sinking into a hot bath. The comfort of it surrounds me along with the knowing that I'm exactly where I want to be. Where I should be. In Adam's arms I am safe, loved and known. Nothing else matters.

Well, nothing except the army on its way to take over my hometown. That matters.

"C'mon," I say. "Let's go."

We start back towards the truck, thinking Radley might want to find a book for the wait. As we near where we parked Adam swears under his breath. It's not like him, but when I look ahead, I understand.

There in the snow is a second set of tire tracks. Either we have company or . . . we both run, not caring about our footprints as we circle the old house. Sure enough, the truck is gone. Against a wall, under the limited shelter of the eaves, our personal bags are piled haphazardly along with some supplies.

On the wall above our stuff is a single word.

Carrigan.

It means nothing to me, and a glance Adam's way shows he's just as confused. He rubs the back of his head, takes a deep breath.

"OK, then. Time for a new plan."

Just what that will be neither of us knows. And, of course, that's when we hear the rumbling motor of a large truck behind us.

Chapter 58 - Jaerish

Lucas Vega and I mar the pristine snow with our boots. We don't speak. There are too many unknowns to strategize, and neither of us are chatty types. So instead, I mentally replay my last conversation with Kessa over and over. I said everything wrong. I don't even believe most of it.

Kessa looked at me like she didn't know who I am. Hell, neither do I. The person I've become isn't the Evan I remember. It's not Jaerish from the army base either. No. This man is numb. And pissed. I'm sure there's pain beneath the anger, but I can't deal with that yet. Not until after I deal with Morton.

Once we reach camp there are footprints through the snow, but way too few. I rub at the anxiety that's building in my chest. A base this quiet means most of the men are deployed.

Our original plan was to find someone I know for information before going to leadership, but we're out of time. I walk directly to the main offices where whoever's been left in charge will be stationed. Out of half-remembered habit I shoot up a quick prayer that it's someone reasonable.

We're stopped at the doors and told to hand over our weapons.

"No blades, no bows?" I ask.

The guard looks at me blankly and shakes his head.

"Do you know who I am?" I ask.

"Yes, sir. Jaerish, Elite Guard."

"Then you know I'm allowed my weapons in camp, correct?"

"I apologize, sir. These were my orders."

I hand over my knife, which I wore out of habit. It's not like I need weapons. The guard glances at me again and then at Vega.

"And you, sir?" he asks.

"I don't carry," Vega says.

The guard escorts us through empty halls to Open Sky's office where Captain Betner sits behind the desk. His eyes flick from me to Vega to the guard, and then he dismisses our escort.

"I expected to see Patner for the negotiations," Betner says. "I was hoping you'd just been caught up in this mess."

"We've all been 'caught up in this mess.' What do you mean negotiations?"

"Please, have a seat," he says. "Introduce your friend.

We sit, and I quickly introduce Vega before Captain Betner continues.

"Jaerish, I always liked you. You seem like a young man with integrity, and it didn't sit well with me when I heard that you were part of a conspiracy to kidnap Open Sky. So, why don't you go ahead and tell me your spin on this, and we can figure out how to move forward?"

I'd been wondering what trap Morton would set. This one makes sense.

"Captain Betner, was Richard Morton your information source?"

"For now, I'll be asking the questions, Jaerish. I'm sure you understand."

"That's fine. But you can't un-know what I'm going to tell you. How much truth do you want to hear?"

"Son, I think you'd better give me all of it. Otherwise, there's not much chance of you and your friend here leaving this base alive, despite all those skills I know you have."

So I tell him everything. A shortened version with less emphasis on Kessa, calling her just someone from my hometown, but everything he needs to know. If I could have hand-picked our first contact, I'd have chosen Captain Betner. Major Merritt has integrity, but no imagination. Captain Betner has both.

"So," he finally says, "You're telling me Morton drugged an entire army, kidnapped Open Sky, and is planning on unleashing us on an innocent ally?"

"Yes, sir," I say.

"And you're saying that *Cov-4N* doesn't exist. If I were to go off of the blue pill I'd remember everything from my past in a matter of days?"

"That's how it worked for me and Patner. Radley took longer, but him too."

"And for Open Sky?"

"Yes," I say, taking a deep breath. "It worked for Open Sky. But he hasn't been the same since."

"In what way?" Captain Betner asks.

I'm grateful when Vega, who's been silent to this point, speaks.

"Open Sky was part of the original drug trials before the pandemic. I'm not sure what kind of trauma impelled that course of action, but the combined weight of his memories then and the guilt he carries now was too much for him. His mental stability is sporadic at best."

Captain Betner nods, considering.

"Also, Open Sky killed Forsworth," I add.

"So not completely insane," Betner says. "And where is Open Sky now?"

"He's nearby. Radley insisted we ensure his safety before bringing him to camp."

"Your story is easily enough proven then," Betner says rising. "Let's go."

Captain Betner chooses four soldiers to accompany us. Vega and I ride in the back of an army truck surrounded by men with guns. I can take them if I have to. Probably. But we want these men on our side.

There's no conversation as we pull through the gates past the posts marking the Big Red One. An empty playground and picnic table sit beneath a flag pole waving nothing.

As we near the house where the truck is parked, I see an extra set of tire tracks in the snow. The weight in my chest increases as I exchange a glance with Vega.

We're motioned out the back of the truck by the not-so-subtle barrel of a gun. There are footprints in the snow leading to a small pile of supplies at the base of a house. There is no note. There is no truck. A single word is painted above the pile. A name, maybe, but it means nothing to me.

I should have expected this. Radley would do anything to keep Open Sky safe, including betraying the rest of us. I can't tell if he left Adam and Kessa here or if he forced them to go along.

Beside me Vega says what I'm thinking.

"I shouldn't have trusted him."

Captain Betner turns to us expectantly.

"Explain."

"Radley's protecting him, sir," I say. "He cares nothing for the entire population of El Dorado Springs, or even for this army, if weighed against Open Sky."

"And why would he think Open Sky in danger?" Betner asks.

I glance at the guards. "In private, sir?"

"Search the area," he says and they fan out. I keep my voice low.

"For one, he would have been facing a murder charge in Salida. But beyond that, what do you think the men will do when they find out the truth?"

"Probably the same things you considered doing. Did you kill him, Jaerish?"

"That's a fair question, but only because you haven't seen him. There'd be no justice in killing such a broken man. I don't have it in me." Or maybe I do. I have all kinds of ugly things in my head now. But he doesn't need to know that.

Betner deliberates, looking at the house and our pile of supplies.

"It's your word against Morton's. And there's still a simple way to prove your claims. How long does it take memories to return?"

I nod slowly, catching his meaning.

"My memories started the morning of the second day, maybe 28 hours from the first missed dose. Patner's took longer, but not much. Radley took two full days. We're assuming there's a base time then it's proportionate to how long someone's been on the pill. You'd take longer than we can wait."

"I couldn't be that irresponsible in my current charge even if I wanted to. But perhaps we can find someone trustworthy who's willing to take the risk."

"Is Gideon still in camp?" I ask.

"He is," Betner says. "Is it just you and Vega here?"

I glance around. Truthfully, I don't know.

"Yes," I say, as we climb back into the truck.

Chapter 59 - Kessa

THERE WAS NO TIME to think. Grabbing our bags and whatever else we could snag quickly, Adam and I darted into the snow. We followed our original footprints and barely got into a nearby house as the army truck arrived.

Now we peer around a dust-coated, disintegrating curtain as a soldier gestures Evan and Lucas from the vehicle with the barrel of his gun. They aren't handcuffed, but they obviously aren't free either. We're too far to hear what's going on, and Adam's single gun wouldn't do us much good against what they're carrying if this were to become a rescue mission. Besides, the only one of us with a chance at pulling off something like that is on the "to be rescued" side of things.

The man who seems to be in charge is having a private conversation with Evan. Then, just like that, the soldiers are picking up the rest of the supply pile and getting back into the truck. Should we run out and throw ourselves on their mercy? The alternative is being stranded here in the cold with minimal supplies and no transportation. Evan didn't describe them as madmen.

A glance at Adam decides it. I don't think they'd hurt me, but I don't know how they'd treat him after they hear what his dad has done. I'm not even sure I can trust this new version of Evan to help. I won't risk it. If it weren't my home being threatened, I might pull a Radley myself and take off.

With the soldiers gone, Adam is kneeling on the hardwood floor by the pile of stuff we'd grabbed, systematically opening bags.

"It could be worse," he says. "We've got our own stuff, food for about three days, a lighter and a blanket. No water, but I bet we could find a pot in this place and melt snow."

"That won't be necessary. Put your hands where I can see them."

I jump and turn to the door where a soldier stands, rifle leveled at Adam's chest. The soldier speaks into a device on his shoulder.

"I've found the two we were looking for. I don't expect trouble, but why don't you join me just in case? The blue house with the wallpaper."

The wallpaper really is terrible, now that he mentions it. Faded pink and white peonies on a black backdrop. They probably use Ogden for drills and who knows what else with its proximity to camp. We never stood a chance.

Turning back to us he says, "I don't need to expect trouble, do I?"

"Not from us," says Adam.

"Any weapons?" the soldier asks.

The gun is in the back of Adam's waistband, out of the soldier's sight. I fantasize about a world where I could whip it out and save us both. That is not this world. Besides, we want these guys on our side.

"I've got a gun," Adam says, hands still in the air.

"Young lady, please retrieve his gun and slide it my way." I get it and slide it clumsily across the floor. It stops about three feet shy of him, and he huffs a laugh. I glare in return.

Another soldier shows up, and they walk us outside. The guns are no longer pointing our way, but they're still out.

"What's the word '*Carrigan*' mean?" the first soldier asks.

"I was wondering the same thing," Adam replies. We're standing in the ruined snow, crushed by feet and wheels, and I can't help but think of the pristine scene of this morning. On the wall of the lopsided house that one word stares back.

"Now what?" I ask.

They've gone through our gear, but only the gun was confiscated.

"Just waiting on transport back to camp."

When the truck arrives, we climb onto the benches in back. The hungry way the driver looks at me has me drawing closer to Adam, who puts a protective arm around my shoulders and pulls me close.

"It'll be fine, Kess," he whispers into my ear, nuzzling his nose into my neck for the briefest of moments.

When we arrive on base, our guards lead us through the halls of a medical facility to a room labeled "Consultation." Several uncomfortable chairs surround a large wooden desk. Two landscape paintings hang from otherwise bare, beige walls.

Adam and I sit hand in hand, saying nothing, until Evan and Lucas enter, followed by the man who'd been in charge out in the snow and a Hispanic guy, maybe Jace's age, with a determined look on his face.

"Yes, this is them," Evan says. "Captain Betner, meet Kessa McKnight and Adam Morton."

"Morton?" Betner asks, looking closely at Adam's face. "Are you Richard Morton's son?"

"Yes, sir. Unfortunately," Adam replies.

Betner turns to Evan.

"Why didn't you mention them while we were at the site?"

"I didn't know if they left with Radley and Open Sky," Evan says.

"Do you think we'd do that?" I ask. "Just leave you here?"

Evan's face shutters.

"I don't know what you'll do anymore, Kessa."

Adam's glaring at Evan, but Betner speaks before it can escalate.

"Kessa, are you the person who first recognized Jaerish in Salida? He's been telling us some very disturbing things about the nature of our reality."

"Yes, sir. It was a shock to see him alive when we buried his body months ago."

"I can imagine so," says Betner, nodding. Turning to the young man he says, "Allow me to introduce Gideon. As Open Sky is no longer available to verify your story, Gideon has agreed to go off the pill to test your claims. We are hopeful that the short duration of his time with us will have a positive impact on how long it takes to reverse the effects of the blue pill and give us the truth, one way or another."

I look at Gideon, who now seems even younger than at first, but his shoulders are set.

"Thank you, Gideon," I say. "I appreciate your bravery."

"Yes, Ma'am," he replies, cheeks flushing.

"How long do you think it will take for Gideon's memory to return?" Adam asks Betner.

Evan answers. "We don't know. He's only been here a few months, so hopefully not long. A day and a half? Less?"

"Where's my dad now?" Adam asks.

"Richard Morton arrived here two nights ago and told us that Open Sky had been kidnapped by his elite guard and was being held in El Dorado Springs. We mobilized as quickly as possible. Your father went with the main battalion, who should have arrived in El Dorado Springs this morning. The tanks are slower and won't arrive until late tonight."

My mind goes blank at the idea of tanks surrounding my town. Adam doesn't have the same problem.

"He showed up with these accusations and you just believed him?" Adam asks, his voice incredulous.

"Some of us were aware that Open Sky had a partner elsewhere who's been part of this endeavor from the beginning. He and Open Sky arranged a code word known only to themselves, Major Merritt and me."

"Carrigan," I say.

"Yes; Carrigan. Though I suppose now they will need to choose another."

"The only thing Morton is going to need to choose is his cell number," says Evan. "And that's if he's lucky. Once the army knows what he's done he won't be safe outside of prison."

I can tell from the steel in Evan's voice that he'd lead the lynch mob. I can't say that I blame him, but it still hurts to hear. The Evan I knew before would have advocated for mercy.

"We need to tell the army not to attack," I say.

"It's done," says Betner. "I sent a messenger advising a 24-hour halt to action before investigating Jaerish's claims. I'll send another now with updates."

"That's not good enough," Evan says. "We're all going."

Betner looks surprised. "You seem to have forgotten your place, and my lenience, soldier," he says.

A strangled laugh escapes me. I can't help it. That was so the wrong thing to say.

"I am not your soldier." Evan emphasizes every word. "And I am also no longer your captive." His flinty grey eyes throw off sparks that just might set this whole camp on fire.

Betner measures him. There are no guards in the room, but they're within shouting distance. No one breathes until Betner says, "Very well. Give me an alternative."

"We bring Gideon with us. And we confront Morton with the truth," Evan says.

Betner gives a sharp nod. "We all go. Rest quickly. We leave in two hours."

I've been running on adrenaline, and my body needs real sleep, but I resent the two hours we're wasting. What if Betner's messengers are waylaid or Morton convinces Merritt to disregard them?

We're so close. We can't come this far and then be too late.

Chapter 60 - Michaela

ADDING TANKS WAS A nice touch. If by "nice" you mean demoralizing.

Tension crackles in the morning air as I walk through the square looking for Jace. When the army showed up yesterday it was shocking. Horrible. But our militia outnumbered them, and we had home field advantage. Tanks change everything.

I finally find someone who saw Jace enter Mae Cartwright's house with Henry and the Professor and "a tall black guy" I'm guessing is Cole. I'd rather stay outside with the tanks. But yesterday when Jace came back from the meeting with his dad, the jester mask was firmly in place.

Everything's fine. Army led by my crazy father? No problem. The sky's falling? We'll just hold it up. Even Jace's optimism has limits, whether he shows it or not, and I'm not going to abandon him now. Straightening my shoulders, I enter the lair.

I don't know what I expected to find. Maybe voodoo dolls or the bodies of past rivals. But instead, it's eerily perfect. Just the right paintings hang on just the right ivory walls above just the right expensive rugs and furniture. There's nothing anywhere that says, 'make yourself at home.'

Patner's in the front room describing what the tanks can do to Jace, Cole and Mae. I'm not sure when Cole and Mae met, but she's leaning into him like she needs his strength to stand upright in the face of such horror. Cole shoots a look at Jace, who is smirking.

As I join the group, Jace takes my hand and brings it to his mouth, kissing my fingers casually as though that's just how we say hello. I want to lean into him for more than strength, but it would seem way too Mae at the moment, so I squeeze his hand and focus on what Patner's saying.

Cole's just asked Patner how he thinks they'll use the tanks, when a messenger from the checkpoint comes in looking for Professor McKnight. Patner directs him to the dining room, and we follow behind.

Professor McKnight takes the message and reads through it. "They're requesting a meeting to formalize terms of surrender," he says.

"They're surrendering already?" Cole asks.

Mayor Cartwright glares at him unamused. "There is no way we're surrendering," she says. "I don't care how many big toys they have. This is our town."

"And how would you have us defend it?" asks Mr. Harris.

"We won't need to defend it," Patner says, "if the army knows the truth."

"It's the only play we have left," says Professor McKnight with a sigh. "We can only hope that Merritt isn't involved."

Plans are made and a reply sent. We'll meet at noon, for the first time allowing a select delegation inside El Dorado Springs. Until then, we wait.

Mae is an unwelcome addition as I stand with the guys. Her arm is looped through one of Cole's and she's looking up at him like she's never seen anything so pretty.

"Aren't you dating Bruce?" Jace asks.

Mae blinks slowly, probably trying to draw attention to her big blue eyes or look innocent or something.

"We aren't exclusive," she says.

"Good," says Jace. "That's just the way Cole likes it."

Cole doesn't even pretend to object, just shrugs in a way that's somehow cocky and nonchalant at the same time. I don't know how this doesn't bother Mae, but she draws him closer and asks if he wants to see the rest of the house.

Jace and I take the opportunity to escape to the porch. The waiting is wearing on everyone, and I haven't had a chance to be with Jace alone since the army arrived.

"How are you?" I ask, knowing it's a stupid question.

"Better now that you're here," he says.

It's a throwaway answer, but he follows it with a kiss right there on Mae's porch where anyone could see. And for once I don't care because there are more important things going on than a little PDA.

The porch is covered in classy patio furniture, but they're all individual seats. Jace scoots a couple aside, and we sit scrunched together on the floor, our backs to the house. The space is cramped, but that makes it perfect. It's just him and me, tucked away from the world and everyone in it. No dads. No armies. Not even a Mae Cartwright.

I don't know how long we stay like that, side by side with my head against his shoulder. Jace has gotten better with silence. Eventually he starts talking.

"When my dad volunteered me for the swap, as manipulative as it was, part of me hoped it was because he believed in me, you know?"

"In a way he did," I say. "He trusted you to represent him and Salida well. And you have."

"Yeah, but it didn't really matter if he was going to send in an army anyway."

"Maybe he wasn't. Maybe when Kessa realized Evan was alive, the plan changed."

"Yeah. Maybe."

"I'm not defending him, Jace," I say. "Nothing he's done is ok. I'm just saying he might have trusted you more than you think back at the beginning."

"Well, he doesn't trust me at all now," Jace says with a humorless laugh. "What gets me, though, is that I still care. Shouldn't I have stopped by now?"

I turn his face with my hands and bring his forehead to mine.

"I hate that he hurts you. But I love that you care. Because you caring about other people is something I love about you." I kiss him on the nose, and it makes him smile, just a little. "But now you need to start caring what God thinks about you. Or what good people like Henry and Professor McKnight think about you. Because we all think you're amazing."

I don't know if he believes me, but his smile grows, and he kisses me. He tells me he loves me. And for now, tucked away together in our little hideaway, that's enough.

At noon I stand with Jace, Cole and Patner outside the main Boardroom at City Hall as the army delegation files past. Patner points out Major Merritt and tells us that four of the six soldiers in attendance are from Open Sky's personal guard. He doesn't say it, but that means those men were his friends. Now only one looks his way, and that's with a scowl.

Richard Morton is there too, of course, but no one needs to point him out. His resemblance to Jace is uncanny, except for the studied blankness of his eyes. They're nothing like Jace's open warmth. Morton barely glances at Jace or me before his eyes narrow on Cole, whose presence must not please.

Once the delegation is past, Patner follows behind. Cole swaggers after him like a meeting to discuss tanks and armies and the surrender of our town is just a normal day. Like everything isn't riding on this.

Jace and I are alone in the hall. He takes a deep breath and reaches for my hand. I softly say his name and Jace looks down at me.

"No matter what happens in there, this is your home now. With us." I mean "with me," and I hope he knows it. I reach up on tiptoes and brush a quick kiss over his lips. He nods once, straightens his shoulders and we enter the room.

The gleaming cherrywood table is circled by eight plush armchairs, four on each side. Morton and Merritt are seated in the center chairs facing the entrance, leaving the outer chairs on their side of the table empty. All six soldiers stand at attention behind them, ignoring the chairs lined up along the wall.

The El Dorado Springs delegates, Mr. Harris, Professor McKnight, Mayor Cartwright and Henry, sit facing them on our side of the table. Patner stands behind Mr. Harris, opposite the soldiers. Cole sits in a chair along the wall, and Jace and I take the seats beside him.

As we sit, Morton notices me for the first time. He looks at our joined hands then gives me a once over. He's not scowling at least, so that's something. His eyes catch on Jace's watch, then flick up to his face, brows drawn. Is this a peace offering? Jace gives an imperceptible nod. I can almost hear his thoughts. *Sure, Dad. I'm still your loyal puppet, despite everything.*

Professor McKnight clears his throat and starts a round of introductions. They're brief, and I notice that he doesn't mention Mr. Harris's connection to Evan, although a couple of the soldiers, and Major Merritt, seem to be studying him already.

I'm not surprised when it's Morton who speaks for team army.

"Once again I see that you've brought my son, but not General Open Sky," Morton states. "Is there a reason for his absence?"

"Having never met General Open Sky, I'm at a loss to answer your question," Professor McKnight replies. "And quite truthfully, Mr. Morton, I would have thought that we'd be meeting under friendlier circumstances. We came to you in good faith, and now you have perpetrated this attack against us."

"There has been no attack," says Morton. "Only an attempt at communication that will not be denied." He says it with a little wave of his hand, as though the soldiers camped on our doorstep are a minor issue.

"I am also concerned," Professor McKnight says, "with the safety and whereabouts of my daughter in light of these new communication tactics."

On the surface Professor McKnight is calm, but I've known him all my life. He hasn't been this upset since we heard of Evan's death. Major Merritt hasn't spoken yet, but he's taking it all in.

"Your daughter is quite safe, Mr. McKnight. I can assure you that both she and Adam are comfortably going on about their lives in Salida. I saw no reason that Kessa should be involved. Yet."

The threat isn't even subtle.

My gaze shifts to Cole, whose jaw is clenched. According to him, Morton knew about Kessa's suspicions, and I can only hope he's not lying about her safety as well.

"Kessa has been 'involved in this,' as you say, since last summer when her boyfriend, my son's, body was found burnt in a ravine along with his best friend."

It's Mr. Harris who's spoken, of course. The ice in his voice has the soldiers along the wall reaching for weapons they aren't carrying. Morton is unphased.

"Mr. Harris," says Morton, "I am sorry for your loss, but I don't understand how it relates to our current situation."

For a minute, I think Mr. Harris might spring over the table and put his martial arts training to use regardless of the guards, but Professor McKnight places a hand on his arm.

"Patner, will you please enlighten our guests?" Professor McKnight asks.

Patner straightens even further, all soldier. His attention is directed fully on Major Merritt, as though he can convince him of the truth of his statements through force of will alone.

"Mr. Harris's son, Evan, was not the body found in the jeep. That body belonged to one of Forsworth's men who'd grown a conscience and had to be dealt with. Evan is alive. You know him as Jaerish."

Morton begins to interrupt, but Major Merritt puts a hand up and, for once, Morton shuts his mouth.

"Please continue," says Merritt.

"Jaerish and I accompanied Open Sky to Salida, where he came in contact with Kessa, Professor McKnight's daughter. He didn't remember her, but she knew him. When we left town, Jaerish went off the blue pill without telling anyone. It didn't drive him insane. Instead, his memory returned. The pill was suppressing it, not keeping a disease at bay. Evan remembered the day Forsworth and his men attacked him, and all of his life before that as well."

Morton opens his mouth but closes it as Merritt once again raises his hand. It's obvious Morton isn't used to being silenced, but I suppose it is Merritt's army in Open Sky's absence, regardless of who built it. That seems like a contingency Morton didn't plan for.

"And how do you know that what Jaerish told you is true?" Major Merritt asks.

"Because I'm also off of the pill. And I remember everything."

The soldiers behind Merritt are shifting as Patner's words sink in. They steal glances at Mr. Harris's face, no doubt seeing Evan there.

"Is this why the two of you kidnapped General Open Sky?" asks Morton.

"We did no such thing." For the first time Patner's eyes leave Merritt's, and the look in them as they focus on Morton is all fire. "We were to wait for General Open Sky in Colby, Kansas. The last time I saw him, he was headed to Salida to confront you."

"Lies," says Morton, again with the hand wave, as though he can swat anything unpleasant away. "He left with you before New Years. That was the last time I saw him."

Professor McKnight interrupts the tension. "I'd also like to have Cole speak to the information he was given by my daughter."

The sneer Morton sends Cole's way would have done Forsworth proud. "I don't know why you're in this town, let alone this meeting," Morton says.

"Gotta visit my boy, Jace," Cole says with a shrug. "And stop you from invading an innocent neighbor. You know, be a hero."

To his credit Professor McKnight seems more amused than annoyed when he says, "Cole, could you please tell everyone how you came to be in El Dorado Springs?"

"Sure," Cole says, rising. "Kessa and Adam, his other son, told me that Morton had an army full of drugged soldiers, including Kessa's ex-boyfriend that she thought was dead. They wanted me to get word to El Dorado Springs. I ran into Patner on my way, so we came together. Evan and their scary friend went to Salida to look for Open Sky."

"We don't even know if you're really Kessa and Adam's messenger," Morton says. "For all we know you could be in on the kidnapping with Open Sky's guards. Jaerish obviously has plans to undermine the army's authority structure. Open Sky told me as much, and now he's disappeared. If this person were Evan and his memories were restored, why isn't he here reassuring his grieving parents that he's alive? Even if he'd gone to Salida like you claim he could be here by now."

"Regardless of the validity of these claims," says Merritt, "I am currently the leader and guardian of an army with no memory. Were word of these allegations to spread, things could get out of hand very quickly."

"Are you confirming, Major Merritt, that the men behind you and in the field outside of my town, also have no memory as Patner claims?" asks Professor McKnight.

"I am. Or rather, they have no memory before arriving at Fort Riley, beyond possibly a couple of days on the road. I myself have two decades of memory, but nothing before that."

There's silence in the room. Maybe everyone is thinking, like I am, about what it would mean to suddenly find out your life had been stolen from you, not by a disease, but intentionally. Suddenly Morton is on his feet.

"My son and I will be leaving," he says.

"I think not," says Professor McKnight.

Merritt nods towards the soldiers and two step forward, but before they can take hold of him, Morton raises something he's clutching in his hand. It looks like a pen, but there's a light in the tip blinking on and off.

"Stay back," he says. "Or I'll push the trigger."

The soldiers pause, looking to Merritt for orders. Mr. Harris is coiled as though to spring. Henry has looked back at Jace, who's staring down at his watch. A light that wasn't there before is pulsing in time to the pen. Jace holds up his wrist, and Merritt's eyes catch on it as well.

"Morton, explain yourself," Merritt says.

"My son leaves with me or neither of us leave this place," says Morton.

"What are you talking about?" asks Professor McKnight. Henry curses under his breath, his face drained of all color. Mayor Cartwright has become a statue.

Jace frantically starts trying to take off the watch, but Morton says, "Stop, Jace. Once it's engaged, removal will trigger the failsafe. And then you'll be useless again."

Jace winces at the words, but then things happen so quickly I'm not sure what's going on. One of the soldiers has moved on Morton. They wrestle, and the pen falls to the floor. At the same time Jace crumples back onto his seat, his mouth going slack and eyes rolling back in his head. The scream I hear is my own.

It only takes moments for the soldiers to subdue Morton, but my eyes don't leave Jace's face. How did this happen? We knew about the watch. Why did he wear it?

Henry is assessing the situation. "It's done, Jace," he says.

With that Jace's eyes open. He straightens, taking off the watch and rubbing at a small cut where its face had rested.

"You're in on this with them?" his father spits. "How could you turn your back on family?"

"Well, Dad, they've never threatened to kill me, so there's that."

"What's going on?" asks Merritt. The soldier holding Morton hasn't loosened his grip, but he's looking at Jace with narrowed eyes.

"The watch was a 'gift' from dear old Dad," says Jace. "But Henry's a history buff, so he knew it wasn't standard issue. We took out the poison that was set to that remote trigger but left the needle, just in case I needed to know when to play dead."

Merritt is looking at Morton with horror now. "You would have killed your own son?"

"Of course not. It was just a tranquilizer. He'd have been knocked out, nothing worse."

"And where is Open Sky really?" asks Merritt.

"I assure you I don't know. I came to you believing that Open Sky had been taken captive by these rogue soldiers, although I had no idea of their true motives. How could I have guessed that Open Sky was perpetrating such a heinous crime upon his men?

"Seriously?" asks Cole. "How do you think you can still get out of this?"

"I don't know what you mean," says Morton.

"I bet you've still got Open Sky stashed in that saferoom. Maybe Kessa and Evan too," says Cole.

"Bro, that totally makes sense," says Jace. And right there they fist bump.

"Explain," says Merritt, voice icy.

"Kessa said Morton took Open Sky down to his safe room on New Years Eve," says Cole. "Maybe he never let him out."

"And why are you just telling us this?" asks Merritt.

"I'm not too chatty with dudes who pull up in tanks," says Cole.

Merritt looks like he'll reply, but Professor McKnight says, "And you must understand that we were uncertain of your involvement. As far as we knew, you were part of the conspiracy and used this opportunity to take control of the army. The full extent and ramifications of what's been going on are only now becoming clear. This information could be very destabilizing, to say the least."

Merritt looks at his guard. "Confidential until we have a plan."

They nod their assent, and a couple of them nod Patner's way. It looks like he may be forgiven after all.

"Professor McKnight," says Merritt. "There's one more thing I need to tell you. Your daughter is safe. As, Mr. Harris, is your son."

Morton's head whips up as Kessa and Evan walk through the door.

Chapter 61 - Kessa

I don't know which is better: finally assuring my dad I'm safe or seeing Morton in handcuffs. Both feel pretty dang good.

Standing with Adam, Evan and Lucas outside the boardroom while Morton spun his lies took all of my restraint, but it was Merritt's condition for bringing us in. He wanted to see how El Dorado Springs answered Morton's accusations as a last verification of our story, and give Morton time to incriminate himself in front of witnesses before revealing our arrival. Morton managed his part well, although Adam almost made it past Lucas when his brother was threatened in some unknown way.

Now, wrapped up in my dad's arms, I know it's finally over and everything is ok. Looking around I see Evan's dad in tears, releasing his son to stare into his face then pulling him back in again. No causal man-hug there. Adam stands by his brother and Cole, meeting Michaela who is all smiles. Morton sits, scowling, surrounded by guards.

There's a lot to tell and to hear, but first I have something important to do.

"Dad, there's someone I want you to meet."

Chapter 62 - Jaerish

Captain Betner was true to his word, and we caught up with the tanks just outside of El Dorado Springs. Morton didn't blink twice as we rolled into camp with their convoy. He made up for it when we walked through the boardroom door.

I haven't seen Kessa since. I'm sure she's having a great time showing Adam around town to all the places we used to go. She's probably kissing him in that bend of the hall where you can't be seen from her dad's office . . . No. I won't do this.

I leave my room, which is exactly as it was last April, to look for Patner or Gideon. Or eat lunch. Or something. Anything to keep my mind off Kessa and Adam.

I find Gideon in the kitchen, staring into space with an open book on the table before him. Suddenly his face contorts and sobs are shaking his body. Hell no. I back out of the room, standing frozen outside the doorway until the sounds stop. Then I count to fifty, slowly, before walking into the kitchen like I just got here. Gideon hasn't moved, but he's not sobbing. It better stay that way. I go to the fridge and look inside.

"Remember anything yet?" I ask.

"Yeah, but none of it's good."

"You want to tell me about it?"

"Nah, that's alright." My back's still to him, but the pain is obvious in his voice. "The good news is, Forsworth didn't kidnap me. He won me fair and square in a poker game."

I swear under my breath but don't turn around. Gideon continues.

"My folks are both dead, but I've got a sister. I need to go get her out of that place. If she's still there."

"I'll help you."

The words are out before I can think them through, but it's been a long time since something felt this right. I repeat it, turning to look him in the eyes.

"I'll help you find her."

Gideon holds my gaze, nods then stares back down at his hands.

"If I'd been more like you, I could have protected her."

I don't know what to say to that, so I clap my hand on his shoulder and fake confidence.

"We'll find her together," I say. "I'll go tell Merritt and Betner that you're remembering things. Figure out how much you want to tell them, ok?"

Gideon nods, and I walk out of the room.

CHAPTER 63 - JACE

I THOUGHT I'D BE nervous when I introduced Michaela to my dad, but the feel of the watch's needle on my wrist finally did it. His approval no longer matters.

I wouldn't be here at all if it weren't for Henry. He wants me to have closure, and he's usually right.

El Dorado Springs used to have a jail, but after the pandemic they started handling crime differently, and the town decided to use the building for something else. They converted the cells into workspaces for craftspeople. The cafeteria became a market where vendors sell everything from vegetables to toys to furniture. It's normal now to stop by jail for eggs on the way home.

I wish I was walking into that jail, but this is the real thing, El Dorado Springs style. A cheery bell rings as Michaela opens the yellow front door of a converted two-story house on main street. A receptionist with thick glasses and grey hair waves to us from her desk and calls down the hallway. Soon the town sheriff is reaching out to shake my hand and give Michaela a hug. Apparently, she babysits his four-year-old.

We follow the big man up a narrow stairwell. At the top are three closed doors labeled A, B and C and an open door showing a bathroom. The sheriff knocks on door A.

"Morton? Visitors," he says. He turns a key in the lock and pushes the door inwards.

Michaela and I step into a very normal-looking bedroom complete with freshly painted walls and a matching bedspread. Were it not for the bars on the windows, I wouldn't know it was intended to hold a criminal. My father.

Dad sits at a desk with his back towards us. He holds up his pointer finger in the universal gesture for "your time isn't worth as much as mine" and keeps writing in the journal. Even now he's chronicling the latest in the life of Richard Morton.

"Did you know that I wanted to name Adam 'Richard' after myself?" he asks. "Your mother stopped me. She said it would be enough to live in my shadow as a father without also bearing my name. So, we gave him the name Adam, after the first son of God."

"Probably a good decision," I say, proof that El Dorado Springs has taught me self-control.

Dad finishes his line with a flourish and looks back at us. As he stands, his presence fills the room. I have no idea how he manages to take up so much space. Michaela squeezes my hand, and I realize I've slouched down without even knowing it. I stand up straight and square my shoulders.

"Ah, Jason, I see you have brought a lovely young visitor to see me." He pauses and in the silence I realize I should be introducing Michaela.

"Dad, this is Michaela Barr. Michaela, my father, Richard Morton."

"It is my honor, Michaela." Dad steps forward and reaches out his hand.

Michaela takes it and smiles. "Jace has told me so much about you, sir. It's good to have you, here, in El Dorado Springs."

Although nothing shows on her face, Michaela's true meaning, as we stand in my father's prison cell, is unmistakable. But not to my Dad, whose other hand covers hers as he looks down and smiles.

"I will be delighted to get to know you further after this whole mess is cleared up. But for now, I am glad that Jason brought you by. It says something, at least, of his remembrance of family duty." Before I can tell him what I think about his type of family duty, Michaela speaks again.

"I've never known Jace to be anything but devoted. It's one of his best qualities."

"Well, I'm glad to hear it, Miss Barr. Perhaps there's hope for him yet."

Michaela's jaw clenches, and I'm reminded of a cartoon where a kitten jumps on a wolf in a fit of anger. Unaware of his danger, my father keeps talking.

"Son, there are times in history that we look back upon as turning points. This may well be one of them. It is my deepest hope that the dismantling of my army is not seen by future generations as the turning point that plummeted society into chaos and war. Without such a force to keep the peace, what will civilized people do when faced with those who would impose their will through violent means?"

I share a glance with Michaela. He's seriously saying this with no hint of irony. I consider pointing this out, but why bother?

"Dad, as much fun as this has been, Michaela and I have some important things to do. If there's anything you need, I'm sure the sheriff will be happy to help."

I turn and pull a fuming Michaela out the door behind me.

"He makes me so mad! How could I ever have cared if that man liked me?"

"Trust me. I get it."

Halfway down the stairs I stop. Michaela's on my heals and bumps into me, but I was braced for it. I turn around. With the help of the step she's almost my height, and I take her face in my hands.

"My dad sucks. You, though, are amazing. I couldn't have gotten through that without you."

I lean in for a kiss, but she pulls back.

"Really?" Michaela asks. "Is that what you want to do when you're mad? Kiss someone?"

I don't know exactly what to say, and for a minute I think she's going to brush right past me. Then her face softens, and she takes a deep breath.

"I'm sorry. I'm not mad at you, obviously. Just give me a second." Michaela closes her eyes, and when she opens them she smiles. "I'm ready now."

It's not exactly the romantic moment I'd been going for, but when she leans just the tiniest bit towards me I give in. I lose myself in the kiss until a throat clears at the base of the stairs.

The sheriff looks up at us with a smirk. "I need to lock your dad's door."

"We'll be right down," I say.

Michaela stares deeply into my eyes, puts one hand on my cheek.

"Your dad's an idiot. Let's go to the jail and get some pie."

Best girlfriend ever.

Epilogue - Jaerish

I'M STANDING IN MY kitchen, leaning against the counter, when Kessa walks in. She looks at the mug in my hand.

"You don't like coffee," she says with a forced smile.

I swish the bitter liquid around then take a drink. I'm still getting used to its harsh taste on my tongue. I'm still getting used to a lot of things.

"I do now," I say. "I guess some things change."

She winces, but nods. At least she isn't saying "sorry" again. Her being sorry doesn't matter.

"I'm leaving tomorrow with Merritt and Betner," I tell her. "I'm going to help keep peace when they tell the men."

"I'm glad you'll be with them. They need you."

"Yeah, it won't be pretty," I say.

"What's after that?"

"After that, I help Gideon rescue his sister. Then back to the army, I think. Merritt's making a place for the men who want to stay at Fort Riley. We still don't know what the black lines on Morton's map mean, but probably nothing good."

"Are your parents ok with it?"

My mom had taken it badly, but that's not Kessa's business anymore. "They'll adjust," I say.

We stand in awkward silence, and then Kessa steps forward and I wrap her in my arms one last time. I kiss the top of her head, breathe in the smell of her. Then I step back and close off my heart.

When Kessa leaves, I pull my grandfather's pen from my pocket. Flipping it through my fingers, I think of my grandfather giving it to my dad when he signed over the deed to this house. My father always assumed he'd do the same one day, but instead he learned his son was dead. He'd given it to Kessa, and she'd ultimately used it to let everyone know I'm alive.

I'm not sure why Dad gave it back to me now. All he said was "Everyone needs hope, Evan. You've lost yours, but you'll find it again."

More than anything, I hope he's right.

AUTHOR'S NOTE

First off, thank you for reading my debut novel. If you'd like to see Evan find healing and his own happy ending, join me for book two. If you're a Cole fan, you'll get to see him too, although you'll need to wait until book three to find out just what kind of girl will finally capture his heart.

To stay updated on future release dates, cover reveals and freebies, visit me at **DogsandCoffeeBooks.com**.

You may have noticed that many of my characters talk to and about God as though He's involved in their everyday lives. That's because He is. I began writing this series after reading a swarm of dystopian novels that either left God out entirely or created some sort of powerless mash-up of multiple religions. That makes sense . . . a dystopia, by definition, is filled with suffering, injustice and oppression. That's an easier scene to paint if you ignore God. But it's not an honest vision of existence.

Reality is a Good Father longing to know his kids, and an Older Brother who sacrificed himself to make that possible.

We, as humans, try to pretend that sin is a hair in our salad. Gross, but you can pick it out, pretend it doesn't exist, and keep eating. Until you find the next one.

A more apt analogy would be a dead rat in your boba tea. It's utterly disgusting and impossible to ignore. You can't work around it. The only solution is a brand new cup. And that's what Jesus offers us.

God won't force you to love Him. He won't force you to admit there's a rat in your tea. But He won't pretend it's not there either. Because He's a good dad, and He loves you.

Practically, if you want to know God, here's what to do:

1- Start talking to Him. Tell Him you want to know Him. That's how relationships usually begin, right?

2- Ask Jesus to point out a Christian who can help. We aren't meant to live this journey alone.

3- Download a Bible App (or go old-school with a paper version) and read the Book of Mark.

You can also find resources I think are excellent or connect with me directly at **DogsandCoffeeBooks.com**.

ACKNOWLEDGEMENTS

Thank you to my amazing husband and best friend who encouraged me every step of the way. I can't express how much I appreciate your selfless love and support.

Thank you to my sons for your insights into the young male mind and for not complaining when dinner was cereal again. Harper, I love your boldness and drive. Rhett, I love your desire to love God and others well. Ambrose, I love your humor and ability to make people feel valued.

Thank you to my parents for encouraging my strengths and framing my weaknesses in a way that didn't crush my confidence. (Remember when you told me I couldn't try out for cheerleading because you wanted me playing my own sports, rather than pointing out that I have the flexibility of a yard stick and the coordination of a drunk beagle?) I'd never have believed I could write a book without that foundation.

Thank you to my sister who was always willing to listen to me snark and sympathize.

Thank you to my non-blood sisters, Christina, Michaela, Courtney and Paige who surrounded me with prayer when I needed it most. And to the many others who so often stepped in at exactly the right time to keep me balanced and somewhat close to sanity. I started writing a list, and it was just too long, so if you think I'm talking about you, I am.

Thank you to my writer friends. I always wanted you. E.F. Spence, I think Kessa and Kat would have been great friends if they didn't live in different futures. C.M. Genton, thanks for being a few steps ahead when I needed guidance. Rebecca Mogollon, your feedback was invaluable.

To my beta readers, I truly appreciate your willingness to read early drafts, point out where tension was needed, and encourage me that it was a story worth writing. Thank you Adi, Hayley, and Elizabeth!

Thank you to Bret for creating a beautiful website in 4.3 seconds flat.

Thank you to Bespoke Books for my cover art. It's even better than I hoped it would be.

Thank you to my dogs who will never read a book, but were there every step of the way.

And thank you to Jesus. You're the reason. May your kingdom come.

ABOUT THE AUTHOR

BEKKI LIVES WITH HER husband, three sons and two dogs in Kansas City. She likes hiking, hosting, baking, decorating, smiles, reading, love stories and Jesus. Oh, and iced coffee. She doesn't like geese or goats, but she's getting over it.

This is her first novel.